MEXICO

IN THE REARVIEW MIRROR

A Psychedelic Travelogue

Michael Tassone

This is obviously a work of fiction. Names, characters, and incidents are a product of the author's imagination or are used fictitiously. Any resemblance to actual persons, living or dead, is entirely coincidental. Like how the author and narrator each have a great head of hair and both spent a year south of the border eating LSD—pure coincidence.

ISBN: 1470078236
ISBN-13: 978-1470078232

LCCN 2012908560

CreateSpace
North Charleston, SC

Cover photograph of *el Tiburón del Tierra* by the author
Author photograph by Emily Rhodenbaugh
michaeltassone@yahoo.com

In memory of my father

Salvatore P. "Chip" Tassone

who never backed down from a fight.

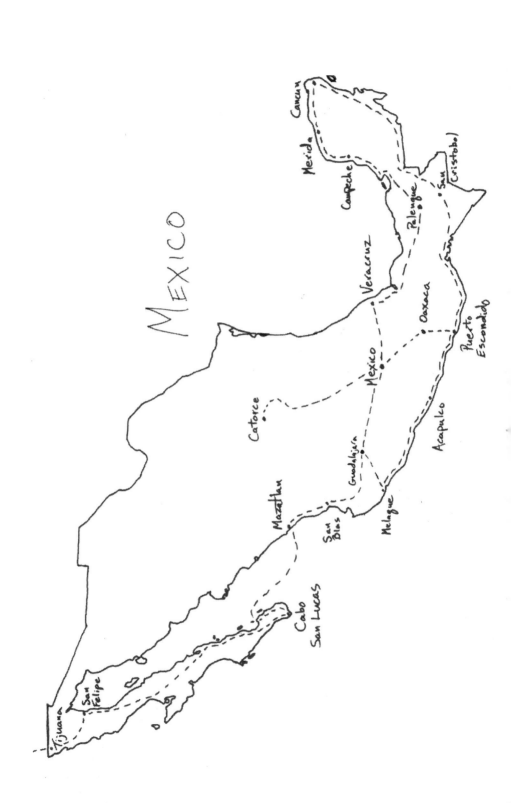

MEXICO

IN THE REARVIEW MIRROR

Part One

Baja California

One

August 1992, Midnight

"Shit—is that the border already?" Rudy's driving. "We haven't hidden the stuff yet." We've been talking and singing, jubilant to finally be on the road again after a year apart and suddenly we're squinting into the bright glow of the Customs and Immigration checkpoint, Mexico expanding beyond.

Rudy's concern is about our possession of the two hundred doses of LSD, the ounce of marijuana, the bag of fast white powder.

"You've got to drive us across," he says, vacating the driver's seat at fifty miles an hour and climbing to the back of the VW bus. I slip in behind the wheel and into Mexico as the border guard waves us through and the familiarity of America recedes rapidly.

Rudy rummages frantically through our stuff. "Let me know when we're coming to the checkpoint."

"We're in," I tell him.

"Customs? Shit."

"Mexico," I tell him.

"Huh?"

"We're in Mexico. We've crossed the border."

"No inspection?"

"No inspection."

"That was easy."

"Yeah."

"Too easy. We're really in Mexico?"

"We're really in Mexico," I say. "You can relax."

Rudy leans into the cockpit, rests an elbow on each of the seatbacks. "So this is Mexico."

We have crossed the frontier under an almost full moon. Rudy breathes a sigh of relief. I am gripped by a strange anxiety. *Mexico—that nebulous terra between shadow and light, that indefinite wilderness, magnet for countless seekers; Mexico—that sanctuary to which outlaws have fled for centuries in the evasion (or pursuit) of justice. What secrets does this land hold? What mysteries will it reveal? What surprises will it spring on you over the course of the year to come?*

Rattling slowly down the dirt and cobbled streets of Tijuana, we take in Mexico for the first time, the air filled with flies and dust, smells of garbage and perfume, the tinkling of unseen bells, the calls of barkers and pimps, and the strangling of a far-off accordion. Cinder block buildings line the streets, storefronts painted red, blue, green, hung with papier-mâché *piñata* and wool-woven blanket, signs painted in unintelligible combinations of letters, *mercados* and *farmacias*. Middle-of-the-night silver cart taco vendors turn bacon-wrapped hot dogs with stainless steel tongs.

I weave the bus through the lethargic flow of foot traffic, which moves in and out of doorways, spills off the sidewalks and into the streets. We pass mule-drawn carts and seventies expatriate sedans painted over yellow and green, working as taxis in their retirement. Cloaked figures close in as we roll sluggishly through. Calm eyes track our passage from *sombrero*-shadowed faces. Open palms stretch from the dark voids of *serapes* towards our open car windows, the children's call of *chicle, chicle,* chimes in my ears.

We roll out of Tijuana, continue south on Highway One, pass through the sleepy borough of Rosarito. And once we're out of the glow of the city and into the dark vacuum of the unclaimed desert it begins to sink in. *We're doing it.*

We drive through acres of low, barren hills, sand dunes extending their tentacles across the roadway. The hulking shells of eviscerated, burning automobiles dot the landscape, echoes of the buffalo indiscriminately slaughtered and left to rot on the American Plains. Black smoke billows across moonlit highway.

Rudy telephoned me one afternoon last June, "I've got the perfect vehicle for the journey." It was never a trip, always a journey. An hour later he chugged up to the ranch on which I was living, stalled in front of my shack in a cloud of smoke and rust. The 1971 Volkswagen Bus was a primer gray beast. Big and roomy yes, and the rear seat folded out into a bed, but the engine idled uneasily and leaked fluids it shouldn't have contained. And as I looked it over it whispered to me, the bus *whispered* something. I leaned in close but couldn't make out the words.

Over the next few months it was in and out of the shop, getting *this* replaced and *that* repaired and by the date of our departure I still didn't have much confidence in it. The week before leaving I went to pick it up at the shop and made the mistake of asking the mechanic how he thought it would perform out there, on the road.

"Well if it was my bus I'd have that engine re—"

"You know what?" I intervened, "forget that I asked. I really don't want to know."

"But you should know. That—"

"You don't understand," I explained to the mechanic. "We have to get out of here. We have to get on the road." With that I stomped accelerator to floor. The engine revved, choked, and stalled. The mechanic gave me a hopeless shrug. A twist of the key and a pump of the pedal and it coughed to life. I forced a smile and was off, southbound down the wide-open highway.

"You think she'll make it all the way out to the Yucatan?" Rudy asks.

"You can't doubt your ride," I say, "once you're on the road."

"Now that we are officially on the road," Rudy says, "we're gonna have to name the bus."

We contemplate it on the drive through the desert, along the coast, and down the highway, deeper and deeper in.

"How about the *Gray Whale*? No, no—*Moby Dick*."

"This thing's more of a shark than a whale," Rudy says. "How about *Land Shark*?"

"Hey, what's shark in Spanish?"

"*Tiburón*—that's it, *el Tiburón del Tierra*, the Shark of the Land." Rudy knows at least a few words in Spanish. I took French in high school—lot of good it'll do me down here. But I am determined to master the Spanish language. We discover early on that a Volkswagen bus is known as a *combi* (comb-bee) in Mexico, and so it shall be.

I ease up on the accelerator outside Ensenada, glide to a stop. We unfurl our sleeping bags on the beach at San Miguel. Surf crashes hard. Orange moon slips through lace veils. It is our first night sleeping on the beaches of Mexico. It's the best sleep I've had in months.

Two

W e awaken in the sand, well rested, sun burning hot. Stumble to the water. Let surf and salt cleanse body, arouse mind. Put on shorts, t-shirt, sandals. Fry eggs and bacon over an open fire, orange juice—*a dream realized!*

I unfold the map of Baja California, peruse it thoughtfully.

"Where we goin' today?" Rudy asks.

"Well, we eventually want to end up here, in Cabo San Lucas," I point to the southern tip of the Baja Peninsula. "The main highway takes us directly there, south along the Pacific Coast."

"Looks easy enough."

"*Or* there's this little fishing village on the Gulf of California I've heard about—San Felipe. We could cut east to there, and then take *this* road south along the Gulf coast."

"You're always so goddamn well prepared for this shit, Clark," Rudy slaps me on the back. "That Gulf route looks more interesting—the road less traveled and all that, eh?"

"But it's dashed."

"Dashed?"

"On the map, the road is dashed."

"What does that mean?"

"Unpaved, for about two hundred kilometers."

"Oh, we're on the metric system now, are we?"

"We are in Mexico," I say.

"Why don't we do this, Clark: Why don't we go into town, have some beers, and talk to people. You know, get a feel for this country."

"Right, we are on vacation."

"We can decide later where to go," Rudy says.

"And a few *cervezas* might help to lubricate the gears of the decision making process."

"We should also try some of that acid," Rudy says, "just to see if it's any good."

"Yeah," I agree, "just to see if it's any good."

I met Rudy a few years ago in London, the both of us there on a college exchange program from San Francisco State. I'm tall and lanky, of English and Italian descent. He's short and muscular, Irish and Mexican. I write quietly, he sings loudly. He's one of those people who makes things happen and I'm the type who lets things happen. He looks for trouble where I try to avoid it—most of the time. Our friendship was instant.

When our semester in London was over we traveled Europe together and developed an effective alliance. He never had any money, I usually did; he was good at getting us *in* (to parties, clubs, fights, jail) and I was good at getting us out (of parties, clubs, fights, jail).

We returned to San Francisco in the fall and both finished our final year of college at S.F. State. Upon graduation we hit the road for a summer trip across the United States of America with all the accompanying trouble and adventure. Back home again we lived our separate lives, seeing little of each other until the next summer when we once again embarked on the hero's journey—north, this time, to Alaska. Our goal was to make some money working a season on a fishing boat. We succeeded, but it almost killed us. Thus we felt our next years' journey should be somewhere warm and tropical, somewhere south of the border.

We cruise downtown Ensenada before noon, park behind a row of low brick buildings and walk along the waterfront, up Boulevard Costero past the curio and souvenir shops, the line of sidewalk stalls where artisans hawk the gleam of silver earring, the shine of snakeskin boot and leather belt, hammocks woven from rainbows, iconic sculpture of seashells glued together and topped with bloody, crucified, plastic Jesuses. Mexicans move about languidly in the heat with overflowing baskets and their wide-brimmed hats. (*There, another Spanish word in your vocabulary— sombrero.*) We duck into a darkened doorway up the block.

The long, wooden bar of Hussong's Cantina is empty except for a few serious locals sequestered in the smoky darkness. Establishing ourselves on a couple of stools at the rail, we take a breath and order a round. Time stands still as the barkeep pours. This cessation of physical movement is the chance it's been waiting for. The acid, which has trailed us all morning, uses this opportunity to climb up our spines and overtake brains.

"Did you feel that?" Rudy asks.

"Oh yeah."

"Hey Clark, you see that set of longhorns on the wall?"

"Must be six foot wide if they're a day."

"I'm thinking' those would look awful nice mounted across the front of the Combi.

"*Garçon!*" I call out. The bartender saunters over, places his palms on the bar in front of us. The longhorns on the wall behind him appear to grow out the sides of his head.

"Whaddaya want for that pair a horns?" Rudy asks.

"Tequila, señor."

"You want tequila for those?"

"No *señor*, *you* want tequila." Two shot glasses of the amber elixir appear in front of us.

"I guess we do," Rudy says. "*Gracias*."

"Welcome to Mexico, *señores*."

We drink the tequila. We are, after all, in Mexico (*on acid*).

We have a beer and a tequila, two, three, four, five, and at some point I look up and around and the bar is packed to the gills. *How long have we been here? Is it nighttime already?*

This small old guy with a tired hat comes in, moves silently through the crowd. He subtly darts in between each patron lined up at the rail so fast that he is at the other end of the room by the time I realize he has dropped something onto the bar in front of me. I pick it up and hold it before my eyes, rotate it to get every angle of perspective.

It's a combination knife, screwdriver, bottle opener, can opener, and nail file, fitted into a fingernail clipper with a loop of chain dangling from one end for your keys. The little sunlight which manages to sneak in the front door and through the dust and smoke, glints on its chromed surfaces, illuminates the image mounted on it: a blue and white enameled Virgin of Guadalupe radiating her own light. It is a beautiful thing. I keep turning it over in my hands, barely able to contain my now-altered self.

"This is perfect," I stutter in excited gasps, "beautiful... Look at this," as if the rest of life is settled, complete.

Then I look down, see on the bar the little green card that came with it. I pick it up and read: "I am a deaf mute. Please purchase this for a dollar to help support my tequila habit." Or something to that effect, written in a dozen languages.

"All this for only a dollar?" My amazement mounts. I look around the cantina but see that no one else is having quite the same reaction as I am— except for Rudy.

"Give me a dollar," he says.

I pull out two.

The old guy sweeps through again as quickly and as unnoticed as the first time, as if he were operating at a different speed, on a different plane of existence. He is already exiting the door when I realize the cards and the dollars are gone. He has collected them and departed before I could pin him down and purchase a gross.

By now it's afternoon and twisted and time to leave though we don't know where we're going. Stumble back to the bus.

"You drive," Rudy says, throwing me the keys.

Into the Combi, I race the engine. Rudy jumps into passenger seat as I pop the clutch, tear out of the parking lot in a fog of gravel and dust, wheels screaming furiously onto pavement. We explode into traffic, clipping a taxi.

"Stop!" Rudy shouts.

Combi screeches to a halt.

"What?" I ask.

"We need more beer."

Rudy jumps out and marches into the *mercado* in front of which we have stopped. I pour some of the crystal white powder onto the dashboard, snort it into my head to cut through the tequila and LSD, to provide clarity for the drive. Gazing through the windshield of the Combi, I take in this slowly moving town, rays of dust shimmering in sunbeams, a man leading a donkey down the street. *Or is that a mule?*

"Clark!" Rudy shouts from the doorway of the market. "What are you doing?"

"Waiting for you."

"Get in here," he says, " and pay the man!"

Rudy fills the cooler with big brown bottles of beer and ice.

"Let's go," he says.

I fire up the engine, pull out with a squeal of tire and finally we're burning down the road, driving into the dusk. Rudy, bleary-eyed, passes out, his head falling onto my shoulder. I shove him over against the passenger door. Grateful for the stereo, I turn the music up loud to guide us around potholes and donkeys, slow at forty-five kilometers an hour in order to preserve the integrity of the Combi's suspension. The road winds through a shallow desert canyon lined with huge boulders and posturing cactus. Thin veils of smoke drift through the air. Beyond the road's shoulders, vertical cliff faces rise, spray-painted with art and graffiti.

La Luna, the moon, pops up ahead of us, filling the mouth of the canyon. Her glow pulls us along. I'm a stereo stylus, a diamond-headed needle dropped firmly into the vinyl groove of this canyon that squeezes us across the blackness of the unknown Mexican desert. A line of drool issues from the corner of Rudy's mouth. My eyes scan the road ahead for hazards, lips sipping at a large brown bottle, the Mexican litre of beer known as a *caguama* (pronounced *coo-wa-ma*, say it with me, *coo-wa-ma*). Rudy bolts upright with a shout.

"You all right?" I ask.

"Yeah," he says. "I was havin' this dream."

"Nightmare?"

"Pull over," he says.

I stop in the roadway, no shoulder. Rudy gets out of the bus, stumbles across sand and sagebrush towards canyon wall at the curve ahead. I'm on my way down, feeling the low aftereffects of the white powder and tequila. Rudy's caught in the glow of the headlights, standing at the foot of the cliff, staring up at it, running his hands over it. I have no idea where his head's at.

He shuffles back to the Combi. "There's candles," he says to me through the open passenger window. "Give me a lighter."

I throw him a book of matches; rest my head on the steering wheel as he shuffles back to the canyon wall, huddles at its base. Struck matches illumine his face in flash and shadow until he gets the candles lit, a dozen of them casting a pale orange glow on the cliff face. I kill the engine and headlights and with the glare removed see it in the silent dusk.

There, in the candle flicker and lunar radiance is the Virgin of Guadalupe, larger than myth in her blue robe, looking down on us, a vision in spray paint on stone, watching over us, an angelic image glowing out of the Mexican night.

Rudy gets back in the Combi, revived. "I was dreaming," he says, "that we were in Mexico."

"We are in Mexico," I say.

"Yeah, and when I woke up, it was like I woke up into the dream. I knew she was going to be there," Rudy indicates the Virgin. "I saw her in my dream."

"What do you think it means?"

Rudy takes a deep breath.

"That it's time to have another beer." He pulls a cold *caguama* from the cooler between the front seats, opens it for us to share as we drive into the evening. After a year apart we're back together and on the road again.

"So you just been peddling fish, huh?" I ask.

"Yup," says Rudy, "workin' the docks in S.F."

"You didn't get enough of fish in Alaska?"

"I guess not. You were working for the senator all year?"

"Yeah."

"And living out at that commune?"

"When I wasn't on the road."

We fly past a cactus.

"How'd you leave things with Virginia?" I ask.

"V.?" Rudy says. "I love that woman."

"What does she think of your spending a year in Mexico?"

"She's not crazy about it, but she knows that I'm gonna do what I'm gonna do."

"And what are you going to do?" I ask.

"We left it like this—neither she nor I trusts me, so we've decided to have an open relationship for now. When we're together, we're together. When we're not..."

"You're gonna do what you're gonna do?"

"Right," Rudy turns and glances at me. "And she doesn't need to know what I do."

A tumbleweed tumbles across the roadway.

"I told her I'd call once we're settled somewhere."

"Settled?" I say.

"Yeah, when we're staying in one place for a while. She's gonna come down and visit us. That is, of course, if it's okay by you."

"It's okay by me," I say.

"I might marry that woman some day."

I swerve around a pothole.

"What happened with—" Rudy begins.

"She dumped me," I say.

"I'm sorry to hear that. You and her seemed so—"

"It's over."

"She wasn't right for you anyway, Clark," he says. "And it's always good to start a journey with a broken heart—nothing heals better than being on the road."

"Hallelujah, my brother."

The highway rolls away beneath our wheels.

"How you dealing with your father's death?" Rudy asks.

"I'm dealing with it."

"You miss him?"

"All the time."

"It's gotta be tough," he says. "You want to talk about it?"

"We just did."

The moon pulls us along.

"You get your court case worked out?" I ask.

"It's not quite resolved."

"Oh."

I swerve around a boulder that has fallen from the cliff above.

"Are you a fugitive from the law?" I ask.

"If I was Clark, it would probably be better if you didn't know, don't you think?"

"*Si señor.*"

We settle into silence.

"Mexico…," I ponder out loud. "What the hell are we doing here?"

"What do you mean?"

"I mean, we don't know where we're going or what we're doing—just that we're in Mexico for a year."

"Do you remember why we went to Alaska, Clark?"

"No. Do you?"

"No, but I can tell you what it was about. It was all about preparing us for Mexico."

"And what's Mexico preparing us for?" I ask.

"That's why we're here," Rudy says, "to figure that out."

"You really don't know anything at all, do you?"

"No."

"Aren't you worried about living in a place where you don't speak the language?"

"I know that *amigo* is beer and *cerveza* is friend," Rudy says. "We'll figure the rest out as we go. Are you worried Clark?"

"No."

Yes.

One Sunday afternoon about six weeks ago I walked from the ranch where I'd been living since Alaska, up to the San Gregorio General Store, stood for a moment in the doorway while my eyes adjusted to the dim interior. It was empty except for an old guy with a long red beard and potbelly sitting at the bar, pondering the Budweiser longneck in front of him.

Laura was behind the bar, stocking the well. Noticing my presence, she leaned over, gave the old-timer a slap on the arm and a, "Hey." He screwed up his face at her. "This is Clark," she said, pointing in my direction. "He's about to drive down to Mexico. You should talk to him, tell him where to go." I ambled up to the bar. Laura turned to me. "This old guy's spent a lot of time down there, fishing."

"Who you callin' old?" he growled.

"Oh yeah?" I said, taking the stool next to him. "Where in Mexico?"

"All over," he grumbled. "Where *you* headed?"

"Don't know," I said. "Haven't planned it yet."

With a grunt and an old man's effort he turned his head and leaned back in order to fit me into his field of vision. "Why should I share my secrets of Mexico with you, huh?" His eyes narrowed to slits. "Why you goin'?"

I wished he hadn't of asked the question, cast about my mind for an appropriate response. Unable to formulate one, I gave him the one answer I didn't want to give. "I don't know. To escape, I guess." His gaze dropped to the wooden bar, engraved with all the local ranchers' cattle brands. He took a slug from his Budweiser, exhaled heavily.

"There's three things you should do every day," he began. "Take the juice of one lime, a shot of tequila, and a clove of garlic. Those will keep you healthy. Don't drive at night. Always have a can of gas with you, and oil. Are ya gettin' all this?"

"Uh huh," I nodded. Laura, who'd been listening from the other side of the bar, extracted a faded invoice from amongst the dusty bottles. She slapped it down in front of me then rummaged through the cash drawer for the dull stub of a pencil, handed it over. I jotted down *tequila, limes, shot a day, garlic*. Laura opened a Budweiser, set the bottle in front of me.

"Skip Tijuana," the old man continued. "Stay away from all the border towns. Head east to San Felipe, it's a little fishing village on the Gulf of California. From there you'll want to go down to Mulegé on the east coast of Baja. That's M-u-l-e-g-é." He stared up at the wall, smiling as he made this trip in his memory. "Then down the peninsula to Cabo San Lucas. You gettin' all this? Here give me that." He took the pencil from my hand and continued the itinerary in bold capital letters.

"From Cabo to La Paz where you can catch the ferry to Mazatlán. Then down the coast to San Blas..." These names and places meant nothing to me, yet each one touched on something deep inside me. I smiled and nodded and took it all in as his pencil scratched across the page and his mind wandered down the coast of Mexico. I had had no idea of where to start this journey and was glad to have this unexpected input. The old guy finished and again leaned back to size me up through narrowed eyes.

"Thank you," I said, extending a hand.

"Don't thank me," he pushed his stool back from the bar. "Just be respectful. Stay open, and be *there* when you're there." He threw a fiver down on the bar. "Thanks Laura," he said and walked out the door.

Wonder if he is what you one day will become.

Three

I had expected to arrive San Felipe in the middle of the night or the beginning of the following morning because so much has happened in the day, time has been so dense. Instead, our arrival is entry into a perpetual twilight. The sun hides behind hills, neither rising nor falling but lingering in shifting shades of orange and apricot. *Are we still in the same day? Or is it the next night already, the sun having failed to shine on our canyon drive?*

It's hot. A wooden sign at the entrance to town announces "San Felipe," and someone has scrawled at the bottom, "The only way to live happy the months of July, August are crazy, drunk, and nude." (*Take warning.*)

San Felipe is a small town. Bars and restaurants line the main boulevard along the Gulf shore. Taco vendors push their carts along the wide esplanade of the *malecón* past old men who lean against the sea wall suspended in eternal conversation. Children peer over ice cream cones with those huge, wonderful, brown eyes. *Mariachis* wander the beach with instruments, hot in sequined jackets.

We drive north along the coast, canvassing the town for a place to camp. After a couple kilometers the road ends, white sand giving way to a muddy yard full of ancient ships. Pirated, beached, and listing moonward, their rusted hulls stand empty except of untold history. Behind this graveyard a hill rises, extends a precipitous appendage that supports a lighthouse out over the water. Beyond it, a steep slope ascends yet higher. Hundreds of stairs meander lazily up to a small whitewashed building topped by a cross. I turn the Combi around and follow the beach south, continuing our reconnaissance.

We find a perfect campground right on the beach. It is empty of campers but several people scurry about carrying firewood and lumber, sawing and hammering together a stage, their activities directed by a short, scowling man. When we inquire about renting a campsite, he shakes his head *no* but we can't transcend the language barrier to the *why* of the matter. He repeats no and directs us next door to another campground.

This one is full of families lazing about. Polkas blare out of portable stereos and open-doored cars. The proprietor is wide and old and friendly and rents us a beachfront site on the end, shaded by a palm leaf roof, a *palapa*.

"What's going on in the campground next door?" Rudy asks him.

"You do not know?" the man shouts.

We answer his amazed declaration of our ignorance with blank stares.

"The moon is full," his finger casts a trajectory into sky. Our eyes follow it up to the chalky orb. "There will be a fiesta tonight—dancing, drink, food..." he leans conspiratorially close and whispers, "*muchachas*. You must go."

We set up camp and then relax in the infinite twilight, roll up whatever victuals we've got into tortillas and ingest them for fuel, all the while maintaining the flow of *cerveza* into systems.

A band strikes up next door, lays a solid foundation of rhythm and builds in volume. We walk the beach and swim the sea to disperse the day until finally and suddenly the night arrives, steps into the scene and yanks her billowing skirts through as the door slams shut on the day.

"Hey Clark," Rudy calls. As I turn, he shoves a tiny square of paper into my mouth—just enough medicine to perpetuate the eternity of this day, saliva dissolving papyrus to pulp.

Now, next door to the party.

The adjacent campground is identical to the one we're staying in—a big, sandy plaza framed by a *palapa* roof. Dozens of inebriated bodies are jammed into the square, rhythmically rubbing against one another in oceanic waves.

A low stage is centered on the beachside of the plaza. From behind a wall of speakers, a half dozen teenagers perform American and British hits from the sixties and seventies, blurting out the Rolling Stones, Doors, Lennon, lyrics rolling out of their throats with barely an accent, words they have heard and repeated a thousand times with only a hint at their meaning, guitar, bass, drums, and keyboard going at the music like a taunted bull pursuing a red flag.

In the center of the square burns a large bonfire, not for the purpose of routing any chill, but as an avatar of the white goddess, *la Luna*, burning above. We enter the lunatic celebration frenzy, work the crowd through to the bar.

"*Dos margaritas*," Rudy orders.

The bartender plops two plastic tumblers of the icy green elixir down in front of us. "Four dollars," he frowns.

Rudy grabs a drink in each hand, "Can you get this Clark? My hands are full." He shrugs with that smirk of his as I reach for my wallet. "Why don't you get a couple for yourself while you're at it?" Typical.

A dusky brunette steps to the bar, an opportunity that won't get past Rudy. "Wanna dance?" he asks. Her red lips part in a smile. The first notes of "Love Shack" echo across the courtyard. Rudy drinks down both margaritas. "Here Clark," he hands me the two empty cups, "hold these," and he drags the brunette willingly into the melee.

I order two for myself, drink them down as the band progresses into the heavy metal classics of AC/DC, the percussionist's sticks blurring through air, lyrics flowing out like a thick, warm chowder. I order two more, drink them down as well.

The music screeches to a sudden halt but the energy of it continues to swarm about like fireflies, a murmur waving through this ocean of people, rising, falling, cresting and breaking. The charged undertone halts as abruptly as had the music, suspended in a pregnant silence. A thick trail of scented smoke curls upwards. Energy rushes away, retreating above and below, sizzles out of the here and the now. Heads drop in the sudden silence, a quietude flooded with the crackle of fire and hum of the moon.

From my station by the bar, I stare across the bent, reverent forms of the crowd, feel the energy channeling back in like an undertow, first through distant, disembodied cries, the clapping of hands, lonely twang of guitar string, rim shot becoming drum roll pumping it all back in, a dog, barking, crowd coming alive as the band launches from out of the shadows and into the music, "Bad Moon Rising," everybody moving now, wavering in the lunar glow.

Consider that the moonlight does not originate from that sphere itself, but is only the reflection of a dying star on the opposite side of the planet.

There, illuminated by the fire and dancing in partnership with the flames is a vision of woman in flowing white. The moment my eyes settle on her, I know she has something for me. But I can't approach her, can't handle any more rejection in my life right now.

There is a subtle tugging at my sleeve. I turn and...

Itch emanates, center cerebrum, extending outward, embracing brain, filling fingers with shooting sparks, declining spine, branching hips, splitting to the tips of the toes of my feet, emerging out, rushing up and over skin, across my scalp, hair on end in one of the most beautiful onsets of LSD there is—the Boomerang.

Take the medicine and ask a question then go on to something else while expectation recedes, slowly withdraws from your foreconscious until you've forgotten you took it. And the moment it's completely withdrawn from the stream of your thoughts, it reappears, perched on your shoulder, whispering in your ear, *remember me? LSD?*

I try to ignore it, turn back to whatever it was I was doing but whatever it was I was doing is now gone forever.

She's cute, go and introduce yourself, exhume that long dormant capacity for social interaction. C'mon Clark, you're in Mexico.

"Hi. I'm Clark."

Yes, that's it.

"Hi," her eyes flash and turn away, back to her circle of friends.

Don't give up. Don't let her get away. Persist. Continue to cast your lines, a different fly, lure, or bait until she bites and your hook sinks. Then reel her to the periphery to talk.

Christina is her name, visiting from Baltimore—a teacher and student, a thinker. We discuss philosophy and life, dance to the reggae beat the band maintains for the rest of the night. She is a beautiful person, but where will it go?

Don't worry, Clark. Just give in to this moment, this night, with her. Don't attempt to make it something it isn't. Enjoy it for what it is.

What was it the senator used to say, "Nothing just happens, everything is brought about?"

Yes, yes, but nothing need happen, not tonight, not now.

What about "everything happens for a reason?"

And que sera, sera, yes, there's a million ways we could look at this but there will be plenty of time on this journey for dealing with the philosophical dilemmas of cause and effect, plenty of space in the remainder of this treatise for healing your broken heart, for ameliorating the bereavement of your soul.

When the crowd thins after midnight—the moon at its apex—I offer to take Christina back to her lodging. We walk, long down the beach, bare feet through warm surf, past bodies snoring away, singles, couples, whole families stretched out on blankets, in hammocks and in the sand, on the hoods and roofs of cars, in the beds of trucks. The music follows us for miles. We lean on one another and laugh under the moon.

Know that you will always have this to return to.

I leave her quickly at her door to escape the uncomfortable uncertainty of a goodnight kiss, and begin the long walk home.

Four

I arrive back at camp just before the break of day. There's no sign of Rudy but the cooler is full of ice and Coronas, which weren't there the night before. Opening a beer I sit on the sand, gaze out across the sea. The moon is still in the sky, low over the hills behind me. It toys with the surf, luring waves up the beach and then driving them back. A gentle light spreads upwards, delineating distant horizon and giving texture to the undulating ocean before me. On the peak to the north, the steadfast shrine glows warmly.

Red leaps suddenly out of the sea and onto the sky like spilt grenadine soaking into a paper towel. The scene fills with color, a canvas streaked in broad brushstrokes of ivory sand, cobalt sea, scarlet sky, and swaths of cottony cloud pushing purple up into midnight shadows. Just before the sun peeks over edge of the earth, blue-white lightning streaks out of the clouds, reaches all the way down to the sea and branches once, twice, three times to herald the overdue arrival of a new day.

Pelicans begin to glide along the water's surface, breaking the night's fast. Two men, out in a boat, throw nets into the silence. Up and down the beach human bodies are awakening, raising heads, sitting up and leaning back on arms. They rub their eyes and gaze in silent awe (with me) at this birth of the day as the sun lifts itself fully out of the sleep of the sea and casts its long rosy arms across the surface of the earth to me, to you, to us all.

Rudy materializes out of the dawn. He has danced all night, played volleyball, run around on the beach. Neither of us has slept.

I slip into the surf with Rudy and float—one day into the next, just like that.

"How'd things go with what's-her-name?" Rudy asks.

"Christina?" I say. "Fine."

"Fine, and…?"

"We talked."

"You talked. That's nice, Clark. At least you talk to someone."

"I just can't handle any more rejection right now."

"You gotta get back in the game, man," says Rudy, looking out across the sea. "What are we doing today?"

"I don't know."

"You haven't planned anything? How un-Clark-like of you."

"We could sleep."

"I'm too tired to sleep," Rudy says. "We gotta do something."

"We could leave."

"Yeah," Rudy weighs this. "Where we going?"

"Cabo."

"Right. Did we decide which way we're going?"

"Not really. We just—I don't know what we did. It was yesterday for a really long time and now all of a sudden it's today and here we are."

"We were either going to take the highway out of Ensenada or go south from here on a dirt road, right?"

"Something like that."

"And which route does Clark think we should take, based on the extensive research I'm sure you've done?"

"The safest and easiest approach, of course, would be to go back to Ensenada and take the paved highway. But the mountains would be more scenic and challenging."

"And?" Rudy says, "Which do you recommend?"

"The highway or my way."

"Clark?"

"To be or not to be—" I say, and dive underwater.

That's one of your issues isn't it, your ambivalence to making decisions, big or small. Decision—the word is derived from the Latin root of incisus, to cut, divide, sever (like the function of your incisors), and that's what it's all about, decision-making. It's the cutting away (or biting off) of lateral impedimenta so as to eliminate options. Take a lesson from arbori-culture, the pruning of trees: thin out the branches in order to suppress lateral growth and encourage apical dominance, the vertical advancement of one main trunk, to narrow down the possibilities of your life to one route forward, one path leading down to the end of your existence. Maybe that's what has led you to this state of indecision—the fear that decisions will lead you closer to death. Journeys, by nature, are transformative. Let's focus on this as one of those aspects of your self to change on this voyage. Take a bite and chew it up good. Here's a hint: The important thing is not to make the right *decision, but to make* a *decision.*

"Well," says Rudy, when I surface for air, "we're already on the east coast. We might as well just head south. Isn't there some road rule about never going back, always moving forward, further..."

"Faster?" I finish. "It's not in the Book of Road Rules."

"It is now—*forward, further, faster.* I like the sound of that. Rule number eighteen—"

"Thirty-two," I correct him.

"Forward, further faster."

"That's not a rule," I say. "That's three adverbs."

"I know you, Clark. You wouldn't have mentioned the eastern route unless you wanted to take it. You just wanted *me* to suggest it so that if something bad happens, I get blamed."

"You're absolutely right."

"Of course I'm right," Rudy says. "I'll make the decision and I'll take the responsibility. What's the worst thing that could happen to us out there?"

"We die in the desert."

"Would that be so bad?"

"I guess not."

"Tell me something, Clark. Where are we?"

"San Felipe, Baja California Norte."

"Could you be a little *less* specific?"

"Oh," I say. "We're in Mexico?"

"Riiight," Rudy smiles, "we're in Mexico. Now, let's go take the road less traveled," and he backstrokes out to sea.

"Okay," I shout to him over the increasing distance between us, "but we should leave soon, so we're not driving in the dark tonight." I move out of the water, walk up to our camp, and open a beer.

We sit in the shade of the *palapa* as the day heats up. Remembering the advice of my travel agent, we each take a shot of tequila and suck down the juice of a sweet, green lime. Haven't gotten any garlic yet.

"Okay," I say, "you ready to hit the road?"

"Let's do it," says Rudy, and the two of us collapse for a well-needed siesta.

"It's too late to get on the road," I say upon awakening in the afternoon. "Why don't we hit it first thing tomorrow."

"Right now," Rudy says, "I say we hike up there." He points to the hilltop shrine at the north end of town.

We trek through the muddy graveyard of lost ships to the base of the mount, stare up the one hundred ninety-six steps (without railing) to the small white temple at the top, sweat our way—step by step—up through the afternoon heat.

The shrine is three stucco walls and a roof, its open side enclosed with bars. Inside stands the Virgin—a meter-high maiden in plaster and paint, wrapped in her robe and gazing at swaddled babe in arms. This is the third time we've seen her this journey: the fingernail clipper, the cliff face, and now here, in three dimensions. It must *mean* something, this trio of apparitions.

Feel the energy invested in her. Imagine the hundreds of feet laying their soles bare on each of these timeworn steps every morning, every hour, grieving mothers and brokenhearted pescadores, chanting children and panting dogs. Think about the burden of dreams they drape around her green, peeling-paint shoulders. Think of the collection of confessions deposited daily at her dust-covered feet. Imagine the multitude of misfortunes shoved into her arms.

"You want to say a prayer or something?" Rudy asks.

"No," I say.

"Aren't you Catholic?"

"I was *raised* Catholic," I say. "That doesn't mean I am Catholic."

Humble yourself anyway. Bow your head in silence. Try, but you just can't ask her to answer your questions, make your decisions. You cannot expect her to take on the additional encumbrance of your anxieties. She is already full, as replete with suffering as you are with guilt and anger and heartbreak. Why don't you instead give her something. Toss her one of the heavy pesos from your pocket.

"What was that?" Rudy asks, the clanging of the coin against the base of the idol having interrupted his meditations.

"An indulgence."

"Oh, like a wishing well," he says. "Gimme a peso."

"It ain't like blowing out the candles on a birthday cake." I fish another coin out of my pocket, hand it to Rudy. He closes his eyes, murmurs under his breath and heaves the coin. It hits the baby in the face with a clunk, drops to the floor and rolls out of sight.

"You hit the baby in the face," I say. "You beaned the baby Jesus!"

"Is that a bad thing?"

"Depends what you wished for."

We turn from the statue of the Virgin, take in the view from atop this mount, the length of beach and all that goes on in the lives of the town below.

Mytho-Historical Departure
An Abridged History of The Virgin of Guadalupe

In 1521, the Aztec capital of Tenochtitlán fell to the forces of Cortés, completing Spain's Conquest of Mexico. The Spaniards spent the following decade dispossessing the Aztecs of their land and culture, repressing indigenous religions, and indoctrinating the *Indios* in their male-dominated monotheism, leaving them little choice but to accept Jesus Christ as their savior (or at least give that impression) and slip into the role of docile peasants. It was in this atmosphere of religio-cultural repression that a miracle took place, a singularity that begat the unstoppable turning of a quiet revolution.

In December of 1531, Juan Diego, an indigenous peasant (and recently converted Christian), was on his way to church. Dawn broke as he approached the hill at Tepeyac, north of Tenochtitlán (modern-day Mexico City). As he passed around the side of the hill, someone called out his name from the mount. "Juan," the beautiful voice sang out. "*Oye*, Juanito..." Intrigued, Juan climbed the hill to find out whom it was calling to him. Towards the top, he was confronted by a floating vision, a dark-skinned woman in a blue-green shawl, radiating a solar brilliance.

"Whoa!" he said. "Who are you?"

"Be it known that I am Mary, the Virgin Mother, who gives birth to all things and receives them back at death. I am the Mother of God, Creator of the Heavens and of the Earth. I am the compassionate mother, protector, and healer of you and all who seek me out and confide in me."

"You fit all that on a business card?"

"Juan, I need your help. I want a temple built here, a *teocalli* where people can come and tell me of their suffering and hardships, unburden themselves of their pain and misery, a place where I can give them my love and compassion, and help them through life's challenges."

"Sounds ambitious. How can *I* help?"

"I need you to go see the Bishop in his palace in Tenochtitlán. Tell him of my miraculous appearance. Tell him you represent me, the Mother of God, and that I want a temple built here, on the hill at Tepeyac where people can come and worship me."

"But he'll never believe me," Juan whined.

"Don't worry, Juan. I'll give you proof that you can take to the Bishop," said the Virgin. "All you have to do is climb to the top of this hill and pick all the flowers you find there—"

"Flowers?" Juan exasperated. "In the dead of winter?! If I find any flowers at all it would be a mira— Oh I get it."

"Gather them in your *tilma* and take them to the Bishop. That should be more than enough proof of my miraculous appearance."

So Juan climbed to the top of the hill and found there big, beautiful blossoms in the fullness of their blooms. He gathered the flowers, cradled them in his cloak, and went down the hill to the Bishop's palace. Holding his *tilma* close against his chest, Juan relayed to the Bishop the story of the Virgin Goddess's miraculous appearance on the hill at Tepeyac and of her desire to have a temple built there.

"Look Juan," said the Bishop, "that's a great story and I appreciate your sharing it with me. But I'm afraid I can't start a construction project based on your crazy tale."

"But you *must*. She's the mother of our savior, the Lord Jesus Christ."

"Don't you blaspheme!" said the Bishop.

"It was a miracle, I tell you!"

"You can't go around proclaiming miracles Juan, unless you've got some proof."

"That's exactly what *I* said."

"And...?"

"And the Virgin told me to go to the top of the hill and gather flowers. She told me to give them to you as a sign of the miraculicity of her apparition so you can fulfill her wish to have a *teocalli* built at the place she asked, where people can come and worship her."

"Flowers?" the Bishop chuckled, "in the dead of winter?! That's impossible. Why that would be a mira—"

On cue, Juan Diego let drop the corners of his *tilma* and the precious blossoms cascaded to the floor. The Bishop's mouth fell open.

"Yessiree, flowers in winter," Juan gloated. But the Bishop was not looking at the pile of flowers on the floor. He was instead staring at the front of Juan's now-exposed *tilma* in which the flowers had been cradled. Juan looked down and saw the stain left by the miracle blossoms, a divine image of the Virgin of Guadalupe as she had appeared to Juan, wrapped in her star-studded green shawl, supported by a black crescent moon on the shoulders of an angel, with the rays of the Fifth Sun emanating from her being.

News of the Apparition spread rapidly through the indigenous community. The dark-skinned goddess quickly garnered a large following among the *Indios* who believed her appearance was a miracle and her Image—imprinted on Juan's *tilma*—a gift divine. The pressure to fulfill her wish to build a *teocalli* on the hill at Tepeyac where people could worship her became undeniable.

Today you can still go to the hill at Tepeyac, visit la Basilica de Nuestra Señora de Guadalupe, and see the original image imprinted on Juan's *tilma*. There also you can worship her, unburden yourself of pain, misery, and suffering, that she may protect you, take you into the fold of her garment, and heal you.

Five

W e're up before the sun, packed and ready. We stop in town to replenish our *cerveza* reserves. At the back of the liquor store is an insurance desk.

"Should we buy some insurance for the Combi?" Rudy asks.

"Might as well."

The insurance agent/liquor salesman sells us a year's policy for eighteen bucks, asks what we're doing, where we're going.

"We're driving south, through the mountains," I say. "Do you know the road?"

"I do," he says. "It's pretty rough—all rocks, potholes and cliffs. You oughta be able to make it in a combi, though. Just take it slow and bring a good spare. Those rocks will eat your tires."

We say nothing to one another as we drive south to the edge of town, stop at the crossroads. One sign points right, Ensenada 265 km, and the other left, Puertecitos 75 km, the little town at the base of the mountains, at the end of the road.

"We do have a spare tire," I ask Rudy, "right?"

"Of course we do."

I gun the Combi towards the mountains.

"It's flat though."

Saguaro cactus dot the western hillside. To the east, there's nothing but white sand from the road's shoulder down to the shoreline. We pass no other cars on the highway as we drive south for an hour on the still-paved road to the tiny, inconceivable town of Puertecitos.

Puertecitos is the last outpost of civilization and gasoline before the high desert wilderness ahead. And it's deserted, a ghost town. There are homes and businesses, a gas station we pull into, but not a single person nor sound nor stirring of dust. We honk, knock on the station door, shout, but no one appears to sell us gasoline. The Combi has three quarters of a tank but there are three hundred miles of unpaved obscurity ahead. We wait around for half an hour, but no sign of life materializes.

"Should we go back?"

"Hell no." *Onward!*

I drive us through to the end of the road at the base of a hill where the pavement, the town, just end. El Tiburón climbs onto the dirt hill and ascends away from civilization, carried along by the momentum that drives us, that force which propels us from behind (*or draws you forward*).

The road isn't even dirt. It's solid, jagged rock, as promised. The twisted, rutted, potholed mess winds its way upward, providing fantastic vistas of the Gulf of California, the Sea of Cortés. The Combi pounds up and over this obstacle course. Hot, dusty air flows in through the open windows as if blown from a furnace.

Although we never move faster than 15 miles an hour, the road beats the hell out of the bus, tires, suspension, us. At the back of the Combi, canned provisions rattle loudly on a wooden shelf. The temperature sizzles up past 100°. An hour of this beating and we're thrashed, stop for a break. Rudy slathers thick gobs of peanut butter and jelly onto slices of wheat bread for our sustenance. Then, I lie down on the back seat, slide into sleep while Rudy takes a turn at the wheel.

My awakening is rude. The Combi pitches steeply sideways and jerks to a stop, throwing me to the floor.

"Wake up!" Rudy yells. (*As if...*)

I pick myself up. The Combi shifts with a groan.

"Don't move!" he says. "We're gonna roll."

"What?"

"See, there was this pothole in the road and I swerved to miss it. But in retrospect, that may have been a bad call." I slide open the side door and tumble out onto the ground, survey the situation. Rudy's swerved off the solidity of the causeway and into the deep sand of the shoulder. The Combi rests at a 45° angle—half on, half off the road. Her rear end is hung up on the raised roadway. One wheel spins freely.

"It's too steep to back up," I say. "We're going to have to go forward," about fifty feet through the sand, "and steer it back onto the road."

"If we can find the road," Rudy says. "It seems to disappear up ahead."

We dig and push and push and dig and soon it's noon, mercury rising to a hundred and ten. Cascades of perspiration drain our inner reservoirs; take us to the edge of dehydration. An hour later we've managed to move it only ten feet onto more level, but no more stable, ground. Not a single car has passed us since we left San Felipe. And there's not a tree in sight to provide us shady refuge, not even a cactus.

"What now?" Rudy asks, as if there is anything else.

"Take a nap," I say and lie down in the narrow strip of shade the Combi provides.

"A nap?!" he says, but can think of no argument against it and exhaustedly throws himself down next to me. "Yeah, nap."

Flat on my back, eyes closed, blood pounds in head.

"Rudy—what is the purpose of underwear?"

"Don't know. Never worn it."

"It's so damn uncomfortable in this heat."

"Then stop wearing it."

"You're right. From now on, it's just shorts and bare feet and nothin' else. I am no longer going to wear underwear."

"That's great Clark."

That was beautiful.

What?

You made a decision.

It was nothing, really.

Yes it was. It was more than a decision, it was commitment to an unequivocal change in lifestyle. I'm proud of you.

"There is one drawback," Rudy chimes into my internal dialogue, "to going *al fresco...*"

"Yeah, what's that?"

"You've always got a handicap at strip poker."

"That's right, you always are the first one out."

Twenty minutes into our sweltering rest we're roused by a distant rumble approaching from up ahead. We leap to our feet and the roadside. From the cloud of dust that moves steadily up the hill, a multicolored Volkswagen squareback emerges bearing two girls and two guys, surfers from San Diego, topless in the heat.

Their oil pan has been punctured by a rock on the rugged road. They've managed to patch it but are dangerously low on oil.

"We've got some oil," Rudy offers. "We'll trade you for a push." Rudy and the two guys put their weight behind the Combi. I work the wheel as it plows slowly but steadily through the sand and back onto the compacted roadway. We thank them, give them half our case of oil.

"You guys wouldn't have any extra gas would you?" Rudy asks.

"No. We were gonna ask you the same thing. They were outta gas in the last town we passed through."

"Same thing thatta way, no gas."

We wish each other luck and continue on down the same path, journeying in different directions.

Late afternoon finds us still bumping over the rocky road, running on fumes, trying to complete the final leg of this nightmare by nightfall. The road begins to curve inland, away from the sandy shoreline, winds its way up into the hills. Landscape shifts suddenly from barren plain to Sonoran desert, the archetypical desert burned into my imagination by John Ford westerns and Wile E. Coyote dramas. Elephant trees hang their copper branches over the roadway. Saguaro cactus stand at attention like columns of soldiers extending up the mountainside. Cirio stretch their arms to the sky. Recent rains have greened the spiny ocotillo, adding color to the desert canvas. Long-eared rabbits scurry across roadway, playing chicken with our radial tires.

Dropped from the sky amongst this flora and fauna are immense, square boulders, leaning into roadway. The setting sun angles across their surfaces eliciting textures, deepening features, revealing faces which watch our passage with a careful eye.

I'm looking at the dashed line on the map and at the so-called road, trying to make the two of them jibe but they won't. I see no need to concern Rudy with this. He's already preoccupied with the reality of running out of gas. Darkness falls and stars appear, guiding us across time, through space.

At midnight, the stone road drops suddenly into the end of a paved cul-de-sac, the same way we'd entered it. Right there is a darkened *gasolinera*, standing alone in the night. We coast the Combi in, pull up to the pump as she sputters dead, out of gas.

Six

We arrive Cabo San Lucas on Friday just as the sun is setting, change the rest of our dollars for pesos and suddenly we're millionaires! After showering and dressing in our cheap hotel room I find Rudy on the balcony, feet up, taking in the town, working a bottle of Kahlúa.

"Well," he passes me the bottle, "we made it."

"Yes we did—Cabo San Lucas."

"How long we been on the road now, a week?"

"One week," I say. "One thousand forty-nine miles."

"We've covered a thousand miles already?"

"Just since Tijuana."

"I guess we ought to celebrate."

The night is warm. A high ceiling of cloud rolls in, smelling of rain. We walk downtown, wander the main boulevard, up and down the waterfront, in and out of shops and stalls, past tourist bars and restaurants, absorbing the town, searching for that which is not seen, the foundations, the energy, the history that drives this place.

For this is what you need do in a strange locale. Look beyond the outward colors and into the shadows from whence those vibratory radiances emanate. You can't just rub up against the glossy exterior. You need to look for the alleyways, the cracks in the walls, the rough, uneven surfaces. These will be your ports of entry to the other side. Approach the town with respect and let it push you a little but don't be afraid to push it back. History and culture are not intractable. They will yield and may only reveal themselves against the coarse grain of your personality.

Alas the night is empty, the town sleeping, and we don't have the drive to awaken it.

Perhaps you're afraid also to awaken that which slumbers in you. Loosen your grip but don't let go.

In preparation for the day ahead, we eat a filling breakfast early Saturday—not just for the nutritive value but to provide us a grounding point of reference (*a point of condensed rational logic from which to move away, forward furthur faster into the chaos of the expanding universe, a point to look back on from the future and reminisce about the carefully ordered sanity which dispersed rapidly in the wake of the big bang*).

Huh?

Back at the room we change into our loudest drinking shirts.

"Why don't we check out of the hotel," Rudy says.

"Where we gonna stay tonight?"

"I don't know, but tell me this—would you rather spend money on beer or on another night in this foot locker?"

"Beer it is."

We hydrate ourselves, load the ice chest with a case and a half of Corona and ice, tune our hand drums, and drive out to the five-star resort at the east end of town. We park in their lot and carry all of our paraphernalia around the building, past their swimming pool crowded with screaming tourists, make our way to the beach.

For it is now the day and the time for us to fulfill a goal, a shared vision which manifested in the frigid air high above the rippling surface of the Gulf of Alaska, a dream which got us through that cold winter, traveled with us from that Gulf to this one, a stereotype we must embody of the ugly, hedonistic American, the capitalistic *Norte Americano* exploiting the vulnerable resources of a developing country. For this is the collective picture we have brought with us in the weave of our culture, the drama we must act out before we can cast it aside.

And so we move again into that space of chemically altered reality, doubling the dosage this time, and lay in the sunbeams of truth, swim in the surf of the ego, imitate with our drums the rhythmic interaction of sea and shore.

We drink Coronas all day on the beach in Cabo San Lucas, reveling in the fact that we have made it all the way down from Alaska, celebrating the success of having disembarked from that rust-bucket of a boat in the noncontiguous United States of America, crossed through three countries (ambassadors of NAFTA goodwill), followed the western contours of North America, through the length of both Californias (*Alta* and *Baja*) here, to the southern tip of the Baja Peninsula. We allow what will come to come. And on it comes.

Etymological Aside
How California Came to be Named for a Queen

Yes, we have traversed this sovereignty, covered the 2,059-mile coast of the Californias. Look at it this way, as one long autonomous tract of land haphazardly riven by state and international borders, cultures. Picture it as it once was, one long, narrow strip bounded by the Pacific Ocean on one side, the Sierra Nevada and Gulf of California on the other. Here is how it was first described (before it was ever seen or "discovered") in a Spanish novel of 1510, *Las Sergas de Esplandian:*

Know ye that at the right hand of the Indies there is an island named California...which is inhabited by black women, without a single man among them... They are robust of body, with strong and passionate hearts and great virtues. Their island...with its steep cliffs and rocky shores...everywhere abounds with gold and precious stones... There reigns in this island of California a Queen of majestic proportions, the most beautiful of them all... The very mighty Queen Calafía, Lady of the great Island of California.*

Imagine the minds of Cortés' men, inflamed with this popular novel as they followed the sun of 1535 across *España Nueva* to the west coast. Then, setting off again across the water (still searching for the Indies?) and coming to this seeming "island of steep cliffs and rocky shores." It was only a short jump from there (no wider than a synaptic cleft) to "gold and precious stones" and a bona fide Queen for whom they named this "new" land.

It's Her *again, the goddess, the virgin, a real queen, if only in the collective imagination real—Calafía ruling the monarchy, California, that island which you at one time (in the past) and may again (in the future) call home, Queen Calafía and her namesake, California.*

My homeland is named after a queen?

Just as this place is. And if you were to ask, the locals here would tell you that they also are Californios, they too are Americans—North Americans—and that theirs also is a country of United States.

How, then, am I to distinguish myself?

Maybe you should stop trying. The important thing is that you've made it this far, to the beach at the end of the Californias, the southwesternmost

---

*Garcia Ordonez de Montalvo, *Las Sergas de Esplandian*, 1510. Translation by the author.

point of land on the Americas. Pause for a moment. Allow yourself to catch up and inhabit your body. Feel the sense of accomplishment. Forget about the challenges of future and past and enjoy this success. Now move on.

Make your presence known. Swim, play and laugh, make too much noise, drink too much beer, take too much acid and engage every person who passes by. Draw a circle around yourselves in the sand of your existence and challenge every passerby to step across. Observe the division of those who shy away, intimidated, and those few who accept the proffered beer, who will share their stories, laugh with you, those who will step onto the bus, if only for a short ride.

The sun sets but we don't realize it until the moon rises, laughing at us. We take more medicine, drink more beer, keep going until we're completely gone, lit up like Christmas trees, sitting alone on the beach at Cabo San Lucas, sipping at a cooler full of ice and Coronas.

We pack the empties into the cooler and leave. And with this done we leave something behind, a part of America washed out of us, a boundary dissolved.

As far as I know we're going back to the hotel, to check-in for another night. But Rudy is driving the Combi and the LSD is driving Rudy. Jim Morrison wails loudly out of the tape player, backed by the Doors. (I have long suspected that Rudy believes himself to be the reincarnation of Jim Morrison.)

As we drive past the hotel turnoff I say, "Hey, you just passed—" but Rudy ignores me. There's another voice in his head, leading him down another path.

He stops in front of a liquor store, engine idling, staring straight ahead, away from me. Without a word, I run in, return with another twelve pack. He drives on through town and up the base of a hill, makes a U-turn and passes back down, through town, again missing the hotel turnoff. A dog falls in behind us, takes up the chase of the Combi.

At the east end of town we start up another hill, make it halfway, turn around and roll back through, faster this time. Another dog falls in for the chase. And another, growing to a pack.

It occurs to me that Cabo San Lucas is situated in a gigantic bowl between mountains. Rudy is driving up one side and then the other of this bowl, higher and higher each time in an attempt to build enough momentum to propel el Tiburón right off the rim, right out of this cereal bowl and onto God's breakfast table. We hit the edge of town and vertical on the last paved roadway until we break from the gravitational field, break free of the pavement and onto a dirt path, momentum carrying us to the top of the mountain.

We stop and get out, high atop the ridge of dark hills surrounding town, take in the view, the electric lights of the city below fading to the water's edge where sandy shoreline glows white in the waning moon.

Breathe.

"Tomorrow we'll go to La Paz," I say, "and catch the ferry to Mazatlán, the mainland."

"Sounds good," says Rudy. "It'll be nice to be on a boat again."

We sip at beers, in the moment. The motley pack of dogs finally catches up, panting and yapping, exhausted from the chase. We feed them all of our hot dogs, share with them our jug of *agua*, invite them to behold with us the *vista*.

Seven

The boat rocks gently across the Gulf of California, the Sea of Cortés as the day reaches its end. The salt air comes to me as an echo of last year's sea voyage—from that ship to this one, then as a wage slave working towards a goal, now as a passenger, relieved to be moving away (*away from a point in the past whence you still were caught in the clenched fist of Time*).

It's late. Run your eyes around the interior of the ship seeking a clock on a wall, a watch on a wrist. Find none. Look out the window for the rising and falling horizon, see that it is obscured by night. Search the sky for some celestial chronometer, as if the angle of the Milky Way will give you the hour, or the juxtaposition of Pleiades to Orion's belt will provide some structure within which to establish a point of reference. Time lurks out there somewhere, hiding in the darkness of the shadow you cast. But you can find no time here. Where has it gone?

Time is elusive, it has run out and you can't get your filthy little hands around its fleeing, fleeting, forked tail. It has escaped you, for now. Don't worry though, you'll catch up to it. (Or it, you.)

Before we go any further, realize this: Time is not stalking you at all. Your infatuation with time is an entirely unreciprocated pursuit. You are pursuing Time, not as a long-range goal, but like a rodent, a rat in your basement to be captured and eliminated from the palette of your fears.

For we fear that which goes unnamed, unframed, unbounded. We've made it our mission to control nature, to subdue our environment. The naming of names is a form of control, a way of separating, isolating, distinguishing entities from their surroundings. This dividing is conquering, and conquering is controlling.

In nature there are only the endless cycles of darkness and light, the phases of the moon and the falling of leaves. But in the human mind we

have epochs, millenniums and nanoseconds. Time is but a massive dividing.
When did we first begin to measure our days, clock our lives and calibrate
reality? When did time begin to turn? Was it with the first systematic
surveillance of sun across sky? Or was it mindfulness of the migration of
shadows across earth? Was it the advent of the sundial? The hourglass? Or
should we date time's beginning only back to 604 C.E. when Pope Sabinus
instituted the ringing of bells to mark the passing of the hours?
     Ah, the ringing of bells, that manifest destiny, divide and conquer,
name and control, the ringing of bells, division of day, that cutting again,
di: divide, decide, dissect, divorce, sever, cut, cleave, Time. *It's inside of*
you, ticking away, gnawing on your intestines. It's tearing you apart, as a
person, a people, a planet, Time. *Ask not for whom the bell tolls. (It tolls*
for thee, motherfucker.)
     Now it is even later.

     I awaken early Tuesday as the boat enters the calm waters of
Mazatlán's harbor. Rudy and I make our way to the hold of the ferry, jump
in the Combi and use the momentum of the docking ship to launch el
Tiburón onto the mainland.
     We travel from one end of Mazatlán to the other but there is nothing
here to stop us. We don't need another tourist trap in which to burn our
money on booze and lodging. We keep rolling, as I peruse the scrawl of our
itinerary.
     "San Blas is next on the list."
     "What's that?"
     "Don't know."
     "Sounds good."
     "Let's go."
     We head south along the Pacific Coast. It's a different landscape and
climate here on the mainland, greener than Baja, and humid. It's jungle,
lush green jungle is what it is. We pass through several small towns and I
try to imagine what life would be like in one of these *pueblos*. Look at
these people—up early every morning, sweeping in front of their homes
and shops, taking yesterday's bottles in for recycling, tossing buckets of
water onto the street to subdue the day's dust—each person tending to their
immediate surroundings until hectare by hectare the whole of their
homeland is heeded.
     Contrast this to the country you've left behind. Do you remember the
self-absorption, the traffic, the noise, the hurry? Do you remember the
tension in the air? The rate at which things moved? Mexicans seem to have
a whole different set of priorities. They seem to understand the importance

of life. They move at a slower, more deliberate pace. It's as if you've gone back in time—that's it, time! *It's slower here, so slow you can barely see it moving. People here seem to have the time to* be—*to be with family, bullshit with friends, to stand on the side of the road in the middle of nowhere and stare at the sky all day for no apparent reason. Look at that old guy—he's escaped time, standing on the side of the road forever. You should try that some day, forever.*

Four hours bring us to small fishing village of San Blas, a significant port up through the nineteenth century. The Spanish long had a fortress here to protect their trading galleons from British and French pirates. (*Keep this in mind: Spanish Conquistadors swashbuckling against Franglo pirates in order to protect the fruits of the land they're raping.*)

We take a narrow dirt road along the bay to the Hotel Bucañero, overshadowed by the oppressive jungle. It's an imposing structure from the outside, its foundation probably raised from the rubbled remains of that former stronghold.

A stuffed alligator creeps out of the shadows at us as we go through the arched opening and down a dark breezeway. We are dazzled, coming in from the darkness of the jungle to this sun-filled courtyard lush with palm, mango, and papaya trees, great colored birds, squawking for attention. Ivy and squash vines grow out of the square and across the arcaded walkway, deliberating our progress. Within the canopy of leaves and vines are the broken stumps of Corinthian columns and rusted cannon, aimed at our groins.

They give us a suite for a pittance, two bedrooms connected by a bathroom. It's dark, cool, and airy, red tile floors and high ceilings. We're tired and hungry after the twenty-four hour journey from La Paz to San Blas. We walk to the *zócalo*, the town square, for enchiladas and pork chops, a couple of cold ones. The heat and humidity zap us. We take the night slow. For dessert get a bottle of Kahlúa, find a roost affording a view of the nightly *paseo*, drink from bottle bagged in brown paper.

Etymological Aside
Zócalo

In 1521, you'll recall, the Spanish completed their conquest of Mexico with an attack on the Aztec capital, Tenochtitlán. The Aztec ceremonial center lay in ruins. This plaza, once full of pyramid-temples honoring the tutelary gods of water and war, had been the social and spiritual heart of Tenochtitlán as well as the symbolic center of the Aztec Universe.

The *Conquistadors* immediately put their newly enslaved labor force to work. Cortés had the Indios rake over the rubble of the ravaged square and — using stones from the destroyed district — lay out a new plaza atop the old, submerging the history, culture, and ideology of Tenochtitlán.

But, like a hardy rootstock, it didn't take long for the Aztec civilization to reemerge, sending out shoots that sprouted between the stones of the plaza. It was impossible for the *Conquistadors* to halt this growth so they pruned these emergences back as far as they could and grafted onto them their own culture and pantheon.

And so the garden grew, filling its plot and extending out of the square. A metropolis emerged from the soil surrounding the plaza, a hybridized garden of civilization which flourished across the island of Tenochtitlán, unchecked even by its shores, spreading across the lake, a rolling wave which emanated outwards from a dropped pebble in the pond of humanity, a rising tide which broke against the foothills and washed back upon itself, flooding the basin with the largest concentration of people on the planet.

On 16 September 1810, Father Miguel Hidalgo issued his famous *Grito de Dolores*, effectively commencing the Mexican Revolution (*that turning again*). "My children, a new mandate comes to us this day. Are you ready to receive it? Will you be free? Will you make the effort to recover from the hated Spaniards the lands stolen from your forefathers three hundred years ago? We must act at once... Long live Our Lady of Guadalupe! *¡Viva Mexico!*"

Propelled by the momentum of this speech, the Revolution pressed forward, enduring a decade before the tide again shifted. In 1821 — three hundred years after the Spanish conquest — Mexico regained her independence from Spain.

Shortly after this revolutionary victory it was decided that a monument (in commemoration of this deliverance from imperial rule) should be erected in Mexico City's central plaza. In anticipation of the installation of said monument, a stone plinth was fashioned in the center of the plaza. With the placement of this pedestal, construction on Mexico's testament and tribute to her liberation and autonomy ceased.

And so it endured — at the center of the plaza, in the center of the city, at the center of the universe the plinth stood — bare, naked, and unadorned, supporting only an invisible tension, an empty stage attended daily by an anxious audience eagerly awaiting the consummation of their sovereignty.

The *Indios* called the pedestal *zócalo*, and so this plinth came to be known. The name was extended to the plaza in general and subsequently to every central plaza in every Mexican town, from the smallest village to the largest city.

The *zócalo* is the central focus of every *pueblo*, the gathering point of the populace, the heart and soul of every community. This plaza usually occupies an entire city block or more. There's generally a stage or gazebo in the center or at a corner where proclamations may be made, pageants held, impromptu dances danced by little girls in blue dresses and patent leather shoes. Always, one side of the *zócalo* is towered over by the church, *el catedral.*

Rudy and I walk back across town, through the cobbled night and jungle murk to the relative coolness of our musty rooms. I strip down to my shorts and lie across the chenille bedspread, let the slow-turning fan breathe down on me from high ceiling.

A light comes on in the bathroom, shimmies under the door, reflects off the floor and shines on ceiling, creating a second fan above. Sound of toilet seat dropping. A voice.

Voices?

"Rudy?" I say.

"Yeah?"

"You okay in there?"

"Well," he clears his throat, "I'm having a Mexico experience in here."

"Montezuma's Revenge?"

"No, no."

"Well what?"

There's a pause behind the bathroom door as he pulls together his tale. "You see, I came in here and sat down to do my business, when this cockroach comes walkin' across the floor. And when he sees me, he stops in the middle of the floor and stands up on his hind legs."

"This is a cockroach we're talkin' about?"

"Yeah, and he says to me, '*What, so I'm a cockroach.*' And I say to him, 'Look, I've got no problem with that.' And I don't. But now he's pounding his other legs on his chest."

"*I can withstand freezing temperatures,*" a small, cockroach voice declares from the bathroom. "*I can survive a nuclear war, swim a hundred miles...*"

"Look," Rudy says, "I'm sorry if I'm a threat to your machismo or whatever."

"*You're gonna be sorry,*" the cockroach says. "*Why are you picking up that trash can?*"

"This? I'm just going to put it on my head like a party hat, see? La la la—" The sudden metallic wham of garbage can on tile floor jolts me. "Take that, you little bastard."

"*You goddamned asshole*," says a muffled cockroach voice. Toilet flushes.

Rudy comes into my room, sits in the armchair by the window, stares up at the revolving fan. "Where we going tomorrow?" he asks.

"I don't know," I say. "Take a look at the itinerary. It's stuck in that book."

He takes it out, unfolds it, grimaces.

"This is it?" he asks.

"Yeah."

"Just the one page?"

"Just the one."

"This is it."

"Yeah, *that's it.*"

"That wasn't a question," Rudy says. "I'm telling you, *this is it.* San Blas is the last place listed."

"Really?" I sit up on the bed. "There's nothing else?"

"Just something about Tequila and garlic and don't drink the water."

You hadn't imagined getting to this point, had you? —the edge of a whole other frontier. Did the old guy at the bar, your travel agent, get no further than San Blas?

"Let me see that."

I look at the itinerary, the broad graphite scribbles drawn up between Budweisers on a bar-top so long ago. I hadn't noticed this before—it doesn't end with a period, but with three. What're those called—ellipses? *An* ellipse? That's no ending. Did he not expect us to get this far? Did *I* think we'd make it this far?

"Let's look at the map," I say, getting it out of my bag and spreading it across the bed.

"Hey look," Rudy points. "Guadalajara isn't far from here. I know people there."

"That's pretty far inland," I say. "We should stay along the coast." I feel better with the ocean in sight.

"C'mon," Rudy says. "Let's go check out Guadalajara, see what it's like."

"But the coast is so scenic—the beaches and the ocean. There's always a place to camp..."

And it provides a shoreline of reference, a boundary to limit your movement. It eliminates at least one direction in which you might move, making decisions that much easier. Keep the ocean at your back and it's one less side to defend (except against pirates).

"We could probably find jobs in Guadalajara," Rudy says.

Ah, there's the rub. You just want to keep moving, taking in as much of Mexico as you can. And Rudy, he wants to stay in one place for a time, find employment, have Virginia come and visit. You're always the one who gets the show on the road and Rudy's the one who creates the opportunities to remain on the road, which usually means being in one place for a while and working. Look where it got you in Alaska.

"All right, we'll go to Guadalajara," I concede, "and see how it is. But eventually we return to the coast and continue on, right?"

"Of course."

Right.

Part Two

Guadalajara

Eight

udy leans the Combi down winding curves, zooms it through the jungles of Nayarit. One of those crazy, multicolored Mexican buses gets on our ass, headlights flashing, air horns blowing. It pulls out to pass us on an impossible blind turn, roars up alongside the Combi and flashes by in a rainbow blur of crucified Jesus and blue Virgin, lengths of prayer scrolling past us like a subtitle, a *message* trimmed in chrome and bordered by an unbroken line of green running lights.

Faces peer down on us from above as they pass, the windows full of straw-hatted men and *rebozo*-wrapped women. A trail of feathers floats out of the crates lashed to her rear and into our open windows as the bus overtakes, cuts in front of us, teetering with a top-heavy load of trunks and bags piled on roof. The bus moves rapidly away, increasing the distance between us, passing every car it comes to without faltering or breaking stride. Rudy isn't going to let her go though, *oh no*. He pushes the Combi to catch up.

Then, the Combi slips right out from underneath his foot, jumps from lane to lane down the narrow highway, duplicating every move the bus makes, passing insanely. I put my faith in the road and the engineers at Volkswagen. (*Know that el Tiburón is distantly related to Herbie the Love Bug, from that same family of fine automobiles.*)

Car by car we close the gap and before you know it we're on the rear bumper of the bus. Rudy lets a straight stretch of asphalt pass away beneath our wheels, waits for a truck to come head-on out of a blind turn then downshifts into third, *into that reserve of power*, second, *that potential for speed*, and the Combi pulls out, moves confidently towards the oncoming truck, flashes the brights of its own accord and moves steadily past the length of diesel burning bus until we're neck and neck. I look over at the driver and he's laughing.

The oncoming truck has varied not in its velocity nor bearing and just before we collide head-on in a 150 kph impact the bus defers, downshifts, and the Combi pulls in front. I can see the driver, laughing in our rearview mirror, laughing until he turns with a honk and a wave and is gone.

Know that the race against time is not always a race to be won. Remember all the footraces you lost as a kid? Your subsequent invention of the slow race in which whoever crossed the finish line last was the winner? Finally something at which you could triumph. Nobody could run slower than you.

It is sometimes better to be behind time, running late, better to sneak up on time's rear bumper. Move fast enough and you'll pass the bus, faster still and you'll come around again and be stuck behind it, inhaling its exhaust because the world is spherical, because space is curved, time is cyclical, because the face on a clock is a circle and the hands always return to midnight.

Stand at the bus stop there on the corner sometime to see this illustrated most vividly. Watch the bus coming down the road, feel its rumble up through your feet, your legs. Absorb the puddle thrown up by its dual wheels as it passes you by with complete disregard. But don't be discouraged, don't leave. Stay there, stand there, it may take years, but if the bus keeps going forward it will eventually circle the globe and pass you by again. (If we had the capacity, were endowed with the perceptions to perceive the end of infinity, the edge of eternity, time would cease to exist altogether.)

We have now reached a point where we can proceed no further without attempting at least a shallow comprehension of Einstein's Theories of Relativity. No, no! Don't change the channel! Please bear with me. I'm going to give it to you in just a few easy steps.

In 1687, Sir Isaac Newton gave us his law of universal gravitation *which described how each body in the universe is attracted to every other body. He postulated that wherever there is a massive body there is a gravitation field. And, the denser the body, the more intense the gravitation. Makes sense, right?*

Then in 1915, Albert Einstein published his general theory of relativity. *He proposed that gravity is* not *a force of attraction (as Newton contended) but is a result of the* curvature of space *around objects. He made the revolutionary suggestion that the three-dimensional space in which we live is actually curved around massive bodies, warped by the distribution of energy and mass.*

Now, we add to the three dimensions of space *a fourth dimension of* time *and things get really twisted. Space and time are inseparable in*

Einstein's relativity theory. Albert called this the space-time manifold *or* continuum. *Just as space is curved around objects, so also is time affected by the presence of matter. As the curvature of space varies from place to place—according to the distribution and density of matter and energy—so does the flow of time.*

Yes, the progression of time is not universally constant but is also curved, warped, moving at different rates in different places. You already know this, have seen it. Time is subjective. People experience differing rates in the flow of time, in body and mind.

That wasn't so bad, was it?

The jungle thins as we enter the state of Jalisco, road straightens, landscape becomes rockier, sandier, more arid. We cruise into the blue fields of agave outside Tequila, *a town actually named Tequila*, the first of several small, dusty *pueblos* heralded with a yellow sign announcing, "TOPE."

"What does *tope* mean?" I ask Rudy.

"I don't know."

"Maybe it's like *town* or something—to alert us we're coming into one?"

No.

We are suddenly jolted out of our seats—bodies rising skyward—as the front tires bounce over the heap of cement and rebar sculpted onto the roadway, front axle jamming into underside, heads jamming into ceiling as front wheels land hard and rear axle kicks up and over.

"I know," Rudy says. "*Tope* means speed bump."

Tequila—this is where the stuff comes from, originated. We stop at one of the multitudinous roadside stands to purchase an unlabeled, three-liter bottle of the thick, amber elixir from which to draw our daily ration. Then onwards to Guadalajara. And oh how good it feels to be moving across the land. (*But you don't want to get anywhere too soon, too fast...*)

Mexican Life and Culture
The Economics of Speed Bumps

There is a *tope* (*toe-pay*) across the road at each end of every *pueblo* in Mexico. That little *hump-hump* beneath you defines your entry into and exit out of each little town. These speed bumps force you to slow your drive that you don't bust your shock absorbers or teeth.

What this means to the community is that you don't stir up their dust, run over their dogs, their children, etc. These beneficial attributes, however, are only collateral byproducts of the *tope's* inherent fiscal implications. Speed bump economics dictate that you decelerate sufficiently to facilitate the extraction of pesos from your pockets by the *pueblo's* entrepreneurs.

Much of the local income is derived from your reduction in speed, your slowing enough that signs may come into focus, a blur of words shouting *Mariscos, Refrescos, Tacos al Pastor*, accompanied by the recognizable radiance of corporate logo—Camel, Corona, and Coca-Cola painted across the cinder block sides of shops and restaurants, roadside stands. But the economics of speed bumps function even more directly than this.

An ever-present mob of youngsters waits in perpetuity at each and every entrance-to-town *tope*. When you slow for the hump, they affix themselves to your vehicle for the ride through town—standing on bumpers, running boards, hanging from mirrors or luggage rack. Their octopus arms extend in through your rolled-down windows, a myriad of open-palms exhibiting the local fruits—whatever it might be that grows on their hillsides, in their ecosystem, pulled fresh from the landscape: strawberries, coconuts, dates or bananas; sodas, nuts or sweets; exotic birds and leathery iguana; deep-fried somethings or other.

These adorable children employ the entire spectrum of the sales pitch from pitiful pleading to cognitive conniving, *un peso, un peso, fresas, cocos, refrescos, un peso, un peso*, and they're always more than willing to direct you to their uncle's taco stand, their neighbor's *cervecería*, or the "cleeeneest bathroom in town, *señor*."

They fall off one by one as you drive across town until only a couple of the desperate appendages remain suckered to the sides of your vehicle, staring in at you with eyes big enough to contain the cosmos. Take what appeals to you, it's yours for only pesos, pennies deposited into a hastily retracting hand. Thus they detach, leap off and examine the tarnished coins, their forms diminishing in your rearview mirror. And by now you've reached the other end of town, the exit *tope*, and a whole new band of gypsies.

After a long stretch of nothingness (*it sure has been a long time since the last tope...*) we mount the western edge of Mexico's great central plateau. Suddenly and without announcement, Guadalajara bursts out of the dry earth before us. We dive right in, drive deep into this sea of more than four million, grope around her gelatinous interior in an attempt to define her boundaries, identify her landmarks, acquire a set of bearings. But it overwhelms us. Guadalajara possesses neither the quaint personality of the coastal *pueblos* nor the tourist-friendly capitalism of the border towns. It's a completely self-absorbed metropolis of hulking buildings, frenetically flowing traffic, and millions of people moving about—the beggar and the banker, scurrying and scrounging.

Guadalajara has the same density, intensity, and tension in the air as that from which we're fleeing. We attempt to embrace the city but she is too immense, we can't get our arms around the overweight bride that is Guadalajara.

Rudy and I collect ourselves, sit down at this sidewalk café, get a cuppa coffee, and try to come up with a game plan. But we can't—the two of us don't share the same vision. Together we've pushed down to the fifty-yard line, fighting through blitzes and the pass rush. But from here, we're looking at two different end zones.

"Let's spend a couple of days here and be tourists," I'm saying. "We'll see the cathedral and the markets and then go back to the coast and continue on across Mexico."

"Continue on?" Rudy looks around. "To where? Our goal was to come down to Mexico. Well here we are. Look, Clark—there's opportunity here. We can get jobs, make some money, learn the language. And this would be a good base from which to explore the rest of Mexico."

"I don't want a base. I want to keep moving." I want to get lost.

"This trip's going to be real short if we don't find a means of supporting ourselves."

"I'm aware of that. When our money does run out I'd like to be as far away from home as possible, in the middle of nowhere."

"That makes no sense, Clark. If we're going to continue traveling, we're going to need some income. And the easiest place to make money is here, in the big city."

"Yeah, this is also the easiest place to spend it."

"Look Clark, we've been on the road together for so many years—it's not vacation for us anymore. It's a lifestyle and we've got to think long-range. We both want to be here a while, right?"

"Want to be or need to be?"

"And we both want to keep traveling. I intend to see the rest of Mexico, maybe Central America, too. That's our plan, right?"

"We never had a plan," I say. "Ever since we got off the boat in Alaska we talked about going to Mexico. We talked and talked about it for almost a year. And then one day we got in the Combi and started driving and now we're there—*here*. But we never talked about what we were going to do once we got here."

"Think about Alaska, Clark. What was our plan for Alaska?"

"Again, we didn't have one."

"Right. We just knew we were going to Alaska. That was the plan. But now I can tell you what it was all about. Alaska was about this. It was about preparing us for Mexico."

"I see. And what is Mexico preparing us for?"

The rest of your lives.

There was one thing we did together in preparation for this journey. Rudy picked me up one day last spring and took me to a seminar in San Francisco. "Teach English in Mexico," the advertisement in the *Chronicle* had announced. The seminar was sponsored by Hardship Hall, a growing franchise of English language schools located throughout Mexico. Maggie, one of the school's two founders, was there trying to recruit teachers.

Here was the deal: If we could get ourselves down to one of their schools, they would train us in their teaching method and give us free Spanish lessons. Once certified to teach, they'd guarantee us at least twenty-five hours of work per week. The only prerequisite is a Bachelor's degree (which we both have), and a grasp of the English language. Not a speck of Spanish is needed. Spanish is, in fact, forbidden in their classrooms. They're apparently desperate for native speakers to better explain usage, idioms, and slang.

Rudy was excited by the prospect but I didn't think much of it at the time. Since that day we hadn't talked about it and it had slipped my mind.

"Remember that seminar we went to a few months ago—Hardship Hall?" Rudy says. "They have a couple of schools here in Guadalajara. We should look into it." I answer him with silence, a silence that carries us through the gray afternoon.

We check into the Hotel Hamilton, downtown. Neither one of us feels like going out. Burned from the road and sick of each other, we rest in the room, windows open to let in the roar of the traffic below, the shouts of children echoing off buildings as the night moves in.

Then, after two or three hours, Rudy jumps right back into the conversation as if we had been talking only five minutes ago. "Besides, if we stay in one place long enough, V. can come down and visit."

"Oh I see how it is."

"What?"

"There's always an ulterior motive," I say, "isn't there?"

"It would be the perfect test," Rudy says. "If she could survive a couple of weeks on the road with us, she might be able to survive the long road of matrimony."

"Fine."

"So we'll call Hardship in the morning?"

"We'll check it out," I say. "But no matter what happens, I *am* going to see the rest of Mexico."

Nine

First thing Friday morning, Rudy calls one of the two Hardship Halls in Guadalajara. "Good morning," he says. "Is there someone there I can speak to about teaching opportunities?" His inquiry is met with a long silence. "Hello?"

"*¿Que?*" The woman on the phone giggles. "*No hablo Inglés.*"

"Isn't this a goddamn English school?" Rudy says. Then, slowly into the phone, "*Estamos... buscando... empleo...*" We're looking for employment, "*como maestros de Inglés,*" as teachers of English. He covers the phone. "Maybe she doesn't speak Spanish either."

Muffled voices gurgle out of the phone then, "*Hablas con un alumno, okay?*"

"Hello?" a young male voice.

"I need to talk to someone in a position of authority there, the director of the school perhaps?" Rudy's disquisition is again met by a long silence. "Hellooo..."

"She say you come here at noon and you talk to Danny," the boy says. "You are my new teacher?"

"Clark, they need us here," Rudy says to me. Then, into the phone, "Maybe, kid, just maybe. Can you tell me how to get there?"

A couple hours later we're showered, shaved, and presentable, careening through the complicated maze that is Guadalajara. And it's unlike anything I've ever experienced. There's live entertainment at each of the intersections. Hundreds of *indígenos* commute in every day from the impoverished settlements at the frayed edges of town. They come burdened with the hope of earning a few pesos by performing between green lights — doing gymnastics, selling candy, inspiring pity.

Here, a girl no more than eight juggles two rubber balls as she stands on the back of her brother who lies face down in the roadway. At another intersection an old man on the meridian sells stacks of fresh tortillas. Through stopped traffic wander women with tamales and Coca-Cola, bags of sliced cactus fruit. *Can one* eat *cactus?* At one red light, a young man steps from behind a tree, stands in front of the line of cars. *What will he do?* Cigarette lighter flicks in front of face, fountain of fire roars from throat. Drivers toss pesos into crosswalk.

Rudy holds the steering wheel in one hand, shifter in the other. I spread my new map of Guada across the dashboard. It's no easy task to navigate this town. Many of the intersections have five or six streets that converge on a hub called a *glorieta*. These cement roundabouts contain fountains and statues and shrubbery, most of them surrounded by a circular walk where the performers and vendors rest, pee, and bathe.

The idea behind the *glorieta* is to decrease the number of collisions. Instead of traffic lanes crossing one another, cars circle the roundabouts and turn off wherever destiny takes them. Externally the theory appears to work well, dozens of cars circling in smooth syncopation.

We wait patiently at the circumference for an opening in traffic. When the opening comes, Rudy jumps us into the whorl, el Tiburón moving into the unmarked lane of cars circling farthest from the center. He smiles at this accomplishment. We circle it once, twice. A car pulls in from the left, pressures Rudy into the next lane. His smile fades. This isn't as easy as it first appeared.

We complete another circuit. Cars continuously pull in from the side streets, merging into the circle. As the vortex absorbs these cars, the Combi is forced to shift further in, closer to the center until her port side is practically scraping the fountain, and her starboard is boxed in by three lanes of traffic, circling the *glorieta* at various speeds.

"Are we just going to keep circling this thing?" I needle Rudy. "I'm getting dizzy."

"We're stuck." Rudy glances over his shoulder for an opening, finds none.

"This is not good," I say. "I think there may be something gravitational going on here."

"What are you talking about, Clark?"

"I think we might be circling some celestial aberration, like a tear in the fabric of the space-time continuum."

"Whatever, Clark."

"Look at the way the water is swirling in that fountain—like a whirlpool. You see the way traffic is spinning around it, and how we're being pulled in closer and closer? The Combi is caught in the gravitational pull of this roundy-round, is being pulled in by the centrifugal force of

Guadalajara. If we don't think fast we could be stuck circling this fountain forever, caught in this orbit for eternity, or worse—sucked in."

"Sucked in?"

"To a black hole."

Remember how, in Einstein's theory of relativity, space-time curves around matter? Well, the denser the matter is, the stronger the gravitation. An intense stellar occurrence like the implosion and compression of a supergiant star can result in a case of infinite density—a black hole—where the force of gravity is so intense that nothing can escape, not even light (hence the name, black). Anything passing too close to a black hole—including space, light, and time—is instantly sucked to the center and squeezed out of existence.

"Some people believe black holes are gateways into parallel universes," I tell Rudy. "Or portals for time travel."

"Shut up Clark."

We complete another circuit.

"You know, Captain James T. Kirk was once in a predicament very similar to this one."

"And what did he do—beam himself up?" Rudy chews his lip, knuckles white on the wheel.

"This is no time for sarcasm, Rudy. Our lives may be at stake. The *U.S.S. Enterprise* was caught in the gravitational field of some celestial body which was sucking them closer and closer in. They couldn't break away from it. So what Kirk did was to cut a path straight *into* the gravitational field. He steered the ship in a trajectory that took them right across the surface of the stellar mass."

"And?"

"And the force of gravity was so intense that it slingshotted them right around the planet—or black hole, whatever it was—providing them with enough momentum to break from the gravitational pull. They were catapulted right out of orbit and blasted into another dimension."

"Gee, that's great Clark. Only we're in a Volkswagen—not a spaceship."

"And you're no Captain Kirk."

"Shut up Clark."

A battered truck swerves in, cuts off the Combi. Rudy throws the wheel left. Front tire bangs into curb, bounces off, jerks steering wheel out of his hands. The Combi angles out from the *glorieta*, squeezes magically between cars, and finds its way to one of the roads leading away from the center of the universe and its multitude of paradoxes.

"You did it, Rudy! That's exactly what I was saying. That's how Kirk did it."

"Clark?"

"Yeah?"

"Shut up."

I have completely lost my sense of direction, but we have broken free, escaped from the exhaust, the honking horns, and circumlocutions into a wooded, residential neighborhood. It's a relief to be out of the traffic but the road ends abruptly in a cul-de-sac. We'll have to turn around, go back to the black hole. Rudy begins a three-pointer. *But no*. There it is! Right in front of us, in big orange letters, "Hardship Hall." And it's noon, we're right on time.

Through the windows we see empty classrooms—lunchtime. There's a young woman behind the front desk, all teeth.

"We're here to see Dan," Rudy says. "I called earlier..." The girl continues to smile. "We have an appointment..." Still, nothing but teeth. She must be the one he talked to earlier.

Slowly and without removing her eyes from Rudy, she turns her head towards the corridor behind her, yells out, "Daneee. *Los Gringos estan aqui.*"

"Just a minute," squeals a male voice.

She turns her head back, smile still glowing, squints at us through pinched fingers to indicate the compression of time. "*Momentíto.*"

"Send them in, Alicia," comes the voice. She makes neither move nor sound nor pause in her smiling, but we take this as our cue to go, and enter the office behind her.

At the veneered desk sits a slight man in his early thirties—thinning red hair and mustache—scribbling in a notebook.

"Good afternoon," says Rudy. "You're Dan?"

"Daniel."

"I'm Rudy, this is Clark."

"And?"

Rudy takes the liberty of sitting in one of two chairs facing the desk. I follow his lead. "We just drove down from San Francisco." I'll let Rudy do the talking.

"Am I supposed to be impressed?"

"We met with Maggie last spring," Rudy continues. "We're here to teach."

"Maggie made no mention of it to me. Does she know you're here?"

"The way we left it was that we were going to find our own way down here and once arrived we'd contact her to find out about available positions. So here we are."

Danny pokes tongue into cheek, leans back in chair. "So you thought you could just drive down to Guadalajara, come waltzing in here, and be offered jobs?"

"Maggie said you needed teachers."

"It's not that simple," says Danny. "I don't suppose you have your work permits?"

"Permits?"

"In order to work in Mexico, you have to have permits from the immigration office—and those could take months to obtain. Then you'd have to get into our training program. And even if you completed it and got certified, there's no guarantee we'd have jobs for you—here or anywhere else."

"Maggie told us there was a shortage of native-speaking teachers."

"Maggie doesn't even work in this district—she's up in Chihuahua. Look, we need people who will make good teachers, people who will take the job seriously. We don't just hire off the street. Especially not a couple of Beatniks on a joyride down from Frisco. Do you think I just showed up here one day and said 'Hi, I'm here, hire me?'"

Oh, this is going well. I'm prepared to apologize for being so brash and walk out of here.

This is where you and Rudy differ.

"Look, you're obviously not in charge here," Rudy says. "I'd like to talk to whoever is."

"Whomever," I say.

"She won't tell you anything different," Danny snaps, "from what I already have."

"Just give me her name."

"It's not going to do you any good," Danny says. "*I* do the hiring."

"Just give me her name, we'll find out for ourselves."

"Lilly," Danny huffs in defeat. "But I'm telling you, she won't want to be bothered with this."

Rudy rises, says, "Thank you for your time," and walks to the door, "Danny." Exit stage left.

"It's *Daniel*," Danny yells behind him, but Rudy's already turned the corner.

I stand and extend a hand. "So nice to meet you," shake the limp paw he offers. I don't want to burn a bridge I may some day have to scramble across.

Rudy is standing at Alicia's desk, squinting into the glow of her smile as she writes something on a pad of paper. She tears off the page and hands it to Rudy.

"Thank you," he says.

"No, no, no." She shakes her head, enunciates, "*Gra-ci-as*," from behind huge teeth.

"*Grassy-ass*," Rudy mocks, barring his own teeth at her.

"You welcome," she giggles.

Rudy walks outside and heads up the street. I follow.

"Well—" I say, "*that* certainly went well."

"What an asshole."

"What do you think his problem was?"

"He's an asshole."

"He called us 'Beatniks,'" I smile.

"I don't think he meant it as a compliment, Clark."

"Oh. What was it she gave you?"

"Phone number."

"You work fast."

"Not hers—Señora Lilly's. I'm not giving up."

"Oh," I say. Rudy walks on past the Combi. "Where we going?" I ask.

"Pay phone."

"You gonna call her?"

"Brilliant deduction, Clark."

"You want this job pretty bad, huh?"

"Not really. I just want to show that asshole up."

"And when we got off the boat from Alaska we decided what we really wanted to do was to come down to Mexico and teach English," Rudy says. "So here we are." Señora Lilly is a much more receptive audience than Danny. Rudy got her on the phone and she invited us to come right over to her office at the Hardship Hall downtown.

"After our interview with Maggie," he continues, "we took a month to get things together. We fixed up this old Volkswagen bus and left San Francisco a few weeks ago, drove the Gulf Coast through Baja, ferried across to the mainland, and then drove straight here, to Guadalajara."

"That's quite a journey," Señora Lilly says, her eyes glazing over. "All the way from Alaska..."

Rudy grins, knowing his words have found their way in. Oh, she can see right through his bullshit and charm, yet is enamored with the two of us. His tales perhaps return her to a restless youth or fan the embers of an unfulfilled wanderlust.

Señora Lilly is a redheaded gringa in her mid-fifties. One look at her set jaw and pursed lips and my shoulders tensed up in anticipation of a reception even colder than Danny's. But once Rudy got into the rhythm of the rap—that particular art at which he excels—she softened. He shares the true tales of our continuing journey, which set her to smiling. She catches herself, straightens in her chair, and redirects her gaze at us.

"And you want to teach," she says.

"Yes ma'am," Rudy says. "And here," he produces a sheaf of papers out of thin air, "are our résumés and references." He hands them to her.

Where the hell did those come from?

She perches a pair of reading glasses on the end of her nose and scans the pages. "Mmmmmm," she says. "Hmmmmm." Finished, she taps the pages into alignment, lays them on the desk in front of her, and drums fingertips as we wait for a verdict. She looks up and inhales.

"Maggie and I began this undertaking over twenty years ago by opening *one* school," she says, raising an index finger as a visual aid. "Since then, we've built Hardship into a corporation with over fifty franchises. We've dedicated half our lives to creating and nurturing this institution. And we've worked hard at it. I don't tell you this for sentimental reasons. You need to know that I demand the same caliber of dedication from my employees that I do of myself. If you want to work here you're going to have to put some time and effort into the endeavor. I want you to commit at least six months to Hardship Hall. And that doesn't mean just showing up every day. I expect you to give your *all*."

"Of course, of course," Rudy says.

"Your résumés are fairly impressive, whether fictional or not. I'm going to check these references and confer with Maggie. We just happen to have a training session starting next week. If you're willing to make a commitment to Hardship, a commitment to yourselves, then I'm willing to give you a chance. The training runs four weeks. We've developed a simple, straightforward method for teaching language. It's fairly structured but once you learn the structure, you just plug in the lesson and the class teaches itself." *Is she offering us a job?* "I can't guarantee you jobs but if you do well in the training, we'll try to find something for you."

"Daniel said something about a work permit?" Rudy says.

"I'll take care of the permits for you."

"What does the job pay?" I ask. (I've got to appear to be at least somewhat interested.)

"Your wages would be twelve pesos an hour," about four dollars. That's less than the American minimum wage—*or is the hour shorter here?*

"It sounds great," Rudy beams.

"I'm not going to ask what you're really doing here," Señora Lilly says. "I am going to ask that you not give me anything to worry about." She lets this sink in with an over-the-glasses glare. "Think about it over the weekend. If you're willing to make the commitment, come and see me Monday, around noon. If not—I wish you the best of luck on your journey."

"Let's go for a walk," Rudy suggests once we're outside the school. "Where the hell did those résumés come from?"

"I typed them."

"When?" I ask. "Where?"

"One day, when you weren't looking."

"Well they'd better check out."

"What are you worried about?" Rudy says. "I thought you weren't so hot on getting a job."

"I'm not. I just don't like to be misrepresented."

"This is meant to be, Clark. We just got here, decided to look into the school, and they just happen to have a training starting next week. It couldn't be more synchronistic. It's like—it's like instant karma or something."

"Don't jinx us."

"We agreed to give this a shot."

"We agreed to look into it," I say.

"Yeah, and we just did and there's no reason for us not to go for it."

"Six months is a big commitment."

"We can always bail if we need to," Rudy says.

"That's your idea of *commitment*?"

"After we complete the training we'll look at our options. You never know what opportunities will arise, what people we'll meet."

"So we waste an entire month here 'training,'" I whine, "with no income—"

"It won't be wasted," Rudy says. "We'll be learning Spanish, experiencing the culture..."

"And then *if* they decide to hire us, we don't get much of a paycheck."

"Look how cheap things are here," Rudy says. "We can easily survive on that salary. And we'll be able to teach elsewhere, once we're trained and have a little experience. Anyway, we've got until Monday to think about it," Rudy says, although the two of us know what the outcome will be. "You wanna drive out to the coast for the weekend?"

"Yeah, let's do that."

"Let's just forget about all this," Rudy says, "and go have a good time this weekend. We can start thinking again on Monday."

Things aren't turning out the way I expected them to.

Or rather, you have been unsuccessful at unburdening yourself of expectations.

Right.

Ten

Combi swerves its way up through misty green mountains. The earth falls away from one side of the narrow road, climbs vertically up from the other. Sun drops out of cloud ceiling, stretches itself in shifting shades of sienna along the jagged horizon, flooding terrain with its radiance. We pull to the side of the road above a valley lake to absorb the reflection of *el Sol's* departure. Several swords of green lightning thrust out of the clouds to the east. Rumble of thunder introduces a brief but thorough downpour, soaking us, sending up scent of wet cement. We drive into the coming darkness.

The Combi transports us through the infrequent village tucked into cleavage of rolling hills. Lonely highway becomes Main Street of each tiny *pueblo*, leads us past *zócalo* and brown brick church where people gather in perpetual fiesta: celebratory shindigs with steaming soups ladled out of ceramic tureens, music dancing up out of handmade, homemade instruments. And up on the steeple overlooking it all stands the great white cross, where it finds us, reminds us, of Mexico.

I drive into the pleasant still night and the lateness of time on the increasingly bumpy road, which stretches itself straighter, carries us through dark mountains to Barre de Navidad.

After sleeping 'till noon Saturday we stroll along the waterfront, take up residence in Alice's Restaurant for a late breakfast. "*Buenos días, amigos*," a not quite middle-aged woman beside our table says. "What can I get for you *theese* morning?"

"How about scrambled eggs with bacon and toast," says Rudy.

"I'll have the same, but fried."

She twists her head towards the back of the restaurant, "*Mama! Dos desayunos.* Anything to drink?"

"Orange juice."

"Water."

She returns with two Cokes, sets them in front of us. Disappearing into the back, she returns with two steaming plates of scrambled eggs, sausage, and burnt toast. "*Buen provecho*."

"I think it's time for a Separate but Equal day," I say. Separate but Equal is a system we've developed completely independent of and unconnected to the Plessy v. Ferguson decision of 1896. When two people spend as much time together as do the two of us, y'all need some dedicated time apart, to be alone with your thoughts or masturbate, or whatever. And so we exit the café and turn in different directions. Rudy heads north into town. I go down along the beach.

As the sand rolls over and between the toes of my bare feet, tears of unknown origin suddenly well up, not from my own ducts certainly, but somehow they end up in *my* eyes, pouring down *my* face. I peel off my shirt and dive into the cool-warm ocean, swimming into the afternoon.

Up the beach, there's a *palapa*, a palm-leaf roof erected over a patch of sand with a few tables and chairs underneath—a little café. I sit and order a Coke, drink it slowly as the ocean approaches and recedes in dancing progression with my thoughts—memories of the past and fears of the future, manifesting in the present.

I have another Coke, and another just to show my gratitude for the privilege of being here. I get wired on cola and embrace the concept of space here, appreciating the openness, the lack of walls and doors. The floor of the café is the surface of the Earth, the sand of the beach that runs right down to the water, flows up into café.

The proprietor snores softly in a hammock behind me while his wife waits on customers. She pulls a strand of dark hair back from the sweat of her cheek, wipes forehead with the back of her hand. Plucking a coconut from the pile in the middle of café, she drops it onto a tree stump and extracts a machete. She raises Excalibur high, brings it down once, flattening the bottom of the coconut, and again to open the top. She fills it with rum, inserts a straw, and sets it in front of a smiling tourist.

Then, straightening apron, she strides out next to my ocean view table, casts a look down the beach to her brood frolicking in the surf. I want to assure her that if any of her offspring should be swept to sea I'm here, willing to risk my own existence to save theirs from the hunger of the ocean. I have the urge to assuage the fears of this anonymous matron, to inform her that I'm watching over everything—from the restless surf before us to the jagged mountain range behind. But the fear of my words being misunderstood holds my tongue, confines me in a prison of language. I nevertheless will continue to protect the children of Mexico and everything else within my range (but nothing beyond), because doing so will be louder than any utterance I could make.

I can't live in Guadalajara. It'll eat me alive. I came to Mexico for this right here—the paradisiacal elements of sand between my toes, rum drunk straight from a coconut, and the cola bottle in front of me. I could rub it now and conjure a genie but I won't, don't need to, because my wishes have been fulfilled.

This is the ultimate escape because it leaves me need think nothing more. It's all right here in front of me—the eternity of ocean, extent of endless horizon, the day, and the sun going down at the end of it— oscillating organs of the universe into which I cast my ruminations.

Oh all right, a month in Guadalajara—fine. I can last a month and will probably absorb a great deal. But that's it—after a month I move on, or return here, or just keep moving forward, going further and furthur until I fall off the edge of the earth.

Eleven

"**G**et up." Rudy wakes me Monday morning at 7:00 A.M., standing over my bed in our hotel room in Barre de Navidad. "We gotta get back to Guadalajara and see Señora Lilly." I roll over; pull the covers up over my head. "C'mon Clark, she's expecting us. We got to at least go talk to her. It's not like we have to commit to anything."

"Oh, I'll talk to her. I like talking."

We leave Barre, drive back over the mountains, arrive Guadalajara shortly after noon, and go straight to Hardship Hall. Rudy strides into Lilly's office and straight up to her desk.

"We're ready to teach," he says.

Oh that's noncommittal, Rudy.

"I was hoping you'd come back," Señora Lilly smiles. "I've checked your references and conferred with my colleague. We're accepting you into the training."

"Well all right," says Rudy.

"Thank you," I add.

"There's an orientation meeting for new teachers this afternoon at four," she says. "You'll report to Daniel, with whom you'll be training."

Oh no, not him.

"Congratulations," Lilly smiles.

I'm impressed with her use of the pronoun "whom" and suddenly fear that my own English may not be up to par.

Señora Lilly tilts her head sideways. "I hope you're ready for this."

"We're ready," Rudy says, shooting both index fingers at her as we back out the door.

It is not an invalid fear. Do *you have enough control of the English language, possess enough of an erudition to pass on a lingo you have employed since shortly after your birth? Are you comfortable with the idea of teaching English?*

In the same way the human body is sixty-five percent water, spoken language is like sixty-five percent of consensus reality. But our vernacular is a totally abstract and prejudiced conduit between human beings.

Go ahead anyway, dive in, embark on this self-devouring journey of attempting to objectively pass on a personal diction, a limiting set of words and the rules that govern them. And here's the rub: communicate it through itself, by using that same binding tongue.

Know that through education you will narrow down the universe, draw in the peripheries of perception by the process of elimination which, at bottom, is all we really have. For there is no such thing as learning. There is only the sketching of boundaries through eternity (time), and around infinity (space) to make the universe more manageable.

"Thank you for taking the time to discuss our careers with me," I say to Rudy. We're driving away from Hardship. "And for taking my input into consideration before giving 'our' decision to Señora Lilly."

"I'm always lookin' out for your best interests Clark."

"You don't even know what my interests are. We hardly talked about this."

"We just had the whole weekend in Barre to hash this out."

"We didn't *speak* to one another this past weekend," I say. "It was all we could do to keep from killing one another."

"This is how it is, Clark. Whenever you take some time to talk or think about something, you don't talk or think about that thing at all. You talk of something entirely different and think of nothing at all, right up until the deadline. That clears your mind. Then when the time comes to make a decision there's enough room in your head for the correct choice to just—" he snaps his fingers, "*pop* into your head."

"Are you referring to the workings of *my* mind in particular, or is this a generalization about humanity?"

"My point is this Clark, I can confidently say we've got jobs or are at least one step closer to having them. Could you at least try and be happy about that?"

I put on my best jeans and cleanest shirt and we return, at four o'clock, to the hallowed halls of Hardship. Students young and old roam in and out of the building, up and down the hallways. The same set of teeth is behind the reception desk.

"We're here," Rudy says slowly as if talking to someone who didn't understand the language, "for the training."

"*Me llama Alicia.*" She stands and extends a hand and that smile. "*Bienvenidos.*"

"I'm Rudy, this here's Clark." I take her hand and there, I've made another friend, it's that easy.

"*El proximo piso,*" she points at the ceiling. "Upstair. *Cuarto número seis.* Room sex."

We take a moment to decipher this.

"*Six,*" Rudy enunciates. "Room *six.*"

"Sssex," she hisses.

"No, no," says Rudy. "Six, siiix."

"Saaax," she tries, unable to conjure the correct vowel.

"Close enough."

"You were right," I say. Rudy and I climb the stairs to the next floor. "They do need us here."

There are three classrooms and a couple of offices on the first floor and four classrooms here on the second. The stairs go higher but this is not the time to investigate. From behind closed doors, quiet murmurings emanate, punctuated by the occasional revelatory shout of another initiate entering into the cognoscenti of a new language. We stop in front of the door with the six on it.

This is the start of a new career. Once you step through this portal, your life may be changed forever, the dream of working in a foreign country—realized. And you are about to meet your cohorts in this adventure—who knows where they'll be from. Your future wife could be behind that door.

"Well?" Rudy drops a boulder into the quiet stream of my thoughts. "Did you forget how to operate a doorknob?"

"I'm mentally preparing myself," I say.

"There's no such thing as preparation." Rudy reaches past me, turns the knob and the door swings into an empty classroom.

"Where is everybody?" I say. The clock on the wall reads five minutes of four. "Señora Lilly did say *today*, didn't she? Four o'clock?"

"Yep, and we're right on time," says Rudy. "We must be the first ones here, is all."

"Everybody else is late?" I say. "Do you think *we* were supposed to be late? Mexican time *is* supposedly different from American time. Maybe it's a language thing." I walk to the window and look down to the grassy yard below. "Do you think they're playing a joke on us?"

"Sit down, Clark. You're making me nervous."

The room contains twenty chairs with small desks attached. A glossy white board is mounted to the front wall. We sit. We wait.

"I've got a bad feeling about this," I say.

Danny enters the room. "I see you two showed up, that's a good start."

"Where's everybody else?" Rudy asks.

"You guys are it, for now." He sets his briefcase on a chair, takes out a notebook and flips it open. "Let's get started." He elevates his gaze to our figures, sprawled in the undersized chairs. "First, I can see we're going to have to go over our dress code. The required uniform for teachers is black slacks, black shoes, white shirt, and a tie."

Tie?

"Now, the purpose of this training is to steep you in our inductive teaching method."

"Your *what*?" Rudy asks.

"I don't know if you've seen our résumés," I say, "but neither of us has taught before."

"I was more impressed with what you *haven't* done in life," Daniel says, "than with what you *have* accomplished. The fact that you're not clouded by past teaching experience means you come to us clean slates upon which we can inscribe our program."

"Sounds like brainwashing," I say.

"And it doesn't answer my question about intuitive teaching," adds Rudy. One nice thing about this is that we've got nothing to lose. I don't give a shit about getting this job and all Rudy cares about is getting this guy's goat. So neither one of us feels compelled to kiss his ass.

"*Inductive* teaching means that you don't just *give* the material to the students. You *lead* them to knowledge, *induce* them to figure out the answers for themselves and from each other. One rule we strictly adhere to is that only English is spoken in the classroom. This encourages students to *think* in English, instead of translating. The main goal is to get the students involved and speaking, through games and role-playing."

"The training is four hours a day for the next four weeks, starting tomorrow at eleven."

Tomorrow?!

"Tomorrow I'll introduce you to Javiér, our lead teacher. He'll be doing most of the training and will go over the entire method with you. And he'll explain the grammar handbook you're required to write. It's a little homework assignment you'll be turning in at the end of the training. Oh— and tomorrow you'll start student teaching."

Tomorrow?!

"Tomorrow I'll assign each of you to a class. You'll be observing for the first week, and then giving lessons periodically for the rest of the *inscripción*. Any Questions?"

"Yeah," Rudy says, "what's an *inscripción?*"

"See you tomorrow."

"Tomorrow?!" I say. We're in the Combi.

"Great timing, huh?" Rudy drives directionlessly.

"It's so soon, tomorrow."

"Yeah."

"I'm not ready."

"I told you Clark, there's no such thing as preparation."

"What's with the big deal Señora Lilly made about this 'training session'? There *was* no training 'till we came along—they're having it just for us. It had nothing to do with good timing."

"Yes sir," Rudy says. "Things are happening just for us."

"And homework to boot!"

"Look Clark, this is how I see the situation. This seems like a decent organization and I like their teaching philosophy. But they're short of teachers. Demand is high, supply is low. It's basic economics. They're playing hard to get, putting up this facade of high standards and rigorous training while in reality they're desperate and will take whatever teachers they can get. Señora Lilly likes us. Daniel is an ass and is going to make it as hard as possible on us, but he's ultimately got to answer to her. If we just play along with their game we can write our own meal ticket. Trust me."

"This must be downtown," I say, *el Centro.*

"Let's park the Combi and walk around."

"Yeah," I say, "and do some shopping. It sounds like we're going to need a new wardrobe."

Experience the city beneath your feet. Circle the seventeenth-century cathedral. Hop from one plaza to the next, like frogs on lily pads—Plaza de los Laureles, Plaza de las Armas, Plaza de la Liberación, the names alone are a history lesson. Pass the nineteenth century Teatro Degollado. From Plaza Tapatía descend the steps to the subterranean Mercado Libertad.

The market spreads out with the labyrinthian confusion of hot and bothered octopi. Pass down between indefinitely extending rows of produce booths, step across wilted leaves of lettuce branded with shoe prints, past bunches of bananas hanging like valances above countertops which support bins and baskets overflowing with fruits and vegetables. Papaya, peppers and pomegranates spill over. All the colors of a Parisian painter's palette present themselves in a feast for the senses. Onions, limes, and tomatoes cascade to the floor. Wonder, if seen from a distance (another planet or another time) the space displaced by these fruits of the earth and their juxtaposition to one another wouldn't spell out some message, or form a pointillist portrait of some revolutionary hero, Emiliano Zapata perhaps, or Montezuma.

There stands a long line of men and women, chins held high, feet on the ground, eyes staring out of creased, sun-browned faces. These are the farmers who have pressed seed into soil with thick fingers, who remained— not doing—until sprout broke surface in front of them, fulfilling the form of food with no thought of future. Here they stand now, silently behind this rainbow, the fruit of their labor beckoning passersby with alluring color and provocative pose. Walk on...

Descend further underground, deeper down, until you come to those providers of instant gratification, the lunch vendors. Pass along the endless aisles of stainless steel carts and sizzling grills, the continuous hardwood counter piled high with fresh rolls and tortillas, like a castle parapet stacked with cannonball. Chef stands behind, on guard—a warrior defending his fortress, silver spatula sword at the ready to produce for you anything your heart desires.

The hand painted signs overhead shout Gorditas! Tacos! Tortas! Refrescos! He smiles from behind his ammunition of bolillos, the soft rolls he'll willingly slice for you and fill from the stacks of pork, beef, chicken, or cheese. He'll gladly shred some lettuce—just for you, slice a tomato, avocado, onion, anything to please your palate, satisfy your soul.

But you are too overwhelmed by it all, too overwhelmed to acknowledge your hunger, to validate the grumblings emanating from your midriff. So you walk on with a defensive smile, an averted glance, on to the next stairwell.

Descend yet further, deeper down, each lowering level darker than the last as you acknowledge your transcendence into the flaming picture Dante has painted in your head. Further down, darker down, pupils increasing in size yet more, down to the next level, ceilings lowering, air cooling, dampening down. More booths, stalls, and women, all women, standing closer to the earth than you, unsmiling, silent women whose owl eyes follow you from unmoving heads.

You must squint, adjust your vision to perceive their wares, but it takes awhile for these perceptions to sift down inside, to translate themselves: jars of earth-toned powders and leaves and herbs and roots; bowls of seeds and nuts and grains, legumes; baskets full of dried insects—grasshopper and beetle and centipede, eye of newt and skin of toad, wing of bat and tail of iguana; elements which, when combined properly (or not), have the power of life—to give or revoke, inflict or heal—a dark repository of craft and castings.

These are the curanderas about whom you've read, the brujas about whom you've dreamed. Don't look them in the eye for fear of seeing yourself reflected (or worse, not at all) as the inverted homunculus in the dark depths of their enlarged pupili. Fear that you may have already fallen under a spell, a trance cast not necessarily by these technicians of the sacred but perhaps by Mexico herself or the spirit of Guadalupe, la Virgen, inspiration and protectora of the people.

Shake it off and find the stairs. Mount them three at a time; ascend out of this hell you have created in your mind. Break the surface and your eyes are flooded with sunlight and the bright colors of terrestrial existence. Hawkers of every stripe fill the plaza with their wares, a huge bouquet of balloons shivers upward, the pink of cotton candy swims to you, ten story birdcage complexes squawk full of parakeets and chickadees, a rainbow of candies, ice creams, and the yellow of pencils. All these bright blooms vibrate against the dark cathedral looming over plaza. And there She is again, the blue-green of the Virgin winking at you from out of velvet portraits.

We have jobs in Mexico and Rudy wants to share the excitement. "I'm going to call Virginia," he says, and we begin a new journey—from one pay phone to the next, feeding them silver. The fat, unfamiliar coins clunk deep within the intestines of these machines which give only a belch of satisfaction in return. Rudy finally gets an operator and goes through the tortuous procedure of getting a call through to the United States of America, to V.

"Guess what?... We got jobs... Yeah..." I leave him alone with a line to the lover he left behind and wander off through the Guadalajaran evening. As I circuit the *zócalo*, the day's colors blur into the folds of twilight's cloak. The cathedral's facade fades into shadow. I stand at the curb and observe the mad traffic, cars whizzing by all around this island plaza.

It's one thing to talk about living and working in Mexico, but it's another thing entirely to be here doing it. We don't know where fate will take us next. It's like surfing the ocean, being out on the edge of a rapidly changing lip of water and moving forward, held up by a wave fulfilling form, held down by the gravity of love, propelled from behind by history (*and the flapping of a butterfly's wings*), all the while being pulled forward towards the unknown future.

Take stock, and find strength. You've secured employment. You live in Mexico. You're fulfilling a dream.

I'm not sure I want this job. I'm not sure I want to live here.
And you're not sure that you don't. You're not sure of anything.
You're right.
Why are you here?
I'm running.
Yes, but from what? You've got to confront that which pursues you or we've got no story. And you will need, at some point, to weigh your fear of death against your fear of life and determine which burdens you more.

I complete the loop back to my friend on the phone. "Okay honey. I love you... Clark loves you too... Bye." He hangs up, smiling broadly. "Clark, we're living in Mexico, we've got jobs, and somewhere in the world there's a woman who loves me."

"Where are we going to sleep tonight?" I ask, but get no response. "Rudy?" He's staring into space, drifting through memories of big red lips and fur-lined handcuffs.

"Rudy!"

"What?"

"What do we do now?"

"We work, we teach."

"I mean, *now*. I'm hungry, I'm tired, and it's cold. Where are we going to sleep tonight?"

"Don't worry Clark, I've got a plan. Remember how I told you I know people in Guadalajara?"

"Yeah."

"Well I don't. But I did used to work with this woman who has family here. And when I told her we were going to Mexico she said that if I should find myself in Guadalajara to give them a call. Well damned if I don't suddenly find myself in Guadalajara. And I've got their number with me." He digs into his backpack. "I'm going to call them right now."

Before I know it, he's got someone on the line. Rudy struggles with Spanish as I suspect someone on the other side of Guadalajara struggles with English.

"*Somos amigos de Anna, de San Francisco... Si... No... Si... el Centro... No... No... Combi...* Wednesday—*Miércoles.*" Rudy jerks the receiver away from his ear as a voice screams out of the phone. "Give me a pen, Clark." He scribbles on the scrap of paper on which he has their number. "Okay... Okay... Okay... Bye." He hangs up the phone.

"What was that all about?" I ask.

"She was sure pissed off." He waits for my reaction which is a while in coming.

"Who? Why?" I don't yet understand this country. Or human nature.

"Nena," he says. "She's upset that we've been in town since Wednesday and haven't called her until now. She expects us for dinner, *muy pronto*."

We follow Nena's directions through the congested, confusing, roundabout roads of downtown Guadalajara out to the relative complacency of their semi-suburban neighborhood, crickets chirping in the pleasantness of the fall night. Nena greets us at the door with a stern smile. All tricksters, these Mexicans. Fortyish, with curly brown hair, she is the cousin of Rudy's former coworker. Her darling daughter Jessica wraps coyly around Nena's leg as they look us over. "Jew are *han*gry," Nena decides. "Come *een*."

She passes through the dining area and into kitchen. We step inside the door. At the far end of the room, with their attention focused on the television, sit two men on couches. Both appear to be in their twenties, one of them languid and fleshy, the other lean and angular.

"Come *een*, seat, seat," Nena yells over the clatter of pans and refrigerator slammings. We step into the dining area. The lanky one shifts his gaze away from the television, redirects it at us. Jessica flits out of the kitchen, crosses the room and plants herself next to *el Gordo*.

El Flaco stands, crosses the room, and extends a hand. "Ramón," he says.

"I'm Rudy, this is Clark."

"*Clark? Como Clark Kent?*" he asks.

"*Si*," I say.

Ramón hooks a thumb over his shoulder, towards his corpulent counterpart. "*Mi hermano, Martín.*" Martín grunts, but doesn't avert his attention from the *telenovela* unfolding across the screen. Ramón steps back to the love seat, motions for us to sit. Rudy and I squeeze onto it.

"Where from?" Ramón asks, settling onto the couch with Martín and Jessica.

"San Francisco," Rudy says. "*Somos amigos de Anna.*"

"*Si*," Ramón nods. "Mi *co*-sin," and a silence falls between us.

I gaze around the first real Mexican home we've been in, the tile floor and the flowered furniture, the statue of Guadalupe in the corner. The living room/dining room is long and narrow with bedroom doors along one wall. Ramón studies us closely, silence underlined by the television's Spanish murmurings.

"Come and seat, eat." Nena floats in from the kitchen with two steaming plates—enchiladas in a red sauce—sets them on the dining table. She holds eyebrows high until we raise ourselves and to the table, sit. She brings out a salad, glasses of Coca-Cola. "Eat, then we talk." We follow her instructions. We are slow and deliberate with our forks, holding back until hunger catches up, overtakes, and we dive in voraciously.

Nena sits on the couches with the others. They lean in close and speak quietly amongst themselves, a suspicious football team going over the next play. The occasional pair of eyes shoots us a quick glance. Breaking the huddle, Nena reaches for the phone, dials a lengthy number as the others look on. "*Anna?*" She speaks rapidly into the phone, alternately scrunching her face and smiling and I don't understand a word said. She hangs up the phone and the four of them lean in again around the coffee table. Rudy and I eat rapidly and heartily, our first home-cooked meal in a long while.

Conference finished, they lean back and stare at us. I stop, fork halfway to mouth. Television laugh track fills the void. But their eyes are empty, empty of malice or suspicion, empty even of wonder. Just big, warm, indifferent eyes taking us in.

"We talk," Nena says, "and we decide that jew will leeve here."

"You want us to leave?" Rudy says.

"No," Nena says, "jew will *leeve* here, weeth us."

"We're *all* going somewhere?"

"No, no, no," Nena shakes her head, "not *leave—leeve.* Jew...weel...leeve...weeth...us."

"Oh," Rudy says. "You want us to *live* here—with you."

"Dat's what I say," Nena says. "I talk to Anna, and she say jew are okay. If she say jew are okay, jew are okay. She say jew are *crazy* but crazy es okay weeth us. *Este es su casa.*"

Nena clears the dishes and invites us to join them on the couches.

"I leeve two summers in San Francisco with Anna," Nena says. "Is how I laern English. But my brothers, they speak only *Español.* You meet Martín, he is oldest, almost thirty." *El Gordo* inserts a grunt. "And Ramón, he is twenny-seven. But there is another—Güero, the jungest, twenny-three. He is wearking tonight. You meet tomorrow." Martín again grunts. The television drones. "My brothers, they leeve here. Yessica and me, we leeve upstairs, another house." Jessica cowers behind her mom on the couch, peering out at us with one eye. "So why are jew here, en Guadalajara?"

"We have jobs, teaching English," Rudy says. "Tomorrow's our first day."

"Oh!" Nena turns to the others, "*Son maestros de Inglés, aqui en Guadalajara.*" Her brothers nod approval. "Jew can leeve here as long as jew need to. Jew will laern us English?"

"We'd love to," Rudy smiles.

"Well, es late. Time for bed. The front room es prepare for you. Jew batter sleep good tonight so jew teach good tomorrow." She shows us to the front bedroom which has clean sheets on the king bed. "Here is jour key. We wake you in morning."

"Good night," we say and get a final grunt from Martín.

Rudy and I settle into our room.

"Well this worked out," I say.

"Told you I had a plan," Rudy can't help but gloat.

Twelve

A reggae beat and the wavering voice of Bob Marley weave themselves into my early morning dreams long before the firm knock on the bedroom door awakens. *"Gringos,"* intones a deep voice. I struggle out of bed and open the door to a stern, white, mustachioed face. His eyes narrow at the paper napkin in hand. *"¿Eres Clark?"*

"Si."

"¿Como Clark Kent?"

"Si," I sigh, "like Clark Kent. *Buenas días."*

"¿Y Rudio?" he asks, squinting at the napkin.

"Yes," I say, "this is the rude one," nodding to Rudy, who climbs out of bed.

"Buenas días," Rudy says. *"Güero, si?"*

"Si," he says. *"Desayuno es listo,"* and he hands me the napkin, a note, written in blue ballpoint. *Güero— Hay dos gringos en su cama, Clark y Rudy. Despiertalos se por la mañana.*

How long has he been here? For what length of time has he paced the house, studying this dispatch (There are two gringos in your bed), attempting to untie the Gordian knot he's arrived home to (Wake them in the morning)? How long has he held off waking us? Imagine coming home to find that *your* bed has been given to a couple of unknown foreigners who dropped in out of the blue. How would you feel? Put out? Pissed off? *(You just may be his ticket out of here.)*

The rest of the household has already gone off to work or wherever it is they go when the sun shines. Bowls of dark, steaming broth await us on the dining room table. We sit and partake.

Güero's is a dry, deadpan demeanor like them all. But this facade is suppressing something, an omnipresent smile waiting in the wings just outside the corners of his mouth, a smile that's felt rather than seen. He sits across the table from us, head bent to bowl, spoon up to mouth. His eyes roll to the tops of their sockets, bounce back and forth from Rudy to me. It feels as if he has something to say, something to ask us, but doesn't have the words—yes, doesn't have the language to communicate it, that's it.

The music rolls loudly out of the stereo all morning (as it will every morning), the Doors, Elton John, Bob Dylan, the Grateful Dead. If he speaks any English at all, this is where he's learned it.

"*¿Listo?*" Güero says. Are you ready?

"*¿Para que?*" asks Rudy, for what?

"*El courso proximo.*"

"The next course?"

With a wink, Güero disappears out the front door, returns with a case of cold Coronas. "Celebrate good times," he says. *Yes.*

We have to be at school in a couple hours.

Güero makes the next course with a bottle opener.

Well, you don't have to be at school for a couple more hours.

We drink a round, but I'm anxious about the training, had planned on getting there early. And sober.

Güero puts on a video of Jim Morrison and the Doors—live in concert. He opens three more beers and distributes them, sits on the couch singing along. Rudy joins him. I busy myself, cleaning out and organizing the Combi (always sharpening the tools of spontaneity, maintaining the ability to move on at an instant's notice).

"*Que es un* Back Door Man?" Güero asks. Rudy fumbles with an explanation. Güero stops him mid-blather with a sharply raised index finger. Leaping to his feet, he bounds across the room to a bookcase, withdraws a large volume and bounds back, drops it on the coffee table, slides it towards Rudy. *Spanish-English Dictionary.* Rudy thumbs through it, pointing out and pronouncing words. Güero nods along.

Thus the morning passes, Jim Morrison growling and gyrating on the T.V., Güero perpetually opening beers, the Spanglish dictionary sliding back and forth across coffee table. Soon it's time for us to leave for school, for the training. In the kitchen, I hear the *ksssh* of three more being opened. "*No mas! No mas!*" I say, but Güero keeps them coming until all twenty-four bottles (as well as the three of us) are drunk.

"Rudy, this is not cool. We just drank a case of beer. We can't show up to Hardship in this condition."

"And you call yourself a Buddhist," Rudy says.

"Actually, I don't."

"You're living in the future, Clark. You need to focus on the present."

"Don't mock me."

"Right now we're here with Güero," who concernedly looks on, wondering what the drunk gringos are bickering about. "We're living with a Mexican family, experiencing their daily customs. It's important that we bond, on both a personal and a cultural level. We're healing the wounds of the Conquest," Rudy slaps Güero on the shoulder, "mending the rift caused by the Mexican-American War. We're interpreting the sociopolitical implications of James Douglas Morrison here."

"You're going to justify our showing up to work inebriated with— with intercultural healing?"

"That's it," Rudy says, "intercultural healing."

"You're amazing."

"I thought you didn't want this job, Clark."

"I don't. But, now that we're here and we've started the training—it's okay. I mean if we're going to do this—teach and all—I just want to do it right. I want to do the best I can."

"Right now, we're drinking beer," Rudy says. "So why don't you do the best that you can at that. Come on Clark, you gotta relax *hombre. This* is what we came to Mexico for, to drink a case of beer in the morning before work, to live like Mexicans, whatever that means."

With this statement, Güero's backstage smile strides out of the wings and onto his face, front and center below the mustache. "Live like Mexican," he bellows, raising his *cerveza*, "Live like Mexican!" he chants and we clink our bottles and toast our lives, the day.

And yes, Clark—do lighten up.

So yes, we do show up for the first day of our training fairly *borracho*. But we get through it just fine and in so doing set the tone for the rest of our journey.

"The training will be from eleven to five every day, with a break from one to three," Danny begins. "Rudy, for your student teaching assignment, I'm giving you a seven P.M. Advanced class. Clark, you've got a five o'clock Beginning level. This," he motions to the pudgy, twenty-something kid sitting in the corner, "is Javiér, who will be conducting the rest of the training. Good luck." And with that, Danny departs.

Javiér rises, pushes glasses up on nose and, in a soft voice, begins the lesson. "You will start each class by writing the day's vocabulary words on the board," which he does, and goes right on without ever saying hello or asking our names.

About thirty minutes into it, Danny sticks his head in the door. "We've got two more joining us." A couple of chicanas squeeze past him into the room. "This is Diane and Maria," henceforth referred to collectively as "las

Gringas." Diane is rail thin with long, straight hair, Maria shorter and plump with dark curly hair. I am eager to talk with these fellow expatriates, get their stories and perspectives. I lean over to introduce myself but Javiér will have no chatter in his classroom.

"Please, we have a lot of material to cover," he chastises. "You may talk on your own time," and on he goes with the lesson. Javiér asks us no questions, nor provides us the opportunity to ask any of him. He just unloads the information, scribbling it across the board. When finished, he simply announces, "That's it," and walks out the door. Hardly *inductive*.

We walk outside with las Gringas, away from the eyes and ears of Hardship Hall. "You guys smell like a brewery," they say.

"We did have a couple beers this morning," Rudy says. "It was part of an intercultural exchange we're involved in. So where you girls from?"

"L.A. We moved here a couple months ago to work on our Masters at the University."

"You speak Spanish?" Rudy asks.

"Duh, yeah," Maria says. "Don't you guys?"

"Ahhh little bit."

"What are you doing here?" Diane asks.

"Hiding from the law," I mutter under my breath.

Rudy clears his throat. "We are here to teach, to give back to the community that has given so much to us." They give him strange looks. "We start this afternoon."

"You're teaching already?"

"*Student* teaching," I say.

"What does that mean?" Diane asks.

"That means we sit in someone else's class," I say, "and try to learn English so we can teach it to others."

"Hey, do you guys need a ride somewhere?" Rudy asks. "We've got a couple hours to kill." They look us over, glance uneasily at each other.

"No," they sing in unison.

We return to Hardship at five o'clock to begin our student teaching careers. I report to my classroom and introduce myself to Gloria, the abrasive, indigenous woman under whose auspices I will be honing my craft. She reluctantly shakes my extended hand.

"Sit there," she points to a chair in the front corner, "and keep quiet." I sit down; keep my mouth shut and my legs crossed to prevent anything from letting loose. The dozen students stare at me from start to finish.

"How'd your class go?" I ask Rudy on the way home.

"Pretty well. The students really do appreciate having a native speaker in the classroom. How'd yours go?"

"I sat in the corner and was real quiet."

"You're good at that."

"So you think it's okay that we stay with la Familia?" I ask.

"Of course. They love us. As far as they're concerned, we're a part of the family." He's absolutely right. We walk in the door and the whole of the family—all three brothers, their sister, and little Yessica—is sitting on the couches facing the television for the nightly installment of the *telenovela*.

Nena gets up and turns off the T.V., goes to the kitchen to warm our dinner. Martín disappears grumpily into his room. Ramón begins questioning us about the launch of our new careers while Nena shouts translations from the kitchen. Rudy tells them everything, with flourishes and embellishments that entertain thoroughly. Nena brings our dinner to the table—hot bowls of pork stew, tortillas, green salad, and all is good.

Thirteen

We've been slogging away at writing our grammar books—deconstructing the language I have spoken for most of my existence, reconstructing it for others in order to perpetuate the life of a *lengua*. The assignment is to write a basic booklet of English language rules and usage, listing and explaining the massive variety of verb tenses, points of view, pronunciation, syntax, etcetera—our own personal "Elements of Style," if you will. And, as I'm coming to realize with teaching, it's a lot easier to speak a language than it is to explain it to someone else.

On our Friday afternoon break, we go to las Gringas' apartment. We have bonded with them in our daily shared torture under Javiér's tutelage. Diane and I work on our grammar books, attempting to isolate the slender differences between *during* and *while*, trying to discern the subtle nuances propelling the divergence of the *present perfect* away from the *present progressive*. Maria translates want ads for Rudy, calls and inquires about apartments for us.

We've got a schedule now, have to be at Hardship every morning and afternoon for the training and in the evenings to teach. It's going great and I'm actually giving entire lessons now. I've got a smooth presentation down: review a past exercise to prime them, subversively bring in new material, give the students an activity, and let them teach themselves.

I awaken before Sunday's dawn, pull on my robe, and venture out of the bedroom. The house is dark and quiet, but I know someone sleeps behind each and every closed door. I flip on the wall switch. A narrow cone of light illumines the dining room table. Settling into a chair, I open my notebook to write.

In the midst of my scribbling, a door at the far end of the living room creaks open. A slim, dark figure steps out, lithely crosses the room. He stands in the shadows across the table from me for a moment, then leans his face suddenly into the light.

"I am also a writer," he whispers, sliding into the chair across from me. "*Me llamo Libertad*. I am a cousin to this family."

"I'm Clark."

"I arrive last night," he says. "You were out. But I meet you *compadre* Rudio. *El es loco.*"

"I agree."

"We go out for beers *anoche* with Güero, to celebrate." He puts his hands on the table, then clasps them together. "Do you know where I've been?" he asks.

A word comes to mind but I don't voice it.

"Jail," he says. "Three years and a half." Libertad produces a worn notebook. "Do you read Spanish?"

"*Muy poquito.*" Very little.

"Then I will translate." Libertad opens his notebook. Every square centimeter of every page is covered with tight, crisp handwriting. "I wrote this in my cell. It is about *soledad*, being alone."

"Solita, I once fought you like an enemy," he reads, "but realizing you *invencible*, made you my ally. In Spanish loneliness is female so I speak to her as a woman."

"I come here alone in my mother's womb and I shall leave alone in the womb of the earth. But to spend the time in between alone, to go through life solo, this is not to live. It is the *interacción* between people, this is the life. It is the family and friends, the lovers—two lives passing through one another and dropping seeds to the soil—this is how blossoms the flower of life. Solita, I once was alone, now I have you."

A bedroom door bangs open and out stumbles Rudy in boxer shorts and chest hair. One eye open, he peruses our suspended discourse, runs a hand through tangled hair, stumbles to kitchen to get some coffee—no I'm sorry, to get a beer. He plops himself down next to Libertad who puts an arm around him.

"I told Rudy I take you guys to my *pueblo* next weekend," Libertad says, "two hours from here."

"Did Libertad tell you where he's been?" Rudy asks.

"*Si*," I reply.

"Did he tell you *why*?" Rudy asks. Libertad removes his arm from Rudy's shoulders, brings his hands together on the table, head down.

"Why I was in jail?" Libertad breathes, brings his head up. "The police, they find a kilo of grass in my car. I tell them I am Rastafarian and need it for my religion. They say okay. But then they find the kilo of peyote. 'Oh, I am *Huichol*,' I tell them. 'That is my sacrament,' and they send me to jail—three years and a half."

"And what did you learn in those three years and a half?" Rudy asks.

Libertad smiles sheepishly. "A man can have only one religion."

During our Tuesday afternoon break, Rudy and I drive out to a quiet suburb with las Gringas to look at what will hopefully be our new apartment. La Familia is great, but we need a place where we can live expansively, cut loose, throw parties, drum, and have orgies—our own place to do with as we please. The landlady, middle-aged Señora Beltrán, meets us on the top floor landing of the three-story, cinder block building.

The apartment has two *recameras* (bedrooms), *un baño* (bathroom), a *cocina* (noticeably lacking a refrigerator) and, "Look at this, a handball court." Rudy produces a small rubber ball and commences to smack it against the cement walls and tiled floor of the expansive front room. "Who's up for a game?"

"Not now, Rude."

"Right. We gotta check the most important thing of all..." he swings his drum around in front of him, "the acoustics." I knew this would come and am prepared with my own *tambor*.

Señora Beltrán doesn't bat an eye as the two of us pound out an unsyncopated rhythm that echoes loudly, lures dust out of the cracks, encourages the foundation to settle.

"You should hear him after he's had a few beers," I say.

"Uh—" Maria cringes, "he has had a few beers."

"We'll take it," says Rudy, when we finish our performance.

"*Bueno*," Señora Beltrán says. "*¿Tiene trabajo, si?*" You have jobs, yes?

"*Si, si, tenemos trabajo*," Rudy says. "*Somos maestros de Inglés.*"

At Hardship Hall everyone's in a festive mood, this being the eve of one of Mexico's biggest holidays. Tomorrow's their Fourth of July, but for some reason they celebrate it on the Sixteenth of September. Okay, okay, it's their Día del Independencia, celebrating the anniversary of Padre Miguel Hidalgo's 1810 Grito de Dolores, the speech what sparked a revolution.

"*My children*," Hidalgo said, "*a new order comes to us this day. Are you ready to receive it? Will you be free? Will you make the effort to*

recover from the hated Spaniards the lands stolen from your forefathers
three hundred years ago? We must act at once... Long live Our Lady of
Guadalupe!... ¡Viva Mexico!" Here's what happened:

History Lesson
El Grito de Dolores
and the Start of the Mexican Revolution

At the dawn of the nineteenth century Mexico's indigenous population, as well as the growing number of mixed-blood mestizos, were experiencing increased marginalization. They were denied basic liberties such as religious freedom and the right to own property. The Catholic Church, on the other hand, had accumulated great power and excessive amounts of wealth and had become the country's largest moneylender in a rapidly growing economy.

Fearing the Church was gaining too much power, Spain's King Charles III passed the Amortization and Consolidation Law in 1804. It called for the immediate transfer of all church funds to royal coffers. To meet the imperial demands, padres all over Mexico were forced to sell off church holdings and call back large sums of money lent to industrialists. The results were economic chaos and the creation of conditions ripe for rebellion.

The opportunity to revolt came when a Frenchman by the name of Napoleon Bonaparte led an invasion of Spain and most of the Spanish authorities in Mexico were called home. The disaffected Mexican clergy prepared for their uprising.

By the summer of 1810, Captain Don Ignacio Allende of San Miguel had raised a clandestine army of rebels. Along with Miguel Hidalgo, a priest from the village of Dolores, they formed a secret league intent on overthrowing Spanish rule. They had planned a coup d'état for 8 December but news of their plan leaked to the government. In September, Spanish authorities began rounding up and imprisoning suspected insurrectionists. Hidalgo had to act at once.

At two o'clock in the morning of 16 September, 1810, Hidalgo rang the church bell, calling all rebels to the parish. There, Hidalgo gave the fiery speech that has been immortalized as the Grito de Dolores. Fasten your seat belts ladies and gentlemen, here it comes again.

"My children, a new order comes to us this day. Are you ready to receive it? Will you be free? Will you make the effort to recover from the hated Spaniards the lands stolen from your forefathers three hundred years ago? We must act at once... Long live our Lady of Guadalupe!... *¡Viva Mexico!*" (I expect you to have that memorized by the end of this book.)

The crowd then took to the streets, a raging torrent serpentining through town, growing as it moved, fed by dozens of tributaries as *Indios* squirmed out from under the boulders of oppression and joined the march. Of one mind in fulfilling a shared destiny, they sloughed off the past like an old skin and released their anger, three hundred years of suppressed hatred against the *Conquistadors*. That night they indiscriminately killed every Spaniard and *criollo* in town. But the blood spilled wasn't enough to satisfy the hunger of their wrath. It would take another eleven years of full-scale war for this emotional conflict to play itself out.

From Spain's Conquest of the Aztecs in 1521 until Spain's surrender to the Revolution in 1821, three hundred years, one month, and two weeks had passed. In 1824, the name of the new republic was officially changed from España Nueva to Los Estados Unidos de Mexico—the United States of Mexico.

No school Wednesday because of the holiday. We break the news to la Familia that we're moving out. Güero decides we should drink some beer and disappears with a case of empties. And—even though it's illegal to buy or sell alcohol on holidays—he returns shortly with a case of beer and ice, fills the cooler.

We pack what few possessions we have into the Combi and the three of us drive over to Señora Beltrán's house where we sign a six-month lease (which I can't read), pay the first month's rent of six hundred pesos (two hundred bucks), get the keys, and go to our new *departamento*.

I put my stuff in the bedroom on the right, the one with the little balcony out the back. Rudy throws his things into the room on the left, the one with the closet. Güero carries the ice chest into the front room. There, we're moved in. We open beers and sit on the floor (we have no furniture).

We have no stereo. We have no couch, no beds, no refrigerator, no chairs, not even a toilet seat fer cryin' out loud. There are bars on the windows. (*Don't get depressed, Clark.*)

"Let's go for a walk," Rudy says, "and check out the 'hood." *Good save.* The three of us wander through our new *colonia*, Lomas Universidad.

We're west of Guadalajara in a residential suburb called Zapopan, close to the University. The neighborhood climbs a low, terraced hillside. The crosswise streets are lined with three-story apartment buildings, each with two units per floor. Our apartment is on the top floor of a building at the end of a block. At the top of the hill are tree-lined railroad tracks, to the east a grassy field alongside our building, and at the bottom of the hill is a row of businesses—the local taco stand, *carnecería, lavandería*.

We wander out to the open west, past the homogeneous rows of apartment buildings, past a dirt soccer field, and along another small commercial strip containing hardware kiosk, ice cream shop, *farmacia, papelería*, and a small but modern *tienda*—the corner market (which will come to stand in for our refrigerator.)

Keep going, walk further—beyond the shops and houses and Mexicans. Keep going until the pavement beneath your feet disintegrates, blacktop peeling away to expose ancient underpinning of gray cobblestones flowing beneath you. Keep on now, across the uneven pavers, studying the pattern they weave.

As you progress, the stones become more irregular, more spread out, the gaps between them widening and the three of you soon find yourselves stepping from one stone to the next until they disappear altogether and your feet pad across naked earth.

Look up—it's different here. The sun is brighter, the skin darker, the dust thicker. Even Güero seems disoriented. The buildings are all low, one-story stuccoes, adobes, many of them uncompleted yet already crumbling. The streets and sidewalks are torn up or unfinished, everything in process. Laundry hangs between trees. Wheel-less cars sit in vacant lots. Bicycles lie in the streets where children have distractedly abandoned them. It resembles one of those seaside towns in which you so desire to live (except there's no sea), tucked away, hidden on the outskirts of Guadalajara.

Continue on until you find the heart of it. Search over the tops of the buildings for the cross, always the highest structure in any pueblo. There it is, in the next block, the church—a perfectly whitewashed structure rising out of the dark soil and broken streets, twin steeples aspiring heavenward (one for Jesus and one for Guadalupe?), leaning against the wild blue yonder (or is it Tonantzin and Quetzalcóatl?). The plaza in front is perfectly, smoothly paved, as flat and as level as the globe on which it rests, benches at its perimeter and a stooped devotee, perpetually sweeping a counterclockwise course.

Walk up to the temple. Its aqua door stands ajar. Look in. Don't enter, but look through the doorway. There, in the vestibule, in her dress blues—Lupita, Guadalupe, her head cocked, gazing at you with a look that says, "Everything is going to be okay."

Forget about the cold cinder blocks and the bars on the windows and the lack of toilet seat and refrigerator. Realize the great privilege it is to have been accorded the opportunity to live here. Now go find the pavement again and follow it back out.

We stop by the *tienda* to get some beer, eggs, tortillas, and juice, some vegetables, *food*. We do, after all, have a kitchen now, a stove in our new apartment, can prepare meals. There's a young man, our age, and an old guy behind the counter.

"Can I open those beers for you?" the kid asks. "You're Americans?" He hands us each an opened *fría*.

"Clark and I are from San Francisco," Rudy says. "Güero's a *Tapatío*."

"I am Carlos. This is my father."

"You speak English pretty good," says Rudy. Carlos' dad comes out from behind the counter, slaps me on the shoulder. With a smile, he begins to tell a tale in Spanish.

"He is telling a joke," Carlos informs us. The old man rambles on with a rapid-fire delivery, gesturing wildly until his narrative slams to an abrupt halt with the line, "*Soy el Gran Jeffe*," with his hand to his head in salute.

"That was the punch line," Carlos says. "It means 'I am the Big Chief.' He would like you to laugh now."

The old man slaps my shoulder again, "*Si, si. Big Chief! Big Chief!*" and begins to laugh uproariously.

Back at the *departamento*, our spirits are higher now that we've familiarized ourselves with our habitat. Güero cooks an omelet. Like all Mexicans, he possesses those great talents basic to survival—the innate ability to coax a great meal out of insubstantial ingredients, to lure beautiful music out of an unsound guitar, to get the cap off a bottle of beer with any implement at hand (or none at all). We hang about our home the rest of the day—inside, outside, on the stairs, the porches, the roof, drinking beer and celebrating *Independencia*, both ours and Mexico's.

"More beer?" Güero offers. We return to the *tienda* but, being late afternoon and a holiday to boot, it's closed. We walk around but can find no place to buy beer. Darkness falls. Güero starts chanting. "More beer, more beer..." and I do wish he'd learn more English. (*But then, that's your job, isn't it—Maestro de Inglés*.) But he's right, the lack of beer *has* become rather conspicuous.

So there it is, the pursuit of cold beer. See how thin your plot gets? It's as if you don't even have one and are trying to obfuscate the issue with all these distracting detours into obscure aspects of Mexican history and quantum physics...

Güero raises an index finger—sign that he has an idea. He goes to the nearby pay phone and makes a call, gives someone directions to our apartment. We return home and hang about and Güero starts in again with his mantra, "More beer, more beer..." until Libertad pulls up in Güero's car. He opens the trunk to a cold case of *caguamas*, far more beer than the four of us could possibly consume in a night. But it can't hurt to try.

We toss all the cushions, rugs, pillows, and blankets on the floor in the front room, light candles, put some music on the boom box Libertad's brought. Each one of us opens a *caguama*, rolls a joint and lights it, passes them around and we're happy, just happy to be here, doing this. Next week we find out if we have jobs. And if we don't, it's okay. We'll make it, one way or another.

We clink our bottles to shared shouts of "Hidalgo" and "*Viva Mexico,*" drinking in the night, Mexico, and *Independencia*, taking advantage of the freedoms secured for us on the anniversary of a Revolution touched off by that humble *padre*, Miguel Hidalgo. (This is the last time, I swear...)

"My children, a new order comes to us this day. Are you ready to receive it? Will you be free? Will you make the effort to recover from the hated Spaniards lands stolen from your forefathers three hundred years ago? We must act at once... Long live Our Lady of Guadalupe!... *¡Viva Mexico!*"

And finally, we get a new mantra from Güero. "*La Noche es larga.*" He keeps on with it until we all repeat, "*La noche es larga...*"

"Next weekend," Libertad says, "we will take a trip south, yes? We go to the beach and you will meet my family. Perhaps we can stop and pick some *hongos* on the way..."

I awaken in my apartment the next morning to Güero's repeated retching in the *baño*, stick my head in the bathroom to taunt him. "More beer, more beer!"

"*Pinche cabrón.*"

The night is long.

Fourteen

O n Friday we turn in those bloody fucking grammar books to Danny. Without a glance, he tosses them on a table behind him.
"Aren't you going to look at those?" Rudy asks. "Clark put a lot of effort into them."
"I'm afraid I've run out of obstacles to prevent you from working here," Danny says. "I'm going to have to hire you." He hands us each an orange tie emblazoned with the black *HH* logo. "Congratulations, you're teachers."

Early Saturday morning we pick up Güero and Libertad and the four of us head south into the day on Highway 80, three hours to Melaque, straight to the beach for sun, sand, and surf. In the evening we walk—sand-dusted and salt-encrusted—into town, to the *zócalo*, seat ourselves on the edge of the fountain to watch the evening procession circuit past. "Mass will be over soon," says Libertad. "The plaza will be full of *chicas*." Cathedral looms over *zócalo*, blue neon cross buzzes on top.
Sure enough, the service ends, church empties into square, and here comes the most clearly defined example I've yet seen of that Mexican mating ritual, the *paseo*. They circle the *zócalo*, the girls in their finest dresses, arms locked in couples, trios, and gangs; the boys decked out in corduroy pants and button-down shirts, boots, thumbs hooked over belts, hats tilted back.
"You see, the girls they walk against the clock and the boys with it," Libertad says, the two genders promenading in opposing directions that they may eye one another, view the merchandise, giggle, and flirt. Aunts and cousins, *tías* and older sisters sit around the track chaperoning the girls, refereeing the boys. Small children run throughout.

It seems funny to me, this whole elaborate and contrived ritual. Yet therein lies its beauty, its effectiveness. Everyone has a role in this society and knows what it is. After all these years I still haven't figured out the American mating rituals nor the nebulous rules which govern them (if they exist at all).

Back at the beach we mix a round of cocktails, twist a joint, and sit in the lunar glow listening to tide's murmuring. Rudy drops his shorts, runs naked into the surf. The rest of us strip and follow, swimming through the moonlight.

Sunday we awaken on the beach, half moon still above horizon, its radiance blanketing us on this bed of sand. A little Bloody Mary seeps over the east end of the bay. Waves wash gently onto beach, float the lingering dregs of dreams out to sea. We share a morning swim before dark clouds roll in, sprinkling rain on our parade.

"Rain is good," says Libertad. "We go now, to the home of *mi familia,* where a fiesta awaits."

I don't yet put it together.

But you will.

I take the wheel, get us on the highway north, Güero riding shotgun, Libertad and Rudy stretched out in back slipping into slumber. Cats and dogs rain from the sky. As we rise gently in elevation, scrub lowlands give way to stands of dark trees separated by fields. No homes and little life along the way. Cows graze unfazed by thunder and lightning, the downpour.

Coming to the crossroads, I look to Güero for direction in his country. But he has slid into his own slumber in the navigator's seat. There is no one to direct me to a destination, not a soul to take us there. But I'm not worried. I've got that innate radar what gets me always—albeit obliquely— from out of whatever trouble I might be in to wherever it is I next need to be in the universe. We roll through a green valley of towering cornstalks as the storm works up to her worst, lightning bolts slamming the ground all around.

We zoom past a trio of drenched Mexicans standing about a red Ford pickup, its hood propped open with a disjoined tree branch. Another quarter mile passes beneath our wheels before Güero bolts upright and yells "*Alto!*" I skid the Combi to a halt, back it up to the men who run smilingly towards us through the rain. "*Mis primos,*" Güero says, my cousins.

He and Libertad jump out, shake hands with and embrace the three men who slap Libertad on the back, punch him in the arm. *So, are these cousins in the literal sense as in "my uncle's kids?" Or is it more figurative as in "my cousins of Mexico, brothers and sisters of the world, a todo mi familia?"* The fact is, they know these men, out here in the middle of nowhere and in their sleep, Güero and Libertad know or are related to these three people stuck on the side of the road, their brothers or cousins or friends—*no hay separación en Mexico.*

They pile in, Güero and Libertad and the three cousins, settling themselves on the floor so as not to disturb Rudy who has remained asleep, sprawled across the seat, slumbering in only his boxer shorts. I gun the Combi back onto the highway. The rain finally ceases, but cloud cover remains. The men talk excitedly with Libertad, chattering in hushed tones. When I hit fourth gear Rudy's eyes open by degrees, all these silver Mexican smiles gleaming over him.

"Clark...?" he says, sitting up.

"Cousins," I say.

"Right," Rudy yawns, stretches and they all shake hands and all is well. Güero directs me off the highway and up narrow, unpaved roads that climb forever into the hills.

"*Aqui, aqui,*" says Güero.

I turn into the narrow, rutted drive, follow it up to a house atop a hill. Out front, a welcoming committee of two dozen mills about haphazardly— brothers, wives, sisters, and cousins, aunts and uncles and nieces and nephews, friends and *compadres*, babies and puppies, a multitude of generations awaiting our arrival with shuffling feet and crossed arms in a delicate tension of simmering anticipation chafing against constrained excitement. In the sky, the sun breaks through the clouds.

As we one-by-one pour out of the Combi, the Committee lines up to receive us. But then, just for a second, no one moves—neither us nor them—two fronts facing off in a mounting silence (a Mexican standoff). Then, Libertad exits the Combi. An elderly woman breaks ranks and rushes forward in tears. Libertad steps up and they unite with a great throwing of arms.

Because, you see, this is his home, his family, and this, the first time he's seen them since his release from prison, the first they've seen him since he was sent up the river three years and a half ago. One by one they embrace and the tension dissolves into gaiety. And though they know neither me nor Rudy, smother us equally with *abrazos* and *besos*. For we are the men who have returned their prodigal son.

We follow the crowd into the rough brick house. It is small, cool, dim, and before my eyes can adjust to the darkness, we have already exited out the back. A low wall of the same coarse brick surrounds the large yard of packed earth. A half dozen chicks peck about the soil, jumping on and off mama's back while papa rooster scouts the perimeter. In the center of the yard a pit has been dug, filled with slender sticks piled dense and high. A cousin loads cases of empty bottles onto his pickup, heads to town to get them "filled."

In an alcove in the wall at the end of the yard stands a statue of Guadalupe, her arms spread wide, an altar laid out around her. One by one family members approach to pay homage and leave offerings—flowers or fruit and kernels of corn, shot of tequila, or agua, or brandy, chocolates or candies, burning candle or smoldering incense, copal, tobacco, wood figurines and clay *animales*. And in the bowl at her feet each person deposits a scrap of paper scribbled with prayer, petition, or gratitude.

There—now that she's available approach her, approach the Virgin with the same apprehension you once carried into the ancient, creaky confessionals of your youth, before your fall from grace. Kneel; bow your head with thoughts of thanks for the fluidity of passage up to this point. Express your yearning for the highway ahead to be as forthright and fulfilling. Search your pockets for a physical object, something material into which you may project your pleadings—nothing but keys and those you need to start the Combi, to access your home—ah this one, the key to your home back home which exists now only as a memory. Roll that llave *off the ring, concentrate into it cogitations of once and future and lay it at her feet, touching her toes.*

Conversation dwindles, silence falls as the clan patriarch comes out of the house and crosses the yard. Gray-haired, mustachioed, and stooped, he kneels in front of Her as I step away. Eyes to the ground, he murmurs quietly, crosses himself, chuckles softly as they share a joke or a memory.

Realize that his are words which date back centuries, back to the warrior sons of Aztec kings and princesses kneeling on the earth in prayer to Tonantzin for success in battle, down through the generations to the migrant worker kneeling in the soil of the field, hands clasped to the heavens in petition to Guadalupe for the health of his family and crops enough to feed them.

Kissing her feet, el patrón lights a candle, drops the burning match in the bowl of pleading petitions and gracious gratitudes. From out of his throat, ancient Toltec murmurings rise with his eyes to the skies, arms stretching along horizon in duplication of her pose. The scraps of paper smolder, catch, burn—black smoke rising, ash and invocation up through the circle of their open arms.

His chants increase in volume until his voice fills the yard, spills over the walls and crosses the fields of corn. Four women emerge from the whispering stalks, each holding the corner of a burlap bundle. They enter the yard with rhythmic steps, dance its periphery to an invisible beat, out to the four corners, raising their burden to the sky, lowering it to the earth, to the hearth in the center of yard, the center of the universe where they release their bundle and spill out dozens of ears of corn.

Two young men set to work poking torches into the pile of sticks. The fire flames high and hot, but the small sticks burn quickly, squirm into a pile of glowing coals. The men converge on the hearth and place the ears directly in the coals. Scattered conversation returns. Someone turns on a radio.

"You know what they are doing?" Libertad has materialized beside me. "Why they cook it this way, so hot in the fire? The corn is still green, the first of the season, so they must soften the kernels to eat." The beers arrive, distribute themselves through the crowd.

"*Listo, listo!*" el Patron pronounces the *maíz*, ready to eat. The men who have been turning it and stoking the coals remove the ears from the fire. The women strip the chaff, serve the ears on their husks, one to each person seated about the yard on logs or benches or leaning against the wall. We wait for *el Patron* to take a bite before beginning on our own. Conversation mutes as we crunch and chew. The kernels are blackened and tough. (*Take a bite.*) Soft, sweet and tender inside, it rolls down my throat. *Corn.*

Look around. Look into the deep eyes of those who have planted it. See the muscled backs that have strained to pick the ripening harvest. Taste the dark earth into which the farmer has placed the seed. Taste the sun and the rain that have nourished it, which nourish you. Look into those eyes and see yourself as you are seen.

"Do you know why we do this?" the gravel road of a voice startles me. *El Patrón* has slid onto the bench beside me (*and here you assumed he spoke no English*).

"This corn," he says, shaking his half eaten ear in the space between us, "it is a gift from the gods. It is our life, and we must honor that. You see this—this kernel? It is the seed that becomes the ear that will feed my family, my people for the rest of the year, the seed that becomes our food. This corn," he stares into my face, inches away, "it is our universe."

El Patrón leans slowly back. His body relaxes, but our eyes don't separate until he turns to the fire. "The whole of our universe is in this ear of corn," he says. "And you must be wondering which came first—the seed or the plant. Well I can tell you. Our universe started the same as yours..."

"Yes?"

"With a big bang."

"A big bang?" I lean in.

"*Si*," he says, and a grin creeps up his chin. "Popcorn," he whispers, "Popcorn!" And the whole of the clan breaks into laughter, mouths full of the yellow stuff spilling across chins, laughing knowingly as if they have witnessed *el Patrón's* masterful setup before.

The sun descends behind hills. Rudy, Güero, and I say goodbye to Libertad and *familia*. They give us each a beer for the road, a touch, and we head north, back to the big city of Guadalajara, to our jobs, our homes, our lives. But we'll be picking the corn from our teeth for weeks to come.

Fifteen

We get back to the *departamento* and neither of us has the house key. We check the Combi, digging into it, through the piles of bedding and clothes that have accumulated, tossing everything out onto the ground. We really tear into it, but can't find the key. And then, overdue for a separate but equal day, we fight.

It starts out innocently enough with the traditional "casting of blame" but quickly escalates into something ugly. Neither of us will remember who throws the first stone, but it flies something like this: "You had them last." "No I didn't." "Yes you did." "No I didn't." "Did too." "Did not." And with the accumulated pressure of two months on the road, constantly in one another's presence, a gasket blows.

A fist flies, connects with a jaw. We stagger. More fists fly. I beat Rudy to the ground. He struggles to his feet, slams me against the Combi and against the ground. I roll onto my back, get a foot in his stomach, send him sailing through the open door of the Combi. He leaps out, knocks me into the dirt, pummels me with fists and feet. I manage to knock his feet from under him, slam him to the terra, get an arm around his neck and bash his head into the side of the Combi with a dull metallic *whack, whack, thwack* 'till blood flows. An elbow to my midriff doubles me over. Fist to head grounds me. Foot in the—

"Wait!" I shout.

"What?" Rudy asks, appendages poised to pound.

"Found it," I breathe heavily.

"The key? Where was it?"

"In my shoe."

"Let's go."

We help each other up the stairs.

*   *   *

It's our first day as certified teachers of English as a Second Language. I roll out of bed in the pitch black of 5 A.M. and stumble to the shower, turn the knobs to open the valves. Ice cold water sprays out of a pipe in the wall, flows over my body, causing me to be more awake than I've ever been in my life. This place didn't even come with a showerhead. There is a hot water heater *somewhere* in the *departamento*, but it certainly ain't heatin' this water.

I pull on my new black slacks, button the crisp white shirt, slip into the shiny leather loafers, knot the ugly orange tie and I'm ready to go by five-thirty as Rudy crawls to the shower. I go out on the landing to wait, take in crescent moon on horizon, stars twinkling in the clear sky, the tortured screams of Rudy being struck by arctic waters.

"You ready Clark?"

"For the past hour."

"Of course," Rudy says. "Let's go, *maestro*."

"Wait—there's something we gotta do first," I say. "We gotta take a picture."

"A picture? Clark, it's 6:15 in the morning—"

"Today's our first day of school. Mom always took a picture of me on the first day, and she would never forgive us if we didn't—"

"Okay, okay. I wouldn't want to upset your mother."

I upend the cooler, put the camera on it, set the timer. We pose in front of our barred front window, straighten our ties, smile.

"Clark..." Rudy says through clenched teeth.

"Yeah?"

"I don't think our water heater's working."

Camera flashes.

"No kidding."

My morning class is an Intermediate composed of five women in their late teens—and Tony. Tony has black hair—slicked back, a crooked grin, and a leather jacket he's never without. I nickname him *Trouble*.

"My name is Clark." I write my name on the board. "I'm from San Francisco."

"Clark," Trouble says. "Like Clark Kent?"

"Yes, like Clark Kent."

"Do we call you *Mister* Clark?" he asks.

"No, just Clark is fine. Now if there are no further questions—"

"What happened to your eye?" Trouble pushes. "It looks like you got hit."

"Were you in a fight?" one of the girls asks. "The other teacher, he was beat up too."

"We had an accident," I explain, hoping to put an end to the matter.

"That's not what I heard," another of the girls. "I heard there was a fight."

"Did you fight the other teacher, *teacher*?"

"There *was* a small scuffle in which we were involved but—"

"What's a scuffle, teacher?"

"Well there's our first vocabulary word," I announce, conjuring my best teacherly voice. "Scuffle." I write it on the board, SCUFFLE.

Good tactic, Teacher—keep things on track. This is your class, you're in control.

"A scuffle is," I say, "...a small fight."

Well that didn't work out too well.

"Who won?" Trouble asks.

"Nobody won."

"Are you friends with the other teacher?"

"Of course."

"What was the fight about?"

"Nothing in particular. It's something we do every now and then to release some steam."

"Oh. It is custom in your country?"

"Yes, it's an American tradition."

"Teacher?"

"Yes?"

"Why are you in Mexico?"

"Look—we're here to learn English. So unless you have questions pertaining specifically to the apprehension of the English language, I'd like to proceed with the lesson." A petite, bespectacled girl in the back row shoots up her hand.

"I have a question about English."

"Good. What is it?" I ask. "Why don't you start by telling me your name."

"I am Lupita—Is it not redundant, Mr. Clark, to say that you had a *small* scuffle since a scuffle—by your own definition—is already small?"

"Am I in the right room?" I ask. "Is this an Intermediate class?

"Teacher—I have English question," Trouble says. "If I meet an American girl and I want to have sex with her, what do I say to her?"

*   *   *

Everyone has been talking about a big festival this coming weekend, the *Cervantino* in Guanajuato, a colonial town two hours from Guada. Las Gringas are going, as well as a number of our students. Güero suggests the three of us go for the weekend. We'll drive to Guanajuato Saturday morning and spend the weekend partying.

"If we're going Saturday morning," Rudy says, "that means I can throw you a birthday party Friday night. We'll invite everyone from school, all the students and teachers."

"I don't like birthday parties. Besides, we've got no furniture, no place for anyone to sit or set their cocktails."

"We'll make it a furniture party then, a B.Y.O.C.!" Rudy exclaims.

"Bring Your Own...?"

"Chair. You see, besides bringing a bottle to the party, everyone will bring a piece of furniture. That way we'll get furniture *and* alcohol."

"You really think people are going to bring furniture to a party?" I ask.

"Everybody in Mexico brings *something* to a party. We just have to convince them to bring furniture—I know! We'll tell them it's a tradition."

"You're going to tell people it's an American tradition to bring furniture to a party?"

"No, we'll convince them it's a *Mexican* tradition, with pre-Colombian roots, one that's been suppressed since the Conquest. Yeah! Whenever someone moves into a new home they throw a party," Rudy continues, on a roll. "And everyone brings a piece of furniture. C'mon Clark, you're a writer, throw me a bone. We can build a whole mythology around it."

"Right," I say. "So the home gets furnished with all this stuff from different people. And each table or credenza represents a person or their soul," I continue, unawares of where I'm going. "Since a part of that person is always in your home, you think of them when you're sitting on the couch or whatever. And then, when a person who donated a piece of furniture comes to visit—no, no, it gives them the *right* to come and visit, any time."

"So if a girl gives me a bed," says Rudy, "she has the right to come over and sleep in it. That sounds okay. I'll slip it into my lesson for tomorrow. I gotta get to work on the history and origins." He gets out a pad of paper and pencil. "I have to convince my students that Mexicans have *always* brought furniture to parties."

"You should put this much effort in to getting laid," I say. "Oh, I forgot—you do."

*   *   *

I meet Rudy after our Tuesday morning classes. "You ready for Spanish?" he asks. Private Spanish classes are one of the perks of our employment. Our tutor is the soft-spoken and dry-witted Edgar, who's studying to be an English teacher, just like us. And, like us in our English classes, Edgar allows only Spanish to be spoken in his classroom. Unlike us, Edgar takes his teaching very seriously.

"*Hoy*," Edgar begins, "*vamos a aprender los muebles.*"

"Edgar," I ask, "what are *muebles*?"

"*Por favor, Señor Clark—habla me en Español.*"

"Sorry. *¿Que son los muebles?*"

"I know, I know," Rudy shoots up his hand. "*Muebles* is furniture."

"*En Español,*" Edgar groans.

"Oh right," says Rudy. "Uh—*muebles es muebles?*"

"*Digame Clark,*" Edgar says. "*¿Qual muebles tienes en su casa?*" What furnitures do you have in your home?

"*No tenemos muebles.*" We don't got no furniture.

"*Ah, no entiendes.*" You do not understand. "*En la noche,*" Edgar asks, "*¿a donde dormir?*" In the night—where do you sleep?

"*Sobre el piso.*" On the floor.

"*En tu casa, a donde sientarse?*" Where do you sit?

"*En el escusado.*" On the toilet.

"No, no, no," Edgar says. "I'm asking what *furniture* you have—in your home."

"And I am telling you," I say, "that we have none."

"Oh. But you *do* understand that *muebles* is furniture."

"Yeah. I caught that."

"None, huh?"

"*Nada.*"

"Well then," Edgar says, with a wink and a hand on my shoulder, "you should have a *Fiesta de los Muebles*. It is an ancient tradition in Mexico."

"Okay," Edgar continues, "*despues su Fiesta de los Muebles,*" after your furniture party, "*vas a tener muchas muebles, si?*" you are going to have much furniture, yes?

"*Si,*" I say, "*muchas muebles.*"

"*Rudio,*" Edgar says, "*la cama es para que?*" The bed is for what?

"*Sexo,*" Rudy says.

"*Okay. La silla es para que?*" The chair is for what?

"*Sexo.*"

Edgar exhales. "*La mesa, en la cucina, es para que?*" The kitchen table, it is for what?

Rudy shrugs, "*Tambien—es para sexo.*" Edgar drops his face into his hands, but Rudy isn't finished. "While we're on the subject, teacher—if I meet a girl in Mexico and want to have sex with her, what do I say?"

On Friday morning the big sign in the lobby—the one that flashes messages in bright red l.e.d.s—is running a banner: "Happy Birthday CLARK! CLARK! CLARK!" Random people punch me in the arm all day. "It is a custom in Mexico." Rudy and I go home on our siesta break, clean the *depto*, install some colored light bulbs, take our cooler to Carlos' *tienda*, fill it with beer and ice, invite Carlos to the fiesta.

"Oh yeah, don't forget to bring a piece of furniture," Rudy tells Carlos.

"Oh, it is a *muebles* fiesta?" Carlos says. "That is a Mexican tradition, you know."

Just before my evening class, I am called into the teachers' lounge where the assembled staff presents me with a chocolate rum cake.

And who is that redhead? We haven't seen her before.

"Clark, have you met Rosa? She's our regional supervisor."

Mamacita.

"Bite! Bite! Bite!" they shout, as per tradition. I bend over to take a bite of the cake and my face is smashed into it, as per tradition. Fun people, these Mexicans. I head off to class. Now here's a strange thing that happens: As I'm climbing the stairs, I run into Javiér coming down.

"I hear you are going to the Cervantino this weekend," he says.

"Yeah."

"I am going with you," he says, and then continues on down the stairs, just like that. He doesn't ask, just tells me that oh yes indeed, he is going with us.

Isn't he the bastard who trained, mistreated, and ignored you for the past month?

Yeah. Maybe Rudy invited him.

I tell Rudy about it after school, as we drive home to the coolers full of cold beer and our *Fiesta de los Muebles.*

"Are you crazy?" Rudy says. "I didn't invite him," and ponders it. "Do you think we should take him?"

"Like I said, he didn't ask—he *told* me he was going with us. I don't think we have a choice."

Before long there is a knock, knock, a knockin' on our front door. I open it and am almost crushed by a falling bookcase followed by Trouble, a

bottle of tequila, and three women. Everybody and more shows up for the party—teachers, staff, and students, people we don't even know.
Do they bring furniture?
"Yes of course, I bring you a lamp. It is ancient Aztec custom to bring *muebles* to a *fiesta*."

Past midnight, the party thins to four—me, Rudy, Güero, and Javiér, who's slumped with a beer and a grin in an overstuffed chair. Güero looks to his watch.
"*Es Sabado*," he says. "*Felice Cumpleaños, Clark*."
"Congratulations Clark," Javiér pats me on the back, "you have lived another year." Maybe he's not such a bad guy after all. Maybe it was Danny making him so uptight.
"Happy Birthday, asshole," Rudy says. "I sure could use a fat joint right about now."
"Well," I say, "I just happened to have found a fat green bud when I was cleaning the apartment today," producing it with a flourish.
"I'm glad one of us is obsessive-compulsive about housekeeping," Rudy says, "or I'd lose a lot of dope." He rolls a joint.
"What— What is that?" asks Javiér.
"*Mota*," Güero tells him. "*Te gusta?*" You like it?
"*No se*," says Javiér. "I will try it." The joint makes a circuit.
"That was a successful *Fiesta de Muebles*, if I don't say so myself," Rudy says, himself.
"Yeah, but nobody brought the most important thing," I say, "beds."
"All good things in all good time," says Rudy. "You want another hit, Javiér?"
"Yes, I like this *mota*."
"*Hav-e-air...*" Rudy muses. "We're going to have to change that."
"What do you mean?"
"Your name—we're going to have to change it."
"Why?"
"Too many syllables. You notice how the rest of us have only one or two syllable names—Clark, Güer-*ro*, Ru-*dy*?"
"Yeah," I say. "You're going to have to change it if you want to be in our gang."
"How about if we just call you 'J.'" Rudy says.
"I don't think I like that."
"*Jota*," says Güero through a cloud of smoke. "*En Español es Hoe-ta*."
"That sounds good," says Rudy. "And it rhymes with *mota*."
"Oh I don't like that at all," says Jota.

Sixteen

We're up early Saturday, despite the late night. I straighten the house (arranging our newly acquired furniture) while Güero cooks breakfast, Jota goes out for another case of beer, Rudy broods. We eat at our new dining table, pack the Combi and get on the road. Destination: Guanajuato, for the Festival Internacional Cervantino.

Guanajuato. Once my students discovered I was going they forced me to repeat the name until I had mastered its pronunciation. "Güwana-*whahhh*-toe," with a karate-chop drawling of the "wh*ahhh.*"

So what, exactly, is a Cervantino?

It's a festival of Cervantes. You know—Don Quixote, the batterer of windmills...

Wasn't he Spanish?

I believe so.

Then what's his connection to Guanajuato?

I don't know. It's a big street festival. You're going to have fun, what more do you want?

Answers.

We stop en route to replenish our *cerveza* supply, empty our bladders. It's shaping up to be a mighty drunken road trip. But then, the very layout of this country encourages drinking and driving. Because at the end of each little *pueblo* through which we pass—right next to the end-of-town *tope*— there's always a squat building of stucco or cinder block, standing by itself with the logo of a national beer painted on its side—Modelo or Superior or some such—and the word *DEPOSITO.* Here, one can pee on the back of the building, and exchange empties for fulls to avoid paying a deposit, purchasing only the beer (*that liquid gold which fuels your great deceit*) in a perpetual recycling of glass, beer, and urine in the dusty middle of nowhere Mexico. They also sell ice but, drinking so fast, we don't need any.

Güero directs us to a house in Irapuato, the home of another cousin who supplies us a stash of the green that Rudy promptly rolls. On the road again and into the second or third joint, Rudy drives, Güero and I stretch out on the floor, and Jota—leaning back into the back of the Combi—rocks with the motion of the road as he sucks another roach out of existence with a beat grin.

"Hey Rude," I say. "I think we're having a bad influence on this country."

"Any influence we have is bound to be bad," he responds. "We're a bad influence on ourselves." Rudy, red-eyed and focused on the drive, swerves the Combi around potholes and animals, dead and alive. "Did you ever notice how driving in Mexico is like playing a video game."

"No," I correct him. "Playing a video game is like driving in Mexico."

"Oh," he says, and quietly considers this for the rest of the day.

The luxuriously straight-flat highway wrinkles as we near the city, curves hugging hillsides, undulating down into ravines out of which houses climb vertical slopes, one on top of another. Rudy steers the Combi onto the cobbled streets of Güwana-*whahhh*-toe, glides it past the long Colonial facade, weaves it through teeming throngs of revelers choking the narrow roadway, parks at the end of a dead-end street on the fringes of *el Centro*.

The four of us exit into the midst of the revelry and heat, meander on foot through the crowd, navigating slender streets until they open onto the laurel-shaded trapezoid of el Jardin de la Union, the *zócalo* where I had loosely discussed meeting las Gringas. "We'll meet you," is how, I think, our conversation ended, "in the square," without much concern by either party of this actually happening as evidenced by the setting of a place devoid of time.

"We'd better get some beer," Rudy says, "before the sun goes down."

"You said the same thing this morning," I say. "Only then it was, 'we'd better get some beer before the sun comes *up*.'"

"That's not the same thing at all, except that we again need to get some beer." We get some beer, loiter in the sun on the broad steps of Teatro Juárez, sipping at the cold life, observing the passing crowds, dramas, and revelry and—*ahhh* but it feels so good down the gullet, *cerveza* cooling throat on this long day's journey into intoxication.

"We're at the Cervantino and it's your birthday," Rudy says. "What do you think about taking some acid." I laugh at this. "What's so funny?" he asks.

"You already took some, is what's so funny."

"You dosed me?!"

"In your beer." I laugh some more.

"Oh yeah?" he says. "If you think that's funny, you're going to think this is really funny."

"What?"

"*¡Igualmente*, in your beer!" and he starts to laugh. We laugh and slap each other on the back and Güero and Jota join in, even though they have no idea what the gringos are laughing at. Rudy produces the LSD and offers a small paper square to Güero and Jota. Güero takes one and puts it on his tongue (and I wonder if he knows...) but Jota—

"What?" he asks. "What is this?"

"It's a piece of paper," Rudy says. "Put it on your tongue and I'll tell you all about it."

"I am not putting that on my tongue. I don't trust you guys."

"Rightly so. Let me get you another beer then."

"Yes, I will have another beer." Rudy pops a top, drops in a square, and offers the can. Jota drinks it down.

"So what are we doing here?" Jota asks.

"We're drinking beer," Rudy says.

"Waiting for las Gringas," I say. "I told them we'd meet here."

"Here?"

"In the *zócalo*," I say, "in Guanajuato."

"Did you know there are other *zócalos* in Guanajuato besides this one?" Jota asks.

"I did not."

"Let's go get more beer," says Rudy.

"Déjà vu," says I.

"Follow me," says Jota.

Yes, follow Javiér back through time and space, across the gridwork of slanting plazas that rise beneath your feet, the steep cobbled streets what connect them. Emerge from a narrow alley which expels you into the European Renaissance of Cervantes—the small plaza of San Roque—packed with a dense, motley crowd of all ages, ilk, and species, costumed thespian and wandering minstrel dressed in leather, satin, and velvet, accompanied by song and proclamation, herd of goat, and clop-clop of passaging horse, all promenading past an empty stage.

Be the drama, wander the crowd with the same timeless intention, walking the earth in the forever search—scanning faces for a glimmer of hope, a gleam in an eye, a slant to the smile, some *indication of another's participation in the great* knowing. *But each visage just morphs into the next under your gaze, chasms which can't be bridged.*

We take up residence at a café table on the edge of the plaza; get a round of green bottles. In the square before us, a crowd of college students has organized itself into a game of Crack the Whip. The long human chain undulates rapidly across the square, cutting through the mob and sending one of their links sprawling into the fountain.

"Hey there's a fountain," I say.

"I could use a good cooling off," says Rudy. We slide back from the table.

"Where you going?" Jota asks. "I have a beer to drink."

As we stand to clear ourselves, the end of the whip comes around and cracks, snaps a young woman off, launches her stumblingly towards us. We grab our beers and leap back before she impacts the table, sends it hurtling into the café's interior, excuse ourselves and to the fountain.

Rudy and I shed shoes, jump in. Güero follows. Jota pauses to consider this turn of events. "What— What are you doing? You can't do that," he protests.

"Shut up and get in."

"Well, if you put it like that..."

We douse our heads and cool our feet. Before long we attract the attention of the police who order us out of the fountain. I rebuke them with a plume of water.

"Clark," Jota shouts. "We don't *do* that in Mexico."

"Maybe you should start," I reply.

Güero slaps bursts of water towards the police who skitter back. Rudy joins in, dousing the plaza with water. The disbanded whip-crackers rush the fountain and join the waterworks, wetting themselves and anyone within range. Crowd sparks to chaos. But the police know the four of us are instigators and close in, trying to get *at* us through the mob.

"*Vamanos!*" Güero shouts and the four of us clamber out, filter through the rapidly condensing frenzy, and disperse in the four directions and the gathering of the night.

I head off alone across the warped checkerboard of plazas that is Guanajuato to another, smaller square with another fountain, settle on a bench and watch. This inertia allows me to descend back into my body and absorb the scene before me—the party proceeding here in the plaza, a merry crowd still milling, still willing, still filling the air with the electricity of festivity as darkness descends.

Across the square the cathedral doors suddenly fling wide, releasing a viscous stream of black which pours forth, gurgles down the steps and into the plaza, parts the crowd and pools in a puddle of people. A white pine box bobs out the doors, floating atop a forest of black-sleeved arms. It cascades down the steps, surfing the black river of mourners—a somber slick of oil surging slowly through the merriment, cutting a path across the square, carrying the wooden box past the reviewing stand (me) and out the other side of the plaza. The Cervantino's rainbow revelers quickly close the chasm, filling the space in the wake of the lamenters' departure.

I up and approach the fountain, climb over the side and into the water, head hung, wade around, circling the statue in its center. On the opposite side I trip over a body in the water—Rudy. I sit in the shallows next to him.

"¿*Como estas?*" I ask.

"Pretty twisted," he says.

"Me too."

"What have you done to me?" a third voice says. We look up to see Jota standing over us, outside the fountain, his pupils like black dinner plates.

"Jota," Rudy smiles. "How are you?"

"I am feeling very strange."

"Strange?"

"Yes. But I like it."

"Why don't you join us."

"Okay." Jota climbs into the fountain, sits down on the other side of Rudy. "I think I'm beginning to understand you guys."

"I'm sorry for that," says Rudy.

"Please don't call me Jota."

Seventeen

Out on the front porch, five forty-five A.M., ready for work and waiting on Rudy, I watch the eternal approach of the distant storm. The eastern clouds sip blood. In the west, a still-full moon hangs between zenith and horizon. Overhead, Orion winks at me. *Twenty-five years.*

We're settling in here—Guadalajara is becoming a home, is settling into me. And I never thought I'd get homesick but, *I miss him.*

Señora Lilly is playing the role of good employer by throwing a Taco and Tequila party tonight, perhaps to institute some team building among the crew. Rudy has offered up our *departamento* as a beforehand meeting place from which we can carpool to Señora Lilly's.

Jota and his brothers Jorge and Joel show up with girlfriends, cousins, bottles, and the festivities begin. We drink up a good storm and soon it's dark and drunk and then, *¡Vamanos!* We caravan grandly over to Lilly's massive hacienda. Lucky for us, the momentum we ride is up to speed with that of Señora Lilly's, her party in as full a swing as ours. She's got a buffet of build-your-own tacos. Rudy, Jota, and I set upon it like vultures. And best (*worst*) of all is right *plop* in the middle of the table there's a wooden barrel, set on its side and equipped with a spigot. Put your glass under the faucet, twist, and—*caramba!*—a free flow of the amber elixir. I've got to give her credit, Señora Lilly knows how to party.

Nourished and fueled, I start to look around, see who's here. It's the usual crowd—teachers and staff, lots of people I don't know (*but all of whom know you*), as well as kids, children, and plenty of booze. Señora Lilly begins to distribute tequila shots and it's downhill blurry from there, thank God. The hard and fast torrent that flows from the barrel forms a river that carries us through the night.

Alicia "the Teeth" tugs at my elbow. I lean down and she whispers in my ear. "Rosa—she want to talk you." Ah, the beautiful redhead from the day of cake smashing in face. Alicia drags me outside to the waiting woman. She is beautiful—slim and sexy with curves in all the right places, shoulder-length red hair, and small, sharp features.

"Hi," she says. "You wanna walk?" The three of us walk down the driveway to the fountain at the estate's entrance, circle it.

"So what'd you bring me all the way out here for?" I ask.

"I just wanted to tell you that, well if you still need furniture—my mom, she just got new carpets and couches, and if you want the old ones— they're in fine condition—you can have them."

"That's very generous, thank you."

"Oh, and there's a bed, too—a queen."

"A bed, huh? I know what it means to give someone a bed in this country."

"Clark!"

"I'll think about it. Now let's get back to the party. I'm thirsty."

I walk back to the house. Señora Lilly hands me a beaker of tequila and we toast.

"Way to go champ," Rudy says. He and Jota have sidled up on either side of me. "A beautiful woman throws herself at you and you turn your back and walk away."

"Besides being my boss," I say, "she's married and twenty-five years older."

"I'm not talking about Lilly, you dumb-ass. I'm talking about Rosa."

"Oh."

"Yes," Jota jumps in. "You dumb-ass."

"You gotta start gettin' busy Clark, and catch up to the rest of us. Look at Jota—how many girlfriends have you got?"

"Three," he says. "I don't see what your problem is, Clark."

"Well—she's engaged," I say.

"Clark," says Jota. "This is Mexico. Everybody fools around. It's part of our culture." He puts an arm around my shoulders, fills my glass from the bottle he holds. "You need to start getting busy."

It takes some effort for Rudy and me to get our newly donated furniture up the stairs and into our *departamento*.

"So who gets the bed?" I say. "Should we trade off once a week?"

"I was thinking we could split it."

"Split it?"

"One of us gets the box spring, the other gets the mattress," Rudy says. "We'll ro-sham-bo to decide."

"You cheat at ro-sham-bo."

"Then this'll be quick." We slap our fists into open palms three times and Rudy—with the old stalling-hand hesitation prestidigitation—throws down two successive scissors to cut my paper.

"That's it then. I get the box spring," he says.

"You *want* the box spring?"

"Of course."

Friday is the last day of the *inscripción*, the first four-week session we've taught. Jota offers to cook us lunch on our break. "It is tradition."

"Ah," Danny says, "the traditional *end-of-inscripción cena*. Just get Javiér back here by four o'clock—*standing*, please. He has a class to teach."

"Is there something I should know about this tradition?" I ask.

"Well," says Jota, "it is traditional to have a few beers with lunch. So if you will get the beers, I will get the food."

"Okay," I say, but Jota is smiling, which makes me nervous.

"Hey Rudy," I say to him as he walks in the room. "Jota's going to make us lunch."

"What's he want from us?"

"Beer."

"That's not fair—I've seen him drink."

"Yes," says Jota, "and I have seen you eat."

"Here," Jota indicates a *supermercado* as we drive to his place in the Combi. "Stop here for groceries."

"Here?" Rudy says. "This place is expensive."

"Yes," says Jota. "That's because people are always shoplifting. Can I borrow your coat?"

I'm at the beer cooler, loading a cart with ice-cold *caguamas* when I look down to the butcher counter. Jota stands over the case, scratching his belly, contemplating a side of beef. At the checkout line he meets up with us, drops an onion in my hand.

"We're going to need this."

"That's all you need to make us lunch?" Rudy asks.

Jota shrugs. I buy him the onion.

At the Combi, Jota unzips the coat, pulls out a wedge of cheese, a bundle of tortillas, avocados, tomatoes, a bottle of sauce. "I'm going to make tacos," he says, extracting two pounds of sirloin from his pants.

"Hence the onion, huh?"

Jota's apartment is furnished with three bunks he shares with his brothers and a T.V. He starts a movie playing in the V.C.R. and goes to work in the kitchen while Rudy and I go to work on the *cervezas*. Man can he cook. We scarf down the feast of *tacos de carne asada con queso*, chase them with a few liters of Corona. Then, satiated on beer and authentic Mexican cuisine, we slip into a satisfying siesta.

"Clark," Jota cuts into my slumber. "I'm sorry, but you have to drive me back to school."

I don't stir.

"Come on—you promised Daniel, remember?"

"Why don't you wake Rudy?"

"Believe me, I tried."

"All right." I rouse Rudy and the three of us down to the Combi, parked in an alley.

"*Hijo de*—" Jota curses. "I forgot my books. I have to go back and get them." And off he goes while Rudy and I wait in the Combi, in the silence of his departure, still digesting lunch. And then, I lose it.

It comes from somewhere deep, out of the silence, suddenly and unexpected, a tidal wave from behind that catches me off-guard, washes over me, through me, tears bursting from eyes, spilling down face in a torrent. I hunch over the steering wheel and weep like I haven't in years.

"You okay?" Rudy reaches out. But he knows, has been waiting for this. He says nothing more—doesn't need to—just sits with a hand on my shoulder, relieved that it's finally arrived. And I'm glad he's here, if only to bear witness.

You left it all behind you (including a death you can't—or won't—accept). You left it all behind for everyone else to handle—ran, fled south of the border and now can't help but think that if you'd stayed and dealt with things, you could have worked everything out for everybody. Know that no matter how far or how fast you flee, your past will always catch up with you.

Jota appears at the end of the alley, approaching the Combi. "Hop in back Clark," Rudy says. "I'll drive." I climb to the back, slump on the seat. Rudy slips behind the wheel as Jota climbs in shotgun.

Jota glances back at me, throws a questioning look to Rudy who says, "He's alllll right," puts it in gear and drives on.

Eighteen

"**M**y back is killing me," Rudy says as we drive to school Friday.
"That's probably because you've been sleeping on a box spring, you dumb-ass."

"I thought it was the soft one."

"Box? Spring?—do either of those terms indicate softness to you?"

I walk into school and run smack dab into Edgar, wrapped from head to toe in white bandages. "What the hell happened to you?" I ask.

"*Soy un momia*," he answers with a huff, and walks away. Rudy stumbles in behind me.

"Who's the burn victim?"

"Edgar, I think."

"*¡Oye!* Clark. Ruuudeee," Alicia "the Teeth" sings out from the receptionist's desk. "*Tengo un* massage for you." She stands, waving a piece of paper.

"Massage?" Rudy says, "I'd love a massage."

"*Mess*-age?" I enunciate at her, "you have a *mess*-age for us?" She continues smiling, waving the piece of paper. I snatch it from her.

"*¿De quien?*" Rudy asks. From whom?

"*Es de Nena*," Alicia says.

I read it silently through a couple times before Rudy's impatience interrupts.

"What's it say?" he asks.

"I don't know. It's in Spanish."

"Of course it's in Spanish." Rudy grabs the note from me. "Both the person who gave the message and the person who took the message are Mexican." Alicia continues to stand there, showing those teeth. "What are you waiting for," Rudy says to her, "a tip?" And he finally gets down to the business of reading the massage.

"Our presence is *required* at la Familia's Monday for a *celebración tradicional de Mexico*."

"Monday?" I say. "We've got school Monday."

"No," says a voice. We turn to Edgar, standing behind us, reading the note over our collective shoulders—or rather through them. "Monday is a holiday," he says. "Day off."

"What the hell happened to you?" Rudy asks.

"I'm a *mummy*," Edgar says. "Tomorrow's Halloween. I thought we were dressing up."

"We get Monday off because of Halloween?" Rudy asks.

Then it dawns on me.

"No," I say and Edgar leans in between us.

"*Es las Días de los Muertos*," Edgar whispers, and a bell rings to indicate the start of classes. Edgar mummy-walks away.

"The Days of the Dead," Rudy mutters and the two of us stand there, late for class.

Of course. How could you have forgotten? (Or did you?) It's a holiday you've pondered for years, a Mexican celebration for which you've yearned for a lost generation, since long before you were brushed by death's cold hand. And now you find yourself in Mexico staring down its throat as the first anniversary of your father's passing approaches. It's all around you, this pall of death, in the markets and the murals, in the language and the lives, the calaveras and the coffins, the mummies and the altars. Death surrounds you here but you've been too god damned blind to see it.

You're bound to visit sacred ground in the forthcoming future, there's no avoiding it. You're going to the graveyard to mingle with the spirits what linger—he among them, no doubt. You're headed for the cemetery with a bottle of memory, an ache in your bones, and in your pockets— stones. And though you may try to skate around it, attempt to dance with death on your tippy tippy toes—she'll trip you up and take you down, cleave your chest and clench your heaving heart, plant a kiss on it, or a tree. Porque estas en Mexico where attendance is mandatory and there's no dodging death.

*   *   *

Mytho-Historical Departure
**The Fifth Sun, Mexico's Cult of Death,
And Why the Aztecs Sacrificed Humans**

Aztec mythology describes a number of eras called "Suns," four of which have already come and gone. Each epoch endured 5,125 years before descending into discord and culminating in the cataclysmic destruction of the world and the stopping of time. But the end of each Sun has, so far, been followed by the birth of a new one and the restarting of time.

Following the end of the Fourth Sun, the gods gathered at Teotihuacán to generate the next. For four days they sat in silence around a blazing fire. Then, the gods spoke to Tecuciztécuatl. "Enter the fire!" they told him and he prepared to do so. But he became afraid and hesitated. Four times he stepped forward and four times he backed down. The gods then turned to Nanahuatzin. "You, Nanahuatzin, you jump in the fire." Seeing this as his shot at fifteen minutes of fame, Nanahuatzin stepped up and hurled himself into the flames.

A great dawn unfolded across the land. After a long time the sun appeared in the east, blazing red. But it didn't move—the sun stood still in the sky. In order to energize it and set it in motion, the gods sacrificed themselves, offering their own blood to the heavens. This caused a great wind to blow and the sun was propelled across the sky. Because of their sacrifice, a state of equilibrium had again been established in the universe. The Fifth Sun had begun—that in which we currently reside—*Nahui Ollin*, the Sun of Movement that, incidentally, is (or was) set to expire on December 21, 2012.

From the get-go, the Aztec believed sacrifice was necessary for life to exist. At Teotihuacán, Nanahuatzin threw himself into the fire in order to become the Sun. The gods offered themselves to start the flow of time. Sacrifice was a due the Aztec owed the cosmos in order to maintain the machinations of the universe, to keep sun moving across sky, to repay the gods for the sacrifices *they* had made to bring us into being.

The prevailing religio-philosophical belief of sixteenth century Europe was that the individual was in control of his or her destiny. Most Europeans subscribed to the Christian concept of perpetual atonement for Original Sin and the belief that living a virtuous life would secure their status in the afterworld. The Aztec, however, believed that their path in life was determined at birth by the gods. They felt that they were but pawns in a cosmic game. Because the gods controlled their lives and actions, the Aztec lacked the concept of sin as a determinant of fate. When things failed to go their way they didn't blame themselves, they blamed the gods. Since the Aztec were merely living out a predetermined life, it didn't matter how they lived. For them, it was the way in which they *died* that determined the destiny of their souls in the afterlife. Unlike the conquering Spaniards who were apprehensive of death, the Aztec welcomed it.

Sacrifice, to the Aztec, did not guarantee them entry into paradise but helped to ensure the health of the cosmos and the continuity of creation. The universe, not the individual, benefited from the spilling of blood. Giving one's life for the good of the community was a noble pursuit, the loftiest act one could perform, and one that was praised. And so varying celebrations evolved across Mesoamerica honoring the souls of the departed, usually during the fall harvest, a time when the fruit of the plant is taken and its seeds preserved for the next season's sowing.

When the Spaniards began their proselytization of the New World, they attempted to supplant Aztec beliefs and rituals with Christian ideals— and there were some glaring similarities. (Did not Jesus sacrifice *himself* for the good of man?) But the Aztec tradition was one that could not be fully suppressed. And so the missionaries incorporated Mesoamerican death ceremonies and harvest rites into the existing Christian holy days of All Saints and All Souls. Thus the Days of the Dead evolved.

The front door to la Familia's is wide open when we arrive, the air full of Mexican fragrances. "Hola *hijos*," Nena shouts from the kitchen. "*Venga, venga.*" Come, come. From the upper corners of the living room the walls are strung with colorful *papel picada* tissue paper banners. A long table has been set up against the far wall of the dining room, its top built up with cloth-draped tiers. Empty plates and glasses adorn the table. On the shelf above sit incense burners, candlesticks, and unfilled flower vases. The next tier holds knickknacks—toys, jewelry, coins, a plastic skull. The top shelf is lined with photographs. And over it all—hanging prominently on the wall—is *la Morena*, the Virgin of Guadalupe.

"*Buenas días compadres.*" Ramón enters from the back room, sweeping a cloud of dust before him.

"How are jew theese morning?" Nena asks from the stove where she stirs a large pot of dark sauce.

"Me?" I say. "I'm fine. Rudy—*el esta crudo.*"

"Ahhh, jew are the hangover," Nena says. "*Bien bien.*"

"What's cooking," Rudy asks, as a cavalcade of aromas gallop out of *la cucina*.

"You know the *mole*?" Nena says. "We have it later with the *pollo*."

"*¿Donde esta Güero?*"

"*¿Güero?*" she frowns and looks at her watch. "He went to the *mercado* early theese morning, *con Yessica*, to get the flowers. And still he is not back." She throws an exasperated hand in the air (the left), continues to rotate the wooden spoon (with the right), staring into the bubbling darkness. "Ramón!" Nena shouts. "*Rudy necesita una cerveza!*"

Ramón brooms the dust cloud out the front door, comes back in and shakes our hands. He motions to the altar. "*Mira a nuestras ofrenda, para los difuntos.*" Look at our offering, for the dead. "*¿Clark, tienes un fotografía?*"

"*Si, Clark,*" says Nena. "Do you have a photograph?"

"A photo?" I ask.

"*De su papa?*" They look to me. A photograph of my father? For their Day of the Dead altar? I don't carry photos.

Yes, you do have one—you came across it the other day when you were cleaning the depto. You put it in your wallet.

I did? Why?

For this. Get it out.

I dig the snapshot out of my wallet, hold it up. It's my father and me, standing on the shore of Lake Michigan, leaning into the wind, the Mackinaw Bridge blurry in the background. I stand a head above him, an awkward arm around his shoulders. It was taken when we'd stopped for a stretch during our drive from Northern Michigan down to the Mitten, on his last visit home for a final goodbye to family and friends.

Ramón indicates the altar. I approach. "In the center," Nena says. "He was most recent." I position the photo on the top tier, lean it up against a candle, and step back. *Are they doing all this for me?* I can't turn to face them. The sudden putter putt-putt of a flat four engine rumbles to a stop in the driveway.

"Güero," Nena says.

Jessica runs in, hugging bouquets of marigolds. Güero follows, toting string-tied bakery boxes and bags of bread, *el pan del muerto*. Nena turns on her trademark sternness, aims a finger at him and scolds in rapid-fire Spanish. But another presence darkens the doorway behind him and Nena drops the tirade.

"Ah—*Theese ease* why you *wear* late!" she exclaims and rushes to embrace Libertad.

There's more to carry in. I help Güero with the bags of fruit, cases of beer, bottles of tequila and brandy. Nena and Jessica disappear into the kitchen. Libertad sits me down on a couch as Ramón brings out a round of *cervezas*. Güero unties the boxes, reaches in with a grin and pulls out skulls made of sugar. Each has one of our names inscribed in frosting across forehead.

"Is he trying to tell me something?" Rudy asks.

"The Days of the Dead are a time for reunion with the family," Libertad says and sips his beer, sitting forward on the couch. Güero busies himself placing bananas, pineapples, and the small loaves of bread on the altar, lines up the sugar skulls and little chocolate coffins. "But it is not only for us, the living," Libertad continues. "It is a reunion with our relatives who have died." Güero fills the vases with flowers, lights candles and incense. "On this day the dead return, the souls of our relatives come to the house attracted by the fragrances, the incense and flowers, the smells of their favorite food and drink that we put out for them." Güero pours tequila into a glass on the altar, spills some down his throat.

"We call this the *ofrenda*. The spirits come and take the essence of the offering, absorb the aromas and flavors." Nena carries in a plate of steaming tamales, sets them on the altar. "We do this to let them know they are remembered and loved, for no one really dies if they are still loved." Libertad rises and approaches the altar, gazes at the portraits of the *difuntos*. "Clark, *este es su papa*—your father?"

"*Si.*"

"He was short, like a Mexican."

"Italian."

"*Lo mismo.* What was his poison? What did he drink?"

"He was partial to brandy."

"Then pour him a *vaso*—he will have traveled a long way to be here with us and will be thirsty when he arrives."

"*¡Movamos!*" Nena shouts, standing behind us with an earthenware pot of steaming *mole*. We part and she sets the *ofrenda* on the altar. "Don't touch," she warns. "We eat soon."

We finish the *cena* at sunset. The women clear the table as Ramón and Güero gather things for the evening's ceremony—a bucket and brush, candles and incense, flowers, tequila, and brandy, all the things needed for another *ofrenda*. Nena and Jessica pack some food. Rudy slumbers on the couch.

"Time to go," says Nena. "*¡Vamanos!*"

"C'mon," I wake Rudy, "we're going."

"Where am I? Where are you taking me?"

"To the graveyard."

"Am I dead?"

"I wish."

Outside, a loose procession makes its way through the neighborhood. We fall in with the neighbors—families bearing bundles, children cavorting carelessly, lovers holding hands, a myriad of musicians, and the spirits of the dead. The crowd leads us through the twilight, towards the cemetery.

"Clark?" Rudy still hasn't quite woken up. Or gotten over his hangover. "If I was dead you'd tell me, right?" Güero hands him the bottle of tequila.

"It is nice for the spirits to come visit us," Libertad says. "But we cannot have them hanging around. So once they have eaten, we lead them back to the cemetery, send them away for another year."

The procession pours through portal and scatters into cemetery, eerily illumined by hundreds of candles. It's already full of people—dead and alive. Boys thread through, selling candles, soft drinks, beer. La Familia leads us to their plot near the center of the hallowed ground. Two graves rest side-by-side, overgrown with grass and weeds with another adjacent, it's headstone listing. We stand on the soft earth.

"This is my aunt and uncle, their parents," Libertad says. "And this is Nena's husband—Jessica's father." We stare at the earthen mounds. "And this," Libertad addresses the graves, *"te presente Clark y Rudio."*

Everyone sets down their packages and sets to work, pulling weeds from around the graves, clearing them of leaves and pine needles as darkness closes around us. Ramón wanders off with the bucket, returns with soapy water, scrubs down the headstones while Güero straightens them with a shoulder. The graves are then swept with a pine bough, sprinkled with holy water, candles and incense set upon them. The work finished, Nena and Jessica set in to praying. Güero hits me, *"Vamanos,"* and off walk the men, passing the bottle between us.

We circumambulate the graveyard, visiting friends—dead and alive— talking with them, joking with them, for this is a joyous occasion, a *celebración*. At the edge of the graveyard there's a bonfire, where one can dump the weeds and leaves they've cleared, warm oneself, take in the music provided by the contingent of neighbors with instruments while *calaveras* and *mummers* cavort through the scene.

"Death is a part of life, you know," says Libertad. "You see how prevalent the *calavera* is in Mexico—the skeleton? Well, we each have one inside of us," he taps a fingernail on his teeth. "Don't forget that. Death is within us our entire lives, just waiting to get out."

Back at the house, the candles of the *ofrenda* have burned down to puddles of hardened wax. Libertad approaches the altar. "How do we know that the spirits have been here?" He points to the glasses of water and tequila. "The drinks." Once full, they now are only half. "Your father," Libertad points to his picture and the glass in front of him, "he was thirsty." The brandy I had poured for him is gone, but for a drop.

Nineteen

I n the evening after school, Rudy and I stop at the neighborhood pay
phones so he can check in with Virginia. I wander around the block,
return as he's hanging up.

"Good news, my brother," Rudy exhales. "She's coming."

"V.? She's coming *here*?"

"In two weeks," he says. "She's coming to Guadalajara."

"That's great," I say. "Isn't it?"

"Of course."

"You don't seem too excited. What's up?"

"I feel disconnected."

"Well, you have been away from each other a few months."

"I think about what you and I have been through down here," Rudy
says, "the ground we've covered. And I worry that V. and I will have
grown apart."

"Did you get that feeling from talking to her?"

"I didn't really get any feeling from her." Rudy looks at the ground.
"She seemed nonchalant about coming to visit."

"And how were you to her?"

"The same, I suppose. I don't know, maybe I'm reading too much into
it. But what if she gets here and we find the spark is gone?"

"You'll never know unless you give it a try. If the spark is gone then
you just enjoy each other's company. You *are* best friends. And if the
flame is still there, then you fan it into a fire and you marry her."

"Will you be my best man?"

I awaken to a quiet Sunday morning. Before I've even wiped the sleep
from my eyes, let alone figured out what I'm going to do today, someone is
banging on our front door.

"Are you ready to take me on a picnic?" Rosa stands there, all smiles.

"Picnic?" I sneer, "I've got nothing for a picnic," at which she produces a basket chock full of picnicstuffs.

We walk along the railroad tracks to that big park with the sloping lawns and pine trees. Rosa lays out a blanket and a spread of homemade comestibles indicative of a late night's effort. We nibble, and savor the sunshine. Rosa lies down, puts her head in my lap, gazes up at me.

"Clark..."

"*¿Si?*"

"I think I'm in love with you."

Shit.

Jesu-Christo, how are you going to respond to that?

I don't know.

Well how do you feel about her?

I am attracted to her—she's beautiful, smart, sexy. And I'd like to get her in bed, but...

But what?

But *love*? I don't know about that. I don't even want to *say* the word.

Why does it make you so uneasy?

Well the thing is this—here in Mexico it's either wedding bells or silence. There's no in-between, no such thing as a casual relationship. You're either on the proverbial bus or off the proverbial bus. And I certainly don't want to complicate my life—not here, not now.

Being in a relationship is nothing more than a complication?

Well it starts with dating, then marriage, then she's gonna want to have kids, paint the house, take a vacation. And I'd have to work to support all that.

But you do have feelings for Rosa, right? (And I'd like to remind you that she's still laying in your lap, awaiting a response, so we'd better speed up this internal dialogue.)

Yes, I do have feelings for her, but... Look, when it comes down to it none of this really matters anyway. She's got a boyfriend, remember? A *fiancé*. And he's a student of mine fer cryin' out loud. Why doesn't she just stick with him, get from him what she wants out of life?

She probably will, after you reject her. But she won't be happy.

I cannot be responsible for other people's happiness. I'm barely in control of my own.

"You know what I love about this country?" I say aloud, diverting my gaze over the tops of the trees.

"What, Clark?" Rosa raises a hand to shade her eyes from the sun, squints up at me.

"You know the eggs are fresh because they come with the chicken shit, still moist on them."

"What?"

"That, and you can buy milk, still warm from the cow."

Rosa sits up.

"That's what you have to say? I express my love for you and all you care about is—is chicken scat?" I shrug. She up and throws everything into the basket, yanks the blanket from under me, leans down into my face. "I don't believe you Clark," and off she storms.

Rudy and I go to Jota's place to watch Monday Night Football, our 49ers taking on the Atlanta Falcons.

"How are things with Rosa?" Jota asks.

"She's not talking to me."

"Yeah," Rudy laughs. "I don't know what he said, but Clark really pissed her off."

"Be careful," says Jota. "You piss off a Mexican woman she will slit your throat."

"Yeah, yeah."

"I'm telling you," Jota says, "they all have knives." He turns to Rudy, "When is your girl arriving?"

"Next week," Rudy says, "or thereabouts."

"What do you mean," I say, "or thereabouts?"

"You know V. She said she'd be here mid-November but she didn't have her ticket yet and wasn't sure."

"So she might not be coming at all?"

"She'll be here," Rudy says. "I just don't know when. But we'd better get things ready."

"What's there to get ready?"

"Like the water heater," Rudy says. "We gotta get that fixed."

"That's suddenly a priority?"

"You can't expect Virginia to take cold showers."

"You haven't worried about *me* having to take an arctic plunge every morning."

"C'mon Clark, it's invigorating. You're supposed to be cultivating machismo, building up a tolerance for the hardships in life."

"Living with you provides hardship enough."

"Don't worry, Clark," Jota puts a hand on my shoulder. "She will be back."

The next week comes and goes without a word from Virginia. Rudy has been unable to get a hold of her and is in a frenzy—a combination of pissed off at not having heard from her, and worried that something has happened. First thing Monday morning he goes into school and confronts "The Teeth."

"*Alicia*," he says to her, "*tienes algo para nosotros?*" Do you have anything for us?

"*Si*." She stands, smiling.

"Well? Hand it over, god damn it!"

"Okay." Maintaining her smile, she picks up the lone item occupying her desktop—a folded half-sheet of white paper. Rudy yanks it out of her hand and reads it. He lowers the scrap and faces me.

"She's here," he says.

"Huh?"

"*She's here*," Rudy says, rereading the message.

"Here, where?" I ask.

"Mexico City," Rudy says. "She flew into Mexico City."

"Mexico City? Does she know that we live in Guadalajara?"

"She's gonna take a bus the rest of the way. She wants me to pick her up at the bus depot. Who took this message?"

"*Yo*." Alicia raises her hand, smiling.

"Did she happen to say what *time* she's arriving, or which *bus* she's gonna be on?"

"*No*," Alicia says, shaking her head and giggling.

"Of course she didn't," Rudy says, "she's V. I guess I'll just have to wait around at the depot until she arrives."

Jota drops me home after school that evening. The Combi is out front. Rudy must be back from the bus depot, hopefully with Virginia. I climb the stairs, walk in the front door and there, strewn across the apartment, is her stuff—skirts, blouses, and bras; lipstick, hairspray, and curling iron; tampons, panties, and eyelash curler; spilling out of bags and suitcases in a layer across the floor, on the couches and tables and it hits me—we're going to have a woman living with us, sharing our Zapopanian bachelor pad for—how long is she going to be here?

You haven't really thought this through now, have you?

Rudy is slumped, unsmiling on a couch. I shoot him a questioning glare.

"In the shower," he frowns, motioning with his thumb. I hear water running and a voice, singing.

"Is everything okay?" I ask.

"Everything's fine," Rudy says, gazing at the mess. "I only had to wait three hours for her." The squeal of a closing valve squelches running water. "But she arrived safely." Rudy forces a smile.

The bathroom door opens and Virginia, wrapped in a towel, steps out, sees me, and screams. "Claaaaark!!!" She sprints her slim Latina body across the room, black hair flying, and vaults off the ottoman. She hits me like an elevator full of coffins (or a coffin full of lemons, take your pick), knocks me onto the couch, lands on top, and smothers me in kisses.

I'm awakened, seven o'clock Saturday morning by a banging on our door—Rosa.

"What?" I ask, still asleep. "What is it?"

"Aren't you glad to see me?" She asks.

"Yeah, but it's Saturday and I was planning on sleeping 'till noon."

"Then it's a good thing I'm here Clark, because we have a seminar to attend."

"A seminar?"

"Yes Clark, the 'Teaching English as a Foreign Language' seminar at the British Institute. It's mandatory for all Hardship teachers."

"What do the Brits know about English?"

"Hurry up and get dressed. Where's Rudy?"

"He's where I should be, in bed with a hangover—and V."

"Should I wake him?"

"Not unless you wanna get hurt. Do you really think Rudy's gonna spend a Saturday sitting in a seminar when there's fun to be had elsewhere? I don't even know why *I'm* going."

"You're going because it's mandatory." Rosa smiles. "And because I'm gonna be there."

"Now Clark," she says as we sit in her car, recently parked alongside the British Institute, "the whole of our staff is going to be here—"

"Except Rudy."

"I know it's going to be hard, but we're going to have to keep a professional distance from one another. We need to keep up appearances."

"Right. We wouldn't want anyone to think we're a couple."

Someone pulls up next to us on a motorcycle, kills engine, removes helmet—Jota.

"Where's Rudy?" he asks, looking in the car.

"He's where I should be—home in bed."

"—with V. and a hangover," Rosa adds.

"Why are you here?" Jota asks.

I glance at Rosa who diverts her gaze. "I understand attendance is mandatory," I say.

"It is," he says, pulling his helmet back on. "Will you sign me in?" He stands the motorcycle upright and kicks it to life. "I'm going to go hang out with Rudy and V."

The seminar is, of course, long and boring—lectures on teaching technique and theory. As per the wishes of my secret, non-girlfriend, I keep a respectable distance from her throughout the day and what happens? My other female colleagues are all over me, making Rosa seethingly jealous. Two of them in particular—Monica and Sophie—have designs on me. But what better way to hide my non-affair with Rosa than to seek refuge in the affections of others.

I sit in the sun on the steps of the British Institute with Monica and Sophie, eating lunch and talking, laughing and smoking, practicing my Spanish.

"Clark," Rosa is suddenly before me. "Can we talk about that curricula now?"

"Curricula?" I say, "What's that?"

She glares at me.

"Sure we can talk. *Con permiso, señoritas,*" I kiss the hands of Sophie and Mo. "*Hasta pronto.*"

"Oh, Clark," they giggle. Rosa and I walk across the courtyard.

"Why don't we go around back and sit on the grass," Rosa says. "We can talk there." As soon as we round the side of the building and are far from the maddening crowd, Rosa cocks her arm and punches me hard in the chest. "You bastard!"

"What did I do?" I ask.

"Do you have to flirt with every woman in Guadalajara?"

"I was only keeping a professional distance from you," I say. "Like you asked."

She punches me hard in the arm.

"Ow," I say. "You don't want to talk about curricula at all, do you?"

"No," she says, "I want to talk about us."

"Why didn't you say so?" I ask, as she cocks her arm to take another swing. "Okay, okay, I'm sorry." She lowers her fist. I put an arm around her, feeling her pockets for knives.

"Do you think it's easy for me to watch you going around with other women all day?"

"It's probably about as easy as it is for me to watch you and your fiancé all day at school."

"That's not fair, Clark. I *love* you," she says. "I'm just confused."

"It's simple, *who* refers to the subject of a sentence and *whom* indicates the object."

"Clark I'm serious. I want to be with you. I'm just afraid you're not going to stick around here. And you won't even tell me how you feel."

"I don't want to complicate things."

"Complicate things?"

"Yeah. You've got a plan. You want to get married, raise a family. You've got Pedro for that. He'll make a fine husband and a good father."

"But I don't *love* him."

"Then maybe you should dump the both of us and start anew."

"You're impossible, Clark."

Twenty

Before you know it, it's mid-December and we're staring down the throat of three weeks worth of Christmas vacation. Our multitude of friends and colleagues are dispersing to the three corners of Mexico. It's time for us to take another road trip as well. But where to go?

"My friend Austin just bought a condo on the beach at Puerto Escondido," Rudy says. "He and his wife are going to be there for the holidays. I'll see if I can wrangle us an invite."

And so we pass the days leading up to Christmas—driving the coast highway through endless groves of palm and banana trees, cruising through *tope*-filled villages, searching the strips for excitement (but finding none), camping on the beach, and then waking with the sun and the surf for a soak and a swim, followed by the inevitable taking of the Combi to a mechanic to harmonize the various components of *drive* that we may limp on to the next town, the next beach, and continue our journey—from Paraíso to Playa Azúl and Zihuatenejo, arriving Christmas Eve at Acapulco where we set up camp at Pie de la Cuesta, a long finger of beach stretching into the ocean west of Acapulco.

As the sun gets low and the day's heat dissipates, Rudy and Virginia stand in the surf, staring into each other's eyes. I swing gently in a hammock strung between palms, a cooler full of iced beer within reach. It's Christmas Eve and I wonder what the fuck I'm doing here, stoned on the beach in Mexico, naked in a hammock with a bottle of Corona in my hand and a history at my back.

And then it's Christmas day and we're moving down the highway, just about to Puerto Escondido when the Combi lets out a clink and a clunk, a belch and a sigh, and settles onto the roadway. We've broken down, are stranded at the crossroads.

"Go talk to it Clark."

I exhale heavily, get out and walk around to the engine compartment, open it gingerly. "Hi sweetie…"

"How is she?" Rudy yells, standing in the bushes on the side of the road.

"Not good."

"What is it?"

"The engine—it's upside down."

"Upside down?"

"Flipped like a pancake," I say.

"That doesn't sound good."

"No."

"I guess we'd better get going," says Virginia, stepping onto the blacktop and extending a thumb. I remain with the steed while they hitch to town to fetch a *mecánico*, the best conjurable configuration of our collective resources. Rudy's the resourceful one and Virginia's command of the Spanish *lengua*—not to mention her charm—should help us to realize our objectives most expediently.

Six hours later I'm still sitting in the Combi on the side of the road in the middle of nowhere, guarding our worldly possessions. It's beautiful out here. The sun has set and it's finally cooling off. The sky is huge and filling with stars. But I am starting to wonder if Rudy and Virginia are ever going to come back. They may have decided that neither the Combi nor old Clark is worth the bother, and left us for dead. But I could stay here, maybe even live here. I could sleep in the Combi, hunt and gather, live off the land or find a job.

I know! I'll shovel a pile of dirt onto the road and create my own *tope*, then go off into the woods and find a banana tree to harvest, sell the fruit to the drivers who slow for the bump.

Just as I'm succumbing to dementia, a tow truck diesels up next to the Combi and out hop you-know-who and that so-and-so along with a mechanic and the tow truck driver. The mechanic strokes his chin and takes a long look at the inverted engine, *hmmms*, and shakes his head.

"What the hell took you so long?" I ask Rudy and Virginia.

"We had a hard time getting rides," Rudy says.

"And we stopped for lunch," says V.

"Lunch?"

"And a couple cold *cervezas*," she adds. "We found this great little bar with a view—"

"This mechanic is from a shop right by Austin and Zelda's," Rudy cuts in. "I figured if they're going to have to work on it for a while, it should be close to where we're staying. Austin said we're welcome to stay as long as we need to."

We get towed into Puerto. The mechanic tells us he'll look at the engine in the morning. Or whenever he can get around to it. But we're already deep into those five unlucky days at the end of the Mesoamerican year and I expect the worst.

Mytho-Historical Departure
Those Five Unlucky Days at the End of the Year

In every culture throughout history—no matter how time was kept or what calendar was followed—the end of the old year and start of the new has been a time of renewal and rebirth, a cycling of death into life. A part of this regeneration is the temporary suspension or annulment of time. It's a period when social rules are suspended, roles are reversed, and chaos reigns—just look at the West's celebrations of New Year's Eve.

The "Vague Year" of Mesoamerican cultures consists of eighteen months of twenty days adding up to three hundred sixty days. The remaining five days of the solar year stand alone and are considered an unlucky and dangerous time. This five-day "month" is known by the Aztecs as *Nemontemi*—the "useless days," and to the Maya as *Yabeb* or *Wayeb*—the "unnamed."

During this period the gods are especially irritable, and one should do one's best not to annoy them. Most activity—including work, commerce, cooking, and the making of love—should be avoided. Fires should be extinguished and conflict suspended. It's a particularly inopportune time to get married, be born, or travel. It's a good time to stay home. The only activities in which one should engage are rituals or sacrifice to appease the gods. It is a time of walking on eggshells.

Rudy awakens me in the dark of the night.

"C'mon, we gotta go."

"Huh?"

"It's gettin' late," he says. "We gotta go."

"Where?"

"Anywhere. It's New Year's Eve, we gotta go out."

"What about Virginia?"

"She's got a stomach ache. She's staying in."

We walk the beach into town, picking up a bottle of Kahlúa on the way, sit on the sand and gaze out over the ocean, watching the waves and passing the bottle.

"V.'s decided to fly home when we get back to Guadalajara."

"Oh yeah?" I say. "What's up with you guys?"

"I don't know, Clark. I'm still trying to figure it out." Rudy sketches in the sand with a stick. "How long do you suppose we'll be here, in Mexico?"

"As long as it takes..." I say.

The sky above us suddenly explodes with fireworks, fanning out across the bay.

"What the hell—"

"Must be midnight."

"Happy New Year."

Felice Año Nuevo.

I sleep in, get stoned, get a chicken—

Wait a minute. Slow down.

Sorry. This is how I spend the first day of the New Year:

"V.'s still not feeling well," says Rudy. "I'm gonna go to the market and get her some food. You wanna go?"

On our way across the field to catch the bus, Rudy and I stop in to say hi to the Combi and smoke a joint with our Mexican mechanic's Chicano cousin.

"What's the prognosis?" Rudy asks.

"It's blown," he says. "Needs a rebuild."

"How much?"

"Eight hundred."

"How long?"

"Couple days."

"Do it."

Then we ride around on a Municipal bus for close to forever, sharing a seat with the faith that it will get us to where we need to go, which it does. At the open-air market I squeeze avocados, see the biggest cabbage in the world (bigger than a basketball), and a gecko runs across my foot. We also get a chicken.

"Hey Rudy, look," I stop him as we walk out of the market. "I'm a Man Carrying a Chicken in Mexico." Rudy looks me up and down.

"You're the Tan Man from San Fran."

"Hot damn, got a chicken in my hand."

On the second day of the New Year we do things like eat pancakes, lie around, read, swim, talk to the mechanic (who tells us the Combi will be ready tomorrow), smoke pot, walk to town, lay on the beach, play volleyball, swim, read, write, watch the surfers, watch the nudists, watch the sunset, smoke pot, and hang in hammocks.

Likewise the third day of the New Year. And the fourth. But the fourth day of the New Year is different in that the mechanic tells us *really* the Combi will be ready tomorrow. And I really hope so because tomorrow is Tuesday and we're supposed to start teaching on the following Monday in Guadalajara, which is a three-day drive from here.

I spend three hours at the bank securing a credit card cash advance (at great expense) of a thousand pesos to pay for the Combi repairs and our return trip to Guadalajara.

Tuesday comes and the engine is still in pieces on the floor of the shop. "Tuesday? I didn't say Tuesday. *Wednesday*. I said it would be ready *Wednesday*. Come back tomorrow."

Wednesday the engine is *in* the Combi, but not yet connected. "This afternoon," *el mecánico* tells us. We pack our stuff, and wait for the Word.

In the evening, the Word comes. "She's ready." And we take delivery of el Tiburón. She runs great, but it's by now so late we decide to spend another night here and leave first thing Thursday morning, riding out in the dawn's early light.

I hang in a hammock across the porticoed balcony one last time, taking in the town and the beaches, the cliffs and the current, thinking of all the shit that's fallen across our path on this journey, this life—all the potholes we've swerved around, all the *topes* we've pounded over. Sun sets in ocean, purple and pink as full moon rises, glows blue on the sand. A lunar wind plays off the ocean, sweeps up my thoughts and meditations, prayers of good passage, carries them back to fill that waxing orb that it may continue its journey around our globe—that same full moon which rises over every country in the world, filling and emptying, shedding its light—and my thoughts—across the Earth.

"You know, Clark," Rudy says from the driver's seat, "I been thinking..." He swigs from a *caguama*. Virginia and I moan and roll our eyes. It's almost midnight and we're just entering the city limits of Guadalajara. "Maybe we should lay off the juice for a while."

"Come again?"

"Get on the wagon," Rudy says. "Sober up."

I turn and look at Virginia in the back of the bus. We lock eyes and smile, burst out laughing at the insanity.

"What's with this crazy talk?" I ask, taking the bottle from him and taking a swig.

"I'm serious," Rudy says. "We're broke and it's going to take us a while to pay off the debt we've run up. If we cut out drinking, we could save a lot of money."

"Just how long a period of dry time are you talkin' about?"

"A couple of months, maybe through February, or the end of the next *inscripción*," Rudy says. "It's a new year, the holidays are over—it's time we get focused."

"Two months with no drugs or alcohol," I say. "No way we can make it that long."

"Slow down, Clark. I didn't say anything about quitting drugs. I'm just talking about laying off the beer and tequila."

"Thank God."

"I'm not *crazy*."

Twenty-One

Virginia left today. Rudy dropped her at the airport this morning. He's been moping around the apartment ever since. I've decided to blow off Rosa (if she hasn't already reached that same conclusion—she's not yet back from vacation). I want to keep my life simple.

It's gray outside—damp, humid, overcast, crappy—limiting what we can do. We're flat broke anyway. And our prospects are bleak. Enrollment is down at Hardship, and so are our hours. I'm teaching only four classes and Rudy only three. Worse, they're spread out from morning to night so we're stuck all day at school.

"Maybe we should look for other jobs."

"Other jobs?" I say. "It was hard enough getting these jobs."

"It wasn't that hard."

"Well it was stressful. For me anyway."

"Maybe we should think about moving," Rudy says.

"Moving? To where?"

"I don't know, Clark. But we moved here, didn't we?"

As if all that isn't enough for us to cope with, we've both—believe it or not—renounced booze for a while, in order to restore our physical and financial health. But after thirty days of destitution and mind-maddening sobriety, the urge to get twisted overpowers us. We find ourselves, however, without any type of intoxicating substance whatsoever nor the means to obtain any. Zero. Zip. *Nada.* We have nothing but chocolate with which to stimulate our nerves.

"What about the LSD?"

"Gone."

"A hundred hits?"

"We took it all, Clark."

"Yeow."

We scour the *depto*, scrape together whatever medicinal residues we can find—some leafy marijuana crumbs from the bottom of the stash box, the powdery dregs from a found-in-the-glove-compartment pill bottle, even a rumpled envelope which once contained acid. We chop it all up and stuff in a pipe, smoke it, inhale it, consume it, absorb it. Still it is only enough to tickle my spine. We'd be eating the paste off the wallpaper, if we had wallpaper.

And so I sit, cross-legged in the overstuffed chair, with my pen and my pad, sipping hot cocoa in the candlelight and worrying. *If I finish this mug of chocolate and want more, is there enough for a refill?* But I'm not motivated enough to get up, walk to the kitchen, and check. This may seem like a strange thing to trouble a man who's been sitting in the dark for three days because the electricity was turned off (due to a disputed bill of $11.45—and that's pesos, mind you), we're almost out of cooking fuel, the boiler is leaking, the rent is due, we're bankrupt, sober, and there's no sign of hope on the horizon. Oh, and we have cockroaches.

I can't see beyond my own shrinking realm of experience, my own dwindling supply of chocolate. I can barely get beyond wondering where our next meal will come from, and a little thing like another mug of cocoa might just be the highlight of my life right now.

Fresh
> flour
> tortilla
> and squeezed
> *limón*
> to fill my belly.

I could stuff it with cheese and call it
> *quesadilla*
> or fill it with *pollo* and name it *fajita*
> or *carne de res* and label it
> taco
> beans, avocado, onion and salsa.

But not tonight.

Tonight it's
> just a squeeze of lemon
> and I call it
> > my supper.

"Good morning," I say to Rosa at Hardship. "And welcome back. I didn't expect to see you until next week."

"I had to come back early," Rosa says. "To do some things."

Alicia looks on from the receptionist's desk, smiling.

"How was your vacation?" I ask.

"Fine," Rosa says. "Look, I can't talk right now."

"Do you want to meet later for lunch?"

"Okay," she says and walks away.

I stare down the empty corridor.

"I think she love you," Alicia giggles. "You love her?"

"Have a nice day, Alicia."

I slide into the booth across from Rosa, take her hand in mine.

"So what's new?" I ask.

"I've been promoted," she says, retracting her hand.

"Promoted?" I say. "To what?"

"Director."

"Director of what?"

"Of the school—of Hardship Hall."

"Wow. What about Daniel?"

"He moved up, regional supervisor."

"So...you're my boss now?"

"More or less."

"Wow. Can I get a raise?"

"Look Clark, I've had a lot of time to think about my life, and about you and me, and—I just don't think we're going to work out. I mean, I *am* engaged to Pedro and he and I both want to settle down and raise a family and you—well as far as I can tell, you're just going to keep wandering the globe for the rest of your life and never settle down."

"You're right."

"Huh?"

"I agree. You and I want different things in life. You're better off with Pedro."

"You bastard!"

"What?" I say. "I'm agreeing with you."

"But I love you!"

"That's nice, but I'm being realistic. Things would never work out with us."

"I don't want a realist." Rosa slides out of the booth. "I want a romantic." And she marches out of the restaurant.

"What about my raise?" I mutter after her.

*   *   *

"'That's nice'?" Rudy says, passing me the smoldering joint. "She told you she loves you and you said 'that's nice?'" Rudy, Jota, and I sit in the front room of our apartment, late night. Jota has just returned from his vacation and—thank god almighty—he's brought us a nice bag of *mota* as a souvenir. I inhale deeply.

"What was I supposed to say?" I exhale a cloud of smoke, pass the joint to Jota.

"You lie is what you do," says Jota. "Never tell a *Mexicana* the truth. They *expect* men to lie. It's how things work here."

"Don't worry," Rudy says, standing up. "She'll be back." He moves to the door. "I'm going for a walk." Jota lies back on the couch, stares up at the dim red light bulb, chuckles to himself.

"What are you laughing at?" I ask.

"You guys," he says, "and your women."

"Yeah," I say. "I'm going to bed. *Buenas noches.*"

In my room I open the window and lie on the mattress, stare at the stars.

Our world has shrunk to the walls of this apartment. But we're surviving. This place is ours, mine. We've got three fucking couches and room for anyone who wants to come and visit, crash out, stay for a week, a month, friends, family, strangers. Like you, mom. Come on down and see for yourself how I'm doing. I'm okay, really. And you? Come home for Easter, you say? Good lord I'm not even sure what *home* is anymore.

Why are you so apprehensive about going home?

Because I'm afraid of getting stuck there. I'm afraid I'll see how easy it all is back home and fall into a groove I can't get out of. I like the struggle here, the challenge of getting by, of being in an alien environment and having to learn the word for water in order to get a drink. Having one's comfort zone encroached upon forces one to compromise, improvise, learn, and grow. It keeps us alive. Rudy and I push ourselves because we don't have to. Maybe it is time for us to move.

"Clark... Clark!"

"What? What's wrong?" I sit up in bed.

"Nothing." Rudy stands in my bedroom doorway, silhouetted in the red glow. Jota's snores drift in from the front room.

"Something's wrong," I say. "It's four o'clock in the morning and you're waking me up." Rudy walks to the far side of the room, sits on the edge of my bed, gazes out the window.

"I called V.," he says.

"How's Virginia?"

"She wasn't home." Rudy buries his face in his hands. "She was out on a date."

"You don't know that. She might—"

"Her brother told me," Rudy raises his head, "without even thinking about it."

"Oh."

"So then I called my ex-girlfriend," he turns his head to face me.

"Did that make you feel better?"

"She asked me not to call her anymore." He shifts his gaze out the window. "She's getting married next month."

"Ouch."

"Then I started walking." Rudy sits up straight.

"Where'd you go?"

"I don't know. I walked three hours in one direction, turned around and walked three hours in the other direction, until I found myself back here." Rudy again drops his head, rubs his eyes.

"You must be tired," I say.

"I'm hungry is what I am. I am so fucking hungry."

"You want me to fix you something?"

"We have no food, Clark."

"Oh. How about a mug of chocolate? That oughta lift your spirits."

"We're out of chocolate."

"Oh. There's an orange."

"Really?" Rudy perks up. "We have an orange?"

"Yeah. You want me to peel it for you?"

"You're a pal, Clark."

It's the end of the *inscripción*. A month without beer. I've just given the last final of the night. I'm ready to go home. A hard rain falls. Rosa, who hasn't talked to me all week, suddenly sidles up.

"Hi," she says. "Do you need a ride home?" I do.

"No thanks."

"I broke up with Pedro," she says. We're in her car, driving through the driving rain.

"Why?"

"I don't love him."

"But—"

"Don't say it, Clark. Don't say anything. I know it's not rational, but I just don't have the feelings for him that I have for you. And I know you're not going to be around much longer, but I thought maybe we could just make the most of it and enjoy each other while you're here."

"I don't know," I say. "What does that mean?"

"It means we hang out, be friends, honeys, spend time together without expecting anything of one another."

"I do like hanging out with you. I guess—if we have no expectations and just want to enjoy each other—then I guess it's all right to see each other now and then, until I move on. I mean, why shouldn't we?"

"Oh Clark, I love you."

"And I love you." Whoops.

Whoops.

"You do?"

You do?

"Of course."

Did you really just say that?

It slipped out.

"Oh Clark..."

Shit.

Wow. Sobriety's really clouding your judgment.

At the apartment I make some tea, light some candles. Rosa has a pack of cigarettes. We sit on the couch and smoke and talk and snuggle and kiss and—

"Do you want to go to bed?" she asks.

"I'm not tired."

"I didn't ask if you were tired. I asked if you wanted to go to bed...," she raises her eyebrows. "With me."

"Oh. *Ohhh.* Really?"

"I'm so glad we worked things out," Rosa says. She spoons me on the bed. The rain has stopped and the clouds have cleared. Cool air breezes in through open window. Stars sparkle in the night sky.

"Me too," I say.

"Besides being in love with you Clark, I also feel like we're really good friends."

"Me too."

"And you know Clark, if you ever want to just talk or get things off your chest, I've always got an open ear and a shoulder for you to cry on."

"Thank you. I do have a lot on my mind these days. I—"

"Oh," Rosa looks at her watch. "I have to go. Bye." And she up and goes, leaving me alone and naked, tangled in bed sheets.

I go sit on the couch in the dark of the front room, light a cigarette, stare out the window.

Did you really tell her you love her?

I think so.

Well do you?

I don't know.

You said the word.

I don't even know what love is. It's so amorphous and inescapable.

Don't start with that.

Do I have a *right* to be in love?

Love isn't a right, it's a feeling, an instinct, and you're either in love or you're not.

Then I am, I am in love with her. But is that fair—is it *fair* for me to be in love with her?

How did it feel?

The sex was great.

How did it feel to tell her you love her—to say, "I love you?"

Good. It felt great—*I love you.* There was something freeing about it.

As if you haven't, for a long time, allowed yourself to be *in love, to* say *you're in love, to* tell *someone you love them?*

It's an extravagance I've denied myself. There was relief in saying those words. *I love you.* I don't have to worry about what I say now, don't have to censor myself because it's been said, it's out there. But does this mean I'm committed to her—to just one woman?

Good Lord no, Clark. You need think of women as pieces of bread, and love as a big jar of peanut butter.

Smooth or Chunky?

Definitely Chunky. Now the thing is this—there's no reason for you to heap it on thick to just one slice of bread when you could be spreading it thin across the whole loaf.

This is your metaphor for love—a peanut butter sandwich?

Yes, but you can't have a peanut butter sandwich without a glass of milk.

You're losing me.

—To wash it down with.

Oh.

Remember what that man at the funeral said? "One cannot live with reservations of love." Don't forget that.

One cannot live with reservations of love... But what is love?

Twenty-Two

Stoned every night now, Rudy and I sit in the apartment sipping tea, reading, writing, rapping, because that's all we have. Rice and beans for our supper, a roll and some milk, maybe only an apple.

"Art is more important than food," I say.

"Said the artist to the starving man," adds Rudy.

Downpours trap us inside every night, confine us with cogitations on that conundrum of love, each of us trying to work out our own personal tug-o-war with the opposite sex. And so we smoke in order to stretch our minds beyond these walls, to gain a perspective that's more objective.

"He scratches his ear."

"Cigarette glowing between fingers."

I'm so pissed off at that asshole. He's such a slob, always leaving his shit all over—his books, clothes, and food—strewn about the apartment. He's never cleaned the bathroom. He never does the dishes. This place was such a mess last weekend and I was so sick of cleaning up after him that I announced I was no longer going to clean.

"No problem," Rudy said. "I'll straighten up." And he lay down to nap. It's been a week now, and the place has gone to hell. At least the cockroaches are happy.

"Can smell the open jar of peanut butter."

"From the other end of football field."

And he's writing another goddamn play. Every night for the past two weeks he's sat down on that couch, picked up the pen, and the words just flow, I can see them. He shuts everything out, puts his head down, and just writes for hours. What really pisses me off is that it's good. I read some pages while he was in the shower. And here I wrestle with the pencil every day and produce nothing but crap. I try to break his concentration, throw a line at him every now and then to distract. But he just throws one right back at me, turns it into haiku.

"Hunger creates inspiration."

"As heartbreak inspires creation."

I shouldn't be so upset. I do have a no-strings-attached lover, for now. But, besides passing hellos in the hallways of Hardship, I haven't heard from her since that night, a week ago. She must be busy what with her new position and all. Valentine's Day is this weekend and I'm sure she'll come by, spend some time with me—in bed, hopefully. Maybe I should clean this place.

"A box of Corn Flakes in the living room,"

"Pass me the milk."

God *damn* him.

Twenty-Three

Fuck this life, these women—don't need it, them. It's St. Valentine's Day and I'm alone. Rosa didn't call, hasn't returned my calls. Rudy hasn't heard from Virginia. Didn't I fear this would happen? Doesn't it always happen this way—you open yourself, start to expose yourself a little, and they turn tail and flee. Fuck it, I don't need it.

We have no food. We have no money. We have no significant others with whom to spend this evening of *amor*. So we get loaded on this Sunday, smoke the last of the grass and then burn through a pack of forgotten Marlboros.

Drinking my tea black in the middle of the night, dry pancakes with no butter, no syrup, I learn what it is to hunger and to take that ache down, clutch it to my chest and sink beneath the waves, descend into the darkness of that watery underworld while the bubbles of exhaustion rise to the surface.

I've taken up harmonica, haiku, and the juggling of limes. I can't spend my life waiting for a woman to come around. Can I?

"Fuck it."

"What?"

"It's time to make a move," raps Rudy.

"Huh?"

"It's time to make a move," he says. "Tell me Clark, what do we have here?"

"Three limes—but they're getting pretty brown from me dropping them."

"Two broken hearts, that's what we've got. We have lousy jobs, broken fucking hearts, and cockroaches. Let's get the hell out of here."

"It's raining."

"Guadalajara, Clark. Let's get out of Guadalajara, move somewhere else."

"Where?"

"I don't know, Clark. You're the one always readin' your guidebooks. You're the one who didn't want to be here in the first place. There's three weeks left in the *inscripción*. I'm going to go see Lilly tomorrow and give her our notice."

"And then what?"

"I don't know."

"I knew this day would come," Señora Lilly sighs. Her eyes settle on me. "I'm losing two of my best teachers."

"You shouldn't look at it as if you're losing two teachers," Rudy says, "but as if you're gaining two sons."

Huh?

"Where are you going to go?" she asks. Rudy looks to me.

"East," I say. "We're going east."

"I see. And what are you going to do in the east?"

Rudy and I look at each other.

"Hold that thought," she says. "I'm going to make a phone call." Señora Lilly dials, talks rapidly in Spanish, hangs up. "Have you considered Veracruz?"

"Veracruz?" Rudy says.

"I've heard good things about Veracruz," I say.

"It's on the beach," Lilly says.

"That sounds all right," says Rudy.

"I hope so, because I've just volunteered the two of you to teach there."

Huh?

"We're opening a new Hardship in Veracruz and they're desperate for teachers. They've got a full schedule of classes for you."

"When do we start?" asks Rudy.

"At the beginning of the next *inscripción*," Lilly says, "three weeks from today."

"Clark, where's Veracruz?"

"East of here. On the beach."

"I gathered that," he says. "We'd better start planning our going-away party."

"And this is probably a good time to start drinking again."

"Hallelujah to that, my brother."

Things happen fast in this life.

The prospect of a move has lifted our spirits. We're doing our usual *no-dinero* Saturday night—sitting around the apartment, drinking tea and writing, ignoring the pangs in our collective stomach—when there's a knock on the door.

"Hi Clark." Rosa stands on the porch smiling, cradling a steaming pot in her arm.

"Hi." I stand unmoving in the doorway.

"I was in the neighborhood and—"

"And you suddenly remembered me?"

Rudy squeezes into the doorway next to me, sniffing the air.

"Hi Rudy," Rosa says. "I'm sorry Clark, but I needed some time to think—everything was happening so fast."

"Uh-huh," I say. "And then you heard I was leaving town and you rushed over to say goodbye?"

"What's in the pot?" Rudy asks.

"Fried chicken and rice. Yes Clark, I was thinking I should follow my destiny and be with Pedro. But then I heard you were leaving town and I couldn't bear the thought of being without you."

"Uh-huh," I say. "So you think you can just walk in and out of my life as you please?"

"Do you have tortillas?" Rudy asks.

"Homemade," she says, hoisting a bundle into view.

"You think you can bribe your way back in with food?" I say.

"Oh Clark, can't I please come in and we'll talk?"

"Dude," Rudy says. "She's got food—let her in."

"Please?" she pleads.

"Please?" pleads Rudy.

"All right. But we're just going to talk."

I kiss her goodbye at the door, early the next morning. Settling in on the couch, I put on some Coltrane, draw a smoke from the forgotten pack of Marlboros. And I have to wonder, is this the same forgotten pack I've been sucking on for the past month, or do new ones keep appearing? Is Rudy buying cigarettes, spending our meager (but hard-earned) pay on tobacco? Is he stealing it?

We're going to Veracruz. We have three more weeks to enjoy the people, customs and life of Jalisco and then it's time once again to tear up roots and head west—uh, east.

"Good moooooorning!" Rudy emerges from his room. "What a beautiful day, huh?"

"What's up with you?" I ask. "I'm the one got laid last night."

"Better than sex, Clark, I had a meal last night, a three course meal — chicken, rice, and beans — man that girl can cook. You should think about marrying her. How'd it go, anyway?"

"Fine."

"I know, I could hear you guys through the wall."

"She wants to visit us in Veracruz for Spring Break."

"And a week ago she wouldn't talk to you. Who can figure women, huh?"

Twenty-Four

I t is the day of our final, grand, Guadalajaran going-away party. Rudy takes the Combi to a mechanic in the morning to get it checked out for the roadtrip east. I use the quiet time to clean the apartment, prepare for the party, get ice for the coolers. We can't afford beer, but I'm sure there'll be plenty.

By midmorning all is ready. No one is due until afternoon. I have free time, nothing to do, probably for the last time in this town.

Why don't you go for a walk, shoot all those photos you've been picturing in your mind's eye?

I load up with black and white and walk, wander out beyond the pavement to that *other* part of the 'hood, shooting architecture and landscape, children and dogs, taco carts and bicycles leaning against walls. At the plaza, the sunlight angles in over the buildings, strikes straight at the church. I stand at the circumference composing a shot.

"*Amigo,*" a voice behind me intones. "You take-a mi *peek*-ture."

I stand slowly from my crouch and turn. Across the street, behind me, a half dozen men loiter in the shade of a building. They lean on the wall, sprawl on the half-paved sidewalk, watching me. A trough of cement sits before them, on the ground beside each lays a trowel, every other hand holds a beer.

"*Amigo,*" repeats the heavyset *hombre* seated on a case of Corona. "You take-a mi *peek*-ture." I can't tell if this is an accusation or a request. "*Ven,*" the seated man beckons. I cross to the middle of the street and crouch, frame him and focus. He raises his chin and sets his eyes, striking stoic. I shoot and lower the camera. None of them laughs, none of them sneers. *Now what's he want?*

"*Nosotros, nosotros,*" one of the standing men says, stepping into sunlight. He puts a cement-stained arm around a *compadre* and beams a smile out of his gray-smudged face. I frame, focus, and shoot. "*Otro, otro,*" they plead until I use up the roll shooting them all, separate and together, smiling and serious, poised and playful.

"*¿Una cerveza, amigo?*" the big man offers. Leaning forward, he raises his butt from the box and pulls out a beer.

"Sit, sit," he says, indicating a dry cement section of sidewalk beside him.

"*¿Tu fumas, amigo?*" he produces a crooked joint.

"*Si,*" I say, he lights it.

Thus we pass the remains of the morning, sipping *cervezas* and sucking in smoke until sun climbs the sky, conquers our shade and we shift ourselves over to stay in the shadows. *Cerveza* swims straight to my head. The smoke relaxes, releases a tension I didn't know I'd been holding.

We speak but little, me *y mis amigos nuevos*, especially as Spanish slowly slips my grip. It is enough for us to sit here together, sharing the day, and the silence of one another's company.

The case of beer disappeared, it's time for me to go. I have a party to get to. I stand on wobbling legs. *Jesu-Christo*, I'm off the wagon. Look what two months of sobriety has done to me. I bid the workers adieu. They send me off with God, or send God off with me, and I walk my way home. Six months in Mexico and this is the most genuine encounter I've had.

I walk home to the party, to our friends, to my lover, goodbye.

Part Three

Veracruz

Twenty-Five

W e're on the road by seven in the morning, Rudy driving, the landscape blurring past. I'm in and out of consciousness much of the way. We're not just traveling this time, we're transferring— from one city to another, one job to another. Having concluded teaching the previous *inscripción* Thursday in Guadalajara, we commence a new one Monday in Veracruz. So we're not doing our usual leisurely tour of the countryside, but are driving fast and straight.

Rudy steers us deep into Mexico City until we're utterly and completely lost—a requisite for driving in, through, or anywhere within proximity of *el Distrito Federal*. It's the black hole effect all over again, the infinite density of the most populous metropolis on earth curving space, sucking the *all* to its singularity.

I take the wheel in D.F., make the hectic drive the rest of the way through thick fog and heavy traffic, day into night. But we do it, make it, hit the coast of Veracruz and head up the boulevard, along the waterfront *malecón* cruising the length of town, from Playa Mocambo to Playa Norte, south to Boca del Rio, and finally to el Centro where we park, and walk through the warmth of the night to los Portales, the colonnaded arcade of cafés fronting Plaza de Armas—the *zócalo*.

Settling in at a table, we order beers and sit back, taking in the tropical colonial architecture, perusing the perpetual parade of transvestites, mongers, and musicians (*marimba y mariachi*), and absorbing the ambiance of Mexico's most historic city—until three in the morning when we drive to the beach and crash in the Combi.

*   *   *

History Lesson
Veracruz, Four Times Heroic

Imbued with an indomitable endurance, the importance of Veracruz in the history of Mexico cannot be overstated. It was site of the first Spanish settlement in España Nueva and is the oldest and largest port in the country.

In 1519, Hernándo Cortés and the Spanish *Conquistadors* entered Mexico through the port of Veracruz. It was from here they mounted their crusade to overthrow Montezuma and the Aztec empire. Veracruz served as a gateway between the Old World and the New for the next three hundred years, up until 1821 when Spain was expelled (again through Veracruz) following Mexico's victory in the War of Independence.

Once the Spanish were gone there were plenty of other regimes lined up to invade, and all of them would enter through Veracruz. The French took the port in 1837 in a conflict known as the Pastry War (more on this later). The U.S. twice invaded and occupied Veracruz, once in 1847, during the Mexican-American War, and again in 1914 during the Mexican Revolution. Through each of these invasions Veracruzanos fiercely defended their homeland and stubbornly resisted the unlawful occupations, earning them and their city the title "Four Times Heroic."

At eleven o'clock Sunday morning we're back at the *zócalo*, swimming in the clinking cacophony of el Gran Café de la Parroquía, here to meet our new employer. Café Parroquía is known less for its *café con leche* than for the ritual that accompanies it. We find Hector and he orders us a round.

A waiter comes by, sets an empty glass mug in front of each of us. He pours a thick, syrupy coffee from a large copper kettle, filling the mugs halfway. Hector picks up his spoon, bangs it repeatedly, annoyingly on the side of his glass, as do many of the patrons. Rudy and I join in at his urging. Another waiter makes his way across the restaurant, carrying another copper kettle. He attends to each glass-clinker, silencing them by filling their mugs the rest of the way with steamed milk. Hector is in his mid-thirties, soft-spoken, balding, effeminate. He welcomes us and begins to eloquently tell us about *la ciudad*.

"The city of Veracruz is a unique mix of cultures. The *Conquistadors* came, you know, and raped the land of hundreds of tons of silver and gold. They shipped all these riches out of Veracruz, sent them back to Cuba and Spain. And when the ships returned to Veracruz, they brought slaves from Africa to replace the *indígenos* who were worked to death in the mines or killed by European disease. These slaves brought with them their own culture—their music and dance, their customs and cuisine. This African influence mixed with the indigenous and Spanish and *voila*, you have the celebratory spirit that is Veracruz. Have you noticed the accent? True Veracruzanos swallow the Z."

"Huh?"

"They are unable to enunciate the Z sound. For example, somebody who grew up here would never say they are from Veracruz, they would say *Veracrú*, dropping the Z and emphasizing the final vowel."

"And this is important?" Rudy asks.

"It is if you're going to teach English in this town. Are you ready for the start of tomorrow's *inscripción*?"

"As ready as we'll ever be," Rudy says.

"Here are your assignments. I've booked you a room at the Hotel Santo Domingo for the next couple nights, to give you some time to get settled."

"Thanks."

"You found a place to stay last night, I take it?"

"We slept at the beach."

"It's true what they say about you."

"What do they say about us?"

Rudy and I check into the hotel, shower, eat, and review our assignments. The classes we're teaching are all levels we've taught before so this'll be an easy *inscripción*. We can leap right into the fray.

We're tired and go to sleep before midnight for the first and only time in Veracruz—excuse me—*Veracrú*.

We're up and at school, teaching first thing Monday morning. To emphasize Hector's point on the local accent, a young woman in my first class shoots up her hand, "Teacher, teacher, oh teacher..."

"Yes?"

"Escu— Escu— Pardon me teacher, may I go to the bathroom?"

"No."

On our break, the Academic Coordinator (second in command at Hardship), Bertha, drives us out to look at an apartment. "It's owned by a woman who used to teach at Hardship," she tells us. "Her name is Tanya. She and her husband live downstairs and they have an empty apartment upstairs—I think it's been empty for a while. She's a *Norte Americana*, like you."

"Except we're not women."

We park around the corner by the marina, suck in the salt air, the seagulls, the clanging of rigging against masts. South of the marina is Plaza Acuario, a mall containing the aquarium, shops, and a food court. Beyond that is the long stretch of beach, Playa Hornos, bordered by the *malecón*.

We follow Bertha around the corner and into a quiet *callejón* (alleyway), climb an enclosed stairway, cross the front balcony, and enter the apartment. The place is huge, more house than apartment. There's a big front room, a big kitchen with a balcony off the back, and two large bedrooms, each with an attached bathroom. To top it off, the place is fully furnished, including queen beds, and—get this—it's even got a refrigerator in the kitchen.

But it's the location that sells us, walking distance to downtown and, ACROSS THE STREET FROM THE BEACH. Our back windows look out over the water. It couldn't be better. We meet with the young, blonde Tanya, and get down to brass tacks.

"Rent is twelve hundred a month," she tells us. "Plus a five hundred peso deposit."

"We'll give you eight hundred a month," Rudy says flatly. "It's all we can afford."

She's flabbergasted.

"C'mon," Rudy urges, "we're fellow teachers. We're fellow Americans. Besides we'll only be here a few months."

"Well..."

"Whaddaya say?"

"I guess, if it's just going to be for a few months—"

"Great." says Rudy. "We'll move in tomorrow. Oh, and we can't pay you until the end of the month. But Bertha here can vouch for us."

"I can?"

Appliance Interlude
Sparky, the Refrigerator

Did I mention that this place even has a refrigerator? We consider it a luxury and a privilege, having endured the past six months without one. It's a regular old full-sized fridge, large enough to hold all our beer and some food to boot. But something's not quite right about it.

If you should happen to be standing barefoot on the tile floor of the kitchen and you touch the metal handle of the refrigerator door, your body will conduct the full force of the current flowing from the wall socket, which is quite a shock. I'm no electrician, but my layman's opinion is that the wiring is screwy—a grounding problem, I would hazard.

We get wise after the first few electrocutions and insulate the handle by looping a dishtowel through it, with which one can pull the door open. Of course, I'm not so naïve as to expect this will eliminate the problem altogether. Seeing as how we live at the beach and are both heavy drinkers, we're bound before long to wander barefoot to the fridge for a cold one and grab straight for that handle.

And what about the mornings? Half asleep and stumbling naked into the kitchen for that wake-up cocktail before work? Will we remember then to grab the towel, or to put on some shoes? Maybe a little charge will help to wake me up. But what if daily juicings cause me to associate alcohol with electrocution, conditioning me against drinking? Good lord, I hope not.

Look on the bright side, at how much fun you can have with your party guests:

"Hey Clark, can I get a beer?"

"Help yourself, they're in the fridge." (*Guest grabs handle, twitches uncontrollably.*)

Twenty-Six

By noon, Rudy is pacing around my bed. "C'mon, let's go to the beach." It's our second weekend in Veracruz and the day after our first big party.

"No."

The curtains part violently to throw vinegar in my eyes.

"Get up, let's go to the beach."

"No." The tenth time my brain gives in.

We drink a couple pints of Venom, smoke a joint, stare at the devastation of our apartment.

"You think this qualifies for federal disaster aid?"

I count the dead soldiers: twelve emptied rum bottles (*not including the one smashed in the street at midnight*). We head down the stairs, cocktails in hand. We're going to the beach.

Tanya's apartment door is open at the bottom—our landlord.

"Hi," she says, suddenly emerging from the darkness of her abode. "It sounded like quite a party you had last night."

"It was," Rudy says. "You didn't make it."

"I had other things...," She looks down. "I may have to get something out of your apartment later."

"Okay."

"From the closet in back."

"That's fine," Rudy says. "We're on our way to the beach but we'll be back this afternoon." We move to break away.

"My suitcase," she says. "I may need to get my suitcase."

"Okay. We'll let you know when we return."

"I may be moving back to the States."

"That's great," Rudy says. "We'll—"

"I'm leaving my husband."

"Oh."

"There are issues."

"I guess so," Rudy says.

"He has a drinking problem."

"Really?"

"He came home so drunk Friday night that he walked into the closet and started to urinate."

"Hmmm." I shift my weight from one foot to the other.

"And he's been cheating on me."

"I'm sorry," Rudy says.

"He went to Mexico last week, said it was for work, for a convention. But I called the hotel. There was no convention."

"Wow."

"I know he's seeing somebody, and I know who she is—"

"Yeah?"

"—the *pinche puta*."

We're standing in the alley, in the heat of the noontime sun, Rudy and I stoned out of our gourds, hungover, a new buzz materializing from the morning's cocktails, and now *I* have to urinate. We just want to get to the beach but here this woman is pouring her heart out to us and we're stuck in this moment of silence that grows longer by the minute.

Don't get me wrong, I feel for her. I sympathize with her situation but—my floating teeth and twisted state of mind aside—I have absolutely nothing to say to her, can think of no words which might offer her comfort or support. I want to ask if I, too, can pee in her closet, but don't think she'll appreciate the humor of it.

Her eyes search us for answers. I fidget around to take the pressure off my bladder, stare down into the melting ice of my cocktail, stir the cubes with a sticky finger but don't take a sip. Rudy will think of something to say. He's good in these situations, he's always got something to say. And he loves to give advice. But the silence continues, stretches… I never thought a woman could be quiet for so long.

Then, Rudy clears his throat. He has something to say to her. I breath a sigh of relief as he swallows, prepares to deliver a golden nugget of wisdom, a solution to her problems.

"Well," he starts. "Uh…," he stammers. "Do you want a drink?"

What? Did he really say that—Do you want a drink? What is he thinking? What kind of advice is that—do you want a drink? But then, what did I come up with? On second thought—it's brilliant! That was the perfect thing to say—do you want a drink. It's nonpartisan, uninvolved, promoting neither a false sense of optimism nor a pessimistic commiseration. And he said it with such compassion.

"No thanks," she responds. "Maybe later."

"Okay," Rudy says. "We'll let you know when we return," and we back quickly down the street, leap into the Combi. I fire the engine, jam it into gear, and go.

"'Do you want a drink?!'" I say. "What the hell was that?"

"It was all I could think of," he laughs.

"She needs to open up more," I say.

"You're tellin' me."

We drive down to Playa Mocambo, swim in the sea and sit in the sand, brain dead. One of Rudy's students appears with a cooler full of beers, forces us to drink. Everything gets blurry. Rudy passes out. I pass out.

I awaken later (hours or days, I just don't know) to a Mexican goddess in a white bikini, standing over, kicking me in the ribs. I sit up. She kneels down, grabs my wrist and twists it around. Biting the cap off a felt-tipped pen, she writes "Julie" and a phone number on my forearm, stands, slides the pen back into the cap clenched in her teeth and smiles. "*Llama me*," she says and walks away.

The beach is almost deserted, the sun about to set. I look from her departing derriere to the new tattoo on my arm. *There's more.* I rotate my arm and there, covering it from shoulder to knuckle, are all sorts of names and numbers in a rainbow of inks. *What the hell?*

"Rudy!" I turn to the unconscious form beside me. His arm, too, is an address book. There are even inscriptions across his chest, embellished with hearts. "Wake up." I shake him.

"Huh?" He sits up, wipes the drool from his chin and turns to me. "Dude, what happened to you?"

"Me? Look at you." He looks down at the black book of his body. "What the — ?"

"I don't know. I woke up and there was some chick writing on me."

"How'd she look?"

"Goddess. What do you think it means?"

"It means we should go home and have another drink. And make some phone calls."

We get home and remember we don't have a phone. Rudy starts in on roasting the goddamned *pollo completo* that's been residing in Sparky the refrigerator all week. He cooks a huge pot of rice, warms tortillas. The house is still a fucking mess. (*What did you expect, fairies were going to clean it?*) I mix another pitcher of Venom and unenthusiastically begin to clean the place.

I haven't accomplished much when the dinner bell rings. Rudy carries out huge plates heaped with steaming heaps of *pollo con arroz*. I pour another round of drinks. We sit to eat. There's a knock on the door—Tanya.

"I thought I'd take you up on that drink," she says. "If the offer still stands. Oh, am I interrupting your dinner? I can come back another—"

"Nonsense," Rudy bellows. "Have a seat. Let me get you a cocktail. Are you hungry? There's plenty of food."

"No really, I—"

"Here you go, one of Clark's special Veracruz Venoms."

"Oh," she says. "Venom. That's nice."

"Are you sure you wouldn't like something to eat?" I ask.

"Really I ate," she says. "But you go ahead. Don't let me stop you."

I dig in with a vengeance, shoveling morsels to mouth. She takes a sip of her cocktail.

"Wow," she coughs. "This is what you guys drink?"

"On the weekends," Rudy says. "So you're going back to the States, huh?"

"I've been thinking about it all day, and thinking about what you guys said. And I've decided to give him another chance."

"Well I hope it works out for you," Rudy says. She's looking around the apartment now, registering the chaos, the marathon of empty bottles, our condition.

"You guys did give me a security deposit, didn't you?" she asks.

"Of course," Rudy says.

You didn't.

"Is that a tattoo on your arm?" She notices one of the inscriptions on Rudy's arm.

"It's more of a notation—to remind me to do something later."

"Well look," she sets down her drink. "I'd better go." She gets up to leave.

"But you've hardly touched your cocktail," Rudy says. "You're going to insult Clark."

"It's a bit strong for me."

"You must take it with you, then," Rudy says. "I don't want you to hurt Clark's feelings."

"But—"

I chew my food with an open mouth.

"I insist," Rudy says. "Believe me, you need this." He picks up her drink, puts it in her hand, and opens the door. "We'll see you later." He shuts the door behind her, marches around the table and sits, begins too inhale his food.

"We gotta make some calls," I say, pointing to the number on my forearm.

We wander the streets, marching up and down the boulevards in the heat of the night, in and out of stores and shops, searching for a functional pay phone. There's none to be found. We hunt through the humidity until exhausted, soaked in sweat, perspiring all those toxins we've so carefully introduced into our bodies

"Let's try this street," Rudy says. "There might be a phone at that store on the corner."

"Forget it," I say. "We're going home."

"You're giving up?"

"Take a look." I hold out my arm, all the names and numbers smeared and sweated away.

"Oh no!" Rudy yells, looking down at his own arms, indecipherably smudged with ink. "I guess we should write them down on a piece of paper next time."

"As if we're ever again going to regain consciousness with women writing their phone numbers on our bodies."

"It happened once..."

Cocktail Break
Veracruz Venom

3 oz. Light Rum
3 oz. Dark Rum (I prefer Meyer's)
3 oz. Pineapple Juice
5 oz. Orange Juice
Dash of Grenadine, to tint
1 Tab LSD (optional)

Combine ingredients with ice and shake vigorously. Pour into a pint glass. Garnish with whatever fresh fruit you happen to have on hand. If serving to your best friend, who happens to be named Rudy, add one dose Lysergic Diethylamide. Or two, depending...

The whole point of consuming this concoction is the inherent advantage of *the juice*. Anyone who pushes themselves, assaults their bodies to the degree that we do (I'm referring to Rudy and myself) knows that the body requires periodic refortification. With a Veracruz Venom (or pitcher thereof), one can become intoxicated (or maintain a preexisting level of intoxication) while simultaneously getting full benefit of the nine vitamins and minerals gleaned from the juice of the fruit.

The apartment is back in order in a couple days but the hangover lingers until the end of the month. Rudy spends much of the week downtown arranging passage and accumulating souvenirs to take back to his family. We've got some time off, Semana Santa (Spring Break), and Rudy's flying home to San Francisco for the week. I've got visitors coming — Rosa arrives this weekend and las Gringas sometime midweek. March blurs into April.

One evening we get some beers, take our drums, and go to the beach — Playa Mocambo — go out to the end of the pier, smoke a joint, and jam. It's the last night we'll have together for a while.

From out of the synchronicity of our drum, in the midst of the spectral rise and fall of rhythmic wanderings, I drop the beat. But Rudy is there to catch it, to carry it to the next measure where I can pick it up again in a microcosmic manifestation of that trust what links us. We will always have each other's back, sustain one another, no matter what.

We pound it out across the water, into the humid warmth of *la noche Veracruzano*. Thunder echoes back, providing a voice to the lightning that spears horizons distant.

Driving home from Mocambo around midnight, we pick up a tail. I park the Combi near the house and a Chrysler full of Mexicans (that ubiquitous Chrysler full of Mexicans which pursues us across all of Mexico) pulls up behind — a bunch of Rudy's students get out. He invites them up, pours Cuba Libres, and we talk and drink until three in the morning at which time they convince Rudy to accompany them to a discotheque. They desperately try to talk me into going, also.

"Hell no," I say. "I've got to be at work in five hours."

"C'mon, Clark," Rudy pleads. "Tomorrow's the last day of the *inscripción*. All you gotta do is give finals and eat cake. You don't need to be cognizant for that."

"Nonetheless, I'm going to stay home and sleep. I'll see you in the morning — *if* you make it home."

I can't feel my legs when I awaken hours later. There's Rudy, passed out across the foot of my bed wearing only his boxer shorts. I can't kick him awake. I get up and shower, am buttoning my shirt when he stirs. He sits up, grunts, thrusts his arms into the air. "Okay, okay," I say, taking off my shirt and pulling it down over Rudy's outstretched arms and head. He passes out again.

It's a beautiful spring morning. I pour myself some juice, warm a couple tortillas on the *comal*, slice a lime for my breakfast. Rudy stumbles into the kitchen as I'm flipping tortillas. He's managed to put on his pants but hasn't yet found his shoes. He stands next to the stove, leaning against the fridge, his mouth hanging open.

"Hey boy," I say. "You want a treat?" He nods vigorously, sucks the drool back into his mouth. I shove a rolled tortilla between his teeth. "Are you sure you can teach this morning?" I ask. Rudy grunts through his mouthful, nods assuringly, chewingly. "'Cause I'm free until nine. I can cover for you if you need—" He shakes his head at my ridiculous suggestion. He's barefoot.

"You want some juice?" I ask. He nods. "Get it out of the fridge. I'll get you a glass." Rudy reaches for the refrigerator handle as I get a glass from the cupboard. His body shudders violently as a hundred and eighteen volts surge through him. "Is that helping?" I ask. "Is that helping you wake up?"

"Help," he mouths. I slap his hand from the refrigerator handle, breaking the circuit.

"Good thing it's the end of the *inscripción*," I say. "All you gotta do is give finals and eat cake." I help him down the stairs and into the Combi, drive us to school, wake him when we arrive.

Rudy is able to get himself into the building without help, into his classroom at the stroke of eight, and for the first time of the day I hear his voice—booming through the wall of the classroom and into the lobby—the shout of his trademark, "GOOD MORNING CLASS!" followed by the yell of their coordinated response, "GOOD MORNING TEACHER!"

I pour myself two separate and distinct cups of coffee; sequester myself in the empty Audiovisual Room to plan classes for the coming *inscripción*.

I'm in the beginning stages of a R.E.M. cycle when the door bursts open. In marches Rudy, followed by his class of a dozen students. They fill the seats in the room. He dumps a videocassette into my lap, mumbles, "Play this movie," and drops into the chair next to me, falls asleep. Before the opening credits have finished rolling, his students are raising hands.

"Teacher," one says to the sleeping Rudy. "Teacher!"

"He's not feeling well," I say. "Leave him alone."

"But I have a question…"

"Save it."

"But teacher—"

"Shhh!"

Nine o'clock rolls around and I elbow Rudy awake.

"Huh? What?"

"It's nine o'clock," I tell him." Your class is over."

"Oh." Rudy stands and turns to his students. "Class is over. Go home." He walks out of the room, crosses the lobby and goes into his next class. "GOOD MORNING CLASS!"

Twenty-Seven

W hen I awaken Saturday morning Rudy is already packed and dressed and ready to go to the airport. He's even tidied up the apartment. We hop in el Tiburón and he drives us to el Aereopuerto Internacional de Veracruz. Sitting me on a bench, he goes and checks in, returns carrying two beers.

"That's it?" I say. "Two beers?"

"Those are mine," he says and steps aside to reveal a Mexican kid— maybe eight years old—carrying two more. "He's got yours."

"Thanks kid," I say, taking the *cervezas*.

"Yeah thanks," Rudy says, tossing him a peso. "Now get lost." Rudy raises one of his foamy cups. "Well here's to…goin' home, I guess."

"And not," I say, raising mine.

"You don't have any desire to go home for the week?"

"None at all," I say, sucking down one beer and starting the other.

"They're calling my flight," he says. "I gotta board." We embrace, he boards, I go to the Combi, get in, pass out.

I awaken hours later and wander back into the airport because, you see, Rosa is arriving soon. How's that for timing? I drive Rudy to the airport, get a few hours sleep in the Combi, and then walk back into the terminal to gather my lover. Rosa walks off the plane and into my arms and, as we stand in embrace, I know it's over. I'm not in love with her. I love her and I'm glad she's here. But I'm not in love with her.

"Welcome to Veracruz," I whisper in her ear and step back. "We're going to have a great week, there is so much to see and do here, so much history—you will love it."

"Clark—"

"We can go to the fortress of San Juan, walk the *malecón*, hang out in the *zócalo*—"

"Clark!"

"Hi."

"Hi," she says. "I'm sick."

"I'm sorry."

"No, I'm sorry. Everybody at school was sick with the flu all week and I'm afraid it caught up with me on the plane. Would you mind if we just took it easy this week?"

"Of course, of course. *Claro que si.* I'll take you right home and put you to bed, make you some soup."

She sleeps through the night and feels good enough Sunday to walk across the street to the beach with me and lie in the sun. In the evening we stroll downtown to los Portales and have a light lunch, catch up over a couple *cafés con leche.*

"So how do you like your new position at Hardship?" I ask her.

"Fine—it's longer hours and more stress, but I'm making more. How's Hardship Veracruz?"

"The teaching is fine. The students are real characters."

An uncomfortable silence settles between us. She's distant and removed in what is perhaps a manifestation of the realization of the fleeting relations between us. We are strangers. I don't know if she has also fallen out of love, or just senses it in me.

I'm awakened early Tuesday by an elbow jabbing into my ribs.

"What?"

"Someone's calling you," Rosa says.

"I don't have a phone."

"Someone's calling you from the street, silly."

"Huh?" I go out on the balcony and look down. Two faces stare up— las Gringas. "What are you guys doing here?"

"Shut up, Clark," Maria says. "You knew we were coming."

"Where have you guys been?"

"Up the coast in Northern Veracruz, visiting the ruins. Are you going to let us in or not? We're exhausted."

They've been on a bus all night. I send them straight to Rudy's bed for a nap (don't worry, I changed his sheets) and then go back to my own, cuddle up to Rosa. Once we're all rested, I cook up a big lunch of *camarones con arroz* and we gather 'round the dining room table, sunlight pouring in through windows.

"Are you guys interested in touring Veracruz this week," I ask, "see the sights?"

Diane lets out a groan.

"I'm with you, Clark," Maria says. "I'm getting tired of dragging this baggage around," she indicates Diane.

"I wouldn't mind so much," Diane says, "if you didn't have to stop and read every single historical marker."

"I love doing that," I say.

"Maybe you and Maria can go do your thing," Rosa says, "and Diane and I can hang at the beach." And *finally*, I have in Maria, an inquisitive partner with whom to explore the cultural-historical dimensions of this formidable Gulf Coast town.

Leaving our respective partners behind, Maria and I embark on a seventy-two hour odyssey, a whirlwind tour of *Cuatro Veces Heroico Veracruz*—from the fortress island of San Juan de Ulúa (site of the *Conquistadors* first landing as well as the last Spanish bastion in the New World), through Plaza de las Artesanías (the market along the *malecón*), el Acuario (the biggest, newest, most state-of-the-art aquarium in Latin America), and finally to el Museo de la Ciudad, soaking up the history that is Veracruz.

In the afternoons we meet up with Rosa and Diane for cooling brews at los Portales, sit in the *zócalo* and share stories of our days and our travels, listen to the wandering minstrels, haggle with the beggars. When night falls, we walk the *malecón* home, picking up seafood and groceries along the way to prepare meals together in our kitchen. Once stuffed, we walk through the warm night to Café Tres Treinta Tres for coffee, dessert, and dominoes.

Mytho-Historical Departure
The Pastry War of 1838 and the Saga of Santa Anna's Leg

In the wake of its liberation from three hundred years of Spanish rule, Mexico was in a period of great political instability and social upheaval. Her economy was in a shambles. The withdrawal of the colonial power created a vacuum in which a dozen different factions battled for power. Externally, protracted border disputes with the United States lingered and the European nations started calling in debts incurred during the War for Independence.

In a manifestation of nationalistic tensions, Mexican soldiers looted a French *pâtisserie* in the town of Tacubaya, outside Mexico City. The French baker tallied the damage to his shop at eight hundred pesos and submitted a bill to the Mexican government. The administration declined to compensate. The baker then turned to his fatherland, registering a complaint with the monarchy of France. King Louis-Philippe was none too happy to hear about it. Mexico was already behind in repayment of the half million pesos it owed France. An ultimatum was in order.

"Give us 600,000 pesos," came the charge from France in February of 1838, "or else."

"Or else what?" Mexican president Anastasio Bustamante replied.

By April, France had blockaded the entire Gulf Coast, from the mouth of the Rio Grande to the tip of the Yucatán. The port of Veracruz was shut down. Trade came to a standstill and the already crippled Mexican economy reeled.

President Bustamante arrogantly refused to have any dealings with France whatsoever. In November, French naval forces commenced a bombardment of the island fortress of San Juan de Ulúa, the port's primary defense. France's newly perfected exploding shells reduced this great symbol of Mexican fortitude to rubble. On December 1, despite the inadequacy of its military, Mexico declared war on France. French troops were already landing on the shores of Veracruz. La Guerra de los Pasteles, The Pastry War, was on.

Because of the disarray of the government, as well as its economic woes, Mexico lacked a strong national military. Each major municipality harbored a garrison for that city's defense, but the only effective *mobile* forces were independent militias, organized and led by independent generals and their whims. The most infamous of these loose cannon leaders was one General Antonio Lopez de Santa Anna Perez de Lebron.

At the breakout of this Croissant Conflict, Santa Anna was to be found hiding at his hacienda in Jalapa where he had retreated into retirement after being saddled with the disgraced reputation of having traded Texas for his own personal freedom a couple of years earlier. (Remember the Alamo?) Mexican President Bustamante knew that Santa Anna—despite his sullied reputation—was the only person capable of raising an army and countering the French. And so he called him out of retirement, reinstated him as general, and charged him with defending the port. Santa Anna responded enthusiastically, quickly raising troops and leading an incursion to liberate Veracruz from the grip of the evil imperialists.

Early on the morning of 5 December 1838, several hundred French troops landed along the Veracruz shoreline in an attempt to capture Santa Anna. The wily Mexican general managed to elude them and the French began a withdrawal back to their fleet. Always the opportunist, Santa Anna—astride a white horse—led an attack against the retreating invaders. The French forces, however, had captured a Mexican cannon and fired grapeshot to cover their retreat. Santa Anna was hit—his horse was shot out from under him, and his leg was severely wounded. It would have to be amputated the following day, just below the knee.

While Santa Anna recouped, the British were busy mediating between the warring powers. In March of 1839 they reached an agreement. Bustamante promised to pay the 600,000 pesos and grant France "Most Favored Nation" trading status. France agreed to the immediate withdrawal of troops from Mexico and a dissolution of the blockade. With his characteristic gift of self-promotion, Santa Anna claimed responsibility for the great victory of routing the French from Mexican soil. He was the savior of Mexico. He had, after all, given a limb in defense of his country.

Claiming this to be his final battle victory, Santa Anna had his amputated leg embalmed and buried with full military honors at his estate in Jalapa. But this wasn't the last Mexico would see of our martyred hero—nor his leg.

In the wake of the Pastry War, Congress appointed Santa Anna President. As chief executive he raised taxes, sold thousands of military commissions, and began to sell off Mexico's natural resource rights to foreigners. The people rumbled with displeasure. It was time for one of Santa Anna's public relations campaigns. The masses, after all, needed to be periodically reminded of his valorous past. Besides having a statue of himself erected and a theater built in his honor, Santa Anna had his amputated leg exhumed from his estate, paraded through the streets of Mexico City, eulogized, and reinterred in a mausoleum in the capital. And then he raised taxes some more. The people revolted.

In December of 1843, a mob rampaged through the capital. They ransacked the theater that bore Santa Anna's name, pulled down his statue, disinterred his leg and dragged it through the streets. Congress voted to *boot* him from office and Santa Anna went into exile in Cuba. (Don't worry, the leg was recovered and reburied—for the third time.)

In 1846, a simmering Texas border dispute boiled over into war between Mexico and the United States. Santa Anna, in Cuba, played both sides of the conflict, assuring both U.S. President Polk and Mexico that he was on their side. The U.S. allowed him passage through their blockade and Mexico allowed him entry into Veracruz, where he once again took charge of the army.

The pivotal battle of the Mexican-American War took place at Cerro Gordo, a narrow pass on the road between Veracruz and Mexico City. Santa Anna positioned his army of 12,000 around this pass in order to stop the American advance on the capital. U.S. General Winfield Scott directed a frontal attack while Captain Robert E. Lee led a battalion in a flanking maneuver that surprised the Mexican troops from behind. 3,000 Mexican soldiers were captured, 2,000 were casualties, and the rest retreated to Mexico City. Besides losing the battle, Santa Anna lost another leg.

Having stopped to enjoy a roast chicken lunch towards the end of the engagement, Santa Anna's meal was interrupted by members of the Fourth Regiment of the Illinois Volunteers who were part of the flanking action. Santa Anna rushed out, got on a horse, and managed to escape. He had, however, left his prosthetic leg behind, a wooden *stand-in*. The Illinoisans sat, finished the General's chicken, and took his leg as a souvenir. When the war ended, the Illinois Volunteers returned home with the leg. If you're interested in seeing it, Santa Anna's wooden leg currently resides in the Illinois State Military Museum at Camp Lincoln in Springfield, Illinois. It can be viewed Tuesday through Saturday, 1:00 P.M. to 4:30 P.M. The museum is handicap accessible.

By Friday Maria and I have exhausted the city's cultural resources (not to mention ourselves) and join the rest of the Semana Santa vacationers (including Diane and Rosa) on the beach, eating, dancing to the ubiquitous live music, and staying out all night in the packed, thriving discos.

Saturday I take las Gringas to the depot early in the morning, put them on a bus. At home, I rouse Rosa and we make love for hours, that bittersweet, heartbroken, saying goodbye, I'll probably never see you again, no holds barred, break the bed, sex. Then she packs. I drive her to the depot in silence and purchase her a bus ticket—direct to Guadalajara. We hug for half an hour. Her bus comes. She boards without a kiss, is gone.

Twenty-Eight

There hasn't been a word from Rudy since he left on his Semana Santa vacation. It is now seven fifty-nine on Monday morning, one minute before the start of the new *inscripción*. I'm about to walk into Rudy's classroom to cover the first hour for him while the director of the school scrambles to find a substitute for my missing partner, when...

The lobby door bursts open, Rudy walks in, drops his suitcase, tosses me a nod, a basso "Good morning Clark," and strides into his classroom. Through the wall I hear his, "GOOD MORNING CLASS!" And all is right with the world.

We pass each other coming and going from classes all day but don't get a chance to talk. Our siesta break is taken up by a worthless staff meeting. But without even conversing I sense a change in him. He's absorbed in thought, immersed in a pensive quietude that makes me wonder what it is he's encountered on his hero's journey home. And it causes me to consider what *I'll* face when and if I return home.

In the evening after classes we finally get the opportunity to talk, sipping *caguamas* in the warm breeze on our front balcony.

"How'd it go with Rosa?" he asks.

"Maria and I had a nice time."

"I asked about Rosa."

"Things were a little tense, but I managed to enjoy myself."

"Did she put out?"

"She held out for the entire week, but by the weekend I was gettin' it day and night."

"You mean one day and one night?"

"Well, one day anyway."

"So it's over between you two?"

"Yeah, but enough about me. How was your trip?"

"The trip was fine," Rudy says dismissively. Below us, the jingle-jangle of an ice cream cart being pushed up the alley punctuates the silence. "It was kind of a downer, though," he says. Children squeal down the alley, running to head off the ice cream man at the pass, encircle his cart, exchange their *centavos* for frozen delight. "It was great to see everybody, especially my folks, but...it seemed like everything was moving in slow motion."

"Compared to here?" I say. "I know what you mean."

"Yeah, you do know what I mean, don't you?"

"I think a big part of it is the time factor. We know this is going to end some day, which makes everything here more intense. And we never know where we're gonna go next, what we're gonna do—tomorrow or next month."

"That's why this is so great," Rudy says. "We never know what challenge we're next going to encounter."

"Or what reward."

"And that's why we've got to keep pushing the envelope," Rudy says, "pushing ourselves, to find out what comes next."

"Yup."

"And that's why I think it's time to make a move."

"Time to make a move?"

"Time to make a move," Rudy says. "We've got to push ourselves, right? So why not push all the way out to the end of the continent."

"The Yucatán?"

"That was the plan, right—to go all the way?"

"Yeah. But I love this town."

"I love Veracruz too. And that's why we've got to leave. If we don't push ourselves, no one else will. We're getting soft here. Look," Rudy pulls up his shirt. "Look at my stomach."

"You're gettin' fat."

"So are you, bro'. That's what I'm sayin'—we're losing our edge. It's time to make a move."

"What about teaching?" I say. "We just started the new *inscripción*."

"We'll finish out the *inscripción* and get another paycheck. That'll give us enough money to get out to the Yucatán. And it'll give us more time to experience Veracruz, have another party—"

"Take a road trip up the coast."

"And then we'll head east," he says. "We should check out Cancún. It's such a big tourist destination for Americans. They're probably dying for English teachers out there."

"That's us—English teachers."

"Think of all the chicks in bikinis, lining the beaches…"

"I like chicks in bikinis."

"Great weather all the time."

"That clear Caribbean water," I say. "It sounds like a plan. We'll leave for the Yucatán in four weeks."

"Four weeks," Rudy says.

"And then what?" I say.

"We spend a couple months in Cancún and then start planning the trip home."

"Wow. We'll have been in Mexico a full year by then."

"Wow," Rudy says. "There's one more thing, Clark."

"Yeah?"

"You know how we ran out of LSD a couple months ago?"

"Do I ever."

"I got some more."

"You didn't."

"I did."

"Another hundred?"

"Yup. And you know what that means…"

"It's time to make a move?"

"It's time to make a move."

On our Tuesday break Rudy appears with a big dead fish. He's a man carrying a fish in Veracruz. At home he cooks the big dead fish. We eat it, take our drums out to the beach, and go for a swim. Coming out of the water, we are beckoned by a group of Mexican *rudos*.

"You are Americans, eh?" says the skinny guy with a mustache. "Play the drums for us." I'm not sure if he's mocking us but Rudy readies to play, nods at me to join in. We jam hard, pounding out a beat across the ocean, a rhythm they groove to. *Oh yeah—we're in Mexico where everybody plays an instrument, everybody sings, talent or no.* They spark a couple joints and put them in rotation. The skinny guy with the mustache hands me one. I inhale deeply. The group gets suddenly quiet.

"Clark," Rudy says, looking beyond me. I turn, exhaling a cloud of marijuana smoke on the two police officers standing behind me. *Shit.* One of them opens his hand.

"You'd better give it to him," the skinny guy with the mustache says. The cop stares me down. I drop the smoldering joint into the palm of his hand. He pinches it between fingers, brings it to lips, hits it hard, blows a cloud of smoke in my face. When it clears he's smiling, passes the joint to his partner.

"Meet my cousin," the skinny guy with the mustache laughs, pointing to the cop. "I am Reynaldo."

Twenty-Nine

I pop some Janis Joplin into the tape deck, some acid into our mouths, and we roll. Highway 180 takes us north to Antigua, one of the first Spanish settlements in España Nueva. It's early Saturday morning, our second to last weekend in Veracruz. (*It's been a year.*)

"Where we going?" Rudy asks.

"Up the coast to Zempoala."

"More piles of rocks?"

"More piles of rocks."

We come on to the acid just as the jungle jumps to reveal the remains of Casa Cortés, former habitation of that Spanish exploiter. Vines, branches, and roots have consumed the construction, saving its shape, a fantastic facade, a house of vegetation. We wander this mangrovian maze, dancing through doorways, roaming the rooms, heaving down hallways, and walking through windows, hands caressing the foliated walls as we weave our way to what once was, and I shoot the scene in black and white.

Onwards, further north to the ancient ruins of Zempoala, former home of that tribe, Totonac, and the site where Cortés first colluded with a local *cacique*. It is a beautiful hot sun day. We sit in the shade of palms, sipping *cervezas*. Then, taking *tambors*, we shed shoes and pray our way, rising from profane earth up across the face of el Templo Mayor through the thirteen levels of the heavens and, summiting sacred platform, we peak atop the pyramid.

Fueled by the sun we lay into the skins, attracting a crowd of *touristas y Totonacs*, scaling the sides, cresting the summit, and breaking into dance at our drum, circling and stomping. High on acid atop an eight-hundred-year-old temple we lay down a beat that brings past and present together in a timeless tempo at the place, *the very place*, where the cultures of Iberia and Indígena allied against the Aztec resulting in their conquest and ushering in three hundred years of Spanish domination.

Our mytho-historical incarnation atop the Great Pyramid of Zempoala completed, Rudy and I bow to the collected crowd and descend, swerve back onto Highway 180, north past the town of Quiahuiztlan, north through the winding, hilly streets and vanilla fields of Papantla as the sun descends. We drive to the coast where we camp on a secluded beach near the mouth of a river, gaze over the Gulf. Rudy passes out under the stars.

It's been a year since he died, one year.

I sit on the sand, look out over the water, my sights on the sparkling sky, the mourning moon, full for the first time in months, glowing powdery peach in a pocket of cloud. Things are coming to an end for us here, our time is up and I'm sad to be leaving but that's our way—always moving, going, going with nothing but memories. Back home I said goodbye, but knew that I'd some day return. Here, we just go and go. It's been a year to the week since my father died.

Oh goddess of the filling moon, wherever you be, look over me, take care of me, fill the last of your capacity with all my anxiety.

Relax, Luna calls back. *Remember that life is short, there are no second chances, it's all do or die. You can swim to the island if the waves don't drown you.*

Sitting on the sand I watch the moon, full, constellations and clouds, the things that fill the sky above the changing waters of the Gulf. I sit on the sand, look out over the water, facing the warm breeze, and the possibility that the future holds.

A Sunday morning swim awakens. After a liquid breakfast of rum and juice, we pick up a six-pac, a litre of Kahlúa for the long journey home, take more LSD, *go*.

"Ah life…"

"Without a wife."

We play the haiku game on the drive home.

"Why am I here," I say.

"And not drinking a beer?"

"You are."

"Huh?"

"You are drinking a beer."

"Right," Rudy says. "Searching my mind."

"The refrigerator's empty."

"Oh, getting heavy now, are we?"

"I am the weed that grows," I begin.

"Between the cracks in your broken heart," he finishes.

"You're killin' me with that."

"A car passes."

"Vroom."

"Okay, we're scraping bottom now," Rudy says. "Last one."

"I'd rather die on the way up."

"Than on the way out," he says. "That was too easy."

"Pass me the Kahlúa."

"It's gone."

"Gone?"

"We finished it."

"That took a whole thirty minutes," I say. "Do you think we drink too much?"

"Definitely."

We hit Veracruz at eight o'clock at night, loaded and on a roll, drive straight out to el Centro, park, and wander the *zócalo*, stopping in every bar, café, and cantina along the way, drinking more, pushing it, hitting on every woman we encounter. Sometime after midnight we're walking along the *malecón*, sucking in sea air. We stop at a high point along the wharf to gaze on the Gulf.

"You see that over there?" I say, pointing across the water.

"What?"

"The future..."

"Clark?" Rudy says, putting a hand on my shoulder. "You're willing to go all the way with me, right?"

"Sexually? No."

"No you dumb-ass, I'm speaking abstractly."

"If you mean in terms of pushing the envelope, I'm with you all the way."

"Good," he says and gives me a sudden shove off the wharf. I am too astonished even to scream as I plunge forty feet down into the murky midnight waters. I surface and he's up there laughing, laughing his head off. Passersby have paused to see if I survived the drop.

"You bastard," I shout up at him but doubt if he can hear me over his hysterics and the slappings of waves against wharf. "I'll get you for this!"

I search for a way out, a way up the sheer wall of the wharf. His laughter is interrupted by a sharp shout as he cannonballs off the pier, yelling down, plunging into the harbor beside me. We find a ladder and climb out, have a good laugh together on the wharf.

"You wanna go again?"

And in we jump again.

And again.

"C'mon, let me buy you a beer," Rudy says, and we walk to the closest *cantina*, enter barefoot and dripping wet. It's one of the scariest, sleaziest bars I've ever been in—full of scraggy sailors, scarred seafarers, and sleazy sluts. As we stand at the rail and order our beers, a puddle forms at our feet. Rudy pulls the pesos from his pocket to pay, wrings them out before passing them over.

Thirty

Rudy walks out onto our front balcony to greet the day, our last in Veracruz. Below, he sees one of his students, Aldo, dragging a case of beer up the alley.

"Good morning," Rudy calls down. "What are you doing?"

"I am dragging a case of beer up the alley," Aldo says.

"Yes, I can see that."

"I am going to sit by my pool and drink beer and smoke *mota* all day."

"You have a swimming pool?" Rudy asks. "I'll be right down. I gotta go, Clark."

"What do you mean you gotta go? We got things to do. We gotta pick up our paychecks, get the Combi checked out, clean the apartment, pack. We're leaving tomorrow—remember?"

"I'm sorry but I've got plans. I've got to drink beer and smoke dope by Aldo's pool today. You're gonna have to pack up by yourself."

"Aldo has a swimming pool?" I say. "You bastard."

I spend the day running errands, getting our paychecks, getting the Combi tuned, sketching out an itinerary for our journey to the Yucatán, packing. Rudy returns late afternoon, drunk and with a bottle of Bacardi Añejo. We mix Cuba Libres and I drink through the entire bottle to catch up to his inebriation.

I'm hammered in the hammock on the front porch. Rudy walks past and bumps me, causing me to spill a splash of my cocktail on him. He pours his on me. I throw the rest of mine on him. He dumps a pitcher of water on me and it's *go* time. We square off in the front room. Fists fly. Bodies are slammed against walls, the floor. Furniture is overturned. Ashtrays, thrown. Glasses, the empty rum bottle, shattered. The razor-pointed *banderillas*—bloodstained bullfight souvenirs—fly through the air. Blood is drawn.

"What's going on up there?" Tanya's out in the street, yelling up at us. "Is everything all right?" Rudy goes out on the balcony.

"Everything's fine," he slurringly reassures her. I'm surveying the apartment, the glass shards carpeting the floor, the *banderillas* embedded in the backside of the front door. "We're just cleaning the place, that's all."

Some of our students show up to take us out for our last night in town. We drink. I mix Veracruz Venoms, hand one to Rudy who gulps it down. "You oughta feel better now," I smile.

"What do you mean?"

"I put a hit of acid in there."

"That's funny Clark, because I just took one."

"You did?"

"So did you—in your last Cuba Libre."

"You fucker," I say. "That means—"

"That means you've gotta take one more if you're going to keep up with me tonight."

Around Midnight we arrive Ocean Discotheque. "We're guests of the mayor," I tell the maitre d' who leads us direct to the *alcalde's* reserved table in front of the stage. (His attorney, Escobar, was a student of mine). And there they are waiting for us, Escobar, his *novia*, and a couple bottles of Johnnie Walker Black.

Our students arrive in a continuous current, fill the booths around us. We get lubed. More of Rudy's students show up, more of mine. They just keep arriving until there are more than forty of us, celebrating our last night in Veracrú.

Everybody crowds in around us, the wait staff flowing by in a constant stream bringing bottles, glasses, ice. As the empties take over the tables, we clear out and take over the dance floor. Rudy gets onto the stage, gets a hold of a microphone and leads the entire crowd in his personal repertoire of dances—the Sprinkler, the I Gotta Pee, the Frankenstein, "the dance that's sweeping the nation," he shouts through the P.A. Management allows us a good degree of leeway. We are, after all, guests of the mayor, and putting away upwards of a case of their finest whiskey.

I retire from the dance floor and back to the booth with Johnnie, Escobar, and his growing harem. A cold shadow falls over me.

"*¿Quieres un otra botella?*" the waiter asks.

"We're good for now, thanks."

"*Entonces, aqui es su cuenta.*" He drops the slip of paper on the table with a thunk, continues to loom.

"*Dios mio*," I exclaim. "Fourteen hundred pesos?! Uh, I believe the mayor is picking this up," and I turn quickly to the women next to me. "C'mon, let's dance," shoving them out of the booth. As I'm standing, a hand clamps onto my shoulder—Escobar.

"There is a problem with your friend," he says, "on the dance floor." *Shit*. Several of the bouncers are dragging Rudy off the stage. I cut through the madness of the crowd, reach Rudy as he and a group of his students are surrounded by security.

"What's going on?"

"They're throwing us out," Rudy says. "You wanna go?"

"Yeah, the bill just came." The bouncers close in, herd Rudy and his class—and now me—towards the exit. "What happened?" I ask.

"I was just being myself," he says. "And they accused me of inciting a riot."

"That's you all right."

They shove us out the door. We stand in front of the entrance. A dozen of Rudy's students look to him with bewildered eyes. The bouncers ready to repel any attempted reentry.

"So what exactly did you do to deserve this kind of treatment?" I ask.

"We were just dancing, that's all."

"You pushed it, didn't you?"

"As far as I could," Rudy says. "You know these kids will do anything I tell them?"

"Teacher, what do we do now?" his gathered students ask.

"The *finger*, you remember the finger? Just like I taught you." His united pupils extend their arms, their middle fingers at the security guards.

"Fuck off," they shout in unison.

"That's good class. You all pass."

"This was their final?" I ask, "Going to a disco?"

"Field trip," he says. "Class is dismissed," he announces.

"Thank you teacher."

We sit on the edge of the fountain in front of the disco.

"Yeah, Clark," he says. "I'm gonna miss this town. We've had good times here."

"Yes we have," I say. "You remember shoving me into the harbor last weekend?"

"Do I ever," he laughs.

"And you remember," I lean down to tie my shoelace, "I said I'd get you back?" Instead of tying my shoe, I grab his ankles, flip him backwards into the fountain, submerging him. "Now we're even." I jump up as he scrambles out of the water, drunk and pissed, furious.

"You bastard." He comes at me, fists flying. The bouncers are on him, one getting a hold of each of his arms as he growls and snarls at me. They urge him to calm down but he bucks at their hold, trying desperately to get at me. I step to him.

"Hey," I say. "You need to chill out or these guys are gonna call the cops and send you to jail."

"Okay," he relaxes. "I'm cool." The guards release him and he again lurches at me. I turn and step away. They again get a hold of his arms, but he's close enough to fall onto me, sinks his teeth into my shoulder, clamps his jaw down and won't let go, even as they choke him. They finally pull him off me—along with a chunk of my flesh.

One of the security guards is on the phone, dialing the police. Rudy's students close in, threatening the bouncers. He's in trouble and there's little I can do to help him. So I save myself, run around the building and up the road to el Tiburón. I catch my breath while the engine warms. Then, driving slowly back, I turn the corner at a crawl and come to a stop. I aim Combi at the mob in front of the disco fifty meters away, throttle the engine.

First gear, clutch out, el Tiburón lurches into motion, tires pulling, turbine turning. Revving it high, I jam it into second, quickly closing the distance, angling across avenue, engine screaming full speed at the collected crowd. Combi jumps the curb with a bounce, ten meters from impact. I announce my attack with a hand on the horn, headlights high.

Suddenly aware of my assault, the assemblage disperses, scatters screaming, individuals careening out of the way, clearing a course for my approach, exposing Rudy in the custody of cops. With the dawning realization of my advance, shrinking the gap to impact, they release their restraint and run, scrambling out of the way. Rudy is left reeling, dazed, staggering in my route of ruin.

I swerve to a stop with the open side door beside him. He falls into the Combi and I gun it, speed away, onto the boulevard, pass a police car sirening past us. (I said there was *little* I could do to help him, not nothing.)

"Hey," I say to Rudy. "You hungry?"

"Yeah."

"Tacos?"

"Yeah. And then we really need to get out of this town."

After eating, we go for a final swim in the Gulf as dawn breaks over Veracruz, sun rising behind fishing fleet, tiny boats bobbing up and down in the harbor. We load our belongings into the Combi and leave.

And we're on the road once again, headed into our futures and the challenges of the great unknown. *Ohhh the freedom of this life.*

Part Four

Ruta Maya

Thirty-One

We take the drive out of Veracruz nice and easy, enjoying the coastal scenery as we cruise south and east, curving around the contours of the Gulf of Mexico. Rain falls sporadically from the dense cloud canopy, but this precipitation provides little relief from sticky humidity.

The combination of tropical climate and the fertile river zones of these Gulf coast lowlands exhibited enough agricultural potential to encourage the development of the first major civilization of Mesoamerica. Our first stop is la Venta, to view the vestiges of this incipient culture. The extent of this Olmec ceremonial center wasn't discovered until the surrounding swamp was drained in the latter-half of the twentieth century in the pursuit of black gold.

We walk the dirt pathway into the jungle. Each turn of the trail reveals another ancient Olmec artifact (the oldest known monuments in Mesoamerica), altar-thrones featuring figures emerging from the underworld, symbolic sculptures depicting half-human, half-animal *were-jaguars*—portrayals of the shape-shifting shaman, conduit between celestial and terrestrial. And of course, there are the heads.

Of the enduring monuments left us by the Olmec are their colossal *cabezas* carved from stone. Some of these huge human heads rise over two meters in height and weigh up to twenty-five tons. By the time of the Olmec downfall, these basalt monuments had been ritually damaged, rolled into ravines, and buried beneath the earth where they remained for centuries. The first *cabeza*, out of a total of fourteen found, was uncovered in 1862. Here in the forest, set atop mounds of dirt, the heads appear to be those of colossal stone warriors, buried up to their necks in the earth.

The Olmec was the first great civilization to arise in Mesoamerica, lasting from 1500 B.C.E. up until the current era. There were earlier cultures and tribes, but the Olmec was the first community to evolve into a complex society with organized labor and hierarchical stratification. They developed urban planning and public works, terraced agriculture, aqueducts, and irrigation systems that were to be the foundation of all subsequent Mesoamerican civilizations. In the astronomically oriented Olmec ceremonial centers they built the first examples of monumental architecture including the original ball courts and the first pyramid platforms of Mesoamerica. Systems of hieroglyphs, mathematics, astronomy, and the calendar were all developed in the Olmec Heartland. Here also were established enduring religious ceremonies and the ritual of human sacrifice.

Back on the road after this pit stop, we head towards the land of another once-great civilization. We're on la Ruta Maya, moving towards the jungle city of Palenque, western frontier of Maya country. We're headed onwards, eastwards into the land of the rising sun, land of the Maya, where time is scheduled to end on 21 December 2012, when the Sun of Movement, Nahui Ollin, will come to a cataclysmic close with a transformative trembling of the earth, the shaking of the *all* to its foundations that something new may come into being.

This pending apocalypse concerns us not (*but is perhaps that fuel which silently drives you on*) as we lurch into the night, through scattered showers, feeling good and on our way.

Around ten P.M. we arrive the small town of Santo Domingo, source of sustenance for the multitude of tourists visiting the outlying archeological site. We circle *el zócalo y* la Casa de Artesanías, make a mental map of the town, then drive the darkened road towards Palenque. In the jungle, between town and the ruins, are a couple of campgrounds popular with hippies and the European backpack scene. This popularity is due, in part, to the myriad of magic mushrooms, *Psilocybe Mexicana*, that flourish in the fields. We check into the Mayabel Trailer Park and set up our camp.

We awaken early, sweating in our tent at the edge of the steamy jungle, have an excellent breakfast of *huevos revueltos con verduras frescas* in the al fresco café of the campground. Then, instead of following the rest of the unwashed masses up the road to the entrance of the ruins, we head off into the vegetated density of the rain forest, on an adventure.

We pick our way along the fields and through the thickets of trees and vines, ferns and foliage, teeming with life. The treetop canopy allows little light, holds in hot humidity and odoriferous putrefaction. Winged things swoop down at us. Monkeys pass overhead from branch to branch on their own elevated freeway system. An unseen choir serenades us with a chorus of chirps, cries, and croaks. We peruse the terrain for a trail, a track, a footpath through the flora, but find at our feet only the ubiquitous magic mushroom carpeting forest floor.

When in doubt, follow the fungus.

Soon we're stumbling across metrical mounds of earth, unexcavated altars and structures digested by the jungle, stelae and sculpture, guarded by forest fauna. A river leads us up past a waterfall to an opening in the trees. Emerging from the woods, we stand at the periphery of the sacred ceremonial center of that Maya metropolis, Palenque.

Nestled into the forest-covered foothills of the Chiapas Highlands, Palenque served as a hub and trading post for the Oaxacan and Gulf Coast civilizations to the west and the various Maya settlements to the east. First settled in the third century C.E., this jungle kingdom flourished between 600 and 900, a period when most of the buildings were constructed. Around 900 C.E., in one of the world's great unsolved mysteries, Palenque was suddenly abandoned. By the time the *Conquistadors* arrived in the sixteenth century, the jungle had all but consumed this once-great city. Palenque vanished from sight but lived on in legend and lore.

After the Spanish rediscovered Palenque in the eighteenth century, several expeditions investigated the ruins, amazed by the art, architecture, and the level of culture they found. Some figured the Mayan civilization couldn't have gotten so advanced without having had outside help. Theories on the source of this help ranged from the ancient civilizations of Rome, Greece and Egypt, to the lost Tribes of Israel and the lost city of Atlantis. There was even a guy who thought aliens had come from outer space and brought extraterrestrial technology to the Maya.

"Clark," Rudy stops to catch his breath, "why do all of your stories have to involve Martians or time travel?"

"This guy claimed that the carving on Pacal's sarcophagus was a portrait of the Palenque ruler at the controls of a spaceship."

"Why are you telling me this Clark?"

"Because his tomb's in there." I point to the Temple of Inscripcións, rising up before us. "All we gotta do is climb to the top of that pyramid and then descend a couple hundred steps to the core of the temple. You ready?"

"Why don't you go on ahead, Clark. I'll catch up."

"I see how it is. You're trying to lose me, aren't you?"

"Bingo."

So I go it alone, scale the nine levels of the pyramid, get to the top, and I'm exhausted, winded, lung capacity reduced from the copious pot smoking of late. I enter the temple, descend the claustrophobic stairway carpeted in guano, sixty-six slippery steep steps down through the dark dampness to the thirteen hundred-year-old tomb of Pacal the Great. His sarcophagus is capped by a five-ton lid of limestone, intricately carved with one of Mesoamerica's most famous reliefs. It depicts Pacal, the Great Lord of Palenque, descending into the maw of underworld (or ascending into outer space, depending on your point of view). Monsters, serpents, glyphs, and gods, the sun and stars surround Pacal. Behind him, the World Tree rises, rooted in the Underworld and branching into the heavens.

I make my own ascent, back to the top of the temple, wander off its backside and into the jungle. Down along the river, I circle through the ball court and into the Palace, up its four-story tower from where the solstices can be calibrated, this entire ceremonial center astronomically-aligned, arrayed against the vault of heaven.

Done with my tour, I find a rock on which to sit near the entrance of the site, consume copious amounts of water while waiting for Rudy to show up. I scan the ceremonial center with my telephoto, scouting for him. There, high atop the tower, I spy several figures, one resembling Rudy and the rest, women. They seem to be stretching him out on an ancient altar. One of the women suddenly plunges a blade into his chest and—but my view is obscured as someone steps into my sights. I lower my camera. Rudy stands before me, an attractive young woman on each of his arms.

"This is Clark, the guy I was telling you about." He introduces me to Anna from Manhattan and Camille from Copenhagen. "They live in Oaxaca," he says. "I told them they could ride with us to Agua Azúl."

"We're going to Agua Azúl?" I ask.

"We are now."

Thirty-Two

The four of us catch a bus back to Mayabel, where Camille and Anna have also been camping. We load our stuff into the Combi, drive into Santo Domingo, and browse the *mercado*. Lunch is had on the grand old balcony of a downtown café from where we can watch the flow through *zócalo*, and become acquainted. Camille is open and upbeat, tall and bouncy with curly hair. Anna is small and thin, anal and uptight, but pleasant enough, for now.

Back in the Combi and on the ancient highway, we carve through rain forest and rolling hills, arriving late afternoon at Cascades Agua Azúl where the turbulent Río Yax Ha tumbles turquoise over limestone precipices, pours into placid pools of emerald and azure. Rudy, Camille, and I jump right in, swim off the morning's exploratory exertions while Anna paces the riverbank haranguing us on the hazards of currents, rapids, and the hygienics of "that filthy water."

As darkness falls, we set up camp in a big field of tall grass. It's warm enough to sleep under the stars. We dine meagerly on tuna salad sandwiches, lie on blankets in the grass, caressing one another, pondering the fate of the Palenquistas. Late and tired, we spoon, and sleep takes us.

A drizzly downpour rudely awakens an hour later. We throw our soaked selves and soggy stuff into el Tiburón to sleep out the night, girls on the bed, Rudy and I on the floor, cramped and damp in the Combi. Rudy tosses, Camille turns, Anna snores all night.

I get up before dawn and the others, go for a swim in the cold, refreshing waters of Agua Azúl. Then, hiking up along the river under overcast sky, I pass backpackers snoring in hammocks and under *palapi*, small Maya shacks with fires smoldering. I throw a *buenas días* to a woman scrubbing clothes by the riverbank and she returns it with a smile, making my morning. Children play in puddles with little plastic cars. I climb to the calm waters high above the falls, sit against the trunk of an overlooking oak, meditate.

When I get back to camp, the crew is just awakening, the clouds abreakening. We all go for a swim, even talk Anna into joining us, fighting the formidable current up to the falls, through the cleansing cascade, and into the sheltered calm beyond. A breakfast of *tortas y naranjada* at a riverside hut. The morning's strenuous swim compounded with the strife of last night's onslaught—that sopping slumber-interruptus—has banded us together, uniting us in fatigue. It's not yet ten o'clock and we're already beat, but we're a crew now, and get back on the road for a most-of-the-day drive north, up the west coast of the Yucatán. We rotate driving duty in short shifts alternated with sporadic siestas but are still tired when we late afternoon arrive the formerly fortified city of Campeche. Anna orders us to a hotel where we get a spacious room with three beds (for the four of us), and a balcony overlooking *zócalo*.

We're tuckered and road-weary, but assertive Anna insists we tour the town before sun sets. (*You may have met your match, Clark—someone who's more driven to tour than you.*) We out and walk, circle the city on Circuito Baluartes, tracing the remains of the rampart what once protected this port. Fed up after years of piratical pesterings, the seventeenth century Spaniards built a bulwark barring buccaneers from Campeche, a hexagonal wall encircling the city.

Back in the room in the evening each of us, in turn, takes a well-deserved shower. We relax, listening to American Beauty and Live from Folsom Prison, smoking cigarettes, and passing a bottle of Johnnie Walker (one I'd purloined our last night in Veracruz) while we amiably argue over sleeping arrangements.

"It's like this," Rudy says, "someone's got to double up. We can rule out the possibility of Clark and me sharing a bed—seeing as how we're both heterosexual males. So that leaves us—"

"Why not?" Anna interrupts.

"Excuse me?"

"Why can't the two of you share a bed?"

"Are you listening to me? I just said we're both heterosexual males—there's taboos against that kind of thing, especially here in the Yucatán. So that leaves us two options: either you girls double up, or one of you sleeps with one of us—which is probably the better arrangement.

"There's a third option," Anna says.

"Yeah?" Rudy asks. "What's that?"

"The two of us could share a bed with Clark and you could sleep alone."

"I like these girls," I say.

Camille emerges, just-showered, from the bathroom.

"I like you too," she says. "Who's next for the shower?"

"Rudy could use a good cooling off," Anna says.

Rudy rises, walks towards Anna. "And you," he snatches the whiskey from her grip, "could use a good shutting up." He goes into the bathroom, gets into the shower, and sings at the top of his lungs, "Roadhouse Blues," I think it is, in his best Jim Morrison voice.

"So what do you think," I later ask Rudy, when the females are otherwise engaged. "Do I have a chance with Camille?"

"Dude," he replies. "These chicks dig you. You got a shot at both of 'em."

"Both of them? You think so?"

"Yeah, these girls really like you. Look at the way they've been cuddling up to you all day, talking about sleeping with you."

"Yeah, but they're just joking around."

"There's a grain of sand in every beer I drink."

"Huh?"

"They're going to be *fighting* over you pretty soon."

"Why don't I ever see these things?"

"You've gotta tune in to the chick vibe," Rudy says. "Play your cards right and you'll do the both of them—the old threesome."

"C'mon, they've both got boyfriends."

"Chicks always say they have boyfriends Clark, even if they don't. It gives them an out if they decide they don't want to sleep with you. Besides, their boyfriends are probably back in New York and—wherever the hell it is Camille's from—"

"Denmark."

"Right, and their boyfriends are probably cheating on Anna and Camille who are here in the exotic Yucatán with a couple handsome and sophisticated young men they've just met. That's how the game works."

"What about you?" I ask.

"I ain't goin' near Anna. And Camille—she's had her eye on you ever since you met."

"Really?"

"Yeah."

"A threesome, huh?"

"You got nothin' to lose."

We drink whiskey and tell stories into the night, lounging on beds until everyone falls into slumber. As it is, Anna and Camille happen to be snuggled up to me on the queen bed when the sandman pays his visit. I pull a blanket up over our tired threesome, throw Rudy a wink.

In the morning we stop at a *panadería* to pick up some pastries, juice, and coffee, take them out to Campeche's waterfront where we sit on cement steps, breakfast silently as the morning assembles itself over the Gulf. Then we're back on la Ruta Maya, driving north into the Puuc hills. We're on our way to Mérida with a stopover at Uxmal, that Maya kingdom where wizards and dwarves and kings once reigned.

We spend hours exploring the Uxmal ruins, weaving in and out of the forest, from building to building, taking in the carvings and reliefs on the ancient edifi—up and over the magical Dwarf-Wizard's Palace Pyramid, through the Nunnery Quadrangle (arranged in alignment with the voyage of Venus), across the ball court where huge lizards sunbathe on stones, through la Casa de Tortugas, and into the Governor's Palace.

"There's a path behind the House of the Witch," Anna refers to her guidebook. "It leads to the Temple of the Phalli, three hundred meters to the south. You guys want to go?"

"You want me to walk three hundred meters into the jungle to see the ruins of a penis temple?" Rudy says. "It sounds like a distinctively feminine trek to me."

"I'll go," says Camille.

"I'm going to pass," I say. "See you *chicas* later." Rudy and I wander up to the cemetery, through stelae of skull and bones draped with sun-basking snakes.

"You see what I mean?" Rudy says. "Temple of the Phalli? If that wasn't innuendo I don't know what is."

"Really?"

"So tell me what happened last night," he says.

"Nothin'," I say. "We slept."

"You slept?" Rudy says. "You had the both of them in bed and you slept?"

"We were tired."

"You're really disappointing me, Clark."

"They both have boyfriends."

"What did I tell you about that?"

"They don't really mean it?"

"Believe me Clark, these chicks are hot for you. It's a sure thing. Tonight's our last night with them, you'd better make your move."

"I'm gonna make you proud, Rudy."

We arrive Mérida, in the northwest of the Yucatán Peninsula, again get a large hotel room, this one with only *two* beds. "I'm not even going to bother trying," Rudy announces, "because I know the both of you are just going to end up sleeping with Clark."

As darkness falls, we stroll the streets, settle in at a sidewalk café where Rudy plies the women with margaritas in an attempt to loosen them for my intended advances. We all get pretty well liquored up, and Anna and Camille do indeed invite me to share their bed. I cuddle in with them. And make my move.

I awaken the next morning to Rudy, standing next to me, peeing in the toilet.

"Good morning," he says. "Slept in the bathtub last night, did we?"

"Yeah," I sit up, "ow," bang my head on the faucet.

"What happened?" Rudy asks.

"I took your advice and made my move."

"And?"

"And they told me they had boyfriends and threw me out of bed. I thought you said this was a sure thing?"

"I guess I was wrong. But you do gotta respect them for being true to their men. Wanna get some breakfast?"

Henequen is a type of agave native to the Yucatán, the fibers of which are used to make rope. From the mid-nineteenth to the mid-twentieth century, Mérida was at the center of the world's henequen industry. Demand was at its highest during World War II when the European powers were eagerly importing textiles and rope. The huge influx of money during the henequen boom transformed plantation owners into an aristocracy. Mérida in the early twentieth century had more millionaires per capita than any other city in the world. The members of this new class tried to outdo each other in building the grandest and most opulent mansions on the Peninsula. At the time, Mérida was virtually cut off from the rest of Mexico due to its remote location and lack of roads. Almost all of the community's external intercourse was across the seas with Europe. Méridians imported not only material goods from Europe, but also an aesthetic—particularly French—which had a strong influence on the architecture, arts, and lifestyle of Mérida.

We spend the morning in exploration of this beautiful colonial city, stroll the Paseo Montejo—a row of the remaining Beaux-Arts mansions. At noon, we walk the girls to the depot for their trip back to Oaxaca. They've got a little time until their bus departs so Rudy and I buy them lunch, exchange addresses and phone numbers, say goodbye.

"If you ever make it to Oaxaca," Camille yells to us as she boards the bus, "call me." *Wink.* We stay until the bus exhaust chokes us.

"Hey," I punch Rudy in the arm.

"What?"

"We're in the Yucatán."

"Yeah?"

"We made it—all the way from the Yukon to the Yucatán."

"So we did, my brother, so we did."

Rudy and I drive from afternoon into evening, east across the Yucatán, east towards the Caribbean, east into the night, bound for Chichén Itzá. We arrive at the ruins, explore the area, search unsuccessfully for campgrounds, wind up in front of the closed, guarded gates of the ancient Maya (Toltec?) city.

"Should we camp here?" I say.

"In the ruins?" Rudy says.

"Why not?"

"Yeah, why not?"

We park the Combi in the foliage off the road. Shouldering our bedrolls, we make our way around the outside of the *ruinas*, machette-hack through a half-hour of jungle until we emerge into the ceremonial center. After scouting scantily, we set up camp at the Pyramid of the High Priest, beautiful under the stars.

We're ahead of the crowds Saturday morning, take our time exploring the structures of Chichén Itzá, clambering up the steep sides of el Castillo, great pyramid dedicated to Kukulcán-Quetzalcóatl. We circle el Caracol, the observatory, gaze into the water of the Sacred Cenote swimming with sacrificial souls. Then into the forest of a Thousand Columns and the Temple of the Warriors where reclining Chac Mools hunger for human heart, settle for solar sustenance.

As Rudy and I complete our tour of Chichén Itzá, a stream of chrome-lined, window-tinted wonder-vessels flows into the parking lot. Doors hiss open to disgorge the hordes of French, Japanese, German, and Norte Americano tourists bussed in from Cancún and Mérida. We escape into town, stop at a bike shop to pump air into a car tire. Then, one of the best breakfasts I've ever had: tortas de pollo on Wonder bread, fresh squeezed orange juice, and LSD for dessert, the first of the day and we're gone, bound for Cancún, the end of Mexico.

Part Five

Cancún

Thirty-Three

O ut of Chichén Itzá by noon and on to Cancún, flat out on the twisting, potholed Mexican highway, tank full of gas, cooler full of Dos Equis, and somewhere around eighty-five hits of LSD remaining. Hitting on all four cylinders, 1600 cubic centimeters of engine hum in unison, as our little tin box humps over hills of no-shoulder jungle road.

The drive to Cancún is only a few hours. We head straight for the center of town, but it's *spinning*, el Centro is spinning so fast it repels us, throws us right out the north end of town, to the quiet fishing village of Puerto Juárez late afternoon. We hit the beach, drop our clothes, and—for the first time—jump into the blue Caribbean to swim off the road, the sweat, and the fever, the hard nights of sleeping cramped in the Combi and beaten on the ground. I swim the road out of my bones, out through the muscles, expelling it from pores, the azure waters rinsing it from my skin.

The sun descends. We're wound up and flying. It's time to attack this town, find its heart, and let it be known: *We have arrived.* So we head back into Cancún but the centrifugal force is still too much, sends us again to the town's periphery, this time to the south, Playa Delfíns.

Have patience; you'll get another stab at it.

Sitting in the Combi at the beach, we smoke the last of the tea (*oh no*), blowing prayers to Chac Mool, Maya god of the good; suck the essence from another tab of acid. Then, as we're walking from the boulevard down towards the water, a huge old car launches from the berm behind us, roars into the air. We duck, looking up amazedly at its underside as it flies overhead.

The Mercury lands hard on the beach in front of us, zooms away with a flash and a growl, lurching over dunes towards the surf and we're *thrilled!* The sedan is halfway to the water when it jerks to a stop with a cough and a quiver. Passenger door kicks open and two young *Mexicanos* and a dozen empty beer bottles spill out onto the beach. The men stand and ponder their vehicle, sunk to its axles in sand. Two women climb from the back seat over to the front, and exit. In tube tops, tight pants, and spiked heels, they stand a head above the men.

Without discussion, one of the *hombres* slides back behind the steering wheel while the rest of them lay thighs to steel in an effort to loose the white beast. Tires spin, dig into the sand along with the women's heels. Rudy and I shake off the shock of our close encounter and approach the scene with dilated pupils.

"*¿Necesitan ayuda?*" we ask. Do you need help?

"*Si,*" they shrug and we lean our weight into the back of the car. The added force of our addled bodies inches the car forward until, wheels out of holes, tire treads maul the beach for traction and the Merc leaps free, sending us tumbling to the sand, sweating and huffing for air.

The driver brings the car around, gets out, and picks up one of the green bottles. I recoil in anticipation of its being smashed into my head. Instead, the driver strips off the label and scribbles it with a pen. "*Mañana,*" he says, offering the scrap. "*Venga para desayuno.*" Come for breakfast. They pile back into their car and open more beers.

"*Un mil gracias.*" The driver guns it, kicking up twin rooster-tails of sand. Arms wave out of windows as they drive off to complete their mission, pitching over steepening, deepening dunes towards Caribbean. They U-turn in the surf and head back up the beach, lurching over berm with a screaming screech as sand-spinning tires grab asphalt, vaulting them down the highway.

Rudy and I are left standing in their wake, holding a beer label scribbled with an illegible note. But as the dust settles I have a realization. The Flying Mercury has delivered a message from the Universe.

Things have gone well for us on this journey. We've faced *some* adversity but whenever we've found ourselves in a time of need we've been provided for, provided with all we require. The Universe has been looking out for us. (*Ask and thou shalt receive.*) But we can't take anything for granted. We still have to *make* it. We still have to suffer and labor and scrape bottom to survive. It won't always come easy. Yet all that we do will come back, maybe not in this life, and maybe not even *to us*, but somewhere, sometime, to some*one*, it shall return.

You can file that away for later because right now we're *on*. We've made it, fucking made it, have arrived back at our journey. We've made it as far as one can go in Mexico, all the way out to the northeast corner of the Yucatán Peninsula, to our new home, our new life, Cancún. And it has been an adventure, a twisted, mountainous road of a journey, everything always as unsure as the nonexistent future ahead.

We steam down sand dunes, dive into the blue-green toothpaste gel of an ocean, swim and swim and then in the sand and drumming, hands rapid and precise on the skins with a rhythm of thanks for safe passage through to here. But I advance too close to a truth I'm not ready to receive and so alter the beat, causing time to shift, cleave, and merge.

The sun leaves town. Waves pound sand to their own rhythm, dragging us off the steep shelf and under water, carrying us out to sea and putting us through a spin cycle. We claw our way up the beach but each time we clear the surf slender arms of foam reach out, wrap 'round our ankles and drag us back under, toss us around, for hours, leaving us laughing at the mindlessness, the mindfulness of it as we lose it, *lose it* trying to escape the Caribbean.

We play and swim into the evening when darkness shuffles over the beach and we finally escape from the sea, drag ourselves out of the surf and slow the tempo as we prepare for our third and final assault on the city of Cancún.

Fortified with another tab of acid (*the third? fourth?*) we head out for the night, away from the beach and the specter of the white Mercury, into Cancún's center. We stroll Avenida Tulum, the main strip, talking to people, each other, ourselves, peering in the windows and doorways of clubs, bars, and cafés, past the barkers' calls and into the interior scenes. But we do not enter. For these are not *our* worlds which one by one will come back to me in the more lucid weeks to follow. We continue on, searching for a veracity that exists not here.

Let's go find it.

We're in the Combi and moving once again, beyond el Centro, beyond the neon and taxis and two-fer-one, three-fer-one, four-fer-a-dollar daiquiris, margaritas, *cervezas*, all-you-can-chew best-deal-in-town today only half-price ladies' night Happy Hour chantings until we're lost in the narrow dark dusty streets on the wrong side of the tracks, lost and worrying. And then we hear the music and follow it to its source.

Ohhh the music—you're never lost if you can find the music, live and in-person, en vivo.

Slamming to a stop, one wheel up on sidewalk under a hazing orange street lamp, we proceed up the rickety wooden steps to the unannounced pair of swinging saloon doors from whence the music issues. I pause outside in anticipation of the culmination of this entire journey (*as every moment is*), awaiting a cue or vibration, a *sign* before stepping out of the apricot-glowing, fly-buzzing, cool-breeze Mexican night.

Something suddenly pushes me into the doors, through the doors, and onto the well-worn, wide-plank floor of the *cantina*. Everything here is wooden: the walls, the bar, and the faces, as if it was built a hundred years ago, populated, and then forgotten. Any air it may have contained was long ago displaced by an India ink of caliginous exhalations, an atmosphere so thick with smoke that a spilt beer would take half a minute to reach the floor.

Rudy stumbles in behind me, losing his grip, knocks me lurchingly forward. A large, firm hand into my chest halts me—the bouncer. He eyes us, displays a tobacco-stained grin, and allows us entry. *In the dawn's early light he'll probably be picking his teeth with your splintered bones as he dumps your bodies (with a hearty laugh) somewhere on the outskirts of town.*

We take another step in and one by one, ninety-nine eyes turn toward us, peering brown, dark, and red out of weathered faces, noses disappeared behind the green-tinted bottoms of beer bottles emptying into thirsty throats, straw hats angled back to expose smooth foreheads reflecting gleam of stage light, as scratchy beards and unkempt *mustachios* reach across dirt-dabbled cheeks, the after work wash ignored on this overtime Saturday. Bodies slump in wooden chairs; cowboy boots rest one atop the other in the aisles for the wait staff to hurdle.

The air clears little as we move deeper into the eye of this storm, our feet shuffling through a carpet of peanut shells, cigarette butts, and bottle caps. One by one the stares turn away from us and back to the serious business of *emborrachando*.

There's one empty table in the middle of the room, glowing under a spotlight. I head for it, squeezing past a severe *vaquero* in plaid shirt, blue jeans, and the hat, always the cowboy hat—soiled from years of breaking bulls, wrenching on the pickup, and sweating in the midday sun. As I pull a heavy wooden chair back from the empty table, I give him a stiff nod, then stand suspended over chair, waiting to see if he'll respond to this gringo who has invaded his sacred space.

His eyes dart to the sides of their sockets, dwell on me momentarily then shift back, staring straight ahead. With an ever-so-slight dip of his head, he stifles a burp. We have been acknowledged. I release the breath I didn't know I'd been holding. Rudy and I sit.

A skinny waiter in white and black materializes tableside, bouncing. His brow leaps upward. "*¿Cerveza? ¿Cerveza? ¿Cubetazo?*"

Rudy inhales to voice a reply but the waiter produces a steel bucket of iced beers, drops it on the table and disappears. We silently scan the room.

The *music*, that's what drew us here, that sultry Latin rhythm emanating from the shadows of the stage—guitar strumming, horns wavering, congas crawling out from under it all. Visible only are the gleam of the hornman's tool, the up and down flash of the percussionist's wedding band, the glowing ember of pianist's *cigarrillo*. The real show is down on the floor in front of them. There, under perpetually changing lights, writhe a few aging prostitutes, eyes heavy with shadow of blue, lips slathered ruby, silver mine mouths. They gyrate endlessly, raising hands above heads to expose bellies rolling over waistlines. A wink and a smile and their curling fingers beckon.

Resist.

The *vaquero* at the next table slides his chair back so he sits beside me, facing in the opposite direction. He mumbles a salutation and raises his bottle. I clink mine to his and we're amigos. He swallows and leaps to his feet, shoving his table against ours and calling for another bucket. *Victor.* His amigos move their chairs in, hardened *hombres* surround our table. We drink. We drink and we talk and we laugh. Rudy amuses them with stories of the road; they entertain us by singing *corridos* in competition with the band, our table a glowing island in this ocean of murk.

A plump young woman, her face thick with war paint, slips off the lap of one of our new friends, saunters around the table and takes my hand, jerks me to my feet and leads me briskly, stumbling to the crowded dance floor. We wedge ourselves into the mêlée of slowly shifting hips and shuffling shoes, some couples squeezing, others circling at a safe span. Smiling *rancheros* leap bowlegged from foot to foot with women clutching dress hems. There are even a couple of men so thick with machismo, history, and drink that they dance with one other, *hombre y hombre*, swinging stoically, everybody moving to a beat different from the one I hear.

We shake it side to side in a widening gyre until she pulls me against her glistening body, sweat soaking through clothes. Her aroma fills my head. I break away, twisting to my own tempo, a rhythm which moves like a mongoose unseen through bandstand, clawing across guitar strings, paws pounding keyboard, its cry screeching out of trumpet, feathery tail jerking from side to side with each beat of drum. Mongoose slithers silently across tattooed dance floor, chasing an unseen serpent, talons digging in, up a cracked plaster column, across the ceiling between steaming flashes of red, blue, yellow, red. Then, dropping to floor, mongoose crosses the room, unnoticed past cowboys, under tables and underfoot, past crumpled cigarettes and chunks of broken bottle, between the boots of bouncer and out the front door, bounding down the stairs and into the cool night air. We, unfortunately, fail to follow the mongoose outside.

Halfway back to the table I'm intercepted by a mellow Maya who pulls out a chair, motions for me to join him. With a cold beer in hand, the questions fly at me: *Where are you from? What are you doing here?* When I have satisfied his curiosity, Miguel starts in on *his* story. I've lost my grip on Spanish (if that's what he's speaking) but it appears to matter not on this night. I smile and nod enough to keep him going while I enjoy the smooth lilt of his vocalizations flowing into ears and the coolness of *cerveza* sliding down dry throat.

I'm jolted out of my daze when his voice suddenly rises. A sullen stare issues from the obscurity of his face, his glare aimed not at me but at my original table where Rudy and our newfound amigos beckon me rejoin them. I slide my chair back, grab another beer from Miguel's bucket—the cool glass long neck kissing my palm. But before I can stand and goodbye, he puts a heavy hand to my shoulder, presses me to chair. "*Espera*," he whispers. Wait.

His glare is being fiercely returned by the residents of the other table. Rudy slides down in his seat. I do the same. Victor rises to his feet. Miguel up and moves toward him. Words are exchanged. Sleeves rolled up. Their faces redden, muscles tighten, steps shorten until they stand bleary eye to bleary eye, red nose to red nose, glowering. Their gangs rise up behind them, *Vaqueros* and *Indios*, shoving chairs out the way as adversaries circle, spitting words, breathing each other's sticky breath. The band skids to a halt.

As far as I can make it out, the dispute is over whose beer Rudy and I are going to drink. They're fighting over who's going to host the gringos.

The room spins around the fulcrum of their exchanging exhalations, a hostility that radiates outward, drawing focus in. Miguel and Victor lean into each other, arms cocked, fists ready to fly. Rudy and I slip discreetly out of our seats and sink to the floor. I grab a bucket of beers from a table and we crawl across the room, following the mongoose's path out the fucking door and down the steps to the freedom of the apricot-glowing, fly-buzzing, cool-breeze Mexican night.

Thirty-Four

When I awaken, I understand how an egg must feel, frying in a pan. The sun is already high as I come-to on the hot tin roof of the Combi. There's a whistle piercing my brain and the whole world feels as if it's trembling beneath me. I sit up uneasily and look around, searching for bearings, a landmark, anything. We're in a Mexican suburbia, in an alley behind a row of houses. No, it's not an alley, it's—

"*Rudy!!!*" I pound on the roof. "*Rudolpho!*"

"What? What? What?" he awakens, understanding how a potato must feel, baking in an oven. He slides the Combi door open and sticks his head out. Seeing the railroad tracks on which we're parked—and hearing the approach of the train—Rudy reaches up and grabs my ankle, drags me off the roof and into the Combi. He fires the engine, wrestles the stick into gear, drives us off the tracks and keeps it moving on through town, keeps it going until we again find ourselves at the beach north of town, Puerto Juárez.

I crawl out of the Combi and down towards the water but don't quite make it, passing out in the white sand. Rudy makes it to the ocean and manages to swim some energy back into himself. Unconscious and exposed, the sun burns me like a side of overcooked bacon. Rudy comes out of the surf, tells me how stupid it is for a person in my condition to be laying in the sun like that, kicks me in the ribs a couple times to drive his point home, then drags me into the shade of a palm tree.

Neither of us says a word all morning. We are timeless and spaceless in the still day, with no point of reference and no place to be or go, no plans for the day, the future. We are nonexistent as far as the universe is concerned and I can't locate a restroom, never will in this day.

Ahhh but is there anything we *need*? And if so what?

Ask and thou shalt receive.

"Food," we simultaneously state. After wandering all morning on divergent paths, our minds have suddenly come together in this realization of requirement. We must eat, get some fluids into our bodies, some nutrients.

"Have you got any money?" I ask.

Rudy shakes his head. "You?"

"Nope." My hand reaches into pocket to confirm its emptiness, comes up with a prize.

"What's that?" Rudy asks.

"A torn beer label with an illegible note scribbled on it."

"From the Mercury guy. What'd he write?"

"Did I not say it was illegible?"

"Yeah, whatever that means. Here, let me see it." Rudy grabs the label from me. "Didn't he say something about breakfast? Yeah, it says Gourmet Chef right there, you dumb ass. But this... I don't know what this is—Pizza Ku-ku-choo? Hey," Rudy beckons a passing lifeguard. "You're Mexican, right? Can you tell me what this says?" The *salvavida* takes the label, examines it, knits his brow.

"It says Gourmet Chef," the lifeguard offers. "Sounds like a *restaurante.*"

"I got that part," Rudy says. "That's in English. Can you make out the *rest* of it?"

"Yeah, that says Plaza Kukulcán."

"Ku Klux Klan?" Rudy says.

"Ku-kul-cán," the lifeguard enunciates. "Plaza Kukulcán is a big mall south of town. It's named after the ruler of Chichén Itzá, the Plumed Serpent who—"

"Thanks, I don't need a history lesson," Rudy says. "Just tell me how to get there."

"Take this road south, to Playa Delfíns."

"That's the beach we were at yesterday," I say. "Where we saw the flying Mercury."

We park our home next to a hydrant, go into Plaza Kukulcán and locate the Gourmet Chef. (*But you don't yet know what it means.*) We enter the crowded restaurant and spy the driver of the Mercury across the room. He's posing as a waiter carrying a tray of drinks, recognizes us with a smile and a nod. He goes and whispers to the maitre d' who leads us to a table with a view of the Caribbean.

It's a huge, beautiful, all-you-can-eat buffet. We fill our plates and our pockets with the multitude of fresh fruits, breads, pastries, meats, cheeses, omelets, eating like the animals we are, drinking gallons of coffee, liters of juice, refortifying the very cells of our bodies, seconds, thirds, feeling better, our amigo bringing rounds and rounds of unrequested Bloody Marys, and we're *on* again and ready to start the cycle anew.

At the end of this bacchanalia there is no bill, only a smile and a thanks again. We walk out to the beach new men; take more acid to bring ourselves the rest of the way out of the heavy hangover. I say something to the effect of, "Now all we need is some free beer and a place to spend the night."

"And some chicks to spend it with," Rudy says.

"Who will buy us breakfast in the morning," I add.

"Now you're talkin."

The beach is packed with tourists. We separate, drift off, do our own things. I swim, continuing to awaken to higher levels, talk to people, conversing in Spanish, English, and Italian (which I don't speak), try to keep the day moving, mounting. In the afternoon I'm walking up the beach half-looking for Rudy, and there I spot him sitting on a blanket, playing the bongos, surrounded by emptied bottles and bikini-clad women who rub oils into his flesh. He's collected a crowd, attracted an audience.

"What the hell is this?" I ask as I approach.

"Clark!" Rudy slurs. "We were just talking about you."

"Oh, this is the crazy guy you were telling us about," someone says.

"I'm the crazy one?" I ask.

"Clark, this is Ross. He's a cop, but it's okay—he's on vacation."

"Where from?"

"Jersey," Ross says.

"I'll put yer frickin' eye out."

"This is the beautiful Tamara, the lovely Rose, and the talented Valerie," Rudy continues. "They're from L.A. Oh, and you gotta meet Ross's partner, Meritt. This guy's great, just look at him." Rudy points down the beach to a gringo building a castle in the sand. And he's *into* it, really into it, letting himself go, under the spell of the Caribbean and venturing into this growing compound. It's magnificent, moated and with a drawbridge, flying buttresses and flagged spires. I look for the lurking dragon. Rudy leans to me and whispers. "I gave him some acid."

"You gave him some or *slipped* him some?" I ask.

"Clark, can I buy you a beer," Ross asks.

It's a good day to die.

We spend all afternoon talking and swimming and drumming with this group, putting away the beers that keep appearing. Rudy's been busy embellishing to them the story of our adventures and establishing our current state of serendipitous destitution. We stay until the sun gets low.

"Tonight," Meritt announces, raising his arms, "I'm taking everyone out for dinner and cocktails—my treat."

"You don't have to do that," says Rudy. "When and where?"

"Let's meet at eight o'clock at that steakhouse down the road."

The cops and women gather their belongings. Rudy and I sit and watch.

"Hey," Rose says to us. "Do you guys have a place to wash up?"

"Yeah," Rudy says, and points to the ocean.

"Do you want to use the shower in our hotel room?" Valerie offers.

"Not bad," I say.

"What?" Valerie asks.

"I've known you girls only a couple hours and you're already inviting me back to your hotel room to get naked."

"Shut up and come on," Tamara says.

Steaks! Big, red, meaty steaks like I haven't had in months. Then on to Carlos y Charlie's for discourse and drink. We talk, with these peace officers from Jersey, these Chicanas from So Cal, listening to one another's stories, all of us brought together from the scattered corners of our native land in a chance meeting on foreign soil. We come to know one another over tequila and music, telling tales we won't remember, sharing our lives—real and imagined—in order to validate our existence.

When words and personalities become moot, we take to the dance floor, giving in to wild abandon. We infect the place with our energy, pushing the context until the whole place is alive and bulging, forcing those who can't move fast enough out the doors.

The bar shuts down at four and they kick us to the curb. But a befriended bartender invites us to a beach party. The lot of us crowds into Combi and we zoom across Cancún, the Jerseyites and Chicanas loving it, finding themselves laughingly being chauffeured across Mexico in the middle of the night, all of us reveling in our newfound friendships. We're rolling, singing down the boulevard all the way out the peninsula to the Hotel Paraíso. The crowd of us, indiscreetly loud, slips through the hotel lobby and out to the beach, down to the bonfire with its few lingering souls.

Standing around the flames, we nurse drinks, decorating the darkness with a constellation of cigarette-glowing stars. When dawn joins the party we sit silently in sand, where the water meets the land, to watch the onset of the day, flowing up, over, and between our toes. Quietly over the crackle of the fire and the sounds of the swells I hear an approaching murmur. A vision of the Flying Mercury floats into view, gliding over the rise of rolling dunes, driving across the beach towards us, tires splashing through moon-reflecting surf. It rolls past, disappears into the distance and depths of my dreams. But again it has delivered a realization.

The people gathered here, this scene and the memory of this moment in the early morning hours are all that we need. Here, in these final moments of the fleeting night, illumined now by firelight, it all comes down to common ground, to sharing sand with this disparate band. And I'm prepared to move forward, to take on whatever is to come next in this life, even if that be sleep.

We drop Ross and Meritt at their hotel and the girls take Rudy and me back to theirs, insist we spend the night—uh, morning with them. Rudy is dragged into bed with Rose and Valerie, Tamara beckons me join her in the other where we kiss and cuddle, twine our bodies to sleep in a sweaty heap for an hour or three.

Awakening later, the spectrum of our first weekend in Cancún comes into focus for me like a scene from a dream or a movie in my head. Yesterday we found ourselves in this paradise on the Caribbean, destitute and homeless, dancing dangerously on the edge, then waking in the path of a steaming locomotive, onto a gratis gourmet breakfast, vacationing cops who buy us steaks and beers and shots all night then, waking here in a four-star hotel spooned with wonderful women. And I smile, begin to giggle, but I'm trying to keep quiet 'cause the others are still sleeping.

"Clark," Rudy whispers from the other bed. "You alive?"

"Yeah."

"This worked out all right, didn't it?"

"It sure did. We got a place to stay, like I said."

"Didn't you also say something about breakfast?"

A loud knock on the door rouses Rose who rolls out of bed, crosses the room.

"You expecting someone?" Rudy asks her.

"Room service," she says. "I ordered breakfast for everyone before I went to sleep."

Rudy and I try to suppress our laughter but can't, get louder and louder until we've awakened them all. Our laughter just grows, and grows, and grows...

Thirty-Five

After a hearty breakfast, we bid the girls *adieu* late morning. They're on their way to tour Chichén Itzá and we won't see them again. Rudy and I—well, we're broke, it's the start of a new week, and we've got to find some work. We go down to the beach for our daily bath in the Caribbean, put on our Sunday best (even though it's Monday). We're homeless, jobless, and near penniless at the beach, resting in the poverty of the *now*. But it's time to move onward, into our lives, find a source of income, some shelter, and live.

Our plan is to hit all the big resorts and see if they have any opportunities for us. Someone's bound to need us for something. We possess a multitude of skills and we're willing to do most anything: English tutoring, answering phones, leading tai chi sessions, cleaning toilets.

Our first stop is the Hotel Casa Maya. We find ourselves standing in front of the huge desk of the personnel manager as she peruses our résumés. Rudy puts on the smooth talk as I stand there showing teeth, each of us exhibiting the best of our qualities. He finishes his spiel, the one that has worked so well up to now, and then it's her turn to show some teeth.

"I have nothing for you now," she says. "But I will keep your résumés on hand just in case. Good luck. Good bye." We keep our heads high and move on to the next hotel. And the next, trudging from air conditioned offices to outside oven—alternately shivering and sweating—making our way through the length of the Hotel Zone and finding nothing but rejection. After the same scene is repeated a dozen times, we begin to grasp the reality of the situation.

"I guess we didn't think this all the way through, did we?" Rudy says.

"What do you mean?"

"I'm starting to think that summer may be the *low* season here."

"Why's that?"

"People come here to escape cold weather elsewhere, which means they'd be coming in the winter."

"I see your point. I guess we didn't think this all the way through, did we?"

We take our afternoon siesta break; have a swim at Playa Chac Mool. It's so fucking hot here that we've already sweated completely through our clothes. We rinse our shirts in the surf, hang them on the Combi and they're dry in a matter of minutes.

We continue the job search until the day is exhausted. In the evening drive south, out to Playa Delfíns—our night beach—where we cook beans over a small fire, throw a blanket on the sand, let the charging and retreating waves lull us to sleep.

Tuesday and Wednesday are more of the same, checking with human resources at hotels, visiting language schools, and the afternoon siesta reading want ads at the beach. We chase every lead down to its dead end. There appears to be *nada* for us in this town. I withdraw my last fifty pesos from an ATM. We feed ourselves on free samples at the supermarket.

Thursday is no different. We visit the last of the hotels, recheck some leads, and then to el Centro looking into schools. No one has employment for us. We take our usual exhausted afternoon break at Playa Chac Mool, rinse our shirts and our bodies. This routine is getting old quick, the beaches and rejections and canned beans over the fire. We have nothing left to eat but hope. And that provides little nourishment.

Thursday night, exhausted, we buy bread and cheese; cruise out to our bedroom, Playa Delfíns. We're both of us in foul moods from lack of everything and the mounting desperation of our situation. Mosquitoes feast on us. As soon as I bite into my sandwich, a pair of headlights pops over the dunes, heading straight for us. *La policia.* It's a couple of clean-shaven youngsters, sharp in their uniforms and good-humored in contrast to the severity of our dispositions.

"*¿Que estan haciendo aqui?*" they ask us. What are you doing here?

"*Viviendo,*" Rudy says. Living. "*Estamos gringos pobres.*"

"I have never heard of a poor gringo," one of them responds with a smile.

"A couple of gringos living on our beach...," the other one says. "What are we going to do about this?"

"Shoot us, please," says Rudy.

"It can't be that bad. What's the problem?"

Rudy snaps out of his mood and explains our situation to them. Deep in the gutter of abjection, I fail to rouse myself from the sand. Exhaustion and malnourishment have drawn me into a stupor. I don't hear their words, but judging from Rudy's broad gestures through the night—and the officers' laughing responses—I know he's enchanting them with tales of our trips and triumphs. I'm starting to think we should have our story printed up on a pamphlet we can distribute. Yeah, we'll get it printed up and then stand on street corners passing them out for a peso apiece.

Rudy's head droops as he gets to the present situation that has forced us to sleep here, on the beach. Then the cops are shaking his hand, wishing him luck, waving goodbye to me, and leaving us unharassed to camp on the sand.

"Look at this," Rudy says. "That cop just gave me twenty pesos."

Thirty-Six

W *hat the fuck am I doing here?* I know I've asked that question many times during my journey through Mexico, but this morning it seems to have particular pertinence. We've been in Cancún a week now and have found nothing to sustain us but the kindness of strangers. We are deep, living on the fucking beach—and I mean *on* the beach. The Combi won't make it many more kilometers in her present condition and if we don't generate some income soon we're going to be trapped here without the resources to get home. We've got no momentum except in the Combi and that's only because her brakes are shot. We've knocked on doors 'till our knuckles bleed and have found nothing. *What have we gotten ourselves into?* Sitting on the beach of this morning's gray dawn I invite the crash of waves to soothe my soul, but *mi alma* is restless, hungry, and tired.

"This is bad," I say.

"Yeah," says Rudy. "It is."

"Maybe I could prostitute myself."

"That's what I was thinking."

"Prostituting yourself?"

"No, pimping you out," Rudy says, "to cougars on the beach. You could offer to rub suntan oil on them and—"

"Maybe we're not so bad off."

"Not yet."

The morning hunt produces nothing. Our afternoon break is in silence. We dress and begin to drag ourselves from the beach. We're bitter at the world but have only each other to take it out on. Rudy begins his caustic mutterings.

"'Let's go to Cancún,' you said," he says. "'There'll be plenty of work in Cancún, lots of money, plenty of beautiful women,' you said. What a great idea this was, Clark. Here we are, withering away in this heat, no work, no home, eating sand to keep our strength up. Oh, this is paradise all right."

"Hey fuck you," I say. "This was *your* idea. *I* didn't want to come to Cancún. I was perfectly content in Veracruz."

"Veracruz?" Rudy says. "I loved Veracruz. I had no reason to leave there. It was you who talked me into going to Cancún."

"No, no, no, no, no," I say. "'It's time to make a move,' you said. 'Cancún,' you said. 'We gotta get out of here before I get someone pregnant,' you said. I remember it clearly." We're strolling past a skinny Mexican guy with a mustache who glances at us. We glance at him. He glances at us.

"Hey," he says. "I know you guys."

"You do?"

"Yeah, from Veracruz. We met on the beach last month. You guys were playing the drums. We got high, remember?"

We give him blank stares.

"We got high with the cops..."

"Oh yeah, I remember you," I say.

"Yeah," Rudy says.

"What are you guys doing here?" he asks, and I again think of printing up pamphlets.

"Looking for jobs," Rudy says. "What about you?"

"Looking for employees," he says with a big silver smile. "I'm running boat tours, taking *touristas* out snorkeling and fishing, to the reefs and Isla Mujeres. I could use a gringo or two to help hustle business on the beach and go along in the boat. You know how the Americans don't trust us Mexicans."

"I hear ya," says Rudy.

"If you're interested in working, meet me here on the beach, tomorrow at ten." He turns on the smile. "I am Reynaldo," he says, offering a hand.

The afternoon job hunt leads us nowhere. "Maybe we're going about this wrong," Rudy says. We're back at the beach, late afternoon. "We don't want to work for somebody else."

"We don't?" I ask.

"No. Why don't we open our own school?"

"Our own school?"

"Yeah, work for ourselves."

"I'll tell you why not," I tell him. "We've got no resources."

"Clark, we've got teaching experience and we speak English. The only other resource we need is my brain."

"What are you going to do, teach classes in the Combi?"

"Listen, we'll market it to hotels and restaurants, all the places that have an English-speaking clientele. We'll pitch it as being good for business—the more English their employees know, the better they can serve their customers. And here's the thing: we'll hold the classes right there in their workplaces."

"Maybe you're on to something," I say.

"All we need is one account to get the ball rolling," Rudy says. "Just one."

"I've still got all my ESL texts and worksheets. And the tests. We can rework them, put together a curriculum geared towards the hospitality industry."

"And we'll use the fact that it's the low season to our advantage," Rudy says, "as a selling point. 'Get your staff up to snuff now,' we'll tell them, 'so they're ready for the high season.'"

"We'll come up with a four-week course—"

"Why limit ourselves? Let's make it six."

"—a six-week course starting with nouns and verbs, and then we'll do sentences and questions and tons of role playing."

"We can do a two-pronged marketing approach," Rudy says. "We'll sell the employees on the idea of better tips, and management on the notion of increased business. That way they can pressure one another into signing up."

"And split the cost," I say. "What'll we charge?"

"We'll have to determine what's fair and then double it."

"A hundred twenty-five pesos a week?"

"Doubled would be two fifty—that sounds good."

"I *was* doubling it."

"There's another facet to this idea we're overlooking," Rudy says. "And it's pure genius. Tell me Clark—what do we need most right now?"

"Money?"

"Money for what?"

"Food and lodging—Oh, and we'll be working in hotels and restaurants—if this works."

"It'll work," Rudy says. "You and me and those old books are going to go a long way."

"What should we call it?"

"How about *Escuela de los Maestros Borrachos*—that's got a nice ring to it."

"The School of Drunken Teachers? I'd say it lacks a little, oh, professionalism."

"How about 'Drunken Teachers with Books?'"

"We'll work on the name."

After our morning bath in the Caribbean, Rudy heads off to market our school. I walk down the beach to meet up with Reynaldo and see what he has to offer. "Just go up to people, talk to them," he explains the job. "Ask if they're interested in snorkeling or a boat tour. Groups of women are good prey. You can try the hotels, around the swimming pools, and out here on the beach. It's whatever they want—one hour, four hours, all day. If somebody wants to fish or snorkel, I've got the equipment. ¿*Claro?*"

"*Claro.*"

"I'm going up the beach this way. You go down there." We part ways. "Like I said," Reynaldo yells, walking backwards away from me. "You are a gringo, they will trust you."

The sky is cloudy gray and *la playa* almost empty of tourists. Within an hour, I feel the first drops of rain. Then the sky rips wide like a prostitute's dress, buttons popping and all, rain dumping on my head. Reynaldo and I reconvene. "C'mon," he says, "let's get inside."

We take refuge in a beach bar, Bananas. And who should happen to be sitting at the bar with a beer and a shot in front of him?

"What are you doing here?" I ask.

"Me?" Rudy says, "I should be asking *you* that."

"I'm workin'."

"—in a bar? Uh-huh."

"*You're* the one sitting here drinking."

"I'm celebrating."

"Celebrating what," I say, "the rain?"

"Here, I got you a Subway sandwich—you and Reynaldo can split it."

"Did you steal this?"

"No Clark, I did not steal it. I am pleased to announce that Subway sandwiches is the first official client of 'Two Guys With Books.'"

"Subway Sandwiches?" I say.

"Two Guys with Books?" Reynaldo says.

"Let me buy you guys a beer," Rudy says. "Celebrate our grand opening with me."

"So tell me about it."

"I hit half the hotels in the Zone and struck out at every one. I was gettin' all bummed out and tired and hungry."

"I've seen you like that," I say. "It is not pretty."

"I stopped by Subway Sandwiches—just to look at their menu and imagine what it would be like to eat something. I got talking to the manager and he tells me he's opening his own Subway franchise and has to take this big test next month, *in English*. So I told him all about my school—"

"*Our* school."

"And he hired me to tutor him. He wants to meet for two hours every morning for the next four weeks. I told him he had to pay half in advance and—I'm not sure if he misunderstood me or what, but...," Rudy pulls a wad of cash from his pocket, "he gave me a full thousand pesos."

"Shit, that's over three hundred bucks," I say. "Bartender! I'll have what he's having."

"*Yo tambien*," Reynaldo says. "If I knew the money is that good, I woulda been a teacher long time ago."

"I figure this ought to be enough to get us a place to stay, at least for the next couple weeks," Rudy says. "And now we've got some capital to build up our business."

"And we can eat again," I add.

We toast our tequila, swallow it down, stare out the window, watch the falling of the rain.

Thirty-Seven

Reynaldo has offered to help us find a place to stay. On Sunday, the three of us start our search at Puerto Juárez, thinking it will be less expensive than el Centro. But a morning of viewing apartments, bungalows, and hotels reveals that vacancies are scarce and rent more than we've been paying in Mexico. So we head downtown Cancún, start at the outskirts and spiral our way towards the center. Everything we look at is out of our price range. Late in the afternoon we stumble upon the Hotel Colonial. It's on an alley connecting the main boulevard to Parque las Palmas, the closest thing this artificial town has to a *zócalo*.

The airy lobby of the Colonial opens into a large central garden full of banana trees and squawking, tropical birds, with a fountain at its center. Surrounding this garden is a three-story rectangle of rooms, with balconies overlooking this plaza. The rooms are small and lack kitchens, but are almost affordable—twelve hundred pesos a month.

"Let me speak to the manager," Rudy demands, and out they drag the old man. "Allow me to introduce myself. I'm Rudy and this is my associate, Clark. We are the proprietors of the prestigious 'Two Guys With Books' English language school here in Cancún. I've noticed that your staff doesn't speak much English. Have you ever considered hiring an English tutor for your employees?"

"*¿Que?*" the old man responds, understanding not a word Rudy says.

"Well today is your lucky day—" and on he goes until he wears the manager down and gets us a room for eight hundred a month plus four hours of tutoring per week for his employees. We pay for a month in advance and have a roof over our heads, a home in Cancún! And we've nearly exhausted Rudy's windfall, are again near broke.

"Damn," Rudy says, surveying the small room, the two beds. "We went from a house on the beach where we each had our own room and bath, to this? *And* we're paying more for it!?"

"At least we have shelter from the rain," I say, looking out at the deluge which shows no sign of letting up. We transfer our stuff from the Combi to the Colonial, get a couple *caguamas*, and relax in our new room, watching the walls close in as the rain drums all night on windows.

Tuesday I meet up with Rudy after his morning Subway class. We set out with a couple of textbooks for props and with a combined sixteen months experience teaching English as a second language. I follow Rudy as he marches into hotels and restaurants and demands, with as much authority and as little desperation as possible, to speak with *el gerente*, the manager. If we should actually locate someone who admits to being in charge of said establishment and of overseeing said employees, Rudy turns it on. "Allow me to introduce myself, I'm Rudy, this is my associate Clark and we are teachers of English."

"As we all know, recent North American trade agreements have dramatically increased international business dealings on both sides of the border. With this in mind, let me ask you—what is the key to good negotiations, if not the key to good life?" (Pause here for victim to ponder whether or not this is a rhetorical question. When he/she opens his/her mouth to reply, continue.) "Why it's communication, of course. Good communication is the key to everything, especially business. So tell me this, how can we communicate if we don't speak the same language? We can't, obviously. So in the interest of improved relations between Mexico, the United States of America, and (clear throat) Canada, we've taken it upon ourselves to travel the length of this vast continent spreading the gospel of English as a second language to as many fortunate peoples as we can."

"After a brief but thorough survey of your primary staff," Rudy continues, "we've determined that, while they're an extremely capable lot, their proficiency in English is insufficient to meet today's business needs. Well is today your lucky day!" At this point he produces a handful of references, résumés, receipts, and recipes (there may even be a parking citation or two in there). "As you can see, we have a long history of experience all across this great country of yours, illuminating the young and old of all vocations in the ways of the English language. So, if you will just give us the opportunity…"

Of course most people don't let Rudy get this far, throw us out as soon as they realize our intent is to sell them something. Many of them don't even speak enough English to understand his speech, which illustrates his point brilliantly (to me) but gets us nowhere.

I accompany Rudy all morning and quietly observe his pitch. Despite the relentless rejections he won't give this up. "We gotta make this work. It's the only way we're gonna survive." There's a fire in his eyes, his mind focused on this one thing and I know we'll see it through to its end, whatever that end might be.

"Okay, we're gonna split up and we're gonna canvass this backwater," Rudy says. "You do downtown and I'll go finish up in the Hotel Zone. Go into every business you come to, talk to everyone you see. Sell it." I want to object but there's no point. I've never been good at selling anything. It scares me. But we *have* to do this. Our situation is worse than I've admitted to. So here I find myself in Cancún, Mexico, working the streets, battling my fear of rejection, trying to sell not only overpriced boat tours, but my insecure self as well.

I attempt to mimic Rudy's parlance but stumble over my words, hesitate, stutter, make just about all the faux pas you can think of. It's one of the hardest things I've ever done. Generally I'm told that the manager is unavailable and can I come back later. Most of the people I talk to are kind but don't need or want or can't, right now, afford English classes for their staffs.

Along the way I pass the small, run-down Escuela Herrera English language school. Just for the heck of it, I stop in and talk to the director. "Yes, as a matter of fact," Erwin tells me, "I've just lost a teacher. I need someone to teach two classes in the evening, five to six and seven to eight. Can you start Monday?" And just like that I've gotten a job, my own little job! The money ain't much, but it's something. I get a boost from this, even though I have failed utterly to sell anyone on Two Guys With Books.

There's one more business at the end of the block, a white-tablecloth seafood restaurant, Hipocampo. They're not yet open, but the staff is inside setting up for dinner. Ricardo, the owner, will see me. After a long day of this I expect nothing and simply lay it out for him. "I'm an English teacher and—"

"Can you start next week?" he interrupts.

"Huh?"

"You can teach a class for *mis empleados*, in the morning?"

"I'll have to check my availability, but I think I can work you into the schedule."

"*Bueno*. It will be good for my staff. Most of my business is with the gringos." He smiles. "*Los Mexicanos* no can afford *theese* place. Come by next week. We work out a deal."

*   *   *

Monday afternoon Rudy and I go down to meet with Ricardo. He's busily gearing up for the dinner rush, asks us to come back in a couple days.

"That guy's wasting our time," Rudy says.

"I don't know. I've got a feeling about this place."

"It's probably your stomach, starting to digest itself," Rudy says. "We gotta eat. Have you got any money?"

"No."

"I got one and a half pesos."

"I got three," I say.

"That's it?"

I nod my head.

"So if we spend this we'll be completely broke."

"*Si.*"

"Let's get some bread."

We go to Supermercado San Francisco and get a couple of rolls, *bolillos*. We're so hungry we eat them right then and there, standing in the supermarket aisle. We get four more, an apple, a small chunk of cheese, and go to the check stand. Our total comes to five pesos. Rudy puts down the four and a half we have. The checkout girl looks at him. Rudy shrugs. She shrugs, hands us our bag of groceries.

"So that's it," Rudy says. We stand in front of the supermarket with our bag of food.

"That is it," I say. "We are completely, absolutely, one hundred percent, broke."

"I always wondered what this would feel like."

We stand in the sun attempting to determine what it feels like to have a loaf of bread and absolutely no money and no idea of where our next meal is coming from. We laugh deliriously in the freedom of having nothing left to loose.

I start my teaching at Escuela Herrera and it goes okay. The classroom is tiny but there are only a handful of students in each session. They're not used to speaking in class, only to being spoken at. I'll change that. There's a new sheriff in town.

After classes Wednesday, I check in with Erwin, tell him the classes are going fine.

"*Bien, bien,*" he says. "Anything else?"

"Yeah," I say. "When do I get paid?"

"At the end of the month."

"This is the end of the month."

"The end of the next month," he says, "after you teach."

"I may have starved to death by then."

"Here." He reaches into his pocket, pulls out some coins, offers them to me.

"Three pesos?" I say. "How generous."

"I'll deduct it from your first paycheck."

Thirty-Eight

Thursday is a day in which I have nothing—no plans, no prospects, no hope. There's no food to fuel me, no gas to move me. All I have is the hunger in my belly, the ink in my pen, and the desire to get through the day. At least we have shelter. I shower and walk out into the Cancún sunshine, walk into what is to become the best day of my life.

I'm hungry, but to eat I need money, and to get money I need work. So it's back to hawking Two Guys With Books. But as I'm walking up Avenida Tulum, before I even get the opportunity to be rejected, I'm stopped by one of the women in the sidewalk kiosks who recruits victims for timeshare presentations. In the past couple weeks I've heard many of these spiels, all of them trying to rope me into attending various sales pitches. Once I told them all I'm broke and living on the beach they stopped harassing me.

I'd talked with this woman, Rocio, the week before. She knows I'm not in the required income bracket for the timeshare pitch but asks if I'll go anyway, "as a favor to me. I get a commission for everyone I send in, whether you sign-up or not."

"I see. And what's in it for me?" I ask.

"You get a free breakfast from the all-you-can-eat buffet, free cocktails—"

"All I can drink?"

"Within reason. You also get a fifty peso coupon good at fine restaurants all over town."

"All I have to do is sit through a presentation?"

"It *is* a hard sell but yeah, that's it."

"You had me at 'free breakfast.'"

"Good, then let me tell you about yourself—"

"About myself?"

"You're thirty-one years old—"

"Thirty-one! I don't look—"

"You live in San Francisco—"

"Can we say Seattle—I've always wanted to be from Seattle."

"You're single and work in computers. You vacation twice a year, usually somewhere tropical, with a beach. Here," she hands me the form she's been filling out, "give this to your escort."

"When is this presentation?" I ask.

"Right now," she says, shoving me into the back of a waiting cab and throwing some pesos to the driver. "And please act like a wealthy tourist. Don't tell them you're broke and living on the beach or they'll think I'm not doing my job." She slams the cab door on me.

"We're not living on the beach anymore," I say through the open window, but the cab has already pulled away from the curb. "We've got a room now."

The cab dumps me in the Hotel Zone in front of a low, windowless building marked "Club Lagoon." I enter the sparse lobby, give my codified profile to the receptionist.

"Good morning, Rudy." (You didn't expect me to use my real name did you?) She presses a button on her console. "Ginny here will give you a tour of the facility."

"Ginny?" I ask, seeing no one else. A curvaceous blonde drifts out of the shadows.

"Good morning," she says, taking my stat sheet from the receptionist, "Rudy."

"If you'll come with me..." She leads me out a side door and through a tunnel into the attached resort. Spewing forth a laundry list of features and attributes (accentuated with florid adjectives monotonously delivered) she drags me past the pool and jacuzzi, through the spa and restaurant, upstairs to one of the "beautifully appointed rooms."

"They all have balconies with ocean views and are available in a number of different floor plans," she says, "from one to four bedrooms. Each unit is self-contained with a full kitchen, bathrooms, and fireplace." She indicates each with a gesture. "It's like your own private condo but with all the amenities of a hotel including room service and a cleaning service." She turns and faces me. "If there are no further questions—"

"I was told about a free breakfast..."

Food, food, food...

"—then we shall proceed to the presentation."

"You mean this wasn't it?"

She leads me on, back through the maze and into a large room buzzing with people. "Why don't you help yourself to the buffet. When you're done eating, someone will attend to you."

The room is pressurized with air conditioning and anesthesia. The rear wall is plate glass looking out on the beautiful beach. There's a breakfast buffet set up across the back. Large, round tables fill the room. I make my way to the food and, not having eaten in days, fill a plate with cheese omelet, sausages, hash browns, toast and jam, fresh mango, papaya, *piña*, a cup of decent coffee.

At each of the tables there is huddled a young, white couple murmuring with a slick *chilango* who sifts through papers, yakking ceaselessly. I find an empty table in a corner with a view of the ocean, and set down my plate. *Maybe I can just eat and then slip out of here without being noticed—*

"*¿Señor?*" Someone has snuck up behind me.

"Hmmm?" I turn. There stands a waiter, holding a tray.

"Can I get you something to drink? Orange juice?"

"A margarita would be great, thank you. Better make it two, I'm thirsty."

I finish the plate and no one's yet approached me. *Dare I get more food? Or should I use this opportunity to escape?*

"*¿Señor?* Another margarita?"

"Yes. Please keep them coming." *Can't leave now, I've got another drink on the way. Might as well get more food.*

I'm into my third plate when somebody comes and sits at my table. "Rudy?" He peruses my file and proceeds to confirm my age, marital status, occupation, penis length, vacation preferences, etcetera, filling in the details of my fictitious life, all of which I grunt affirmatively to, around mouthfuls of pancake and jam. I realize now why Rocio had briefed me so thoroughly. But this is fun. There's nothing "hard" about it. I must keep in mind, however, that I'm playing a role, pulling a scam, performing for my meal.

"Thank you, Rudy." He gets up to leave. *What—that's it? Nobody's tried to sell me anything.* "Margaret will be right with you."

Margaret's got a bone-breaking handshake and a smile that blinds. "Before we start, can I get you anything?"

"Ummmaah—"

"Another margarita maybe?"

"Double," I say. She snaps her fingers and it appears before me.

"Are you enjoying your vacation?"

"It's pretty good but it sure rains here a lot."

"I see you're from Seattle, one of my favorite cities."

"Have you been?"

"Let me tell you about our timeshare program..." and on she goes, repeating the list of amenities, luxuries, and options available to me as a member. I keep my hands and comments under the table, giving her an occasional *hmmm* or *ahhh*, straw sucking at empty glass like a Hoover between icebergs.

"It sounds nice, but like I said, it sure rains here a lot. I don't know if I'd want to come back here every year."

"Oh, you're not limited to Cancún. You can use your timeshare at over fifty billion resorts worldwide."

Oh.

She starts adding up numbers, gives me a figure.

"That's a little over my vacation budget—"

"Hmmm...," she hums, perusing my growing file. "Let me assure you, Rudy, it's well within your budget."

"What exactly is my income?"

"I'm willing, if you act now, to give you three weeks of timeshare vacation per year for the price of one."

"You know, I don't think I'm interested right now but thank—"

"Can you wait here a moment? I'm going to get my supervisor."

"Your super— What have I done?" *This may be the moment to escape.* My eyes scan the scene, past the peopled disks levitating about the room. Sumo wrestlers have moved into position at each of the exits, arms crossed on chests. They've got every escape guarded, every loophole sewn up.

"This is Rudy." Margaret has returned with a woman who breaks the rest of the bones in my hand.

"What seems to be the problem?" she asks.

"Problem?" I say. "There's no problem. I'm just not—"

"Sir, you can't let this opportunity pass you by." And she's right, you know. If you look at the number of Caribbean vacations my character takes per year, add to that my income and compound it with the embellishments I've given over breakfast and margaritas—there really is no reason why I shouldn't buy in.

"You *have* to take us up on this offer."

Actually no, I don't. I'm broke and living on the beach (no, no, no, you've got a room now) and I won't stand for this indignity. I rise and throw my napkin down.

"Thank you very much," I say. "But I've heard your offer and I'm not interested."

"I don't believe this," the woman says. "Nobody turns us down."

"I just did."

"Margaret will show you out."

Margaret indicates a side door.

"What about my free dinner?" I ask. The nameless supervisor exhales heavily, opens her folder, tears out a coupon and holds it to me. I latch onto it but she doesn't let go.

"All I ask," she leans in, "is that you leave a tip for the waiter. It's the *least* you can do." She releases my free dinner.

I reach into my pocket, feel around and—lo and behold—besides sand there's coins in there, money! *Where did that come from?* It's only three pesos (and I'll need two of those for the bus downtown). I pull one out, flip it in the air and slap it on the table. With that, she nods to the Sumo wrestler guarding the exit. He steps aside and I stride out into the heat of the Cancún morning, buzzed immensely, stomach full, and two pesos rubbing against one another in my pocket. I walk onto Playa Chac Mool thinking, *it sure would be nice to keep this buzz going.*

"Help! *Help me!*" a deep voice shouts from up the beach. "Help!" It's coming from the shadows under a *palapa* bar. I make my way over. "Get over here, I need help." There sits a heavyset black man with graying hair, straw hat and aloha shirt, waving a bottle of tequila.

"Are you okay?" I ask.

"No I am not okay," he demands. "I need help with this, god dammit. I'm outta here in a little while and I gotta finish off this liquor. I figure I'd come down here to the beach and give it away. But—shit, I don't know what's wrong with people these days. See them kids down there, the ones kickin' the ball?"

"Yeah."

"They from Ohio, just graduated high school. I offer them some free beers," he indicates the cooler beside him, "and they didn't wanna give me the time o' day. I had to drink them myself. Shit. *Fuck* them. *You'll* have a drink with me. Don't even think about sayin' no."

"I guess it's yes, then." I pull a chair to his table, a table covered with empty beer bottles, squeezed-out lime wedges, and spilt tequila. He looks me up and down.

"Say, you ain't by any chance Clark, are you?"

Someone knows your name.

"You *must* be Clark, god damn, I knew it. Name's Cheyenne. It is a pleasure sir, to make your esteemed acquaintance."

"How do you know my name?"

"Awww, I met your friend Rudy here on the beach yesterday. He told me all about it. Told me to keep an eye out for a guy like you, wanderin' the beach with a fucked-up haircut and a crazy Hawaiian shirt. And here you are."

"Fucked-up haircut?"

"Rudy, he's a diamond in the rough, that boy. *He* drank with me, yes sir. And you know, I was just sayin' a myself, 'God damn, where is that Rudy, where is that boy when I need him. *He'd* drink with me.' That was when I seen you walkin' up the beach and called you over. Here, *you* need a drink." He twists in his seat, towards the bar behind him. "Yo, my man," he calls to the bartender. "Can we git another glass and some more Squirt? And yo, get the brother some ice." The bartender is promptly upon us, opening Cheyenne's beers, pouring his tequila.

"Thanks, Max." He slips the barkeep a twenty. "Yes, sir, I been out here all week, soakin' it up. But all good things must end, huh? I got to get me on a plane in a couple hours, get my black ass home. That's why I'm out here trying to finish off this tequila."

"Looks like you're ready for takeoff." I say.

"You know, from what Rudy told me, it sounds like you boys've got the right idea," Cheyenne says. "I gotta lot of respect for y'all, travelin' around like this." He gazes out over the Caribbean, speaks to the waves rolling one on top of another onto the beach. "I was in Europe when I mustered out of the Navy. And I thought about takin' my duffel and just travelin' 'round the continent a few months. I thought about it long and hard. But in the end, well, I ended up gettin' back on that boat and comin' stateside."

"But y'know, I've always regretted that. I've always regretted that I didn't stay there and hop around Europe for a while." He looks out to sea. "I'd like to think you boys are doin' it for me." He raises his head. "C'mon now, have another drink." He refills our glasses. "Yeah, you boys have figured out how to live, all right. You got something most people don't— courage." Cheyenne slaps his hand on the table. "Now I gotta go get on that plane." He stands, wobbles. "I want to wish y'all the best of luck. Why don't you take the rest of this tequila. And you give my greetings to that Rudy. He sure is good people—a diamond in the rough, that boy."

I spend the rest of the afternoon on the beach, swimming and sunning, getting to know the bartender and lifeguard, then walk to the Boulevard to catch the bus. While I'm waiting, up pulls the gray Combi, Rudy at the wheel. I climb aboard.

"I was gonna keep going," Rudy says. "But I saw you had tequila." He puts out his hand.

"Nice." I pass him the bottle.

"Good news, Clark." Rudy takes a swig. "I got us another account—Lorenzillo's, that fancy-ass seafood place on the lagoon."

"Good job."

"I couldn't get an advance though." He hands me the bottle. "What have you been doing?"

"I went to one of those timeshare presentations this morning."

"How was that?"

"It was a lot of work for a free breakfast."

"You had a free breakfast this morning and you didn't—"

"Of course I brought you something." I produce the napkin-wrapped strips of bacon, bagel with cream cheese, the orange I smuggled out for him.

"I don't care what they say." Rudy takes the food. "You're all right Clark."

"I've got to go teach at Herrera right now. Do you want to meet me at Hipocampo tonight to talk to that guy?"

"Clark, that restaurant's a dead end."

"We've got to pursue every lead. You said so yourself."

"All right."

"I met your friend Cheyenne on the beach."

"No shit."

"That's where the tequila came from."

"What a character that guy is, huh?"

"He sends his greetings," I say. "He was on his way out of town."

"The world should have more Cheyennes."

Halfway through my second class at Herrera I stop and survey my students. They're glad to have this opportunity and eager to learn, but they're bored to death with these lessons the school has provided. After a moment of silence, I toss the text out the open window and shift gears. "We're going to do some role playing now." And the classroom comes alive. And it hits me, this is what it's about, this is what I signed on for, the teaching, educating, the light in a student's face when they make a connection. I can't lose sight of that.

I leave the class lighthearted, meet Rudy at Hipocampo. Ricardo sits down with us and we hammer out a deal. I'm going to teach a class for his employees every morning from eight to nine.

"I would like you start Monday," Ricardo says.

"You know we require a fifty percent deposit," Rudy says. "Five hundred pesos."

"Sure, sure," Ricardo says. "Come by Sunday—I pay you then." We shake on it.

"You want something?" Ricardo asks, spreading his arms. "*Una cerveza?* I tell you what—I send out some food." Rudy and I shrug at one another. *¿Porque no?*

A waiter brings us a couple Dos Equis, some nachos, salsa, guacamole, more beers, quesadillas, fajitas, enchiladas, *camarones*, more beers. Our eyes bulge as each steaming plate is carried out and set before us.

Hours later, satiated and oh so happy, we stroll up Tulum towards the Colonial, our home.

"You know what?" I say. "This was the best day of my life."

"It was a good day," Rudy says. "We had a great meal, free beers, tequila. We've got some decent job prospects, a roof over our heads, and we're completely broke. The only thing that could top this off is if someone were to hand us a big fat joint right now."

"*Oye Clark*," says a passing *hombre*. "*¿Que onda?*" It's the lifeguard I hung out with at the beach all afternoon. "You need some *mota?*"

"Yeah. But we're broke right now."

"*No hay problema*," he says, slipping a bag of herb into my hand. "Pay me when you can. *Adios!*"

"Who the hell was that?" Rudy asks.

"Joel, the *salvavida* from the beach."

"He's a life saver all right."

Thirty-Nine

*W**here the fuck am I?* Somewhere in June, in Mexico. Yeah, living in Mexico—can't forget that. I've got to appreciate it now 'cause in a few weeks or months I'll be back in the U.S. of A. goin' *fuck, what am I doin' here? It was so much better in Mexico.* And I do, I do appreciate this, here, now, more than you'll ever know.

It's almost midnight, Sunday. I write in the dim light of our hotel room. Rudy drifts off to sleep in the other bed. A silhouette moves past our pebbled-glass window. A sudden pounding on the door bolts Rudy upright. "*Policia! Abre la puerta,*" comes a muffled demand through the door. Rudy leaps out of bed, but I recognize the voice.

Reynaldo shuffles in red-eyed, smelling of tequila. "*¿Que onda,* man? Hey, I just took these five girls out to dinner, these gringas," he says, shuffling past us and into the *baño.* Behind the closed door we can hear him fumbling for the light switch, cursing, giving up, and opening the door for some borrowed light. Then the sound of him peeing in the bowl, across the seat and on the floor as he teeters sideways.

"They were beautiful, man," he continues, zipping, exiting the bathroom, and plopping down on the edge of Rudy's bed. "They booked a snorkeling trip for tomorrow and then asked me where to eat." Reynaldo pulls out a bag of *mota* and sprinkles some liberally into a Zig-Zag. "So I take them to this seafood restaurant, where my cousin is the manager." He rolls the joint, pops it in his mouth, and searches pockets until he locates a lighter. "He give me commission, when I bring people in." Reynaldo snaps the lighter repeatedly—big sparks, but no flame, his face tightening until Rudy lights a match, holds it up for him. Reynaldo inhales, holds in the smoke and whispers. "And the girls, they insist I eat with them, they buy me dinner." He coughs violently, blowing out a cloud. "And you know what we have? Lobsters! Can you believe that, man? I get a free lobster dinner *and* my commission—what a night!" He passes the joint. "How you guys been?"

"We're gettin' by."

"So listen, if you're still interested in making money, I'm taking these five girls, five beautiful girls, snorkeling tomorrow and I could use some help. You guys want to go?"

"I can't," says Rudy. "I got Subway in the morning and Lorenzillo's in the afternoon."

"What about you, Clark?"

"I've got Hipo until nine, and then school at five."

"We're leaving at ten," Reynaldo says. "We ought to be back by three. C'mon Clark—a day on a boat with five beautiful women. And you'll be making some *dinero*. How can you pass this up?"

"I'm there."

"*Orale*. Meet me at the marina at ten o'clock. Just wait until you see them—five cuties from Houston, just graduated high school."

I teach my first class at Restaurante Hipocampo. There are ten men and three women, wait staff and cooks and they're great, friendly, affectionate people, so much camaraderie amongst them. They're always ribbing each other, hugging, and hanging on one another.

"What do you want to learn?" I ask them. "What do you need to know in order to better perform your jobs?"

"Can you teach us how to pick up American women, Clark?"

"Why don't we start with food and work our way up to that, okay? All right. First off I'm going to pretend I'm a tourist who's come here to eat breakfast..."

After class I ride the bus out to the marina. As I arrive at the boat, a taxi pulls up to the end of the pier. Reynaldo gets out of the passenger seat while the five teenage girls unfold themselves from the back. We board the boat—a new, open-bowed, eighteen-foot outboard.

The ride across the Caribbean is smooth. I talk to these young women—America's future, addressing their recently commenced lives. *What are you going to do?* I ask them. *What do you want to accomplish in life, get out of it, put into it,* trying to get a pulse on their dreams, find out where lay their passions. And they all have a plan, but their plans are all the same.

"Marry my boyfriend, have three kids, and live in a big house."

"That's it?"

"Uh-huh. And get a dog. What else is there?" *What else is there?* There's adventure, excitement and danger, pain, suffering and sadness.

There's ennui and cogitation, protest and debate. There's elation, sadness and passion. Where has the fire gone? Where fled the passion from our youth—their whole boring lives planned out for them. Furthermore, where is the *love*? They're the best of friends but the only way they can express it is to antagonize one another, bitch at, and cut each other down. I worry about our world.

"Would you excuse me? I must to speak with the captain." Leaving them to bicker, I go sit by Reynaldo who steers the boat with a smile. "So what, exactly, am I supposed to be doing out here?" I ask him.

"You're already doing it Clark," he says. "Entertain them, challenge them, make them feel comfortable. But you know," he opens the cooler next to him, "we should probably have some beers." He hands me a Corona. "*Muchachas! ¿Quien quieres una cerveza?*" He has me pass beers to the girls, opens a cold one for himself. "That's the second part of your job," Reynaldo says, "drinking beer. The third part is snorkeling. I'll stop when we get to the reef and pass out the gear. You help them put it on and show them how to snorkel."

"Reynaldo," I lean towards him and switch to Spanish. "*Yo nunca esnorkel. No lo conozco.*" This is apparently the funniest thing Reynaldo's ever heard. *I've never snorkeled. I don't know how.* His laughter rocks him back and forth, works itself up to a knee-slapping roar.

"Clark, you know how to swim, right?" Reynaldo cuts the engine and jumps to his feet. "If you look there," he points in the water, "you can see the reef." The girls and I lean over the side of the boat, see nothing. The gear is distributed and I'm on stage. But it's okay; *I am a teacher, right? I can do this.*

"Okay," I say. "The mask goes over your face and tightens with these side straps. But before you put it on, you need to spit in it and wipe the saliva around the clear part."

Reynaldo suppresses laughter.

"That's gross," one of the girls says. "Why do we have to spit in it?"

"Are you questioning the wisdom of the greatest snorkelerer of all time?"

"The what?"

"Didn't you ever watch 'The Undersea World of Jacques Cousteau'? Jacques was always spitting into his mask. And if it wasn't below Jacques Cousteau to spit in his mask, *you're* going to spit in your mask. Is that understood?" I stop and breathe. "Now put it on. Make sure it's sealed around your face. Put this tube-thing in your mouth and jump in."

They don the apparati and splash into the water.

"Stay relaxed and breathe normally," I shout from the stern. "Any questions?" They poke their faces into the water, searching for reef. I turn to Reynaldo. "There really a reef down there?"

"That's what they tell me," Reynaldo shrugs. "Now you'd better get in there Clark. Make sure nobody drowns." I pull the mask over my face, stick tube in mouth, jump in. And inhale a lung full of water. I come up, coughing water out of nose and mouth. Reynaldo, in the boat, laughs hysterically. The girls, with their heads underwater, have missed my performance.

"Maybe I should have the girls teach *you*," Reynaldo chuckles.

Once the girls are engaged with the reef, I swim back to the boat and hang from the side.

"How'd I do, Reynaldo?"

"You're a natural, Clark." He lights a joint. "I wish I'd found you sooner. You are the funniest gringo I ever meet." He leans down, puts the joint in my mouth that I may inhale. "By the way," he says, "that tube thing—that's called the snorkel." This again sets him off laughing.

Their exploration of the reef complete, the girls board boat and we motor out to Isla Mujeres, the Island of Women. Reynaldo takes us ashore, leads us to the market, settles us in one of the food stalls where his "cousin" brings us roasted chicken, rice, and beans.

"Wow, this is really Mexican!" The girls are amazed at the meal.

Reynaldo picks up the tab for lunch. "*A todo inclusivo*," he tells them. "Lunch is free with the tour, especially after that lobster last night." They are delighted. He sends them off to shop the market. Reynaldo and I return to the boat to finish the beer.

"Hey, thanks a lot," I say.

"For what?" he asks.

"For all this—lunch, the beer, the boat trip."

"You're doing me a favor, amigo." Reynaldo reaches into his pocket, extracts his money clip, and peels off a fifty-peso note. "I almost forgot your wages."

"I don't get it," I say. "You don't need me. You could do this by yourself."

"Sometimes it's best not to question a good thing, Clark. Besides, it's nice to have the company. And the entertainment." And he starts to chuckle all over again.

"Where've you been?" I ask Rudy, when he shows up at the hotel Friday evening. He's an hour and a half late in meeting me.

"My students from Lorenzillo's took me to the beach," he says.

"Have they paid you yet?" I ask.

"They bought me beers all afternoon."

"Is that how they're paying you?"

"So far."

"C'mon, let's go down to el Hipo, see if we can't get some money out of Rico."

"That guy's not going to pay us," Rudy says.

"He feeds us."

Besides the thousand advance from Subway—which we promptly squandered on the hotel room—none of our clients have so far "paid" us (in hard currency) for the teaching we've done. Some money has trickled in from various sources, almost enough to squeak by on, but not enough to get us ahead, not enough to propel us out of this place—if and when we decide to depart. We're basically broke, but the universe provides for us. Meals seem to miraculously appear just as we're on the threshold of starvation.

El Hipocampo is hopping. Ricardo is too busy to talk to us but he sends over Salvador, the maitre d' and best student of my morning class. "Ricardo is sorry that he doesn't tonight have the money for you Clark," Salvador rolls his eyes. "But he said to have yourself some dinner and some beers, whatever you want, on the house."

"No kidding."

"Come, I have a good table for you."

We load up on fajitas, prawns, and beer. As we finish the meal, Ricardo comes to our table with a bottle of mezcal.

"Everything—it was okay?" he asks, pouring shots.

"Very good," we say, raising our glasses.

"Do you have the five hundred pesos for us?" Rudy asks.

"I am so sorry. I am a little short this week. If you will come back—"

"If we will come back next week," Rudy says. "Yeah, yeah, yeah, *si, si, si.*"

"Thank you for understanding," Ricardo says.

"Feel free to pour us another shot."

If we're hungry and have a few pesos in our pocket, there are a couple places we frequent that will feed us on the cheap. My favorite is down Avenida Tulum, at the intersection of Uxmal. The sign over the door says "*el Rosticerio del Caribe*" but we call it the "Den of Hungry Men" and it is where we go when we're *hungry.*

The rotisserie is visible in the window of the modest storefront, always chock-full of poultry carcass skewered on spindles and slowly circling.

Beyond the brick oven is a long counter where you pay your pesos and take your plate—a thigh and a breast or a wing and a prayer, beans and rice—and then walk to the rear where it opens into a soaring cinder block temple, quiet but for the low hum of the few fluorescents which stripe the ceiling (but do little to combat the dimness).

Long rows of heavy wooden picnic tables line the hall, two and three men sharing a bench, friends and strangers alike, observing the unspoken vow of silence, eating—jaws unhinging from skulls, their chins shift down and away, swinging across and up in masticatory movement. A fork in one hand, rolled tortilla in the other, arms moving in the arcs, pitching out, down and around to nudge nodes of nourishment, *frijoles* onto fingered fork which swings up and around with a Swiss synchronicity to the opening orifice where dissolves saliva-saturated *pollo con arroz* in gear-meshed maws, teeth turning food into fuel with a sometimes slurp of the included Coca-Cola to ease the passage through alimentary canal.

At the end of my Thursday night classes at Escuela Herrera, Erwin appears, asks to see me in his office.

"You've been doing a great job here, Clark," he tells me from behind his desk. "You've really turned things around. And the students—they have only good things to say about you. But you don't need to come in tomorrow."

"What?"

"Or ever again."

"Why not?"

"The school is bankrupt."

"What does that mean?"

"We have no money," he shrugs.

"So I'm out of a job?" I ask. Again he gives me the shrug. "Am I going to get paid?"

"Come by next week," he says and stands, extending a hand.

Once again I'm broke, hungry, and out of a job. Shuffling home I run into Rocio, working late on the Boulevard. She hooks me into another timeshare presentation. "Free lunch, dinner, and drinks." I'm not in the mood but I owe her. Besides setting me up with free meals at sales presentations, she's taken me out to breakfast and once, when we were really down, she dropped off some groceries at the hotel for us. Here I am, living on *their* streets and the Mexicans are taking care of *me*. Also, I know my attendance at the presentation will get Rocio her commission and help to feed her family. And I'm hungry. "Ten-thirty tomorrow," she says. "The Oasis Resort." She stuffs a twenty-peso note into my pocket. "Be there."

"You must make one hell of a commission."

Having been through the timeshare ordeal before, I'm prepared for the second go-round. The woman who tours me through the place is a sexy and nice *chilanga* who, at the end of the tour, asks me out. But after telling so many lies and stories in my role as the vacationing Rudy, it just wouldn't feel right. And if I copped to the truth or slipped up and my true identity were revealed, it wouldn't look so good for Rocio.

The free lunch is a cheeseburger—a little disappointing, but it is lunch and it is free. I bullshit my way through the sales presentation. I lie. I drink my free drinks. I turn down their offer. I get my coupon for a free dinner and walk out. I'm buzzed, but something is missing.

I walk to the beach, have a good swim, relax on the sand but still the picture is incomplete. I walk to the Boulevard—but what? *Where to go, what to do?* It's four o'clock on a Friday afternoon and I no longer teach in the evenings, have nothing to do for the rest of the day, the rest of the week.

The *real* Rudy—that's the missing element! I haven't seen Rudy all week. And, at this very moment—unless his schedule has, unbeknownst to me, changed—he should be right up the road teaching a class at Restaurante Lorenzillo's. It's only about a mile away. I'm going to walk up and wait for him to finish, see what he's been up to, how he's doing.

Rudy emerges from Lorenzillo's looking beat, smiles when he sees me.

"Hey Buddy!" he says. "What's up?"

"Long time no see," I say. "How you been? You hungry? I've got another coupon for a free dinner."

"I'm starved," Rudy says. "You did another timeshare presentation, huh?"

A couple of right good steaks and baked potatoes put us both in a better frame of mind.

"So what's going on with you?" I ask. "You were in a mood the last time I saw you."

"It's just been getting to me. Ever since we arrived here it's been such an uphill struggle. It was practically a crusade to get jobs and now we're fighting to get paid. I'm worried we're not going to make enough to get us home."

"There's worse places to be stuck," I say. "What's really on your mind?"

"I talked to Virginia this week."

"Yeah?"

"She's coming to Cancún."

"Right on. That's great."

"I don't know, Clark. She's being weird about it."

"What do you mean?"

"She's not sure if she wants to go out with me anymore."

"If she doesn't want to go out with you, then why would she come to Cancún?"

"That's what I'm sayin'. She's coming with her friend Karen. Says it has nothing to do with me. Says it's just a vacation."

"It's just a coincidence that she's vacationing in Cancún," I say, "where her semi-ex-boyfriend lives?"

"According to her, yeah."

"Does she want to make the drive home with us?"

"She says she'll decide when she gets here."

"Do *you* want her to make the drive home with us?"

"At this point Clark, I just don't know."

Forty

After morning class at el Hipo, I go by Escuela Herrera to see if I can collect the money owed me. I don't expect to find anyone there and I'm not disappointed. We're still broke, have so far failed to collect any more money for Two Guys with Books. In the afternoon I meet up with Rudy at the Hotel and he's got a plan, another scheme for free food.

"What's up?"

"What's up?" he says. "Free dinner is what's up."

"You're in a good mood."

"I've stopped caring, Clark."

"Good move."

"We're going to the Krystal."

"That fancy-ass resort on the point?" I say. "What's going on there?"

"I don't know why we didn't discover this earlier Clark, but—get this—every week they throw a T.G.I.F. party, poolside, with live music, free appetizers, and…"

"Free drinks?"

"You got it, my brother."

"Why didn't we find out about this sooner?"

"That's what I'm sayin'."

"Don't you have to be a guest at the hotel to attend?"

"Clark, where there's a will…"

"There's a way," I say. "And where there's free drinks…"

"There's us."

"You said it, my brother."

The Krystal is a right-on scene. We hang by the pool, swimming serenely, nibbling nachos, picking at pizza, imbibing beers, discussing our destitution.

"What we need is to find a wallet," Rudy says, "a big, fat wallet bulging with money and no I.D., no way to return it to anybody."

"That would be nice."

Ask and thou shalt receive.

"Maybe V.'s got money," I venture.

"Don't go there."

"When's she coming?"

"Monday."

"Are you ready?"

Pregnant pause.

"How about another free beer?"

Reynaldo pounding on our door awakens us Saturday morning.

"You guys don't have any plans today, do you?" he asks

"We have big plans for today as a matter of fact," Rudy says. "We're going to go to the beach to swim and drink and lay in the sand and hit on women all day. Why?"

"You can't," Reynaldo says. "I need you to work for me today."

"Sorry, no can do."

"C'mon, there's this new resort, the Oasis. I need you guys to help me work the crowd."

"Oasis?" I say. "I went to a timeshare presentation there."

"It's virgin territory," Reynaldo says. "I'll buy you guys breakfast, get you some beer."

"Let me get this straight," Rudy says. "You're going to take us out to breakfast, buy us beer, and in exchange you want us to hang out at this resort and hit on women?"

"I'm also going to pay you, of course."

"I don't know," Rudy says. "What do you think Clark?"

"I don't work on weekends."

"I tell you what," Reynaldo says, pulling out a joint. "Why don't we smoke this, while you guys think about it."

While Reynaldo and Rudy work the crowd, I sit in the sand and watch the surf, sip *cervezas*, thinking about my life, the journey so far, and its looming conclusion.

The three of us meet by the pool late afternoon. We're all in good moods. Rudy and Reynaldo have generated no business but managed to persuade people to buy them margaritas from the poolside bar all day. It's a tough job, this.

We're preparing to go eat somewhere when a woman's voice comes sailing at us from across the pool. "Rudy! Rudy!" she's yelling.

"Who's that woman yelling at me?" Rudy says. "Do I know her?"

It's the chilanga from that timeshare presentation you attended here.

"I think she's yelling at *me*," I say.

"You?" Rudy says. "She's yelling my name."

"Rudy!"

"I, uh, used your name," I say.

"You used my name?" Rudy says.

She moves around the pool towards us.

"Yeah. You know all those timeshares I've been scamming?"

"Yeah?"

"Well I think we'd better get out of here."

"She looks kind of sexy," Rudy says.

"Now," I say.

We grab the cooler full of empties and the three of us flee the resort, doing an end-out around the hotel to the parking lot and into the Combi, the *chilanga* sprinting after us. I start the engine and back the Combi out of the parking space as the woman approaches, jam it into gear and squeal us onto the boulevard, leaving her standing there empty handed.

"So you've been using my name, huh?" Rudy says.

"You told me never to use my own," I say.

"Yeah, but I didn't tell you to use *mine*."

"It's probably a good thing you guys are leaving town," Reynaldo says, lighting another joint. "But I'm going to miss you."

"Shit," I say, looking in the rearview mirror. "There's a roller behind us."

"Probably that bitch called the cops on you," Reynaldo laughs. "I wouldn't worry about it, we're cool."

"Cool?" Rudy says. "We're loaded, *you* just lit a joint, and Clark here pulled some scam on that place—using my name."

"They're pulling us over." I say.

"Just bribe them, man," Reynaldo says through a cloud of smoke. "You're cool." Two cops get out of the cruiser. One approaches each side of the Combi, hands on their guns, as Rudy and I roll down the windows.

"*Amigos*," the passenger side cop smiles broadly through the window at Rudy and me. "*¿Cómo estan?*"

"*Bien*," says Rudy.

"You don't remember us?" The cop asks and they simultaneously remove their sunglasses. "We talked to you on the beach one night, about a month ago."

"Oh yeah," Rudy perks up. "Yeah—when we were camping on the beach. You gave me twenty pesos. Clark you remember these guys?"

"We recognize your combi is why we pull you over," says the other cop through my window. "So how things are? You working now?"

"We couldn't find work," Rudy says. "So we opened our own school is what we did."

"Your own school?" the passenger cop says. "That's great. Still you sleep on the beach?"

"No, no, we've got a room now," Rudy says.

"I'm glad to hear it."

"Hey, let me get you back," Rudy says, and turns to me. "Clark, you got twenty pesos?" I hand over the crumpled bill Rocio had stuffed in my pocket earlier. "Hey thanks a lot," Rudy says to the cop, handing him the twenty. "*Un mil gracias.*"

"Look at this," the cop says to his partner through the cab of the Combi, "a gringo who pays his debts."

"You guys take care," says the partner. "*Y, di no a las drogas, eh?*"

"*Vaya con dios.*"

"What the hell was that?" Reynaldo says, after a requisite moment of shocked silence.

"That was a Cancún cop," Rudy says, "stopping us to check on our well being. You got a problem with that?"

"No. It's just strange to me," Reynaldo says, "that a cop would pull you over to ask how you're doing. But strange things happen around you guys. I've noticed that."

"You like seafood?" Rudy asks. "I know this nice restaurante downtown, Hipocampo."

"I know that place," Reynaldo says. "*Es muy caro.*"

"Don't sweat it. Dinner's on Clark and me."

Ricardo squeezes his head when we walk into the *restaurante*. "*Ohhhhh*," he moans. "I am so sorry. Still I do no have your *dinero*."

"I'm not buying it, Rico," Rudy says. "Are you trying to tell me that all these people in here are eating for free, that you make no money?"

"Next Wednesday, after class I will have it for you. Today, you eat." He sits us down at the best in the house, sends over a round of *cervezas*.

"You guys really got some clout in this town," Reynaldo says. "You got the cops in your pocket, you squeeze the local businesses for protection—"

"We've probably eaten more here in food," I say, "than he owes us in *dinero*."

"Yeah," Rudy says. "But the Combi doesn't run on rice and beans."

Forty-One

R udy is up and out early Monday, gone to the airport to get the girls. He appears at the end of my morning class at el Hipo—alone.
"What happened?" I ask. "Didn't they show up?"

"Can I get a cup of coffee?" he asks my gathered students, who observe our conversation as if it is a play for their benefit. "And a tequila?"

Salvador brings us coffees and tequilas.

"They showed up, all right," Rudy says. "As soon as they got off the plane Virginia informed me they'd made a pact. 'This is girl's week,' she said. They've got a *toto inclusivo* package at one of those fancy-ass resorts in the Hotel Zone. 'I'll see you at the end of the week,' she said, 'when Karen gets back on the plane to fly home.'"

"She doesn't even want to *see* you this week?"

"Yeah, and get this—she said she'll think about whether or not she's going to make the road trip home with us."

"Isn't that for us to decide?"

"As far as I'm concerned," Rudy says. "She's got a return ticket on the plane and at this point I'd say she'll be using it."

"She thinks she can put you off for a week and then—"

"Us, she's putting *us* off Clark, for a week."

"Then she thinks she can come around and everything will be peachy? That ain't right."

"You're tellin' me Clark. They wouldn't even let me drive them in from the airport. They took the god damn shuttle bus from their fancy-ass resort. It was part of their 'package deal.'"

"Package deal?" I say. "I'll give them a package deal."

"We gotta start planning our departure," Rudy says, "without regards to Virginia. And the sooner we leave the better."

"All right," I say. "I've got two more weeks here at Hipo—"

"I'm thinkin' we should get out of here next weekend," Rudy says. "We need to cut our losses and go."

I think about this for a moment.

"Okay," I say. "Then we need to do some accounting, make some collections."

"Right. How much have you got?"

"Me? Nothing."

"Same with me. The guys at Lorenzillo's owe me a thousand."

"And Ricardo here owes me a thousand, but we can't count on that."

"All the more reason to cut class short."

"Oh no," says Salvador, who's been eavesdropping. "He is going to pay. Wednesday, he said. Wednesday he is going to have your money."

"Thanks Chava," I say. "But we've heard it before."

"What about that school you were working at?" Rudy asks. "What happened there?"

"Bankrupt. Out of business."

"What did that guy owe you?"

"Three hundred," I say.

"So we're broke, people owe us twenty-three hundred pesos, and we can probably expect to collect about a thousand. That's not nearly enough to get us home."

"Yeah," I say. "And the Combi needs brakes and tires."

"We may have to skip the brakes," Rudy says, "and downshift a lot."

"So we'll have about two or three hundred dollars to get us twenty-five hundred miles across Mexico? That doesn't sound good."

"We still need to find that wallet..."

"Oh I am so sorry Clark," Salvador tells me Wednesday. "We do not have your money."

Strike one.

"No kidding. Tomorrow we're going to have the final. Friday is the last day of class."

"Friday? But we were supposed to have *six* weeks."

"And I was supposed to get paid."

"Okay Friday, *Friday* we will have the money, *sin falta.*"

"Sure you will."

Next I go to Herrera one last time, looking for Erwin. The school is not only closed, but is now boarded up. *Strike two.* However, I walk around the back of the building and there find a woman loading boxes out the back door and into her car.

"*Estoy buscando para Erwin*," I say. I'm looking for Erwin. "*¿Conoces?*"

"*Si*," she says. "Erwin *es mi* bro-*there*."

"Do you know where I might find him?" I ask.

"*Claro que si*. He *es* leaving on *mi* couch."

"And where, might I ask, is your couch?"

Rudy's been experiencing his own slump. Every day he's attempted to get together with Virginia, or at least talk to her, and she has rebuked him at every turn, insisting he wait until the end of "Girl's Week." It's worn him. At this point, there's no way I want her along for the ride home. Poor Rudy—the woman he loves toys with him like a puppet on a string. It's painful to watch. Logic dictates that we leave her behind, but love is led by other laws.

Friday I show up for the final class at Hipocampo with a bottle of Kahlúa and a box of doughnuts. Someone mixes us all Kahlúa and coffees. I raise mine in a toast. "I don't care that your boss hasn't paid me," I tell my students. "I know it's not your fault. You've been a great class and today I'm going to teach you how to get American women into bed."

"But Clark," Salvador says, "we have your money."

"*¿Que?*"

"We have your money." He hands me an envelope full of cash—one thousand pesos.

"Good news," I meet up with Rudy at the Colonial, show him the wad of cash.

"That will help," Rudy says. "Lorenzillo's is gonna pay up today—or so they tell me."

"We can probably afford to get brakes and tires now."

"Let's do it tomorrow," Rudy says. "And then head out of town Sunday."

"Sunday it is."

"Did you have any luck with that school?"

"I ran into the guy's sister and she gave me an address," I say. "I want you to come along in case we have to strong arm anybody."

"It's been a while since I've gotten to strong arm anybody."

"Any word from V.?" I ask.

"Fuck her."

"Okay then."

"It's our last Friday night in Cancún, Clark. You want to hit happy hour at the Krystal?"

"Meet you there after class."

I'm into my third or fourth free drink at the Krystal when, "Clark!" Rudy appears. "Look at this." He pulls out a wad of money.

"Jesus, how much have you got there?"

"Two thousand."

"Where'd you get it?"

"There's a story. But first things first—Barkeep! I need a free drink." Rudy wets his whistle. "So I go to teach the class at Lorenzillo's and I tell them it's going to be the last one, right? And everybody's all broken up and sad that I'm leaving, of course. So we just sit around and bullshit. After a couple hours I get up to leave and they hand me this envelope. 'Here's a thousand pesos,' they say, and I thank them. And then, they hand me another envelope, 'And here is another thousand for the rest of the class,' they say. 'Wait a minute,' I say, 'there aren't going to be any more classes. This was the last class, today. You only owe me one thousand, *nada mas.*' 'It's okay,' they say. 'Take it.' 'But I haven't earned this,' I say. 'I can't take it. You understand that this is the last class, yes?' 'We understand,' they said. 'This is your money. Take it.' Then they walk me to the Combi and say goodbye."

"I was halfway here and didn't feel right about it. So I turned around and went back. These are good people and I didn't want to take advantage of them. So I go in and again try to return the money. 'No I'm sorry,' they tell me. 'That is your money and you need to take it.' 'No,' I said, 'I didn't earn this and I can't take it.' 'The money is yours,' they tell me. 'We collected it for you and we talked about it and nobody wants their money back, even if there's going to be no more classes. And if you don't take it we are going to throw you into the lagoon with the *cocodrillos.* Now take the god damn money and get out of here.'"

"That's a lucky break for us."

"Luck?" Rudy says. "Don't you know what this is Clark? It's the wallet I asked the universe for—the no-strings-attached wad of money we needed in order to get home." (*Ask and thou shalt receive.*) "It's our karmic payback, you asshole."

"Payback for what?" I ask.

"For all the shit we've gone through the past couple months. For all the suffering we've suffered through to get here."

"You believe in that stuff?" I ask.

"I learned it from you," he says.

Forty-Two

e awaken Saturday morning on the beach at Puerto Juárez, still drunk from the night before and unsure of how we got here, just like the good ol' days. There's a mechanic right there by the ferry terminal.

"Why don't we drop the Combi off to get brakes and tires," Rudy says. "And then take the ferry over to Bitch Island for the day."

"A little bitter, are we?"

"We can rent a couple bikes, get some exercise."

"Yeah, and you can burn off some of that anxiety."

"What anxiety?"

On Isla Mujeres we wander through the market at the north end of the island, then rent a couple bikes and ride like wild men down the coast, slicing through the heat, burning through the tension and desperation, sweating out all the frustration and apprehension (and much of the LSD, THC, and C2H5OH) that has stockpiled in our fatty cells over the past few months. We ride all the way out to the southern tip of the island, swim it off our skin and then sit back on the beach, staring across expanse of ocean.

"V.'s agreed to see us tonight," Rudy breaks the silence, "on our last night in town."

"How gracious of her. What do you think about her going with us on the trip home?"

"Here's the thing, Clark. I'm really pissed off at her right now and feeling really hurt. But—if she doesn't go with us I'm going to be heartbroken. And that's a long trip to make with a broken heart."

"Not to mention your mood," I mutter.

"What's that?"

"I said 'right on dude,' I know how it is."

"Anyway, we'll have to see how she is tonight, and make a decision before sun up."

We get back to the mainland and pick up the Combi.

"How shall we spend our last afternoon in Cancún?" Rudy says.

"We've got to pack the Combi. And pay a visit to Erwin."

"Who?"

"The director of the school that screwed me."

"Is it worth the bother?" Rudy says. "We've got enough money to get us home."

"It's the principle of the matter," I say. "He owes me money for the work I performed, and I damn well intend to collect it."

"All right, Clark. It might be worth it just for the chance to work someone over."

"What have we got for a weapon in here..." Rudy searches the Combi as we drive across town, comes up with the *banderillas* we've been carrying around since that bullfight in Guadalajara. I find the house and bang on the door until it opens. Rudy stands behind me with the harpoons. Erwin looks haggard in a wife-beater and boxers when he opens the door, is shocked to see me. *Good.*

"I'm here for the money you owe me, two hundred eighty-eight pesos."

"I don't have it." Erwin looks scared.

"Rudy," I say over my shoulder. "Put the hurt on him." Rudy advances.

"Wait, wait, wait." Erwin backs away from the bloodstained *banderillas*. "Don't do that. Maybe we can trade. Come." We follow him around the side of the house to a shed. He opens a massive freezer. "Take all you want," Erwin says.

"What is it?" I ask.

"*Jamón.*"

"You want to pay me with frozen meat?"

"It's all I have. Please, I'm just a poor Mexican."

"Save it," Rudy says, brandishing his weapons.

"All right," I say. "Let's load up."

"What?" says Rudy.

"Meat, grab some meat, put it in the Combi. You too, Erwin. Load it up."

"So tell me Clark," Rudy says as we drive back to our hotel. "We're about to load all our worldly possessions into this Volkswagen bus and then drive twenty-five hundred miles across Mexico to San Francisco. What, exactly, are we going to do with twenty-five pounds of frozen ham?"

"Oh I think we made out better than that," I say. "I think we've got close to forty pounds back there."

"You're missing the point Clark. We haven't got a freezer and there's no way we can eat that much meat before we leave town in the morning."

"I think *you're* missing the point, Rudy. The point was to put the hurt on that bastard. It was a symbolic act. That was retribution against all the bastards who wronged us in this town."

"So what are we going to do with the meat—just throw it out?"

"Of course not," I say. "We're going to give it to all the kind people who helped us out here."

"Like who?"

"Like Rocio, she's got a family to feed, Reynaldo, the staff of the Colonial, the cops who showed us kindness, the guy who gave us dope, and those who gave us hope."

"Jesus Christ Clark, you're like the Robin Hood of frozen ham."

"And I don't even like pork."

After distributing the meat and saying goodbye, we clean the hell out of el Tiburón, wash her windows, shine her hubcaps. Rudy takes a bus out to the Hotel Zone to meet Virginia. I'm left to pack up and move our belongings out of room #23 of the Hotel Colonial, our home for lo these many weeks. I finish and we're done, ready to go, ready to leave this place and head back into our lives. I drive out to join Rudy and the girls, our last night in Cancún.

I find Rudy alone at the lobby bar of the girls' hotel, his head in his hands.

"All I want is a little time to talk with Virginia—alone," says Rudy. "I just want to find out what's going on, where she's coming from."

"So what's the problem?"

"It's her friend Karen—she won't leave V.'s side. Every time we start talking, Karen buts in."

"She's probably a lesbian," I offer. "Or a vegan."

"That's not helping, Clark."

"All we gotta do is separate them," I say. "I'll distract Karen while you whisk V. away somewhere private to talk."

"They're going to meet us in the hotel restaurant at eight," Rudy says.

"It's too exposed to do a smash and grab there," I say. "We'll have to get them in the bar after dinner whence the inebriated crowd will obscure our actions."

"Sounds like a plan," says Rudy. "Even though I don't know what you're talking about."

"You just keep an eye on me. When I've distracted Karen I'll shout 'stack of meat.' That's the signal for you to hustle V. out of here. You can take her through the back door and drag her somewhere down the beach to have your little chat."

"How are you going to distract Karen?"

"Tequila and charm, my brother—no woman can resist that combo."

"You're a pal, Clark."

"We need to synchronize our watches."

"I don't have a watch."

"Me either. Barkeep! *¿Que hora es?*"

"*Seis y media,*" the bartender says.

"We've got an hour and a half until we meet them," I say. "What'll we do until then?"

"Four Dos Equis," Rudy orders from the bartender. "And two shots of tequila. Same for you Clark?"

Virginia and Karen finally appear, without apologies, at nine-thirty— an hour and a half late. It's good to see Virginia, but I immediately pick up on the strange vibe from Karen. Everything goes according to plan. We have dinner—with Karen interrupting nearly everything Rudy or I say. Then we get them into the crowded bar, wedge our way up to the rail.

"You want a what?" I yell over the crowded commotion to Karen.

"A Tanqueray and tonic with a twist of lemon, a squeeze of lime, and an olive," she shouts.

"You'd better explain that to the bartender yourself," I say. "It's too much for me to remember." I step back so she can squeeze up to the bar. While she orders her cocktail I turn to Rudy behind me.

"Stack of meat," I say.

"No thanks," he says. "I'm stuffed."

"No," I say. "Stack of meat."

"Oh right," he says, grabbing Virginia by the wrist. "C'mon." And he drags her away. I step up behind Karen, put my hands on the bar—one on either side of her.

"What are you doing?" she says, struggling to turn around in the corral. "Move," she demands. We stand face to face. I tighten my grip on the edge of the bar. "Hey where did they—will you get out of my way?!"

"I know you like me," I say.

Two hours pass before Virginia and Rudy return to the bar, smiling expansively. Virginia comes up and throws her arms around my neck. "Oh Clark I love you," she says, and quickly steps back. "Your shirt's all wet."

"Yeah."

"Where's Karen?"

"She got upset about something and went to the room."

"I better go check on her," says V. "I told Rudy you guys are welcome to stay in our room tonight." She kisses me, kisses Rudy, and goes.

"Way to go champ," Rudy says. "What's on your shirt?"

"That is a—let me think... That is a Tanqueray and tonic with a twist of lemon, a squeeze of lime, and an olive. It's two of them in fact."

"Someone actually drinks that concoction?"

"Not that I've witnessed," I say. "So what happened?"

"Everything's cool," Rudy says. "We're good. I don't know what the hell was wrong with her all week. But she's fine now—sweet and affectionate. She's her old self again."

"It's that Karen. She cast a spell on V. I think she's a black witch, maybe a lesbian, and quite possibly a vegetarian."

"Anyway Clark, you have the final say. But it's okay with me if Virginia goes with us on the road trip home."

"If it's okay with you," I say, "it's okay with me."

"That's it then. We leave Cancún in the morning, with V."

"With V." I say. "We head home. Do you think it's okay for us to stay in their room tonight?"

"Sure," says Rudy. "But I've got the feeling you may be sleeping in the bathtub."

Sunday I'm up and gone early from the room, before anyone wakes. I take up residence at the lobby bar before dawn, force the night manager to conjure a flow of Bloody Marys while I write. *Why the fuck not?* It's my last morning here and I might as well leave it the way I lived it.

We drive Karen to the airport to catch her flight home.

"Now Virginia," I say, "you're sure you want to go with us? You sure you can handle it? It's going to be a long journey home."

"Handle you guys?" she says. "No problem."

Rudy, Virginia, and I walk back to the Combi.

"Here Clark," Rudy hands me an envelope. "Put that somewhere safe. It's the last fifty hits of acid."

"Don't worry," I say. "I'll put it somewhere safe."

We board el Tiburón del Tierra and go, leave this town.

We did it. We *pinche* did it.

Part Six

Going Home

Forty-Three

W e shoot south down the coast for Playa del Carmen, a few hours distant, Rudy driving, Virginia riding shotgun, and me bouncing around in the back of the beast. Being on the road again together melts away our tensions and apprehensions, wears down the walls between us and again we're a trio, a triumvirate, a triad, the three of us coming together as a team.

I start to drift. V. feeds me ham sandwiches to ground me, but already I can hear the distant ringing of a bell. *Maybe I should take some LSD to regain that edge, maintain the celestial balance. The acid—where is it? Oh yeah, I have it right here. Rudy gave it to me for safekeeping...*

There's something about being on the road with this crew, the conviviality enclosed in this crucible of Combi, the openness of the land and the motion of the drive, which opens us. Once open, the jostling, jerking, and jolting of tires jumping through potholes, jars junk loose, takes me into memories of road trips past, reveals rememberings of those station wagon stories of my childhood, those formative years when the World was impressed upon me, body and soul.

My Discovery of America
A Station Wagon Story

The Year Was 1972. I was five going on six. We were on a family vacation back to Michigan, our second summer after moving to California. And the car (I'll never forget it) was a 1969 Chevrolet Impala station wagon, metallic green in color. Back then it was a just a wagon, but today it's revered as a classic, a work of art.

This car deserved the name Impala. She had a nimble V-8, as all American cars did back then. And talk about style! She had a grill that snarled and fenders that flowed—long, smooth, sculpted fenders that begged one to press cheek against. Inside, her control panel contained but one gauge, and what a gauge it was—a speedometer which spanned the width of the dashboard in front of the driver. Its fluorescent orange needle had to make quite a journey—sliding slowly from the left of the wheel over to the right—as the sleek machine got up to speed, her gauge topping out at a whopping one hundred twenty miles per hour.

Yes siree, the only variable one need monitor back in the summer of 1972 was the speed of one's travel—oh, and the distance covered—how far and how fast, nothing else mattered. "The Godfather" was number one at the box office, "The Joy of Sex" had just hit bookstores, and all across the AM dial, Don McLean was driving his own Chevy out to the levee.

Apollo 16 had just returned from a successful trip to the moon, Richard Nixon had just returned from a successful trip to the U.S.S.R., and five men arrested for a "third-rate burglary" at the Watergate complex had yet to be linked to the C.I.A., the Republican National Committee, or the President. There were no concerns of fuel economy or air pollution, just time and space baby—how far and how fast. These were heady times in America.

The hum of tires across asphalt hypnotized me as we rode that beautiful beast across North America and back, my bare legs stuck to the black vinyl of the back seat where I was forever wedged betwixt older brother and sister. I was always told where we were going, but instead of the stated destination, my ears locked only on the word *GO*. For it is not the places we visited that have stayed with me but the *movement*, the motion— it was this rolling across America that forged my character. To be in the car and moving, that was the thing!

When I did, on those rare occasions, succeed in securing a window seat, the glass was immediately cranked down (and car windows rolled *all the way down* back then). I'd stealthily wriggle out of my seatbelt and kneel on the seat in order to boost my head into the airstream. From there I watched America blowing past at eighty miles an hour—the America of my youth, the America of 1972, the America of big cars and fifty-two cents-a-gallon gasoline, the America of no worries and dad behind the wheel, a smile on his face and the wind in his beard, mom frowning over a map, brother and sister beside me poking and provoking one another.

When I finished college I found myself in control of my life, free from responsibility, and with the whole of the world before me. And when I asked the heavens, *what am I gonna do now?* Rudy was there to channel the answer, the only answer there could be—

Road trip.

And so we left, Rudy and I, got on the road and headed east across America, through the Southwest, Texas, and the Deep South, up the Eastern Seaboard to that Mecca of New York. We returned via Canada, the Midwest, Great Plains, and Sierra Nevada, returned home to *now what?*

North to Alaska we went, through Oregon, Washington, and British Colombia, with all the accompanying adventure. And with the Northwest conquered, the only way left for us to go was south, young man. And here we be. Now it's Mexico blurring past our windows, Anáhuac at the turn of the century, Mesoamerica in the dawn of a new millennium.

Life is different now, from what it was. The same, but different. I've moved from the back seat to the front. I now hold the wheel in my hand, tap the gas underfoot while my best friend rides shotgun, trying to fold a map. But *I* control our course and still don't know—or care—where it's leading us.

Rudy and I got on the road seeking to lose ourselves but instead I've come face to face with my past, my childhood. I've found myself, caught up with myself, have *become* myself. We are where we are, but we still have a long way to go in this paradoxical journey of body and soul, mind and spirit, car and driver. And neither of us knows where any of those will end up.

We arrive Playa del Carmen and check into a motel on the beach. A sense of relaxedness and general well being creeps up on me. It's beautiful and hot here, with the same clear water as Cancún, the same white sand, but without the droves of tourists, without the impending loom of skyscraper crowding us onto the beach.

Rudy and Virginia carry our bags up to the room. I head straight to the sand, wander dazedly along the surf until I end up in Coco's Beach Bar where there are swings in place of stools, individual swings suspended by ropes from the ceiling and it's *Hora Felíz* with two-for-one Dos Equis, Bob Marley playing loudly out of speakers hidden high in the rafters. The music is not loud enough, however, to drown the ringing of the bell in my head.

There are only a few people in the bar and the proprietor attends lovingly to my needs. Before long I see Rudolpho and Virginia wandering outside past. Rudy sees me at the bar and holds up a bottle of Kahlúa, an invitation to join them on the beach. But I shake my head no, order another twofer and watch them settle in the sand. I leave them down there with their

Kahlúa and their cups and the sand and the surf because this place is *my* bell ringing.

I pull out my journal, my pen, start to write, catch myself up on the last couple of months in Cancún, get up to speed on my life, catch time now that we're out of there and moving on. That's it—we're gone from that place, have left, departed, are traveling, journeying, we're on a road trip. We're going home.

It's Monday in Playa del Carmen and my bell is ringing. I write for hours, going drink for drink with the voice in my head (*el Voz en mi cabeza*). I'm on a roll and it feels good and satisfying, as if I'm accomplishing something, here at this bar, with this beer and this pen in Playa del Carmen.

And when I look out again, there's a circle around Rudy on the beach. He's talking, telling, entertaining. He's found an audience. Having pulled them out of the dim corners of their existence he entertains them, and this is all he needs, is all he *ever* needs. It's all any of us ever need, an audience.

I get up late on Tuesday—hell I'm on vacation—eat a cantaloupe and go out to the beach. Rudy and V. are already in the ocean. I sit in the shade of a palm, and think. There're topless women everywhere. I survey their beautiful breasts, the rise of the nipples. I hear many bells ringing on this day but don't know whose they are. What shall I do?

You should take some acid.

I'm down on that white sand looking into the blue water, staring at these overlapping elements, watching the colors vibrate one against another. I've got to do something creative, express myself.

Why don't you eat more acid and paint the Combi?

Virginia and Rudy are off swimming in their own world. I'm free to do my thing, unharassed. (*I fear I may be going crazy.*)

I walk up the beach to where the Combi rusts in the summer sun. Rummaging through the bottles under her rear seat, I come up with two cans of aqua blue spray paint, a can of primer gray, a litre of Añejo rum, grenadine, and a roll of masking tape—supplies I acquired weeks ago and stowed for just such an emergency.

After making a withdrawal from the conveniently located motel ice machine, I fix myself a drink, rum and pineapple juice garnished with lime and LSD. I step out of the Combi and slide her side door shut with a satisfying *click-clunk*. Standing back, I sip the electric concoction, stare at the side of el Tiburón del Tierra. Like the rest of us on this trip she's weathered her fair share of wear and tear, dents and dings, scrapes and scratches. Rust creeps through her gray flanks, speckling her skin. She's served us well and I need to acknowledge that.

I wave a spray of primer gray over her cancer spots, get her a uniform *gris*, and with just this she glows. Again I stand back, stroking my chin, staring at my canvas. A couple gulps of nectar and the energy sizzles out to shivering skin. *Now, what to paint, what to paint... Something that will protect us, streamline her, help her slip through weather, traffic, and adversity.* And then I see it on her bare sides—*lightning bolts.* Yes! Lightning bolts, streaking down from her upper rear to the wheel wells in front—*Greased Lightning!*

I peel the tape from its roll, transferring an outline of the image from my mind to the steel sides of this German-built box. Wanting the energy of the inspiration and the instant to come through in the art, I wing it, stretching tape in straight strips angled with jags to form bold streaks of lightning narrowing to precise points.

Here I am, in the sandy parking lot of the motel, on the beach, flipping cans in the air, and whacking tops on bumper, lids popping, aqua flowing. Escaping the pressure of spray can, tiny blue droplets fly at the side of the Combi, fling themselves at it, fill-in the lightning bolt template, affix themselves to the gray undercoat in multiple layers in accordance with my vision of velocity. I'm *on* and it feels good because I've let go, have permitted myself to take this leap of faith, do something unplanned, imperfect, impulsive. It's got me by the horns and I'm rolling, fucking rolling. I'm an artist and I paint like my life depends upon it—because it does, sucking away at rum and tabs of LSD.

I finish one side of the Combi and leap back. And I realize I'm being watched—from the balcony of the motel, the beach, and parking lot, people have congregated, murmuring amongst themselves, my own little audience of piqued curiosities. I start in on the next side, still flying. Rudy and V. are suddenly there, next to me.

"What are you doing?" they ask evenly.

All I do in response is to flash my eyes and they have no more queries. They know that I'm *on* and this is my thing, my bell ringing. They climb into the Combi, mix themselves cocktails, another round for me, and then stand back to watch as I paint the other side and wonder, *why the hell didn't I do this a long time ago?*

I finish, peel off the masking tape, and get a round of applause from my audience. Rudy and Virginia smile, commend me on my work. I toss the empty spray cans in the garbage and we walk to Coco's for Happy Hour where they've upped the ante to three-for-one.

We drink all night until the town goes to sleep. Something in me has opened and I feel alone. Back in our motel room, V. hands me a cigarette. I step out onto the landing. In the quiet of the hot night, the cool ocean of stars I smoke, admiring my artwork below.

We drive our new paint job south down Highway 307, la Costa Turquesa, four hours to the quiet countryside of Baccalar. As the sun goes down, we find a little Tudor hotel on the Laguna de Siete Colores. After settling in our room I excuse myself, leave the lovebirds to their devices.

The small, darkwood lobby is full of poker-playing European women—English, Irish, Spanish, and German—I can tell by their accents. I figure I oughta be able to strike up some good conversation or at least get laid, but they spurn my advances, are too self-absorbed to heed me.

The proprietor is quite a character though, and I find in him a companion. A sixty-four year old *Veracruzano*, he's a bear of a man, scurrying about to answer phones, check-in guests, serve up food, drinks, and conversation. I pull up a stool to the bar/front desk and buy us a round of *cervezas*. "I have American music," he says hopefully, and puts on a scratchy Glen Campbell album. I smile as if I like it. He shuffles over to deliver another round of Mint Juleps to the women, attempts to penetrate their coven with a joke but they snub him as well, too engrossed in their poker game to acknowledge us.

"*Pinches tortillas*," he mutters, returning to the bar. "*I* have *cartas*," he says. "You want to play *cartas*?" he asks me, rummaging beneath the bar. He comes up with an oversized card box, removes a worn deck and slaps it down on the wooden countertop—Tarot.

"You," he says to me. "I will tell you your *futuro*." He shuffles the deck, flips the cards over one by one, laying them face-up in a crucifix pattern.

"Hmmmmm," he studies them. "Mmmmmm."

"What is it?" I ask, "*¿Suerte? ¿Viajes? ¿Amore?*" Luck? Travel? Love?

"*Si, si, si*," he says, "all of *theese theengs*. But there is more, *mucho mas*. Here, peek a *carta*, any *carta*." I draw a card from the deck he fans before me; turn it over onto the bar.

Muerte.

He sighs.

"*Señor*," one of the women calls out from across the lobby, "*otra mas*," holding up her glass and shaking it to rattle the ice.

Without taking his eyes from the cards, the proprietor shouts back, "*No me molestes*," dismissing them with a wave of his hand. Finally, with a shake of his head he looks up from the cards. "*¿Quieres una otra cerveza, señor?*" he asks me, jostling the cards into a pile.

I look at him evenly. He won't meet my gaze.

"Am I going to die?" I ask.

"*Claro,*" he says. "We are all going to die."

He opens a couple Superiors, sets them on the bar. Suddenly discerning the silence, we gaze across the lobby. The women have departed hastily, leaving spilled drinks and salsa splatters across their tabletop. "Don't worry," he yells to their absence, "I'll put it on your beel," and he goes to clear their table. Returning to the bar, he exchanges the Glen Campbell disc for Paul Anka—Put Your Head On My Shoulder.

"What is it breengs you to Baccalar?" he asks, turning back to me.

"Oh," I say, "it's a convenient stopover on our way to—on our way home."

"Baccalar is convenient to nowhere," he says. "Where are you coming from?"

"We left Cancún a couple days ago. We're headed to San Francisco by way of San Cristóbol and Oaxaca."

"You take the long way, eh? *La ruta scenica.* It must be that you do not want to go home," he chuckles.

"You didn't tell me about the cards," I say.

"*¿El tarot?*" He exhales. "You want to know what the *cartas* say?"

"I drew the death card," I say.

"*La muerte, si.* But you must know that *eat* has more than *wan* meaning."

"It sounds pretty definite to me."

"You must keep in mind that for one thing to live, another must die. Here we call this *sacrificio.*"

186 west out of Baccalar, we drive along the Guatemalan border, through Quintana Roo, Campeche, across a corner of Tobasco, and into Chiapas, blowing past Palenque, and out to Agua Azúl where we camp the night beside the thunderous, roiling *cascadas.*

A morning swim in the cool rushing waters and we're on the road early, out through Ocosinco and up into the mountains, munching on peanut butter and jelly sandwiches. The lushness of the jungle quickly fades, giving way to pine trees, groves, forest like I've not seen in I don't know how long. As Greased Lightning climbs the mountain, the air cools, grows crisp and fresh, and the Combi chokes on the thinness of the atmosphere. We hump over the pass, and begin a winding descent, picking up speed as we serpentine towards valley floor.

Rudy glides her around a steep-sharp curve and there, across the expanse of the road stands a colorful crowd of peasant *Indios* and officials. Rudy slams on the brakes, skids the Combi to a halt. Around an overturned Coca-Cola truck the flock mills about, drinking Coca-Cola.

The throng turns its focus away from the carnage, away from the capsized truck and broken glass, away from the unmoving body that lays uncovered in the road. The cola-imbibing crowd redirects its attention at us, in Greased Lightning. Two police approach, lead the crowd of fifty in surrounding our vehicle. Hooking hands on our open windows, they peer in the Combi.

"¿*Touristas?*" a cop asks.

"*Si*," says Rudy, and the cop turns to the crowd.

"*Touristas*," he announces, and the crowd *ahhhs* an acknowledgment, running their hands and eyes over the sides of our machine.

"What's up with them?" Rudy mutters.

"It's the Combi," I say.

"Huh?"

"The lightning bolts, the paint job. They must think I'm the god of thunder and lightning."

"You?" says Rudy.

"I'm the one being chauffeured."

The crowd parts and passes us through. We continue on, descending towards valley floor.

"Don't you think it's more likely there's two gods," Rudy says, "one for thunder and one for lightning?"

"You mean like the separate gods of peanut butter and jelly?" says Virginia, biting into another sandwich.

Rudy and Virginia in the shower for hours, I mix a pitcher of Veracruz Venom, kick off my shoes, and take some LSD. Taking in the expansive view of San Cristóbol de las Casas, I park myself on our hotel room balcony, put my feet up on the railing, and do some drinking, thinking, writing, and drinking. Fat gray clouds swell with rainwater which falls to gorge gutters, fill forgotten buckets, barrels, and bottles.

Este no es mi vida. This is not my life. It flees from me, lurking over my shoulder left, hiding up ahead, around the corner, hanging from the crook of a waning crescent, leaping out of reach as I stumble through life, grasping at straws. *That's it*—I'm forever chasing, trying to get hold of a life that eludes me. *Este es mi vida.* This is my life.

By the time I awaken Sunday, the sun has already done its bit, leapt clear into the sky. I pour myself a pint of Venom, take more acid. *Did I take more acid? I'd better take some, in case I didn't.* We hit the beautiful highway west, out of San Cristóbol and across the Isthmus of Tehuantepec, 190 to 200, the Pacific Coast Highway. Rudy drives us out of the morning sun, hitting his groove, zooming up and down twisting coastal hills like we're in a slot car, scaring the hell out of us, exhilarating us.

At sundown, we roll into the small town of Huatulco, where we'll camp on the beach. Tomorrow we head north into the hills for Oaxaca. The moon is right for traveling.

Forty-Four

We're out of Huatulco at dawn and rolling east. The Combi's headlights glow dimly in the soon to vanish shadows of the coastal range. At Puerto Angel, we aim north towards Oaxaca, begin a beautiful, winding ride up through misty green mountains. Slithering with a serpentine directness, the Combi smoothes the wriggling ramble of road, rides rapid inclines up through tropical fog. Rains come and go with the decisive quickness of a provident groundhog taunting the seasons. I sleep through this drive, up and up and up we go.

Rudy pulls over at a roadside concession stand on the jungle incline at the edge of nowhere. He buys us sandwiches and *refrescos*. The proprietor is out of coinage. With a shrug gives Rudy a handful of *chicle* for change. Gum. Mexican money. The ancients traded cacao beans.

Rudy swerves Greased Lightning all day up steep elevations, through dense rain forest, under damp gray skies until finally we summit and lo and behold, the Valley of Oaxaca opens before us. Like a great zipper being drawn, the clouds part to reveal bright blue underclothes. We drop into the valley. Forest thins. The hills flatten into a plain stretched taut between distant mountains, like a dried animal skin across the head of a drum. We drive on through endless fields of agave, acres of the blue-green blades bursting forth from the earth. (*It's the mezcal…*)

The Valley of Oaxaca contains one of the largest bastions of indigenous peoples in North America, a continuous lineage maintained for millennia, rooted deep in the nooks and crannies of these hills. Their enduring presence has outlasted the ceaseless onslaught of tribal intruders from outside the valley: Aztec, Toltec, and Teotihuacáno, British, French, and Spanish, not to mention the current assault of gringo tourists such as ourselves. They've managed to hold onto their traditions, the way of the corn and the loom, their ceramics and textiles, their basketry and cuisine, their zoomorphic art. Through everything they've perpetuated piety, cults of transcendence that allow them to move unbounded between, through, and within the worlds of the living and the dead, the above and the below, providing them access to an array of sacred wisdom and divine counsel.

This is mushroom country, *hongos*. You can hear their hum in the air, feel their vibration in the land, smell the fungi putrefaction of the recycling earth: *Teonanacatl*, the "flesh of the gods" in the form of a fungus eaten as sacrament, washed down with the blood of the *magüey* (*it's the mezcal...*).

You can see where the azure arteries of psilocybin have worked their way up out of the ground and into the adobe walls that support the roofs that shelter the people. You can see it in the sure steps and gleaming eyes of the women carrying baskets in from the field. You can see it in the designs embroidered into the shawls that weigh them down along the side of the road. You can see it in the confident grins of the men, pick or shovel, *machéte* or *coa* in their loose grip, teeth glowing white out of sombrero-shaded faces as they stand to the knees in the fertile soil of life.

The openness of the farmland ends as abruptly as had the density of the jungle and we are suddenly in the city of Oaxaca. It stands alone in the late afternoon, isolated in the valley and appropriately overlooked by Nuestra Señora de Soledad, Our Lady of Solitude. We locate el Centro, the *zócalo*, circumambulate the plaza, the three of us road weary, stumbling past the white colonnaded architecture of cafés, galleries, and restaurants, through throngs of *indígenas* and *touristas*, each in the unique dress and colors of their ancestral tribes. We're moving rapidly back through a history of conquest, rebellion, colonialism, and restless tectonic plates. But whichever way we go now, east or west, forward or backward in time or space, we're getting that much closer to home (*that much closer to death*).

We push ourselves until hunger and fatigue and lack of purpose overcome.

"Where are we going?" Rudy asks.

"In circles," I say. "Let's find a pay phone. I'm gonna call Camille."

"Who's Camille?" asks Virginia.

"She's this cool Denmarkian chick—" Rudy begins.

"Danish woman," I correct him.

"—we met at Palenque."

"And the last thing she said to us when we parted ways—"

"The last thing she said," Rudy interrupts, "was that if we should ever find ourselves in Oaxaca—"

"—to give her a call," I say.

"—to give her a call," Rudy says. "She's in love with Clark."

"She's not in love with me."

When I find a phone that works I call Camille, get right through to her. "You're in Oaxaca!? You've got to come over. We've just opened a hostel; there are people from all over. You've got to come and stay here."

"Okay." I raise an eyebrow at Rudy.

"I'll meet you in front of the Cathedral," she says. "Ten minutes."

I hang up.

"She's not in love with me."

Camille is gushing when we meet her. We exchange hugs and introduce her to Virginia.

"Our place is only a few blocks from here," Camille says. "And we've got plenty of room for you." She takes my hand and drags me, turning at every intersection, down narrowing cobblestone streets. Virginia and Rudy shuffle behind.

"Diego's mother owns the building," she explains. "It was a dance school for many years but she recently closed it and retired. The building was empty and we begged her to let us do something with it." She stops halfway down the block lined with contiguous facades shuffling out to the narrow street.

The building has huge wooden doors, rusted iron hinges and pull rings. She tugs at an invisible string and a small portal in the middle of the door pops open. *Who is Diego? (A metaphor?)* "We filled the empty rooms with bunks and opened it as a hostel." Camille crouches and steps through the portal. We follow her into the vast building and down a hallway of hushed sunlight. "We have four private rooms here," she motions to the open doors on the left, "with four bunks each." We turn the corner at the end of the hallway.

"And here," on the right, "is the Grand Hall." She stops before the open double doorway. There is an actual breeze from the exiting snores of sleeping travelers. The high-ceilinged room stretches to the end of the building. Windowless walls are bathed from the top down in a soft, surreal, Tuscan-yellow glow, an eternal twilight beyond night and day. Two rows of double-decker plywood and two by four bunks extend down to the far wall. Scattered on them throughout the hall are a dozen or so amorphous, blanket-covered forms, inhaling the scent of fresh sawdust, exhaling unconscious visions that coalesce in the rafters.

We continue to the end of the hallway where it opens onto a walled patio. Europeans, Mexicans, and Americans hang about, sipping beers on the steps, smoking cigarettes in hammocks. "The kitchen is here," Camille points to the open wall on the far side of the patio through which I spy a long wooden table, "and our room is there." She indicates the hallway out the back. *(To whom do you suppose she is referring with all these plural, collective pronouns? She and Diego? She and you?)*

"Everybody," she announces to the half dozen souls present. "This is Clark, Rudy, and Virginia. Friends I met at Palenque." They acknowledge us with mutters and raised bottles.

"I am sorry that we have no more beer," intones a deep voice behind me, "but you are welcome to drink from mine."

I turn to confront a large, brown man.

"This is Diego," Camille smiles, putting her hands on him. Diego holds out a *caguama*. I take the large brown bottle.

"*Mucho gusto*," I say, and drink of the warm offering.

"Cigarette?" someone offers and each of us takes one of the proffered white sticks, our initiation into the tranquil fecundity of this cabal.

"You are tired," Camille observes. "Please, claim a bed or a room, make yourselves at home."

"I will go out and get more beer," Diego says.

"Thank you," Rudy says, "but we've been on the road all day. We're going to go eat."

"You will come back," Diego says. It is not a question.

The three of us return to the *zócalo* to satiate our road hunger, end up in a vegetarian restaurant with bad live music (the town seems to be full of them), eating voraciously, silent except for our mastications.

"So you're okay with this?" Rudy asks me, wiping his mouth on his sleeve. "Or would you rather get a hotel room?"

"I'm fine with it," I say. "I mean—she's offering us a free place to stay. Why would we pass that up?"

"Because she's in love with you," Rudy says.

"And she's got a jealous boyfriend," Virginia adds.

"She's *not* in love with me," I say. "How do you know he's jealous?"

"I just don't want to get in the middle of anything," Rudy says.

"Look," I say. "We've got a small budget to get home on and if someone's offering us a free place to stay, I think we should take it."

"Okay, Clark," says Rudy. "But remember—you are the God of Thunder and Lightning. And that position comes with a lot of responsibility."

We find the Combi where we left it upon entering town, drive it back to the hostel, and park up the street, pointed towards the highway out. It's past midnight. Camille and most everyone else have already retreated to darkened rooms or darkened corners. Rudy and V. jump into bed in one of the private rooms. I grab my notebook and pen, suck down another tab of LSD for sustenance, and steal off to the kitchen, to that long table, to write.

All around the walls of the kitchen there runs a low shelf, its narrow surface crowded with a myriad of small appliances, neither the functions nor the purposes of which are identifiable. Electric cords twist and snake, vying for access to those two slits in the wall that provide electricity, that spirit which drives our motorized adjuncts. In the back of the kitchen there's a breakfast nook containing a small Formica table around which a trio of Mexican *chicos* harass a couple of young gringas.

I glare at them as I stake my claim, barricading myself behind the huge Last Supper table that takes up the rest of the kitchen. It is a beautiful work of art, dark wood deeply tattooed with indecipherable hieroglyphs carved by the obsidian blades and butter knives of countless famished travelers. This table and bench become the altar and throne from which I rule the kingdom of *pluma y cuaderno* for the rest of the night.

I dive from the cliff edge of this table, through my exhaustion and intoxication, into my notebook, recording these events in an attempt to beat history, stay current, in sync, one step ahead of my nemesis—death, and the virgin what brings it. The group across the room heckles me sporadically throughout the night in an attempt to draw me into their sphere of association but I ignore them, swimming underwater across the unlined pages until I lose time and self (*¿lo mismo?*), not surfacing until oxygen runs out, when sun breaks horizon.

Peeking in on Rudy and Virginia in the private room, I find them cuddled tightly in sleep. I grab a blanket and slink off to the twilight of the Grand Hall, that temple of suspended consciousness. Disappearing anonymously down a long row of bunks amidst the chainsawing of other seekers, I stretch out in the dawn of a new day, gaze up at the canopy of dreams coalesced above.

Forty-Five

Sometime in the night something has shifted—the Earth's lithosphere or a paradigm. Perhaps it was a realignment of parallel universes. When I awaken, Rudy and Virginia are up and out, doing things. I'm on a different schedule now from the one they're following. Our wake/slumber tempos are in opposition. *But are they aware of just how deep the discrepancies go beyond this*? Perhaps the only connection I'll have with them now will be in the dream world, when they're asleep and I'm awake or when...

You'd better take some acid.

"It's somebody's birthday," Camille tells me as I somnambulate into the morning, "one of the German girls. We're having a party tonight. You *will* be here, won't you?"

"*We're going to Monte Alban,*" is all I can say. But these words are not my own. Someone or something has got hold of and is manipulating my tongue. *We're going to Monte Alban.* It's whispered in my head, but I know not from whence this order has issued. Nor do I know what Monte Alban is besides a cheap *mezcal.*

"Oh good," Camille says. "It's easy to find. Just get on the highway south and follow the signs. See you tonight," and she ducks out the door, just as Rudy and Virginia are entering. *She's always leaving.*

"Good morning Clark," Rudy and V. venture cautiously, unsure of my state.

"*We're going to Monte Alban,*" I again enunciate, but it feels as if I have yelled this at them. I pause to watch the slow motion effect of these loosed words penetrating the veil of perception that separates us, hoping our individual languages are not so out of sync that we can no longer communicate.

"Okay," responds Rudy, sensing the authority that speaks through me. Then, instead of futzing around to prepare themselves, they just stand there. "We're ready," says V.

"Let's go," Rudy says. "Do you know how to get there?"

"*Yes, I do.*" And that's it. I, myself, am scared into obeying this directive that has issued from my cakehole. "*We're going to Monte Alban,*" I mutter. And we are, and we do.

Dark gray clouds delineate sharply against slate sky as we venture into the day. I follow Camille's directions and my instincts through the semiarid countryside, up the winding roads, and back in time twenty-five hundred years to the convergence of the three arms of the Valley of Oaxaca, to that disembedded capital of the Zapotec—Monte Alban, the first true city of Mesoamerica, the first significant metropolis of *North* America. By the time we get to the ruins I'm worn out from the chattering of voices, the ringing of bells in my cranium.

"Why don't I drop you guys off here," I say, stopping at the main entrance. "I'll go park the Combi and meet you inside."

"Okay," says Rudy, getting out.

"Clark?" asks V. "You're not going to go paint the Combi again, are you?"

"Not today."

Parked around the side of the ruins, I sit alone in Greased Lightning, the car radio blaring Bob Marley. Unconsciously, I poke a big toe into the outlet for the lost cigarette lighter. For this, I receive a nice jolt of juice as a fuse blows under dash with a flash. The music dies, and up come the voices in my head. I wrestle them. I lose.

I partake of the sacrament of the valley, the aforementioned flesh of fungus, wash it down with the blood of the *magüey* (*it's the mezcal...*) to experience true communion. The waves of history suddenly swell behind, sweep me off my bare feet and carry me forth in a crest of foam. Dumping me on the shores of antiquity, they recede rapidly, leaving me abandoned and befuddled in this ancient city.

The ruins suddenly come alive, teeming with souls. Monte Alban is a dream realized, a Zapotec dream that envelops me, a millenniums-old city standing on the tabletop of the world, 1,550 meters above sea level, close enough to heaven to eavesdrop on the gods' mutterings.

One by one the gathering spirits move into me, merging minds and manipulating muscles until my shoulders bounce to a silent rhythm. Hips gently join and soon my whole body is inhabited, arms swinging, legs moving me into this city of the past, carrying me closer to home. I dance in, following a beat that is felt, a rhythm that emanates from deep within the earth. I dance on, surrounded by the invisibility of spirits that lead me, unseen past the scattering of archeologists, anthropologists, astronomers, and tourists. We dance through, legs stomping a reply to the planet beneath our feet, me and the Zapotec stamping flat the mountaintop in reclamation of our collective domain.

I follow the dancing spirits into the ball court where the hard rubber globe bounces off a thigh and arcs high, like sun across sky, deflects off a torso, touching neither earth nor ocean but staying in motion in a patronizing imitation of the divine perpetuation of celestial orbits.

The lives of men will always attempt to imitate the actions of gods.

We descend to a tunnel, *subterráneo*, where sun travels nightly, *nocturno*. The beat becomes audible and we waltz through underworld, emerge from this cave and circle the observatory as earth circles *Sol*. Up the steps of a pyramid platform we mock the moon as vistas of green valleys zoom down and away from us on all sides. We dance on past dozens of carved *danzantes*, reliefs depicting the blood gushing corpses of captives— hearts removed from chests, souls separated from bodies. As I pass, these dancers peel themselves from the walls, leap to the ground revivified, shake themselves into three dimensions and join forces with former foes, the Zapotec, and me in a battle to retake time and space.

We move to the continuing vibrations, the rhythm of the seasons, dancing with the dead, *el baile de los muertos*—in order to ensure the stability of the solar system, to perpetuate the clockwork flight of fireball across sky, to maintain the gravitational balance of orbiting orbs, Earth against Sun, *Sol* against *Luna*, Man against the moon and the continued rising of *Tezcatlipoca*, the morning star. (*Creation comes from destruction, order out of chaos, for one thing to live another must die...*)

I dance on across the lawn, invisible past Virginia and Rudy, doing their own dance back in time, ten, fifteen years into childhood, hands linked, the two of them spinning in widening circles, laughing, frolicking on the green grass in the openness of the plaza, in the openness of the valley, of the sky, the world, the day. But I'm farther back in time, two thousand years and passing them in the fast lane at two hundred fifty kilometers per hour. They're here though, in a different lane, at a different speed but here, yes, the same place, the same space, but at a different *time*.

These are the last ruins we will visit in Mexico, and that is fine.

The sharp grays of morning have blurred into afternoon mud. I gather Rudy and Virginia and return us to our lodgings. The kids lay down to nap but not me; I have a mission to accomplish—to get the car radio working again in order to drown the voices in my head. For this I'll need to find a twenty-five volt Volkswagen fuse (one of the blue ones) in Oaxaca, Oaxaca. *Gottafindafuse.*

It starts to rain. I'm out in the streets, bare feet slapping cobblestones, sloshing through warm puddles, padding past cathedrals and hotels and cafés, the same long line of colonnaded, colonial architecture. Big, soft drops fall heavily from the sky, washing the paint from the Spanish facades, dissolving plaster from the grooved columns, streaming it down where it swirls white 'round my feet. A majestic face appears from beneath the stucco overlay. Drizzle develops deluge and veneer falls away from the columns in long chalky strips, revealing ancient stone figures within, righteous Atlantean *telamons*, warriors at the ready, supporting the lintels and roofs with their stature alone.

I move on past this columination but the pillars continue to melt rapidly as I pass, shedding stucco skins. Enormous feathery serpents emerge, heads resting on ground, bodies extended upward, tails crooked to support cross members holding up the sky. I try to ignore their unhinging jaws, their lengthening fangs which stretch towards me, snapping shut mere millimeters from my bare, blackened feet.

There, between the serpents—a small storefront with a muffler hanging in the window. I dart quickly inside. The walls are covered with shelves supporting carburetors, gaskets, lubricants, hubcaps, chrome, and spray paint, a grandmother's face. "*Digame*," she barks from behind the clutter. Tell me. But I am ready for this, for her.

"*Necessito plomos, para Volkswagen.*" I need some fuses. "*Vente-cinqos.*" I return her stare, proud of my grasp on the Spanish language after almost a year. (*But she would have understood you in Mandarin as well because she's simply reading your mind.*) Her gnarled fingers claw through a cigar box full of switches, relays, and fuses.

"*Azúles*," I add in order to aid her. The blue ones.

"*Conozco!*" she barks, I know. She extracts three of the little fuses, presents them on palm.

I scoop them up in my fingers.

"*¿Combien?*" I ask, how much?

"*Nada*," she barks. "*Vete!*"

Placing a couple packs of *chicle* on the counter (remember the gum?) I go, hike back to the Combi, which sits alone on rain slickened cobblestones. Snaking in under the dash, I replace the fuse easily with another slight shock, then find myself sitting in the back of the Combi, the side door wide to let in the warmth of the afternoon. Raindrops down the windshield sketch a highway map of future. *What now?*

The body needs further infusion.

I lift up the rear seat to find leftover bottles from San Cristóbol, mix up a big jar of Venom, heavy on the grenadine to tint my liver, electrify the concoction to brace myself for whatever is to come next upon me in the gray Combi, in the gray street, under the gray sky.

I grab my notebook and fill my pockets with pesos and more of the *chicle*—mediums of exchange—and repair to the *zócalo* where the circuit is completed, where the serpent opens wide and commences to swallow its own tail. We have bumped the diamond-headed needle out of the scratch and into the next groove, past the cleft in time, *past the fucking scratch* and onto the next song. I sit myself at a café table at the edge of the plaza, under the portico, and order a coffee to add to the mix, *"con crema."*

Or did you say "au lait?"

Late afternoon, gray afternoon, wet afternoon in the slate green *zócalo*, Oaxaca, Oaxaca, with a coffee in front of me. I am here, now, twisting at a café, *al fresco*, under the portals of los Portales, gouging black coffee (because the waiter forgot the milk) from a chipped ceramic mug, wondering what to do with my life. It is with a head full of LSD, a heart full of confusion *con la vida*, and engine grease under my nails that I write to you from this *zócalo* on top of the world, from this afternoon, this day, thank you very much. This is becoming my life. *No es pregunta.*

This place is different but the same. It's the same trees and buildings, the same fountain spraying sporadically, the same laughter and rain and colors and costumes. It is the same young woman slapping her overzealous boyfriend, the same old man hobbling across plaza, the same toddler, pushing an empty stroller. It's the same tables and chairs, the same waiters and barkeeps, the same vendors, beggars, and bootblacks, the same blue smoke rising from those smoking with the blues, a life heavy on their *pechos*. This place has the same life beat as everywhere.

Afternoon smears into evening. Synapses fire spontaneously, concurrently—nervous chasms bridged by lightning. Cardiopulmonary flows in reverse—a Byzantine network of highways and byways pumping evil truckloads of evil chemicals in the wrong direction through my bloodstream, caffeine and psilocine, lysergic diethylamide into heart-pounding head.

I continue my swim across this sea of green, going nowhere, writing, trying to kill off this vicious cycle, which has been spinning me for days, ever since I first began the feverish shoving of pen across page. I've poured more energy into it than I have, more than the notebook can take and the excess force has created this twister. Yes, I've created my own tornado, started it spinning, an endless cycle that sucks me in, spins me now like an out of control roulette wheel.

The rain falls. The café fills. Empty cups and saucers pile high on the green tablecloth in front of me as my head whirls past. I continue scribbling, attempting to reach an unknown deadline I know is unreachable, but I continue on with the knowledge that even the strength of a tornado must diminish, with time will lose velocity, decelerate, disintegrate, stop blowing. Yes, some day soon those winds shall cease.

Indígenos and *extranjeros* alike wander the plaza. Music drifts out of cafés. The rain comes again, falling out of the sky and into my mug, diluting my coffee, filling my cup, overflowing it, spilling across table, cascading to ground, filling the plaza in a rising tide which quickly ascends above ankles.

You won't leave now, can't, bottom too deep in chair, cobblestone gravity reaching, pulling, yanking the sky down, while reality changes yet again, shifting gears, up or down, slamming, jumping, grinding, cogs, gears, years, horses through stained glass and the fiery hoop of our id fears. Can this go on, another day, page, minute, zooming into dusk, rattling tree leaves past? This is the question we all should be asking ourselves as we dive into our drinks, scuba tank strapped to back, descending down to the bottom of that huge stein, chalice, coffee cup, kicking through the liquid of our personal Holy Grails. Come join me if you're not already here, if you're not already with me, swimming through this rain, this life, this bog of black coffee, leche the waiter never brought. It's raining in my coffee. The rain falls in my coffee. Insects—bugs with legs, wings, stingers, antennae, blacks, browns, and evil sounds hop, move, move like lightning, all these insects fly, crash, pour into my cup, drown in my coffee, disappear into the no-cream black.

And I—I shall drink it.

Forty-Six

Through the front door of the hostel at midnight, I pass Camille and a giggling *gringita*, both drunk, heading out for more bottles of *mezcal. (It's the* mezcal *doing that, you see?)* Ah yes, the birthday party I was warned about. They surround my last supper table in the kitchen, maybe twenty of them. Smoke hangs from the ceiling like an indigo tapestry tacked at the corners.

Camille and the *gringita* return with large clear bottles of large clear *mezcal*. I lay low for an hour or so while the crowd works itself out, the heavy sediment settling to the bottom and the cream, rising to the surface. One by one they exit until the crowd is perfected and only the hard rubber core, the dregs, remain—nine of us, half and half.

The Poet is there. A couple from Britain, Diego, the German women. Camille comes and sits by me. She doesn't need to say anything. But she does. "I'm so glad you're here. You don't know..." But I do know. And she knows that I know.

Tired of asking and giving, someone grabs all the packs of cigarettes off the table and out of purses and pockets, pours them onto a plate which makes the rounds—stubby fingers poking about white French fries. Diego keeps my glass full of *mezcal*. The music picks up, shifts from old school Mexican to Santana, into a whirling reggae mix. Everyone is up and swinging, dipping, shoving tables out the way, tiny whirlwinds knocking unwashed dishes and unused appliances from countertops, the fiesta spilling into courtyard where the light changes, drops to almost darkness before candles ignite, throw shadow distortions on the high stucco walls. Clothes come off, costumes appear, everyone's face different now. (*Did they put masks on or take them off?*)

The Brits are in glee, the German birthday girl rubs her crotch against everyone, looking for a bedmate, and Diego has just too much fun *con la gringa.* Seeing this, Camille is on me. And the Kid, a *poet*, is watching, seeing everything from Jesus' seat at the Last Supper table. *It's the* mezcal *causes this*, he'll tell me later.

And so the night passes, beating like a slow heart, the platter of white sticks making the rounds, clear *mezcal* pouring from bottle to glass to glass to mouth, hormones boiling until the gray ceiling of sky is suddenly torn apart, opened by blue-white knife slashes of lightning and everything moistened with a layer of rain as the dark walls of kitchen and courtyard are sucked inward with our collective breath. Thunder rattles window panes, crescendo after crescendo shakes plaster from the walls as this spinning dervish orgy reaches its peak of frenzy and the room, the planet, reverse their gyration, begin rotation in the opposite direction—until five in the morning when we let go the spin (or it, us), fly off in the pairs that have or haven't formed.

A silence comes, expands to fill the void left by the departed rain. Freshness descends into courtyard from above the rooftops, pours into the open kitchen. One of the last to leave is Diego, not with his girlfriend, but *con la gringa.* Camille pretends it doesn't bother her. I'm ready to retire but she pleads with me to stay.

Camille and I situate ourselves side-by-side, foot-to-head in the hammock suspended at the side of the rain-freshened courtyard. Balancing the platter of cancer between us, we bite at *mezcal* dregs from the last intact clear-smooth bottle. *(You see? It's the* mezcal.*)* I wait a few moments for the silence and post-diluvium lucidity to seep down, absorb into her bosom, and float it to the surface.

"He cheats on me," she puts forth. I take another cigarette from the pile, suck life into it from a damp match as she launches into their history of love-at-first-sight, the whirlwind courtship, the blatant unfaithfulness, the abuse, and of how much she loves him.

When her tears clear she straightens with a sigh, tells me I can have the room off the courtyard (as if I could sleep) and we say goodnight. (Good morning?) I stretch out alone on the feathery bed; watch the sky bluing through window. Five minutes and I might finally fall asleep after two days, when she knocks on the door and slips in.

"I forgot," she says. "He's in *my* bed, with *my* friend. Can I lay here?" But she has already slipped between the sheets. A few minutes of laying in each other's arms, and a banging on the door commences.

He's looking for her, hunting her. Diego enters graciously. "I am so sorry to bother you, Clark." He turns to her, spits a *magüey* venom. "You will come to bed with me, *ahorita!*"

"*Pinche cabrón*," she screams back with equal vehemence. "I'm staying here with Clark. I love him." Goddamn, Rudy was right. (*You see? It's the* mezcal *does that*.) But Diego loves me too, I know that.

The screaming match intensifies, shifts from Spanish to English to Danish, she throwing him out, he throwing her out (of *my* room), I can't keep up with the ever-shifting dialect. Camille stamps out to the courtyard. Diego counts ten and follows. Relieved, I pull the blanket up to engage in some sleep. But the screaming match resumes outside my window. He comes in, sits on the foot of my bed, begging, weeping, asking me, himself, no one, "What should I do?" Camille storms in, melts at his sobs, kneels, takes him in her arms. They are talking it out, though in what language I don't know.

Taking advantage of this break in the storm, I grab the quilt and slip out to the courtyard, take up residence in a hammock. But as soon as I'm comfortable and drifting off, the screaming again erupts and she chases him out, their voices echoing off the four walls and into my *mezcal*-drenched, sleep-deprived head. I bundle myself back into the room, bury my head under pillows. Door slams and she throws herself onto the bed next to me. (No—the door doesn't lock, I tried it). I glare dark eyes at her from under my pyramid of pillows. I know he can't be far behind and isn't, throws himself down next to her, the three of us on the bed.

"I'm sorry," Diego says, "it's the *mezcal*..." (*See, I told you...*)

It is this morning at dawn when, walking barefoot under the lightening sky and with schoolchildren staring through me as I pause to slosh soiled feet in a rain puddle in front of Oaxaca's grand old cathedral, that I finally and deeply understand Janis. Tomorrow never does happen. It really is all the same fucking day.

Here I am, six fifty-three in the steel morning, back at the *zócalo* as day breaks, arriving at the same goddamn café as it opens, sitting at the same table with the same green tablecloth and the same cold beer on it's way here now, I can feel it. I'm writing with the same pen, scribbling in the same black ink, right this instant. You see, I'm still trying to get it down, pin it to the mat, comb back its earlobes even though I don't know what *it* is, can't put it into words, always one dark step out of my grasp, like brown eels slipping through river shadows.

I gotta eat something this morning, gotta bring it down, touch the ground, been three days now I've been twisted, three weeks wondering *what am I doing with my life? Why go home?*

A liquid breakfast of coffee, juice, and *cerveza*, chased by eggs, bacon, and toast helps to bring me around. Gotta keep those vitamins coming in (caffeine is a vitamin, no?) as I groove into the day where I left off not eight hours ago. I'm completely, 365° twisted. Feet and nose point in the same direction, good, but there's one complete revolution between them, bad.

I return to the dance hall. The place is destroyed. The quarrel must have escalated after my early morning departure. I run into that kid—a poet for cryin' out loud—tiptoeing through the mess. He looks around, looks at me, whispers. "It's the mezcal causes this. You see that? It's the mezcal." I sneak to a bunk in the back of the hall to catch forty winks. I'm hiding, but Rudy finds me just as dreams of the open highway are passing in.

"What the hell happened here last night?" he asks. "Whatever it was, I know you had something to do with it."

"I'll tell you all about it later."

"Hey, you still got the acid, right?"

"Uh, yeah."

"Let me have it."

I pull out the envelope, hand it to him. He opens it and looks in.

"What the hell—? There's only like five hits left. There were fifty in here when I gave it to you in Cancún. Did you—Well this explains a lot. When I told you to put it somewhere safe I didn't mean your bloodstream."

"Can we just get outta here," I say, rolling to the edge of the bunk.

"Hold on," says Rudy. "We've got a flat."

"A flat?"

"Yeah, but don't worry—Virginia's going to change it."

"V.?"

"Yeah, and it'll probably take her a while. So why don't you get a little shuteye. You look like you could use it."

"Yeah."

"It's her first time," Rudy says. "She's excited."

"Her first time?"

"Changing a flat. She's out there now, loosening the lugs." He looks at me. "I'll come get you when we're ready." Eyes closed, I can see Virginia's bright face, a smile playing across those big red lips, bouncing anxiously on tiptoes. Excited about changing a tire. I roll over and the dream slithers back in, a desert highway rolling away beneath me.

Rudy wakes me an hour later. "Let's go."

The Cathedral of Dreams is quiet except for the enduring harmony of snores. Rudy has already packed the Combi. We exit without saying good-bye. To anyone. In the car I pass out immediately, out of future necessity, as we head for points north.

Mytho-Historical Departure
The Aztec Migration and How Mexico Got its Name

For two hundred years, the military empire of the Toltecs dominated northern Mesoamerica. They fought off invaders from the northern steppes and provided protection to the smaller tribes around them. At the end of the eleventh century, frost, drought, and famine all contributed to the decline of the empire. When the Toltec capital of Tollán fell, the city was abandoned, sparking massive migrations southward to the more fertile and protected Valley of Mexico.

Of the many to participate in this migration was a tribe that had dwelled at Aztlán, an island surrounded by marshes. They abandoned their homes, paddled their canoes across the swamp, and commenced nomadic wanderings. Under the command of their chief Méci (*Mé-see*), they were known as México (*Mé-see-ca*). Their spirit guide on this journey was the tribal deity Huitzilopochitli, the god of war, who dwelt in a medicine bundle borne by four priests. These four "god-bearers" interpreted Huitzilopochitli's decrees and led the way (which sounds fishy to me).

Somewhere during their walkabout the México stopped to rest under the shade of a tree and—*Crack!*—right then and there that tree split down the middle, mysteriously cleaved in two.

"What the heck was that all about?" Méci asked Huitzilopochitli, via the priests.

"Hold on, let me check with Big H.," said the head priest, and he questioned the bundle. "The Big Guy says that was a sign that the tribe is to change its name from México to Aztec, after the place we left, Aztlán."

"Why's that?" Chief Méci asked.

"We need to separate the past from the future, myth from reality," said the high priest. "Also, the name Aztec has fewer syllables, easier to remember."

"Where, exactly, are we going?" asked Méci.

"Huitzilopochitli says we must keep wandering until we find a lake with a cactus growing out of it and an eagle perched on the cactus, holding a snake in its beak. That place will be our new home."

"That's a common sight," Chief Méci muttered, and the Méx—uh, Aztecs proceeded to wander for the next two hundred years (I'm not kidding, either). When they finally arrived in the Valley of Mexico (as it later came to be called), the Aztecs received a cold welcome, as immigrants often do. The only marketable skill they possessed was warfare. So they bounced around the valley, hiring themselves out as mercenaries to the various tribes. Notorious for their talents as warriors, they gradually became a force to be reckoned with. The local tribes got nervous and gathered in council to discuss the growing threat.

"These Aztecs are getting brazen," said one of the chiefs. "They're gaining power and prestige and if we don't do something soon, they're gonna walk all over us."

"We should find someplace for them to go," said another chief. "A remote place of their own, where they can settle. Otherwise they're going to just hang around here and cause trouble."

"Hey, how about that swampland on the west shore—it's far enough away that they'll be out of our hair, and barren enough that they won't be able to grow anything. They'll still be dependent on us for food." And so the Aztecs were banished—uh, offered a discounted plot of real estate on the edge of Lake Texcoco. They went down one day to check out the property, a swampy islet surrounded by water.

"Holy Huitzilopochitli," Chief Méci exclaimed. "It's a god damn swamp." He bent down to taste the water. "Yuck," he said and spit it out, then looked up across the lake. "Holy shit," he exclaimed. "Look up everybody." Everybody looked up. "Ha, ha—knew I could make you look. But seriously, look across the water." There, in the middle of the lake grew a cactus. And on that cactus sat an eagle. And clamped in the beak of that eagle was a snake.

"This must be the place," said the head priest. "Let's start building our city."

"You've got to be kidding," said Chief Méci. "It's a god damn swamp."

"Yup," said the priest. "We're going to need an awful lot of landfill."

The swamp was filled, they proceeded to build, and soon raised up a city, Tenochtitlán. The Aztecs persevered and eventually kicked the collective ass of all those tribes around the lake and of anyone else who fucked with them. Before long they were the dominant force in the valley, having built an empire that surpassed even that of the ancient Toltec. The Aztecs established trade routes and exacted tributes all across Mesoamerica—out to the Gulf Coast and the Pacific, into the Yucatán and Central America. Soon, Tenochtitlán was the largest city in the world.

Once the nineteenth century Revolution ended Spanish dominance, the People's first act was to rename the city, the valley, and the entire country Mexico, after the México tribe that had left on a walkabout more than half a millennium earlier. They also adopted a new flag featuring the Mexican coat of arms—an eagle perched on a cactus with a snake in its beak.

Forty-Seven

"We can't just leave him here," Virginia says, shotgun.

"It's what he wants," Rudy says from behind the wheel.

"But it's the middle of nowhere." Rudy zooms the Combi down a valley through the middle of nowhere. Sun descends towards mountaintops.

"V.—it's what he wants."

"What is a vision quest, anyway?" she asks.

"It's when you go off into the desert or the mountains," Rudy says, "somewhere desolate to…to seek visions."

"But why?"

"Why don't you ask him."

"Clark, why—"

"To find meaning in life, direction, answers," I say from the back of the Combi, stuffing a blanket into my backpack.

We've been on the road for days now, out of the mountains of Oaxaca and through the museums of Mexico City. From there we cut through Querétaro and San Luis Potosi, north through thinning civilization on ever-narrowing highways, across the Tropic of Cancer, past Matehuala and Cedral. The more the distance between the border and us has shrunk, the more excited Virginia and Rudy have become, and the more anxious I've grown. I'm not yet ready to leave this land. And so I have taken charge of the navigation, have followed the directions of the voice in my head to here, the middle of nowhere.

"Turn here," I say. Rudy steers the Combi off the paved highway and onto a wide, roughly cobbled road that leads to hills distant.

"You think you're going to find answers here?" Rudy asks, leaning over the steering wheel to gaze at the mountain range ahead.

"Maybe," I say, "maybe."

"What are you going to do, Clark?" Virginia asks. I take a deep breath.

"I'm going to walk...," I point up into the hills and exhale, "up into the hills."

"But why?"

"Because."

"I'll drive you to the baseline," Rudy says.

"You can drop me here."

"Here?"

"Here."

Rudy rolls the Combi off the cobbled road and onto the sandy shoulder, puts it in neutral. Engine rumbles roughly. We're at a crossroads, desolate and deserted—no sign of civilization save the road. Just cactus and creosote, sand, sagebrush, and tumbling tumbleweeds. It's hot, but cooling with the dawdling departure of the sun.

"We can drive you to the hills," Virginia says.

"I'm going to walk." I slide open the side door and step out.

"You want us to come back in a couple days and get you?" Virginia asks, getting out of the Combi.

"No."

"But how will you get home?"

"I don't know."

"U.F.O.s," Rudy says. "U.F.O.s are going to pick him up and fly him home."

"Maybe," I say, "maybe."

"Here," says Virginia, "why don't you take some food."

"No."

"You haven't eaten in like, two days," she says. "A coat, you're going to need a coat to keep you warm."

"I've got a blanket, that's all I need." I pat the lightning-streaked side of the Combi.

"A sweater?"

"Tobacco, I'm going to need tobacco."

"There's half a pack in here somewhere," says V., rummaging through the glove box. "Here," she hands me a crushed pack of Camels and a book of matches. Rudy kills the engine, gets out from behind the wheel and comes around to the side. We stand in the desert.

"It won't be the same without you," he says. A chill wind whistles past.

"It'll never be the same," I say, squinting into the sun which disappears completely now, behind the hills.

Virginia throws her arms around my neck. "Be safe," she says, and kisses my cheek.

"I'd give you some advice," Rudy says, "but I don't have any more."

"That's novel."

He steps up and we wrap our arms around each other.

"Take care of yourself, Clark."

We step back and look at one another.

"Be careful at the border," I say.

"C'mon, it's me."

"I know. *Adios*."

"*Adios*. — Clark?"

"Yeah?"

"If a U.F.O. does pick you up," Rudy winks, "let me know how the Martian women are."

"Will do." I shoulder my pack and turn, gaze down the straight road to the hills ahead. My path is hard and bumpy, paved with river-smoothed stones. I glance at Rudy and Virginia one last time and then start on my journey, one foot in front of the other down this riverstone road. I don't turn back but in my mind can see Rudy standing there, watching me disappear, Virginia at his side, trying to understand.

I'm a good half a mile down the road before I hear the faint sound of the Combi firing up, grinding into gear and revving off. *One foot in front of the other*.

Flat and straight across hard stones, I cut the desert playa toward the foot of the hills.

Where are you going?

To a sacred place — in the hills beyond town.

Town? I don't see any —

It's the other side of that range.

I am not climbin' over that mountain.

There's a tunnel, this road leads to a tunnel bored through the hill to a town on the other side. The only way to get there is through the tunnel. That or hike over the mountain.

There's really a town in them thar hills?

It's high on a plateau, nestled in the mountaintops. During the silver boom a hundred years ago it was a bustling mining outpost. Now it's practically deserted — a ghost town.

I can see why you'd want to go there.

But it's beyond there that I'm going, into the hills above the town, beyond the deserted mines to a sacred space, a semi-mythical place of power.

How do you know this place?
I've read about it in books, studied it in Anthropology class. And Libertad told me about it. Every year, the Huichol Indians of the western Sierra Madre set out on a pilgrimage from the borderlands of Durango, Jalisco, and Nayarit. They travel some four hundred kilometers to a place here in the hills, a sacred ceremonial center they call Wirikuta.
They walk three hundred miles to visit this barren place?
This is the land of their origin—the place they were created as a people. Their pilgrimage is a sacred journey, a reenactment of their cosmology, mythology, and history. Wirikuta is the birthplace of the sun, abode of the gods, domicile of the tutelary spirits of deer and maize.
A-maizing.
It's where their souls go at death. It's also where they come to collect their sacrament, enough to last them through a year's worth of ceremonies.
Their sacrament?
Peyote.
Oh, I see. That's what we're doing out here, looking for another high.
It's a sacred place. I'm on a spiritual journey.
And the peyote just happens to grow here—what a coincidence.
It's the perfect locale for my vision quest—a foreign environment, remote and isolated in the high desert wilderness. And it was a convenient place for Rudy and Virginia to drop me on their way to the border.
Are we ever going to see them again?
I don't know.
The sun has completely disappeared behind peaks, casting an orange alpenglow across the undersides of wispy clouds. As I near the base of the hills I stop and stare at the mountain. From here the road makes a zigzagging ascent that switches up to the mouth of the tunnel. I breathe.
What are you waiting for?
I'm not ready.
Not ready?
Not ready to pass through that tunnel.
For fear of what might lie on the other side?
Yes, fear. I'm going to have to face my fears before passing through.
Good luck.
I need to find a place to spend the night.
Where?
Here.
Here? In the desert?
Vamanos.

I leave the road and wander into the desert, deeper into the shadows cast by the mountain range ahead. Amidst the mesquite and Joshua tree, I find a clearing in which to spend the night with my thoughts.

The sky darkens as I pull the Baja blanket out of my pack. It's the only thing I've brought besides a bottle of water and the tobacco. I spread the blanket across a crust of sand and kneel on it, facing east. Extracting a cigarette, I crush it between fingers, pinch offerings to the four directions surrounding me, to the forces of the above and the below, praying for strength.

I lay down, stretch out in the openness of the desert, the openness of the night, let sky envelop me. *I haven't seen so many stars since I was a kid.* It's huge, this world, expanding from the jungle to the desert, from the city to the mountain, from sea to shining sea and me, a part of it all, from the skies above to the earth below, the infinity of space unfurling before me. I am scared, scared to pass through that tunnel, afraid to pass through that town and into the hills beyond not because of what I may confront there but because of what I may encounter within.

For what do you seek?

I'm not running from anything.

Nobody said you were.

I'm seeking something.

Yes, yes, I can see that. For what do you seek?

The Huicholes seek a return to their origins, a reconnection with their past, communion with their gods, their ancestors. They seek oneness.

What do you hope to gain from this experience?

Truth, love, clarity, purpose, a goal. All of the above and none below.

All right then—what is it that you fear?

Rejection. Failure. I am afraid of failing, in my own eyes and in the eyes of others. I am gripped now by the fear that I may fail at this endeavor, that I may come out the other side of it having failed to change anything, crushed under the weight of this dream, this ancient quest for transformation.

Yes, yes, but for what do you seek? Your whole life you've ransacked the world's religions, all year you've sought meaning in the cultures of Mexico, ancient and modern—

Because I've found none in my own.

You've looked for it in the ancient mythology of the Aztec, in the glyphic inscriptions of the Maya, even in the patterns of the astral plane. You've aped an array of faiths with your explorations into religious intoxication, your attempts to circumvent the ecclesiast—

Because there can be no secondhand epiphany. Revelation, divine communion must be a direct experience, or none at all.

Is that what you seek—an experience of the divine?

It's owed me.

Owed you?

It was the empty promise of the Catholic Church. For years I waded through the torturous ordeal of weekly mass to get the promised reward of First Communion. *Oh*, to take the body of Christ in mine, to drink the blood of divinity itself, what revelation would that bring! But the Eucharist turned out to be nothing more than a stale cracker and some sour juice that caused me to pucker.

What is it that you seek?

Acceptance. Approval.

From whom?

My father.

He's gone.

And I need to accept that.

Yes, you do.

I rouse before dawn and stuff blanket into pack, hike through the desert twilight back to the desolate road, the riverstone road which leads me to the foot of the mountain. From here the course serpentines up the base of the hill to the entrance of a tunnel. Day breaks over the range and I begin my ascent, one foot in front of the other. The trail twists and switches as I twitch and sweat, slaloming up the steepening incline. All morning I trek up this dusty, rugged road as sunlight descends the mountain's craggy face.

Finally I mount the final rise, round the final bend, and before me looms the dark opening, Túnel Ogarrio, a mouth in the face of the mountain. I stop, huffing heavily. A chill breeze blows from the tunnel.

"*No puedes a caminar por el túnel*," a voice announces from the shadows beside the dark entrance.

"*¿Que?*"

"*No puedes—*" A fat, mustachioed man emerges from the *sombras*. "You no can walk through *el túnel*," he says.

"Oh." The tunnel has a guardian. "Then how—"

"*¿Necessitas un ride?*" someone shouts from behind. I turn to see a Volkswagen Beetle, a taxicab, pulling up beside me. Its driver leans across the front seat, peers at me through the open passenger window.

"I guess I do," I say. "*Pero no tengo dinero.*"

"*El ride es gratis*," he says.

"*Bueno*," I say, offer a cigarette to the cabbie, one to the tunnel man, and slip into the taxi. The toll-taker tunnel-man cocks an ear towards the earth's opening, listens for the distant rumble of oncoming traffic. The tunnel is only wide enough for one vehicle and his job, I take it, is to ensure that traffic flows in only one direction, thus reducing the number of subterranean head-ons. He nods us the clear sign and the cabbie puts the Beetle into gear. I take a deep breath and we lurch into the maw of the underworld.

The walls and ceiling are rough and chiseled, close and claustrophobic, the floor carpeted with rubble. It appears to be a straight shot, more or less, but there's no light at the end of the tunnel, nothing for me to focus on, nothing to draw us forward, no illumination at all. Dim headlights jab into pitch. *What if the engine dies? What if we run out of gas in here?*

"*En* 1897, two crews on opposite sides of *la montaña* start digging," my driver says, "through the solid rock of *theese heels*. Nobody know if ever *theese túnels weel* meet. But they keep going—two and a half kilometers and four years—until the two *agujeros*, they meet. Such are the lengths to *weech* man *weel* go in order to get *el tesoro*, the treasure."

The tunnel bends—where the bores finally met—and alas, a light at the end of *el túnel*.

"Do you know of the cathedral?" my driver asks. I do not.

"La Parroquía de la Puŕisima Concepción," he says. "At the height of the *seelver* boom, it is ordered that five percent of all *ganancias* from the mines is to be *geeven* to the church. They build—for over thirty years—a big *barroco* cathedral *en* el Centro. *Eat es feeneshed en* 1817. The temple *es* beautiful, but *eats* main attraction *es* a sacred and powerful *emage* of *Saint Francis de Asis*."

"San Francisco?"

"Every year for the past cen-*too*-ree, thousands of peoples come to here to make homage to *hees* shrine. Mostly they come on foot, some on their *niece* and *hans*—how do you say?"

"They crawl?"

"They crawl here, from far away to confess they *seens*, to give thanks to the *emage* for the prayers he has answer, for the miracles he has perform on their behalf. For *hees* followers truly believe that Saint Francisco does *theese theengs* for them."

I can picture them, a parade of toothless women in shawls, bent *viejos* with hunched backs, dragging their broken bodies, their bloody stumps up that long cobbled road to worship a wooden idol, to invest in it their prayers, deposit their hard-won wages in the coffee can at its feet.

Taxi in tunnel, engine echoes off walls.

"*¿Para que buscas?*" the driver says suddenly into the silence, for what do you seek?

"Release," I say without thinking, *release*. I need to release my father's soul that I may release my own, crawl out from under his shadow and get on with my life.

There it is.

What?

Your declaration. Was that so hard?

It was.

"*Bueno*," says the cabbie, "you will find that here," and we blow out the end of the tube and roll onto tarmac suddenly struck by searing sunshine. A fat, mustachioed man awaits us at the other end of the tunnel. He could be the twin of the guardian from the other end, could be the same man. But he wants nothing from us, is there simply to tip his hat and smile, welcome us to Real de Catorce.

My driver turns the taxi up a small rise. The road passes through an opening in the low wall that surrounds the town. We drive straight on through el Centro, up the narrow cobbled street, past the closed doors and boarded windows of a people living in the shadow of their ancestors. At the far end of town we slide to a stop at edge of the steep, deep canyon that forms the northern boundary. Here the Potosino Plateau drops into the void, isolating us between mountain and abyss.

"Now my friend, you have seen Catorce." The cabbie guns the engine, kicking us towards the cliff's edge, spins the wheel, turning us around and sending a cloud of dust over the gorge. We head back to el Centro.

"I will drop you at *el cathedral*," he says. "Before continuing your journey, you must pay your *respetos á Panchito*, confess your sins and *purificas su alma*, purify your soul."

The car rolls to a stop in front of the church. I turn and look at the cab driver. He laughs. "*Suerte amigo*," he smacks me on the shoulder and then holds out a hand for me to shake. "*Suerte en su búsqueda*." He drives off in a cloud of dust, leaving me alone at the curb, staring up at the spired structure that rises before me. It's still morning. Sun burns in sky.

I step to the vestibule and head for the nave. But before I can enter, my body stops, dips fingers in bowl of holy water, charts the four directions from forehead down.

What are you doing?

I don't know. Washing away my sins of iniquity.

Regaining control of my body, I drag it into the church proper. The walls are perforated with niches sustaining a multiplicity of forms and figures—Jesus, Mary, and Joseph, the Christ in his many guises—standing, sleeping, and nailed to a tree, blood-drenched and with thorns around his head, his nagging wife beside. There, halfway down the wall in his own special alcove, sitting on his own special throne is Saint Francis de Asis, patron saint of my hometown. I pause before his image and again without thinking drop to my knees, bow head.

What's all this—the holy water, the crossing, the genuflection? From what do you need absolution?

Myself.

You have asked for release.

There was a trail by the tunnel.

A trail?

I saw a trail beside the tunnel that went up the mountain, disappeared over the ridge. That's where I'm going.

Didn't I tell you I am not climbin' over that mountain?

You don't have to. You can stay here.

I walk back through town, back to the trail that rises beside the mouth of the tunnel. It ascends so steeply that I have to use my hands, climb it like a mountain goat. The trail levels over the crest, dips into a saddle before curving up the next hill. I pass a horse ranch in the flat of the basin. Two *caballeros* shout to me that I will need a horse; I will need to rent a horse from them in order to get up the trail.

No, I shout back, I will not need a horse.

Si señor, if you are going up there of course you will need a horse.

Gracias, I shout back, but I do not need a horse, and walk on.

Up the next rise and the next, all afternoon hiking up hills, scrambling across shale on steepening inclines, past fallen mines, through the standing walls of once buildings, aiming up, up, all the while scanning the slopes for tracks of the little deer.

The altitude and sun wipe me out. In a few hours I've passed far up into the sierras, past the faded *el Dorado*. I'm exhausted and in need of a rest. Up over the next summit there's a small plateau, marked by a tall wooden cross. I climb to it. The cross is crude and sagging, maybe twenty feet high, a couple of weathered boards rustily nailed together. I sit in the narrow shade of its trunk and sip water. Picking up a stone I consider it, toss it aside, and begin to clear a space that I might unfurl my blanket and stretch out for a rest before—What's this?!

Bulging out of the earth at the foot of the cross in front of me is a blue-green pincushion—*peyote*. Holding breath, I withdraw from imaginary quiver an invisible arrow, reach for my bow. Drawing back the bolt, I release, send it sailing straight and true, as Huichole would do. The arrow does its part, lands its mark, peyote through the heart, releasing into flight ripples of rainbow light, spirit of *Híkuri*. Freeing the fruit from its root, I take it from the soil, raise it to the sky, the directions surrounding, press it to lips with a prayer—*mitakuye oyasin... a toto mi familia... all my relatives... Dios y Diosas...*

Suddenly, more of the little blue cactuses pop out of the ground around me, surround me, here at the base of the cross. I gather a baker's dozen, put them in my pack. The view behind and below me is the empty bowl of Catorce, the abyss, the beyond. Around and above me looms the mountain ahead. Sun is low and soon I must stop for the night. Adobe remains top the next hill, possessing position prestigious. I proceed. Sun slides out of sight as I arrive the ruins—nothing but a couple of low walls to block the night's breath. I clear a space in which to sit, and sit.

Now what?

Here I am, finally arrived at a destination and—*what do I do now?* I've been so focused on getting here, on doing this, that I didn't think about what I'd actually do once I got here, once I gained my wilderness solitude.

Don't just do something, sit there.

I know, I'll sit is what I'll do. I'll meditate mindfully—breathing in, observing the flow, breathing out, letting go, watching the world ebb and flow, come into being and dissolve, so slow. I must be alert, pay attention to the signs what come, and not be distracted by thoughts that arise. I must observe without attaching. I must not miss any messages what the universe dispatches—nor the messengers what bring them. And so I sit down, work it around, into a lotus on the ground, and fall into contemplation.

I remain so thus, for the life of the night. It comes to me easy—all the years of meditation having trained my body and mind, just for this.

Sit and do nothing. Breathe, relax, let go. Release. *Pay attention to the rising and falling, the passing of phenomena.*

Spiritual practice is something I've neglected on this journey. I've been mindful of my surroundings, focused on others, but have failed to heed myself, failed to attend to my own soul's needs, my own mind.

What are you running from?

A chill wind blows. I bring my intention to mind. *Release.*

And so I sit, on the side of a mountain, in the middle of nowhere, unmoving, just breathing, my chest barely heaving with attention to nothing as the day does its leaving from that sphere what surrounds me, that canvas around me, sky shifting red as the sun goes to bed, stars creeping up high overhead to texture the transfer of day into night. Then—*bam!*—moon escapes obscurity and the me what once was realizes I've been observing progression, that parade march of *time*. And in this witnessing time has again ceased to be. All night airstream, I shoulder through shivering, blanket wrapped 'round, letting go of the me, the now, *set it free.*

Current catches memories, careens them downstream from fathoms afar and fuck-deep within launching one thing after another to float down the river, remembrances and revelations, recollections long gone, forgiveness forgotten I wait for the dawn, unfounded fears forever enduring the twilight of years in life's sweet cessation, the losses and gains of gambles untried, dreams that were dashed in love lost on you; the pain of broken bones, broken promises, and broken fucking hearts, the dog you never had and the monkey you never will.

Sky shifts from red into purple, blue, black, and at some point it peaks, this process of change, and slowly shifts back (at the rate it's supposed to) from black into purple, red into orange, and *el Sol* taps my shoulder, good morning, good morning, good morning to you.

I've made it through the night. But did I gain anything? Clarity? Release? Transformation? Did the stars bring a message, the night revelation? I get up and stretch, walk around, move until the blood again flows and the chill of the night is expelled from my bones. Again, with a nod to directions surrounding, the earth below and the sky above, I sit for the day.

Two ladybugs alight on my arm. *Is this a sign?* A raven lands in front of me, slowly pecks towards me, cocks his head curiously, lets out a *caw* and flies on. Morning mist dissipates, revealing the distance. Sun rises behind me, climbs overhead. Coyote comes crouchingly creeping 'cross hillside, steers a wide berth. A Golden eagle sweeps in low from behind, glides over shoulder, her wings cutting air with an audible *shush*. It arcs widely in front and soars back on out, dipping low towards my left. *Is this a message from the universe?* Breathe in, breathe out, let go, watch flow... Sun soars across sky.

Late afternoon the wind shifts, slips around the low-walled break where I shelter, blowing into my face, colder and colder and not yet the night. It's the last of the light and I think I must move. I fold up the blanket and sling it on back, head down the hillside to plateau below. It's a round disc of mesa, jutting out of the slope. There's a sheltered spot by the hillside, surrounded by pines and bordered by boulders. I put down my blanket, settle in, sit. Tonight, *el peyote.*

Cleaning earth from the cactus, I bring intentions to mind: *clarity, release.* Sun touches hilltops and I make sure I cast shadow before day disappears. Reducing the peyote to bites I accept sacrament in mouth, chew the bitterness of all thirteen buttons—*goddamn!*—wash them down with the last of the water. Numbness in mouth. Heart beats in head. A Mexican revolution in stomach. Body becomes desert, dirt, ocean, and mind. I ground myself again in the lotus, watch night come on.

As moon clears horizon, the spirit Híkuri emanates earth, fills me, dissolves me. It tells me to rise and I do, acknowledging directions, saluting the stars, regarding the planet. *Let go.*

Bundling up against the wind and the cold of the night, I sit again against the hill and open, observe the stream flowing through, let go the flotsam as death creeps upon me. *What am I waiting for? This is my life to be lived, here and now, everywhere and always. So get on with it, get into it, jump in the river and swim. The rest of your life will follow. For today is the first day of the rest of...* Let go also of this. Moon reaches apex, begins its withdrawal.

I'm worn from the fasting, the wind and the chill, the complete lack of sleep and the thoughts that still creep. No visions have come, no message, no answers. *Have I asked any questions?* The sky is clear of clouds. I shiver in the cold. In the wake of Luna's departure the tides of darkness gain ground until they vanish the planet beneath me. I drink in the stars from the now orbless night, ponder whether Híkuri has run through its flight, when a rumble of thunder jolts me upright. The sky is cloudless, no lightning, just thunder, its volume a wonder.

Here, the thunder's here *with me* on the plateau, a thunder of hooves from silhouette stallions—a herd of wild horses rearing before me, storming and stamping and dancing and prancing, their hooves making thunder, producing a storm, tails whipping wind, manes flying wild, eyes loosing lightning, blue bolts of energy flashing the night.

What if they trample me? *Fear.* I'm supposed to let go. But is this *real?* Are the horses here or is this a vision?

Things just are, don't judge them, accept them, let go.

Of course they're real, I'm perceiving them. *But am I real?* This is happening, and I need to accept that. But what are they doing here, this herd of storm stallions, the middle of night, the middle of mountains, the middle of mind dancing dervishly? What does it *mean?*

I struggle to feet. At the sight of my standing, my rising in east, horses break from their dance and drop to all fours, whinny like wildfire and gallop on out, disappearing down hill. Everything rushes my mind all at once. I'm hit with a vertigo taking me down, down to the ground, hands, knees and head. Starting to shiver I violently wretch, a wave of convulsions from gut to my soul. I cough up my innards, my organs, my past, my future, my fears and my father, my heart oh-so-sore, the hurts that I've held for so many years, I vomit it up, let it go and release, collapse to the earth, and roll on my side.

At the first hint of morning I find legs underneath me, stand myself up, make ready to leave. *Did that really happen?* There's something to check before I head down. In the middle of mesa, at the center of clearing, I squint through the twilight at ground underfoot. The bare light of dawn reveals the sign that I need. In the soil of earth there's a message to read: a pattern of hoof prints from shadowy steed.

The day breaks hard and red, the morning unfolding as I move down the mountain and aim through the tunnel, which leads back to life.

Acknowledgments

In gratitude to all those who provided me shelter, sustenance and inspiration—feeding my stomach, mind and soul while completing this work—I thank you.

To Mike Jasen—traveling partner, instigator of trouble and good times, *amigo por vida*—without whom neither this adventure nor this book would have happened. To Veronica Chaname, for hanging in there with us. To Leonard Ardoin—copilot of the Cadillac and member of the congregation—for seeing the light and pointing it out to me. To Tawnya and Sean Martin for holding me hostage and kicking my ass all the way through to the end. To Mark Dyson and David Mulholland of MDM Limousine, employers extraordinaire, for granting me numerous sabbaticals in which to "finish that god damn book." To Heidi Cortese, patron of the arts. To Tomas Zavala and Karen Trowbridge for providing refuge and mezcal at the el Tee Ranch. To Roberta and Dave Cootes for writing retreats in the redwoods. To Steve, Jain, Grace and Tommy Dolan, for home-cooked meals when I most needed them. To Laszlo Rohrwild for cups of coffee, games of chess and for reminding me what's important. To dancing philosopher George Cattermole. To Lauren Smith for vital research, Diana Medina for reminding me to breathe, Elissa Mendenhall for her wisdom. To all those coffee shops in North America what poured a strong cup and gave me the time and the space to write. To all those in Mexico who opened their hearts and their homes—la Familia, Reynaldo, Roberto Matosas, Linda Hamilton, Henri and Rosa. To Tara Austen Weaver, editor *especial*. To the memories of those who loved, supported and inspired—Lesley Laura Cootes, Christopher Clader, Monroe Mark Sweetland, and Javiér Sommerz, *mi hermano Mexicano*.

Last but not least, thanks to my mother who gave me a thesaurus for Christmas and never gave up.

Made in the USA
San Bernardino, CA
19 September 2017